I dedicate this book to the memories of both mum and dad, whom I loved very much.

To my wife's parents Dorothy and Lajos.

All missed deeply by our family.

And also to my grandchildren, Jack, Dylan, Jon, Bailey and Lauren.

A special dedication to Chloe, our wonderful granddaughter taken too soon from us before she could shine, no doubt she is a beacon of light in heaven and is always in our thoughts.

Jonathan Andrews

ATTICUS FIGHTER OF ROME SERIES – DEATH BEFORE DISHONOUR

AUSTIN MACAULEY PUBLISHERS®

LONDON * CAMBRIDGE * NEW YORK * SHARJAH

A CIP catalogue record for this title is available from the British Library.

ISBN 9781035882694 (Paperback)
ISBN 9781035882717 (ePub e-book)
ISBN 9781035882700 (Audiobook)

www.austinmacauley.com

First Published 2025
Austin Macauley Publishers Ltd®
1 Canada Square
Canary Wharf
London
E14 5AA

A big thank you to Martin Hardcastle and the many customers of Hardcastle Cleaning Services for their great and continued support, many of whom are looking forward to this second book.

Introduction

Rome's eastern borders were being attacked; the Parthian king Artabanus felt his army was now strong enough to take on the might of Rome. The fort at Tadmor, garrisoned by the legion 111 Gallica Raphanea, was under siege. The fort sat above a natural underground reservoir fed from the river system of the Tigris-Euphrates far underground.

The large stone wells within the fort were essential, supplying the legions and forts protecting the outer regions of the Roman empire to the east.

The fort also housed large granaries to feed its army, keeping Mesopotamia under Roman law.

Atticus had arrived at the fort in Ostia to take up his post as 1st Centurion of the Legion 11 Augusta with his new wife Naomi at his side.

General Maximus had gone to Rome to be honoured by the Emperor Augustus for his recent victories in Gaul, putting down the uprising and reasserting Rome's dominance in the region. But it had been at great expense; many Roman soldiers had paid with their lives. Atticus believed above all in the glory of Rome, but honour was paramount; he wouldn't stand for injustice and would always defend the weak.

But make no mistake, Atticus would kill the enemies of Rome without hesitation.

He would not tolerate any dishonour from the men under his command.

Maximus's legions would soon be back to full strength, and with Atticus fighting from the front, watched over by the gods Mars and Jupiter, a new chapter in Rome's glory would begin.

Chapter 1

Atticus rode Fury into the fort with Naomi, as Edelgard and Asken rode at either side of them, followed by the cavalry of the Legion Augusta 11, as the soldiers at the gates promptly stood to attention with the Centurion in charge of the gate detail, Sextus, saluting.

Atticus returned his salute, smiling, and dismounted from Fury.

Tribune Matias of the Legion 11 Augusta walked over to the gate to meet them, "Good day, 1st Centurion, Atticus," said Matias with a smile.

Atticus saluted and replied, "Sir, it's good to see you so soon." Matias clasped forearms with Atticus, "And who is the young lady I have the pleasure of meeting?" enquired Matias.

"This is my wife Naomi," explained Atticus, as Naomi bowed her head towards Matias with a smile while still sitting on her horse.

Atticus then helped Naomi dismount, "Well, I must say, Atticus, you are a very lucky man to have such a beautiful wife," and took hold of her hand and kissed it.

"It is I who is the lucky one," answered Naomi, going a little red in her cheeks.

"I will escort you both to your married quarters at our legions barracks," said Matias.

"Thank you!" replied Naomi, eagerly wanting to look at their rooms and see how comfortable she could make them, knowing full well they would be rather basic.

"Sextus!" shouted Matias, who was standing to one side at attention, "SIR!" replied Sextus.

"Take Atticus's and Naomi's horses to the livery and make sure they're fed and watered."

"Yes, sir."

He walked towards Fury gingerly as he'd met with Fury before and knew the big black stallion had a temper to match his size.

Fury snorted loudly and stamped one of his front hooves into the ground, Atticus smiled and began to stroke Fury's neck, "Come, Fury, you know our old friend Sextus here; go with him, and I'll come and see you soon."

Then Atticus handed Fury's reins to Sextus, and Edelgard began to laugh, "What's so funny?" asked Sextus.

"Nothing, my Roman friend. It's just that Fury seems to have that effect on all of us." answered Edelgard with a grin.

Sextus led the horses to the livery, Edelgard and Asken bid their farewell and told Atticus they would come to his quarters later and rode with the cavalry to their barracks. Matias walked with Atticus and Naomi down to the barracks, and as they did, Atticus stopped to watch the training of new recruits on the training ground.

They were being shown how to form battle lines and the testudo, and when they got it wrong, many got a clout with a vine stick from the Centurions performing the training. Atticus noticed that one of the Centurions took great pride in dishing out the punishment and seemed only to be enjoying the training when one of the soldiers made a mistake.

"Who's that Centurion over there?" asked Atticus.

"That is Brutus, why?"

"He's a bully and has no interest in those recruits; from what I've seen in such a short time, he is only interested in handing out pain." Matias paused for a moment.

"Your judgement of him is probably correct, Atticus, and I've noted he doesn't like leading from the front in battle," replied Matias.

"Then why not deal with him?" asked Atticus.

"You know how things often work in Rome. Brutus comes from a wealthy background. His father is one of the senators." replied Matias.

"We need those men trained and ready to fight, and that's not the best way."

Matias looked at Atticus again for a while before replying, "I see you're a man of conviction and straight to the point. I like a man who is not afraid to air his views…but don't worry, I will deal with him." reassured Matias.

"Men need discipline, and some men need a clout with a vine stick from time to time, but in a measured way to get the best out of them," replied Atticus.

Their conversation was interrupted by a loud scream coming from the training ground. One of the new recruits was lying in a heap on the floor as Brutus kicked him hard in the ribs, shouting, "You useless fucking piece of shit!"

"STOP!" shouted Matias.

Brutus turned and looked over at Matius, then walked over and saluted.

"SIR!" he replied, then stood to attention, trying to keep the anger burning inside of him under control. Atticus looked Brutus up and down and walked around him, and he towered over Brutus by a good ten inches. He was broader than Brutus, his muscles flexed and twitched as he circled Brutus, making him feel very uneasy. Brutus felt an aura flowing from Atticus; he now realised he was standing in the presence of a formidable killer. Matias stood back for a moment, watching Atticus prowl around Brutus, and liked what he saw, knowing full well the discomfort Brutus was feeling.

Matias finally broke the silence, "Keep your temper, and I don't want to see those men in the infirmary! We need them ready for battle, do you understand?"

"But…"

"Silence! Do as I say!" growled Matias, cutting him off.

"Yes sir!" Then he turned and walked back to the centre of the training arena, barking out further orders, and the training commenced minus the recruit who'd been carried off the field probably with a couple of broken ribs.

"If it's alright with you, sir, I'd like to take over the training tomorrow?" enquired Atticus.

"Certainly, you're in charge, training starts at six in the morning," replied Matias, who now addressed Naomi, smiling, "Sorry, for any delay Naomi in getting you to your quarters." Naomi smiled in response, and off they went to be shown their rooms. When they arrived, several soldiers were sitting outside their barracks who immediately stood to attention and saluted.

"Sit, gentlemen, and carry on," said Matias.

As they walked a little further and came in front of a building set slightly back, Matias announced, "This is your quarters." Standing at the door was a servant dressed in a grey tunic; he was tall and slight of build with brown hair. He was clean-shaven, and like Zuma, as black as nightfall.

"This is Doukasi, your servant! He is responsible for cleaning your room's clothes, armour, and making sure all your personal needs are attended to."

"Good day, master, and good day to you, lady," said Doukasi and bowed.

"Right, I will leave you two to get comfortable; there will be a meeting with myself and all our legions' officers to fully introduce them to you and for you to get to know them at seven in my office with the legate."

"Yes, sir!" replied Atticus.

"Doukasi here will show you the way; it won't take you long to find your way around." Matias then bid his farewell to Naomi and left.

"One thing, Doukasi!" asked Atticus.

"Yes, master, what can I do for you?"

"Please call me Atticus and my wife Naomi."

"But the other officers will punish me if I do not call you master," replied Doukasi, bowing his head.

Atticus put his hand under Doukasi's chin and lifted his head up and looked him in the face, "They won't anymore, so it will please both me and my wife if you would call us by name."

Doukasi smiled and said, "It will please me also, Atticus."

"Good, will you help Naomi bring our things in and show her around. I'm going to take a walk and explore the fort a little and get to know my way around."

"It will be my pleasure," replied Doukasi.

Back in Rome, the celebrations honouring Maximus had finished. Maximus and the Emperor Augustus were sitting in his private rooms. They had many things of great importance to discuss.

Optio Paulinus was instructed to guard the door and, under no circumstances, allow anyone to interrupt them.

Emperor Augustus was reading some dispatches that had arrived during the celebrations with great trepidation as Maximus poured them both a glass of fine wine.

Maximus sat down on a wonderful couch made with the finest gold thread silk and ostrich feather cushions. Augustus let out a long sigh. Maximus knew all too well that the news wasn't good.

Augustus spoke without looking up as he read the reports.

"How has Atticus settled into his role as first Centurion?"

"I haven't had the chance to speak with him. I'd already left for Rome before he arrived," answered Maximus. Augustus carried on reading for a while, "and where do you think young Atticus's future main aspirations lie?"

"In what sense?" asked Maximus.

"Do you think one day he would wish to become a leader of Rome rather than a fighter of Rome?"

Maximus laughed and answered, "If you mean a threat one day to your leadership, I'm sure he has one objective, and that is to serve you and Rome without reward. He is a proud soldier of Rome and wants nothing more."

"That's what I wanted to hear!" replied Augustus, who then paused to drink some wine and put down his last dispatch onto the desk.

"There are so many schemes for the role of emperor. I trust your judgement beyond all others, so I needed to ask; his name already commands respect even at the age of eighteen! Last night I had a dream and felt the gods had spoken to me," said Augustus.

Maximus looked at Augustus, feeling very surprised at his revelation. Maximus had been a close confidant of the emperor in private but had never heard him mention the gods in such a manner.

"In what way?" enquired Maximus.

"They told me Atticus is the sword of Rome and will fulfil the wishes of Mars and Jupiter."

Maximus looked at the emperor, and thought for a few moments before he answered.

"If the gods demand it, we must follow."

Maximus and Augustus drank their wine and sat in quiet reflection for a while.

"What news have you received in those dispatches?" enquired Maximus.

"Our spies in the east have revealed how the attempt to assassinate you came about!" Maximus immediately focused his full attention on Augustus and put down his glass of wine.

"And?" asked Maximus, almost forgetting he was addressing the emperor.

"It appears we have a Centurion with a loose tongue after a few drinks who has been coerced into revealing your daily routine amongst other matters regarding your legions."

Maximus jumped up and began to pace the room, "The spy goes by the name Adrian, a tavern owner in Ostia, but whether or not that is his real name is still a little bit of a mystery!" Augustus revealed.

Maximus sat down on the couch again, still contemplating the revelations.

"And which Centurion can't hold his piss?" asked Maximus angrily.

"The name of the Centurion is Sextus." answered Augustus.

"Sextus! I thought he would have more sense," replied Maximus.

"Even the best of soldiers falls short of our expectations while under the influence of a fine wine or a beautiful woman, and in some cases both."

The room fell silent, Maximus was deep in thought, it wasn't long before Augustus broke the silence.

"What punishment do you regard as fitting?" asked Augustus while refilling his glass with wine.

Maximus ran his fingers through his neatly cut beard before replying, "We can turn this to our advantage; he's probably, although unwittingly, been telling this spy various amounts of information for months now!"

"Certainly, looks that way to me," replied Augustus.

Maximus stood up and began to pace the room again, then turned to face his emperor.

"We will feed Sextus various pieces of false information as to our intentions for dealing with our enemies in the east…and as to the strength of our legions' capability and readiness for war."

Augustus began to smile at Maximus's train of thought.

"Very well, I will leave that to your total discretion, but keep me informed daily," demanded Augustus.

"Of course," replied Maximus.

"The most pressing matter I have received is from the Legate Marcellus of the Legion 111 Galicia Raphanea, based in the fort at Tadmor, supplying our eastern forts with grain and water. It is under siege and requires immediate reinforcements and more heavy weapons."

"Never a dull moment," answered Maximus.

"General Felix of our legions based in Thracia has sent the legate Titus and two thousand men to Mesopotamia to support Marcellus." Maximus looked a little angry.

"Titus is not one of your best officers, and to be blunt, he is a fucking idiot! Whose idea was it to put him in charge?"

"Felix is a friend of Titus's father and probably wants some glory for his son. You know unfortunately how some things work in the upper classes of Rome's elite," replied the emperor. Unfortunately, Maximus knew all too well the dealings that went on in the senate.

"I better organise a force to leave for Mesopotamia at once in case Titus fucks up!" answered Maximus.

"I will give you two hundred of my Praetorians and Tribune Marcus to lead them; you may use them as you see fit, let me know of your plan without delay."

"Yes, emperor. I will, but I better get back to Ostia and make plans quickly," Maximus finished his wine, saluted, and left with all haste.

Chapter 2

Maximus arrived back at the fort in Ostia late in the evening. Atticus had met with all the other officers of the Augusta 11 legion. Atticus required all Centurions and men to be on the training ground in full armour and carrying their shields and a spear at six in the morning. He had then retired to bed with Naomi, wanting to be rested for the early morning training. Atticus awoke at five and began to dress in full armour, which Doukasi had laid out the previous evening; he'd also laid out his tunic with the gold eagle pinned to it.

Doukasi walked to the small kitchen and prepared breakfast for Atticus, "Good day, Doukasi," said Atticus as he walked into the kitchen.

"Good day, Atticus. I have made you some oatcakes containing fruit for your breakfast. It is a recipe I've used from my village back home. I hope you will like them."

"If they taste as good as they smell, I am sure I will."

Atticus picked one up and devoured it in seconds, then ate a second one a little slower, and said, "They are very nice."

Doukasi smiled with satisfaction, "Look after Naomi if you will; I'm going to be busy all day."

"Yes, Atticus, it will be my pleasure to make her wishes my priority," answered Doukasi. Atticus smiled and left for the training ground with shield, and spear in hand.

He arrived just as the barracks were emptying and the soldiers began assembling in the training arena. The Centurions and optios marched up to Atticus and saluted.

"Centurion Brutus!" commanded Atticus.

"SIR!" came his reply, "Where is your shield and spear?" all the other Centurions and Optio's were standing to attention with spear and shield in hand. "I thought it was the legionaries and auxiliaries to carry them, sir."

"I said everyone, now go and get them, and leave that vine stick in your quarters; you won't be needing it today."

As he left the training ground staring ahead with the look of anger on his face, several of the men began to laugh, and young Linus, one of the Optio's, couldn't help but grin. Brutus had made his early days since arriving at Ostia a living hell.

Brutus looked over at the men standing in ranks, trying to see who was laughing, Atticus shouted, "At the double Brutus!" who turned his eyes back to his front and quickened his pace.

"Centurions, I want the men separated into two sections, with new recruits at the front of each of their cohorts and the rest behind at the double."

While the men were organised quickly by the Centurions, Tribune Matais and Tribune Tiberius entered the arena.

"Good day, Atticus," said Tiberius.

"Good day, sir!"

"What have you planned for the men today?" asked Tribune Matias with a grin.

"We're going on a fifteen-mile hike in full armour, carrying a shield and a spear. I want to find out their fitness—who's capable and who is not, sir," answered Atticus.

"I see you're fully equipped for the hike yourself," said Tiberius.

"I lead from the front; the men might not like it in the heat today, but they can't moan if the officers are joining in," replied Atticus, smiling.

Just as Atticus finished speaking, Brutus returned to the arena carrying a shield and spear, much to the delight of the men; some even cheered.

"Silence in the ranks!" shouted Tribune Matais, trying not to smile. Brutus glared at them, thinking, "Just you fucking wait!"

"Centurion Cyrus!" shouted Atticus.

"Sir!"

"It's your job today to write down all the names of anyone falling behind and not up to today's task."

"Yes, sir!" replied Cyrus.

"We'll leave you to it then!" said Matias, then he and Tiberius left for a meeting with Maximus.

"The men are in their two groups. Sir, new recruits in the cohorts at the front," said Centurion Sextus.

"Thank you, officers, join your units."

"SIR!" came the reply as they all quickly joined their ranks.

Atticus marched to the front and shouted, "Forward!"

Five thousand men began the march out of the fort as many onlookers of the other legions admired the sight of a full legion in full dress leaving the fort.

As they marched down the road, a cohort of Hispanic auxiliaries and a contingent of Cilician archers were marching towards the fort, having just arrived from Germanica to bolster Maximus's legions.

Back in Rome, Tribune Marcus had set off for Ostia, leading two hundred Praetorians as promised by Emperor Augustus, accompanied by his wife Aurelia, who'd talked him into taking her to stay at the fort with Naomi.

Centurion Metelus and Optio Paulinus were amongst the troops heading to join General Maximus. The sun was burning brightly in a clear blue sky, making it a very hot day. Atticus led the men on the forced march up into the hills; they'd been marching for a little over three hours. Sweat poured down their faces from underneath their helmets, and the sound of weapons clattering against armour filled the air.

Atticus now upped the pace; a few had started to struggle in the heat and were breathing heavily. Atticus had noticed some of the new recruits falling behind.

"Sextus on me!" shouted Atticus; he quickly joined Atticus at the front panting quite heavily.

"Yes sir!"

"Keep the pace going. I'm going to the rear to see for myself who can't keep up."

"Yes sir!" came the reply.

Atticus jogged back along the ranks of men marching, taking note as to how they were coping in the heat at the pace he had now set. Many of the men noticed that Atticus didn't seem to be struggling in the conditions and was clearly not out of breath when jogging past.

One of the new recruits dropped his spear as Atticus passed, "Pick that up, you horrible little man!" shouted a burley Centurion.

Atticus stooped down and grabbed the spear and handed it to the soldier, "Thank you, sir!" the soldier responded, feeling very uneasy that the first Centurion himself had picked it up and waited to be reprimanded. Atticus turned back to the front and marched at the soldier's side and asked, "What's your name?"

"Thaddius, sir!" he answered while gasping for breath.

"Keep a firm grip on that spear. I know it's hard in this heat, but that weapon might save your life one day…you will get fitter! So, eyes forward, and keep the pace. Those that fall behind are the first to die!"

"Yes, sir, thank you sir!" replied Thaddius.

Atticus quickly turned and arrived at the rear, where Centurion Cyrus marched with his wax tablet in hand, taking the names of those who fell behind and out of the ranks. Further back, he could see a dozen, at least, who were dragging their spears and walking very slowly and recognised one of them as Centurion Brutus.

"How many have fallen behind so far, Cyrus?" Cyrus quickly calculated and replied.

"Twenty-three, including Brutus," answered Cyrus with a grin.

"Better than I thought, we've got about six miles left before we get back to the fort, so when we get back, bring the names on that list to my quarters for me later."

"Yes, sir."

Atticus then made his way back to the front, passing by the ten cohorts of men marching four abreast.

"Fuck me, our first Centurion doesn't even look out of breath!" stated Decimus, one of the legionaries, to his friend Demitri marching at his side.

"He's not human; look at the bloody size of him," replied Demitri, gasping for air and trying to keep up with the pace.

"How's the pace affecting you, Sextus, my friend?"

"It's the heat, not so much the pace, that's bothering me, sir."

As they marched back down from the hills towards the road heading to the fort, Atticus could see Tribune Marcus leading his Praetorians towards the fort along the road with his wife Aurelia at his side.

"See those pretty Praetorians ahead, Sextus."

"I do, sir."

"Well, we can't have them reaching the fort before us, can we now?"

"No, we can't, sir," Sextus replied, smiling. Atticus had shouted so the soldiers marching behind in the front ranks could hear many of the veterans grinning, knowing full well what was about to happen.

Atticus turned to his front cohort and shouted, "Are we going to let those pretty Praetorians reach the fort first, men?"

"NO!" came the loud response; word soon filtered back through the ranks to the other cohorts and the officers leading them.

"Right men, time to quicken the pace on me!" Atticus shouted, then he began to trot a shield in one hand and a spear in the other. The sound of their hobnailed boots crunching the ground was quite deafening.

The men who had seemed to be breathing heavily suddenly found renewed energy, smiles had now replaced the look of discomfort on the soldiers' faces.

"That's it, lads!" shouted a burley Centurion leading the front century of the second cohort, and all the ranks of the legion were now moving as one at the double; many had started to shout encouragement to those still struggling a little.

The front rows of the legion being led by Atticus could quite easily make out that they were gaining fast and were soon only a couple of hundred yards behind the rear of the column of Praetorians marching three abreast.

The rear ranks of Praetorians could hear the noise of the marching legion and were turning around to look as one of them tripped, causing several of them to fall over each other.

This caused great amusement to both Atticus leading and his men in the front ranks who could see. Optio Linus had burst out laughing even though he found the pace draining all his reserves of energy but again found that extra momentum.

The sound of jeers erupted from the ranks of the Legion 11 Augusta Tribune Marcus had pulled his horse to the side of his marching Praetorians to look back and see Atticus leading at the front at such a fast pace and knew exactly what Atticus was up to.

Aurelia moved her horse to Marcus's side and said, "My, that's a wonderful sight. Such a large body of men marching so fast, isn't it, my dear?" Not realising what was going on. Marcus looked at her while raising his eyebrows and letting out a deep sigh, and replied, "Better get that horse of yours to move a bit quicker, my dear."

Aurelia turned her horse back to face the front as the Praetorians began to march past and asked, "Why do we have to go quicker, darling?"

"Never mind, just do it!" retorted Marcus. Then he shouted "PRAETORIANS! At the double," Metelus barked further encouragement.

"Come on, lads, don't let those legionnaires inbred goat fuckers catch us up, move yourselves." Atticus and the front of his legion were now beginning to pass the rear ranks of the Praetorians; obscenities were now being shouted from the ranks of both the legionnaires of the Augusta 11 and Praetorians. Optio Paulinus looked over and smiled at Atticus as he trotted past, leading his men. Atticus grinned and nodded to him.

Then Atticus began to shout out a chant, "AUGUSTA" and banged his spear twice loudly against his shield; this was quickly taken up by the ranks of the whole legion, which caused a deafening crescendo.

The fort was now insight high up on the hill; he turned his men to his left and started to take a shorter route to the gates, peeling off from the side of the column of Praetorians' zigzag amongst the brush and rocks.

Atticus still led the chant "AUGUSTA" banging his shield with his spear; the guards at the gate were now looking down towards the duel taking place. The guards on the fort's towers and walkways began to shout encouragement for the Augusta 11 legion. They had a good view and could see the legion was going to reach the gates first. But due to having a column of almost five thousand men, it still strung out way beyond the two hundred Praetorians being led by Tribune Marcus and his wife. Aurelia had decided to keep out front to her right, making sure she was not in the way of the impending race to the fort's gates.

Many soldiers had now appeared on the walls hearing the commotion outside and were now joining in the chant for Augusta; there was only a small contingent of Praetorians based at the fort. They were trying to shout support for their fellow Praetorians but were easily being drowned out by the greater number of legionaries and auxiliaries. Even though they belonged to units of Maximus's other legions, there wasn't much love lost between the ranks of Praetorians and legionnaires.

Tribune Matias and Tribune Tiberius had climbed the stone stairway leading up to the top of one of the towers, and we're watching the duel taking place. They were in fact quite enjoying the scene taking place outside the fort. Edelgard and Adelar walked over and now joined them.

"What do you think, Edelgard, who will make it into the fort first?"

"I'm not sure yet!"

"Tribune Matias fancies a wager to try to win some of your coin back?" asked Adelar with a grin.

"What's the bet?" replied Matais; he enjoyed betting but rarely ever won.

"Who gets into the fort first, the Praetorians or the Augusta legion."

"And what odds?" enquired Tribune Tiberius, he was feeling a little lucky and not wanting to be left out.

"Five sesterces to one that Atticus and the Augusta 11 legion make it into the fort first," answered Adelar.

"The whole legion, not just the front ranks?" enquired Matais.

"Yes, other than any stragglers not in line," Matais and Tiberius looked down from the tower at the race to the gates.

Atticus was reaching the gates first, but the cohorts of the legion were strung out way past the rear of Marcus and his two hundred Praetorians.

"Two hundred sesterces on the Praetorians," shouted Matais, feeling confident.

"I will have two hundred also on the Praetorians to win," said Tiberius.

"Done!" replied Adelar, rubbing his hands. Edelgard smiled and shook his head at Tiberius and Matias.

They all now leant over the fort's wall watching the duel unfold, "First cohort on me and form a line two deep shields locked, and block their path to allow our boys in first!" shouted Atticus.

"Yes sir!" replied Sextus, "I don't want them getting through, and then when I order, I want an organised retreat through the gates." shouted Atticus, adrenaline now pumping through every fibre of his body.

The first cohort quickly formed a battle line as ordered, with Atticus and Sextus positioning themselves in the front row dead centre.

The Praetorians slowed their pace, and Centurion Metelus shouted to the Tribune Marcus, "What's your order, sir?"

"HALT!" cried Marcus as he pulled his horse to a standstill facing the wall of five hundred men, shields locked together. Thinking *I see what you're up to Atticus,* and smiling, knowing full well Atticus wanted to check how well his first cohort could defend and retreat in an organised manner.

"Metelus have the men form a wedge, and let's see if we can penetrate that wall of shields; attack their centre."

Metelus faced his Praetorians and shouted, "FORM A WEDGE! Let's see if we can part those shields and push our way through those bloody inbreds and into the fort."

Up on the wall Tribune, Matais was feeling a little unnerved at the sight of Atticus's shield defence. The other cohorts of the Augusta 11 legion had now started to march through the gates to the sound of cheers from the fort's battlements. But there were still several thousand men to reach the gates in their orderly march being shielded by their first cohort.

General Maximus had now arrived at the tower, "Sir!" shouted Tiberius as they all stood to attention.

"What's going on down there?" enquired Maximus.

"There's a bit of a duel as to who's getting into the fort first, sir!" exclaimed Edelgard, grinning.

"The Augusta legion seems to be getting the upper hand due to Atticus's smart thinking, which looks like it could also hurt me in the pocket," groaned Matais. Maximus looked at Adelar, raising an eyebrow. Adelar just held his hands up as if it had nothing to do with him.

"Well…we'll see firsthand as to how the men's training has been going, no doubt that's what Atticus has in mind, and it looks like Tribune Marcus is obliging," said Maximus.

"Looks like I might lose the wager, but at least it will be entertaining," said Tiberius, as the Praetorians quickly formed a tight wedge.

Atticus shouted, "Shoulders and shields, nobody gets over excited and sticks somebody with a spear."

Many of the soldiers laughed out loud as they dug their heels into the ground and put the weight of their bodies behind their shields.

"Second row shields aloft I don't want any of them climbing over and getting into the fort," shouted Atticus.

The Praetorians started to attack the centre of Atticus's line. Metelus shouted the order.

"ENGAGE! And push those fuckers to one side." Atticus smiled on hearing Metelus, "Did you hear that men on my order take a step back, put them off their stride, then punch their shields forward into them, pass the word on," said Atticus, not wanting Metelus to hear, but that was unlikely due to the noise of the Praetorians' boots crunching the ground as they charged forward towards Atticus and his men.

Just as the Praetorians were about to clash with Atticus's cohort, the order rang out to step back; at once the two lines of legionnaires did with perfect timing and as one. This took the front of the Praetorians by surprise, and were immediately punched with the shields from Atticus and his men, "Fuck me!" shouted Metelus, shuddering as they clashed. Atticus grinned at seeing the look of surprise on Metelus's face as his shield smashed into Metelus's. Atticus's six-foot-six frame of pure muscle and strength came into play, sending a ripple through the Praetorians' attack.

Sextus, with sweat pouring down his forehead, grunted loudly as the two sides clashed, then pushing with all his might into the Praetorians slipped slightly, but Atticus quickly grabbed him with his free arm and pulled him back in line.

To Atticus's left was a burly Centurion by the name of Decimus, who was in his early twenties, only five feet five, but was as wide as an ox. Decimus pushed his shield into the Praetorians just as one of them tried to jump onto the shield covering above his head from the second row. There was a loud scream as he fell to the floor and was about to be trampled on. Atticus's long arm covered in sweat and dirt took hold of him and hauled him up with a grin and said, "You're a prisoner, don't you try running into that fort."

"No sir!" replied the Praetorian gasping for air and spitting out dust. He was a little shocked but thankful that he had not been trampled on.

Obscenities were now shouted between the two opposing sides as they pushed, grunts and groans rang out. Atticus's wall of shields held firm. Centurion Cyrus arrived at the back of Atticus and shouted, "The last cohort is entering the fort, sir!"

As Atticus pushed with his shield replied, "As soon as they are in, give the order for an orderly retreat." Just then another Praetorian climbed on to Atticus's shield but was immediately knocked back into the throng of Praetorians. He fell on his arse but was quickly dragged back by Metelus before being stamped on. Up in the fort's tower, Adelar teased Matias.

"Looks like you will owe me some more of your coin."

"Don't worry, I will win it back from you!" replied Matais, Adelar grinned and looked at Edelgard, who just shook his head with a smile.

Maximus was engrossed in the confrontation taking place below alongside Tiberius and was analysing the whole situation, looking for any flaws.

"Legionnaires commence retreat!" came the order from Centurion Cyrus. Quickly, the second row started the orderly retreat by sections led by their officers barking out orders. Then the front rank began to disengage into their respective units, leaving the Praetorian adversaries standing, placing their shields in front of them. Some leaning on them, breathing heavily, watching the Augusta 11 legion retreat through the gates to cheers from the fort's battlements.

Atticus walked over to the Tribune Marcus and his wife Aurelia, who'd been sitting on their horses watching the confrontation.

"Good day, sir! And greetings to you, Aurelia," said Atticus, covered from head to toe in dust and sweat.

"Good day! First Centurion Atticus," replied Marcus, grinning.

"It's nice to see you, young Atticus, looks like you're in need of a bath," said Aurelia with a smile.

Marcus dismounted and shouted, "Metelus, have the men form ranks and take them into the fort."

"Yes, sir, at once," Metelus turned and shouted the order, and the Praetorians began to march into the fort with a few jeers still being shouted from the fort's battlements, but they were quickly silenced by their officers.

"Have you spoken with General Maximus?" asked Marcus, as they walked towards the fort's gates.

"No, not yet, I've been out since dawn with the legion to see how our recruits are progressing, and he was in Rome when I arrived yesterday," replied Atticus.

"How is Naomi finding her new surroundings?" enquired Aurelia while riding her horse just behind as they walked.

"Fine, we have reasonable quarters, and I'm sure it won't be long before she has everything just as she likes it."

"Wonderful, I can't wait to see her," answered Aurelia, "How come you are here today?" enquired Atticus.

"We've been sent by the emperor no less to bolster Maximus's forces for the upcoming campaign of which I'm not privy yet to reveal. I am in no doubt Maximus will be informing us sooner rather than later. Things are getting a little wild, to say the least, with the Parthians."

The guards on the gate stood to attention and saluted as they walked into the fort, Maximus had come down from the tower, closely followed by Edelgard and Adelar.

"Good day, gentlemen, and not forgetting you, lady Aurelia, how is your father well, I hope?"

"Thank you," Maximus turned his attention to Atticus.

"I need you to come to my office as soon as you have washed and changed Atticus!"

"Yes, sir, I will be as quick as I can sir."

"Good!" replied Maximus.

"Marcus…Adelar will show you and your wife Aurelia to your quarters, and I will send for you in due course," said Maximus.

"Yes sir," Marcus replied.

"Edelgard, you may as well come along with Atticus as soon as he's ready,"

"Sir!" came the reply from Edelgard with a polite nod.

Maximus then left to return to his quarters. Tribune Marcus bid his farewell to Atticus and left for his quarters, following Adelar with his wife.

Naomi had spent the day with Doukasi cleaning and making her rooms just as she wanted, though Doukasi had protested that it was his duty, not Naomi's, to clean, "Nonsense!" she replied. Doukasi and Naomi were returning to her quarters carrying two buckets of water when one of the Hispanic auxiliaries standing outside his new billet talking with two of his comrades shouted over.

"You slave, come and clean my boots!" pointing a finger at Doukasi, who immediately put his bucket down and was about to walk over and comply.

"No, he won't! Come back here, Doukasi! Clean your own boots," Naomi said abruptly.

The auxiliary looked at Naomi, who had dirt on her face and arms from the hours spent cleaning.

"What's it to you, girl?" he retorted, thinking she was a mere servant, "It has everything to do with me! What's your name?" enquired Naomi with a smile.

"Please Naomi, it won't take me a minute to clean his boots!" pleaded Doukasi.

"My name is Centurion Pablo; why do you fancy coming to my room and attending to me?" he replied, licking his lips as the other two soldiers began to laugh. Naomi was by no means fazed by the soldier's comment; or the laughter from his comrades.

"NO! I just need to let my husband know your name so he can come and find you and teach you some manners!" scolded Naomi. Pablo walked over towards Naomi and Doukasi.

"Is that so…and who might be your husband? That would make me tremble at the knees. May I ask?"

"First Centurion Atticus," replied Naomi with venom in her tone of voice.

"Come, Doukasi, pick up your bucket; we have things to do," she said with a smile.

The blood seemed to drain from Pablo's face and the look of fear in his eyes at the mere mention of that name. He had heard all too well the story of how and who had saved Maximus's life.

"Please, my lady...I'm very sorry I didn't realise, I thought." Naomi cut him off before he could utter another word.

"Carry these buckets of water to my quarters and maybe I will not bother my husband, but if you ever see my friend Doukasi again, treat him with respect!"

"Yes, my lady," replied Pablo, picking up the two buckets and swiftly began to follow several yards behind Doukasi and Naomi.

"See, Naomi...your husband already has a great name!" said Doukasi with a big smile. Just as they arrived, Atticus and Edelgard were approaching, and Pablo's heart almost stopped beating. Naomi ran up to him and as she did Atticus took hold of her tiny waist and lifted her up and gave her a kiss and smiled.

Then he put her down and looked at the Centurion carrying the buckets, "I see you haven't taken long to get soldiers doing your bidding," Naomi turned around and said, "Pablo just leave the buckets there that will be all."

"Yes, my lady, glad to be of help, oh and it is very nice to meet you Doukasi." Pablo quickly turned and strode off back the way they came, "What was all that about?" asked Edelgard, looking at Pablo rushing off.

"Oh nothing!" replied Naomi who then began to laugh.

"Don't suppose you had brought any of your father's wine with you?" enquired Edelgard with a grin.

"Doukasi, this is my friend Edelgard who is quite taken with the flavour of my father's wine," said Atticus.

Doukasi smiled at Edelgard in response and bowed slightly.

"Would you please fetch him some wine while I get washed and changed? We have a meeting with the General straight away."

"Yes, Atticus, I will fetch the wine, then I will get you a clean tunic."

Edelgard sat down and began to guzzle the wine as soon as Doukasi had brought it. Atticus, with the help of Naomi, got ready. He then kissed Naomi goodbye as he left Centurion Cyrus arrived.

"Here you are, sir, a list of the men who fell behind."

"How many?" asked Atticus.

"One hundred and three."

"Better than I thought!" answered Atticus.

"Have these men on the parade ground for extra training at seven in the morning, the rest can have a day off, but check with Tribune Matias if that will be allowed."

As Atticus and Edelgard made their way to Maximus's quarters, on arrival Adelar and Asken were standing guard outside.

"Greetings boys!" said Atticus.

"Nice show outside the fort, I hear Adelar got richer today," said Asken looking over at Adelar, with a grin.

"Yes, and the drinks are on him later," said Edelgard.

"Is there anything you won't bet on?" asked Atticus. "Can't think of anything," replied Adelar stroking his long unkempt beard.

"The General is waiting, so you better go in!"

"Sir!" said Atticus while saluting as soon as he entered the room, "good to see you could make it, Edelgard!"

"It's been a busy day," replied Edelgard realising due to Maximus's demeanour it must be important.

"Please sit down, you two, we've lots to discuss; nothing that's planned or discussed today is to be related to anyone for the moment, understand?"

"Yes, sir!" answered Atticus.

"While it is just us three, Atticus, Maximus will do." Maximus quickly told them of the web of spies working out of the Merry Sailor led by Adrian the owner and how unwittingly Sextus had been plied with wine and women to reveal the daily routine of Maximus's hunting trips, the legions strength, and readiness for battle. Atticus felt a little bereft at his friend's stupidity and sat in deep thought.

"Atticus, would you care to share your thoughts as to what we should do?" Edelgard sat staring at an amphora of wine that was noticed by Maximus with a grin.

"What's up? Not had a drink in an hour? Help yourself." said Maximus.

"I think we can use it to our advantage," said Atticus.

"Yes, we can; that's exactly what I told the emperor," replied Maximus. While helping himself to a glass of wine and pouring another for Atticus, and then giving Edelgard a dark look for only pouring his own.

"Oh, err, sorry Maximus…" Edelgard tried to apologise but was cut off.

"Never mind, we need to organise a swift force to travel to the fort at Tadmor which is under siege as we speak. We need to take some badly needed ballistae, vipers, and men to strengthen the fort's defences until my legions are fully equipped and ready for the campaign in Mesopotamia," said Maximus.

He then unrolled a large map across his desk of the eastern empire and the Mediterranean with all the ports highlighted.

"We need to get to Tadmor virtually unnoticed, surprise and speed is of the essence," Atticus and Maximus pondered over the map in deep thought.

"General Felix of our legions in Thracia has seen fit to send two thousand men to their aid."

"That should help!" said Atticus.

"Yes, but in my opinion has made the mistake of sending a Tribune by the name of Titus to lead them!" Maximus slammed the palm of his right hand down on the map.

"Who, in my opinion, is not up to the task and has no real battle experience to speak of, especially for something of this importance!"

Atticus still gazed at the map without saying a word, Edelgard licked his lips and filled his glass again, "Go steady with that and pour me another!" demanded Maximus.

"How many men do you propose sending?" enquired Atticus, "Five hundred led by you with Edelgard and Adelar to keep you company."

Atticus continued looking at the map then said, "I have a plan but first when do we leave?"

"You have six days to be ready to leave and prepare the first cohort of Augusta11, so what's your plan?" asked Maximus.

"We leave Ostia aboard two tyreims in full view of Adrian's spies. I will fill Sextus's head full of false information as to which route we take to Mesopotamia. Where we land etcetera then I will take him to the Merry Sailor for a few drinks, hopefully while we're there he will unwittingly pass on all the false information. Once at sea we transfer our men, horses and equipment here at Corinth, onto several merchant ships which I'm sure you will be able to acquire and change our route and head for Tarsus in Cilicia cut straight across the desert bypass Niblis and head for Tadmor," Atticus looked up at Maximus who was looking at the route.

Maximus agreed.

"I'll arrange for local guides who are very loyal to Rome...at great expense I might add. They will meet your force outside Amat here!" pointed Maximus.

"I will make the necessary arrangements with the captains of the ships; speed is now paramount to put this plan to action. I need to inform the emperor we will be ready to leave and give him all the details." Atticus finally took a long drink of his wine and said.

"I hope that the Tribune Titus makes haste and arrives well before we get there."

"Don't count on it, if I had any confidence at all in him being successful with his mission I wouldn't be sending you," replied Maximus, with a deep sigh.

The next couple of days were frantic with all the necessary arrangements, messengers were sent to the guides, the ship's captains were fully informed and were sworn to secrecy, the Emperor Augustus met with Maximus and was fully informed and the merchant boats had been sent to Corinth quietly in the night from Brundisium.

All it needed now was for Sextus to get drunk and spill the false information to Adrian and his web of spies. They would later be put to death when the mission was complete, or even before. Atticus couldn't wait for that day of reckoning.

Atticus spent the afternoon walking with Naomi and Fury outside the fort's gates in the warm sunshine.

"What's on your mind?" asked Atticus as they strolled.

"It will be the first time we will be apart for so long since the day I first met you all covered in dirt and smelling like a pig at play in the mud." Naomi had a tear in one of her eyes and a pain in her stomach as she spoke.

"I would love for you to come with me, but it is going to be very dangerous, so I have no choice," Atticus replied, also feeling a deep pain in his heart as he spoke.

Naomi took hold of Atticus's free hand and squeezed it hard. Fury, who was being led by Atticus, hung his head and long neck between them, and his big brown eye blinked and he gazed at Naomi as they walked.

This seemed to make Naomi feel a little better, knowing whatever Atticus was about to face, Fury would be at his side.

The piece of red jasper that hung around Atticus's neck always began to glow, and its reflection shone in her eyes as a great bald eagle swooped down and sat on Fury's saddle.

This made Naomi jump slightly. Atticus squeezed her hand reassuringly, smiled, and spoke, "This eagle has been sent by the gods to watch over us. So don't worry too much, my love. We have a duty to perform for Rome; this is our destiny, not just mine."

Fury snorted quietly, which took her out of her trance as she felt a warmth inside her, filling her heart and transcending all over her body.

Naomi hoped it was a sign that the gods would watch over Atticus and Fury. "I will stay with Romulus and Zuma at the farm while you're gone and take Doukasi with me if that is allowed?" enquired Naomi.

"Don't worry, I will get Maximus to sort that out. I would feel more at ease knowing you're at home with family," answered Atticus with a smile.

"Can we go see them before you leave?"

"Yes, we'll go tomorrow, but tonight I have business in Ostia!" replied Atticus.

"You better not be too late, back I have plans for you tonight my love, so you better not come back drunk or tired," Atticus laughed out loud and said, "Don't you worry, I have plans for you also, so don't get a headache."

Atticus and Naomi returned to their quarters, where Doukasi sat outside enjoying the warmth of the sun on his face. He made to stand up, but Naomi said, "Sit I want to talk with you about a change of our surroundings for a while." She then promptly sat down beside him and began to tell him of her home and what she had planned, while Atticus went in search of Sextus.

Chapter 3

"There you are, Sextus, I've been looking for you!" shouted Atticus; as Sextus played dice with Optio Linus. They both stood up and saluted.

"Are you winning some coin, my friend?" asked Atticus.

"Yes, I'm a few sesterces up."

"Good, we're off for a drink to that tavern of yours later first drink is on you."

"Sounds good to me, sir!" replied Sextus.

"Meet me at the livery in an hour. I've got one or two things to do first!" shouted Atticus as he walked off.

Atticus then made his way to the General's quarters. Edelgard and Adelar were standing outside, "Greetings, my young Roman friend!" said Edelgard, looking like he'd had a fair share of wine.

"Good day, Atticus," said Adelar.

"Afternoon boys, do you fancy a trip to a fine tavern in Ostia tonight, my German friend? Or is that a silly question?" asked Atticus.

"When?" said Edelgard, licking his lips.

"We meet Sextus in an hour at the livery!" replied Atticus, who then knocked on Maximus's door.

"Enter!" came a shout from within; Atticus entered his large quarters.

"Sir!"

"Ah, good you're here. I've set all the wheels in motion, and you will be leaving for Tadmor the day after tomorrow, have all the men been informed?"

"They have their orders but don't know anything about our destination, route, or departure yet. I will brief the officers first thing tomorrow."

"Good!" replied Maximus.

"I leave for Ostia shortly with Sextus and Edelgard, I will fill him in with the details of our alleged mission and route," answered Atticus. Maximus finished reading the dispatch then said, "We've been loading the two tyreims in full view of the Merry Sailor for two days now with all the equipment. Adrian must be itching to find out what's going on," Maximus smiled and poured himself a drink.

"Well, I won't keep you any longer, have fun!" said Maximus, grinning.

"Just one more thing while I'm away, Naomi is returning to stay with my father at the farm and wishes to take our servant Doukasi with her, so if that is fine with you, I will take them in the morning?"

"Good idea, how is she with your imminent departure?" enquired Maximus.

"As well as can be expected, but knows I have a destiny to fulfil and an emperor and the gods to serve."

"I will report the outcome of this evening as soon as I return."

"Good no matter how late…As soon as you give me the details, I will head for Rome to see the emperor and will see you before you leave. Oh! And before I forget, I've instructed the officer in charge of the Cilician archers to have his men ready to join the mission," said Maximus. Atticus smiled and bid his farewell. He was looking forward to the meeting with Adrian.

Atticus quickly returned to his quarters, where Naomi and Doukasi sat in the kitchen eating some of Doukasi's oatcakes with a cup of water.

"I have to leave for Ostia straight away. I will return as soon as I can," Atticus kissed Naomi.

"Farewell, my love; take good care of her, Doukasi."

"I will!" he replied, smiling. Atticus left as Naomi smiled at him.

Atticus arrived at the livery and saddled Fury. Edelgard was next to arrive, "Don't know about you, Atticus, but I'm ready for a drink." Atticus shook his head.

"We've got a job to do, don't forget, and it's an important part of our plan!" reminded Atticus.

Edelgard nodded his head and replied, "Yes, I know, don't worry. I won't bugger it up." It wasn't long before Sextus came walking in.

"Good evening, sir!" "No need for any formality tonight Sextus time for a night of drink and merriment," said Atticus.

"I'll second that!" bellowed Edelgard, followed by a loud belch while mounting his horse.

Sextus led his horse out of one of the stalls, and all three left the fort for the port and the Merry Sailor. As they rode enroute towards the city, Atticus made light of the coming mission, giving him plenty of false information, saying they were heading for Tyrus and a completely different route they would take to Tadmor. Atticus now hoped Adrian would use all his powers of persuasion at hand to get the information out of Sextus as to the destination of the Roman warship's.

As they arrived at the harbour, Atticus could see the two triremes were still being readied for the voyage. In the shadows of an alleyway, he noticed two hooded men skulking, taking notes as to what was being loaded aboard the ships.

It was a warm evening. The clouds had blotted out the evening sun. It would soon be dark. Atticus could hear the sound of the sea splashing the harbour wall, and the sound of birds flying above squawking looking for scraps of fish waste as the fishermen gutted and unloaded the day's catch.

As they passed a tavern called the ship's mate, the sound of sailors laughing and singing songs rang out.

"Sounds like there's plenty of drunken sailors already if you ask me," said Edelgard.

"Can't wait to join them!" shouted Sextus with a chuckle.

The Merry Sailor was quite full, mainly with off-duty marines and local fishermen. The atmosphere was pleasant, and there was a burly man in his mid-forties standing inside the door. He had a heavy club in his hand to deal with any drunken fights, and brandished a tattoo of the legions on his arm, so it was quite obvious he'd served in the army.

Atticus was the first to enter, followed by Sextus and Edelgard. Atticus, standing over six feet six and as wide as the door's entrance, made the man look quite insignificant as he walked past him into the tavern, which made the man with the club feel a little uneasy and take a second look at him.

Adrian was behind his counter with two girls serving drinks and food; the smell of fresh fish filled the air.

There were three other girls waiting on tables and offering other services to the men sitting down at their tables. They giggled when they got a playful smack on their backsides or one of their breasts groped. One of the girls, who is only about sixteen and very pretty, took hold of one of the men's hands and led him off up some wooden stairs to the cheers of his companions.

"Sextus, my friend!" came the shout from Adrian when he saw them walk in.

"Come, I have a nice big table free in the backroom. I will bring my finest wine," then he rushed from behind the counter.

"It's good to see you again, young Atticus. My that is a fine uniform you're wearing, officer no less."

Atticus quelled the anger arising inside of him and politely smiled and replied, "Yes, it's good to see you also."

"And who is this fine gentleman?" enquired Adrian.

"This is Edelgard, who has a thirst for fine wine," answered Sextus.

"Well, he has come to the right place."

"Here you are, sit down!" then, one of the young girls brought a tray holding a large jug of wine and three glasses.

"I will bring fresh fish and meat over, enjoy the wine," said Adrian as he rushed off behind the counter.

Sextus immediately filled a glass with wine and drank it all in one go "I needed that!" said Sextus smacking his lips together and wiping his chin.

Then he began to fill all three glasses, "Fuck me, did you even taste that wine," joked Edelgard, "And I thought you could drink Edelgard." Atticus joked joining in setting the mood.

Adrian quickly sent for Amaya; while he waited, he took the tray of food and another large jug of wine to Atticus's table.

"Here you are gentlemen, enjoy if there is anything you want, please feel free to ask," then he winked and nodded towards one of the girls before returning behind the counter and into his kitchen.

Moments later in walked a beautiful Persian girl with long brown hair in her early twenties; her eyes were brown and lined with dark charcoal, and her eyelids were painted light blue with long dark eyelashes fluttering as she blinked. Her cheeks had been blushed with a gold tint. She was tall with very large breasts, which hung loosely in a low-cut white toga tied at her narrow waist with a gold cord, making her breasts stand out even more.

"Amaya, I have a job for you, and with your expert talents. I am sure you will deliver the result I require."

"And what may I ask, do you require," purred Amaya, fluttering her long eyelashes.

Adrian smiled and replied, "You know, Sextus, my dear, who is totally infatuated with you probably holds some vital information my paymasters require shall we say, and will pay a very healthy sum of gold for it."

Then Adrian paused while Amaya walked towards him and stroked his chest with one of her fingers and asked, "How much will you pay for this information?" as she tapped him on his nose provocatively.

She then blew into his ear while tickling his earlobe with her long tongue. Adrian began to feel an erection grow in his loincloth as she rubbed one of her thighs against his groin.

He quickly drew open his purse fastened to his belt and placed two gold coins in her hand.

She looked at the coins and said, "Give me three, and I will treat you to something special when I'm finished with him and bring you the information you seek."

As she looked him in the eye, she placed one of her hands inside his loincloth, feeling his erection, and gently stroked it between her fingers. Adrian began to tingle all over his body. Adrian quickly took out a third gold coin and pushed it into the palm of her hand with the two other gold coins.

"Your wish is my command!" purred Amaya. She then pushed one of her fingers inside her mouth and then placed it in his. Amaya slowly turned and, with a smile, left the kitchen and walked towards the table where Sextus sat with Atticus and Edelgard.

As she approached, Sextus almost choked, drinking his wine as soon as he saw her.

"My Sextus, I wasn't aware of your intended visit," Sextus's mouth fell open, unable to answer gazing at her beauty. As Amaya sat down on his knee, she gently stroked one of his thighs almost touching his manhood, teasing him.

Amaya looked over at Atticus thinking to herself what a pity it wasn't you who had the information Adrian required. Sextus drew her attention back to him by saying, "Amaya, please let me introduce my friends, this is Edelgard from Germanica, and this young man is Atticus." Amaya's eyes lit up slightly at the name of Atticus, thinking to herself, "So this is the Roman warrior who saved the Roman General Maximus."

"It's my pleasure to meet you both," replied Amaya, she then returned her gaze and attention to Sextus.

"And where is my glass of wine? or are you keeping it all to yourself," she gently stroked his cheek with her hand.

"No, I'll get you a glass!" replied Sextus all flustered.

"No need...my love, I will share yours."

Amaya took his glass and drank from it, then seductively licked the rim of the glass with her long tongue before placing it back into Sextus's hand. Edelgard's loins were about to explode, he grabbed his glass, filled it and drank it down in one. Atticus just grinned at his friend's discomfort.

"Come, Sextus, let's go to my room," and as she stood up, brushed one of her breasts against his nose, Sextus could smell the perfume on her body and almost fell off his stool. Edelgard struggled not to laugh at poor old Sextus.

"It's been nice to meet you boys, but I have plans for your friend Sextus, so I bid you farewell."

Amaya then took Sextus by the hand and led him upstairs.

"Bloody hell, I almost feel sorry for old Sextus, I hope he doesn't have heart failure," said Edelgard, wishing it was him climbing those stairs with Amaya.

"I can see she will have no problem loosening his tongue," whispered Atticus.

For the next hour, Atticus and Edelgard sat waiting, drinking the wine and eating the food. Atticus drank sparingly while Edelgard drank freely, which didn't seem to have any effect on his demeanour. Atticus noticed Amaya come down the stairs and go straight to the kitchen.

"Edelgard, wait here for Sextus! I will return as soon as I've checked something."

Atticus left the tavern and hid in the shadows watching the alleyway running to the rear of the tavern. It wasn't long before the two men he'd seen earlier, now accompanied by a third, made their way down the alley. One of them knocked on the door several times in a manner that Atticus took to be a prearranged code. The door opened, and the three men entered, the door quickly closed behind them.

Atticus crept down the alley unnoticed and stood below an open window, listening to the conversation going on inside.

As soon as he'd heard all he needed, Atticus smiled to himself and quietly left the alley unnoticed and went back inside. Sextus had returned to the table and was sitting laughing with Edelgard.

"Right boys, time to be back at the fort," said Atticus.

"Where have you been?" enquired Sextus, "For a piss but if I'm not back soon Naomi won't be pleased so drink up."

"Are you leaving us so soon?" asked Adrian who'd walked up to their table carrying another jug of wine.

"Atticus, here is on a promise from his wife and doesn't want to be late," replied Sextus with a grin, "But I've brought you another jug of wine, gentlemen!"

"Not to worry, I'll take that with us," Edelgard answered as he took the jug out of Adrian's hand.

"How much do we owe you?" asked Sextus.

"Nothing, nothing, it's been my pleasure to have you as my guests."

"That's very kind of you, Adrian," said Atticus. Once outside, Atticus quickly mounted Fury, followed by the others making their way out of the city.

"You are in a rush to see that wife of yours!" shouted Sextus feeling a little sick with the momentum of the gallop after drinking too much wine.

It wasn't long before Sextus threw up leaning to one side of his horse which made Edelgard laugh loudly.

"Looks like you're going to have a sore head in the morning, Sextus!" said Edelgard, pulling Sextus upright in his saddle so he wouldn't fall off his horse.

He also took hold of the reins of Sextus's horse leading it towards the forts gates, "I will see you two later tomorrow," shouted Atticus as soon as he'd entered the fort, Sextus muttered a reply.

He hung his head again at the side of his horse's neck, throwing up again this time all over one of the guards feeling very ill. The guard was not impressed with Sextus but due to his rank thought it better not to complain. Edelgard apologised on his friend's behalf and placed a couple of coins down into the guard's hand.

Edelgard knew exactly where Atticus was going, took hold of Sextus's horse's reins again and led him to his barracks.

Almut and Asken were on guard duty outside Maximus's quarters. "Greetings boys is the General in?" asked Atticus, jumping down from Fury.

"Good evening, Atticus!" replied Almut.

"He's been pacing up and down like a caged lion for the last hour," said Asken.

The door opened and light shone out from the torches hanging on the walls. Maximus appeared in the doorway, "Come in, Atticus, what news?" Atticus tied Fury to a wooden rail and followed Maximus inside.

Atticus closed the door. Maximus filled two glasses of wine and passed one to Atticus, "Well, don't keep me waiting or are you doing it on purpose?" chuckled Maximus.

"They've taken the bait, Sextus spilled everything he knew to one of Adrian's girls. He's then given the information to his messengers. I overheard everything …they will waste no time in reaching their paymasters and be on their way as we speak," "Good!"

"It also seems Adrian is quite high up in the pecking order!" said Atticus.

"Is that so?" Atticus looked at the map still laid out on Maximus's desk and pointed at the sea at the bottom of the island of Creta.

"One of the messengers has been instructed to meet with pirates to ambush our trireme from there."

Atticus pointed to an inlet shown on the map.

"Well, they're going to be very disappointed then," said Maximus with a smile.

"We will have transferred to the merchant boats and landed at Tarsus while they're still scratching their arses wondering where the fuck we are," answered Atticus.

"I will visit the emperor first thing tomorrow; take your wife to your father's and don't forget you need to be ready to leave in two days."

"Yes, I will…better get back, Naomi's waiting," Maximus smiled and replied.

"I will see you on my return from Rome and fill you in with all the final details have fun."

Atticus left and went quickly to the livery, he fed and watered Fury before returning to his quarters. Doukasi was asleep in bed, all her belongings already packed, when the call came.

Naomi appeared at their bedroom door smiling in an exotic silk see-through gown.

"You look amazing, my love," whispered Atticus. He entered their bedroom, closed the door and with the help of Naomi undressed and made love with his wife for several hours.

Chapter 4

The following morning Maximus had set off for Rome early. Atticus had seen Tribune Matias to let him know of his trip home sanctioned by Maximus. Edelgard and Adelar accompanied Atticus and Naomi along with Doukasi.

Tribune Tiberius had taken charge of the day's training of the new recruits and was already instructing the drill in the training arena; at the far side, the Cilician archers were practicing their skill with the bow.

Sextus was in charge of the guard detail at the gate and looked like a bear with a sore head, and along with the soldiers at the gate, saluted as Atticus rode out.

Edelgard and Atticus did not discuss the events of the night before. They could wait until they were alone.

"So Doukasi, are you looking forward to seeing your new home for the next few months?" asked Edelgard.

"Yes, if it is half as beautiful as Naomi has described it, I will be very happy, but my priority is to attend to all her needs while Atticus is away." The remark from Doukasi made Naomi smile, looking over at Atticus.

"Looks to me you will be looked after very well, but you might put on a little too much weight!" Naomi gave Atticus a look of bewilderment.

"All those lovely oatcakes Doukasi bakes you won't be able to resist," teased Atticus, which made Doukasi smile.

Naomi laughed, "If I do you will still not be able to resist my charm when you return my love!" responded Naomi.

Atticus grinned, gazing over at his beautiful wife.

The road towards Rome was very busy with merchants who'd arrived in Ostia heading to the markets to sell their goods. A merchant's waggon had lost a wheel at the side of the road and was having a struggle trying to change it. He was accompanied by two weak, undernourished-looking slaves whom he was berating and cursing for their lack of strength. Atticus pulled Fury up and jumped down. The merchant lashed one of the slaves with a bullwhip, making him scream out loud, feeling the burning sting cutting through his skin across his back. The merchant flicked the whip back, ready to strike the other one.

Atticus grabbed the merchant's arm and ripped the whip out of his hand. He twisted the man's arm backwards causing him immense pain and pushed him to the floor. The merchant looked up at Atticus towering over him, holding his arm, gritting his teeth with the searing pain he felt throbbing from his wrist to his shoulder.

"What was that for? They are my slaves, it is my right to punish them!" said the merchant, trying to get up but finding it almost impossible due to not being able to put any of his weight on his injured arm.

"Not in my presence you won't," retorted Atticus.

Atticus turned to the two slaves standing in silence, bowing their heads low towards the large Roman officer who was now addressing them.

"Fetch me that wheel strapped to the side of your waggon!" requested Atticus in a gentle tone. Quickly they both went about their task as Atticus took hold of the rear of the waggon.

"I better help Atticus; that waggon is heavy!" said Doukasi, climbing down from his mule.

"No need, watch Doukasi!" said Edelgard. The two slaves rolled the large wooden wheel towards Atticus. As soon as they were near enough, Atticus placed his shoulder under the side of the waggon and seemingly without effort stood up, lifting the waggon high enough. It creaked as it elevated; Atticus kicked the remains of the broken wheel off the axle as he held the waggon up. With a struggle, the two slaves managed to place the replacement wheel on the end of the axle. Atticus lowered the waggon, letting the wheel take the weight, then he let go. One of the slaves got hold of a large wooden hammer and hammered the iron pin in place to keep it from coming loose. Naomi had dismounted her pony and removed a small satchel from one of the mules carrying her belongings. She beckoned the slave who had been whipped to stand in front of her so she could attend to the wound. The merchant had managed to get to his feet, standing, holding his arm.

"Thank you, sir!" the merchant said sheepishly looking at Atticus.

"I didn't do it for you, I did it for them," replied Atticus, pointing at the two slaves. The merchant felt a little ashamed of himself.

"I am sorry for my actions," replied the merchant. Atticus picked up the bullwhip.

"You will not be needing this!" retorted Atticus.

"No sir, I will not! You are right to be angry with me. It will not happen again!"

Naomi had finished treating the slave and remounted her pony. Atticus mounted Fury. Adelar nudged his horse forward to the side of the merchant, looking down at him with disdain before riding on down the road followed by the others.

"Why do you think Edelgard is looking forward to visiting my home with us?" asked Atticus.

"Naomi has told me of your father's vineyards and how they produce the finest wine in all Italy. I have come to know that Edelgard loves his wine," answered Doukasi with a big smile.

"Seems like everyone knows you too well my German friend," joked Atticus, Edelgard just held his hands up as if to surrender.

Naomi quietly spoke with Atticus as they rode in front. Doukasi and the others rode further back. Doukasi told Edelgard and Adelar of his homeland and how he'd been taken into slavery. Having his home burnt to the ground by the slave traders and his parents being killed because they were regarded as too old and worthless.

Several hours later they arrived at the big, gated door of Romulus's home, and before they could even knock the door swung open.

Zuma stepped out to one side, "Missing us already? You've only been gone a matter of days," teased Zuma. Atticus jumped down off Fury and slapped Zuma on his shoulder.

"It's good to see you, my big friend!" Zuma burst out laughing as they all entered the courtyard.

Doukasi marvelled at the wonderful courtyard with its fountain, ornate stone benches and fruit trees in full bloom. Romulus came out of the main house and immediately hugged Naomi and then Atticus before shouting a greeting to Edelgard and Adelar.

Aramea and Seema then quickly fussed over Naomi.

"Figo you better fetch some wine for that big German bugger, he's already drooling in the mouth in anticipation!" joked Romulus.

Edelgard dismounted and shouted to Romulus, "Why else would I come…I didn't come to see your ugly face," he then dismounted and clasped Romulus's forearm.

"It's good to see you my friend."

"It's good to see you and who is this fine young man?"

"This is Doukasi, our new friend from the fort. We've come to stay while Atticus is away fighting for Rome," answered Naomi. Zuma noticed the mule laden up and looked over at Romulus. Figo arrived with the wine and handed it to Edelgard.

"Figo! help Naomi and Doukasi unload the mule, Aramea, and Seema can help."

"Let's go to my private room and you can tell me and Zuma what is going on."

After they had all sat down on the comfortable couches, Atticus relayed the events of the past week and as much as he was allowed to tell them of his mission and the reason Naomi and Doukasi would be staying until his return.

Romulus and Zuma realised it would be some months before they would see him again, hopefully with the will of the gods he would return safe.

The atmosphere in the room became more jovial as the subject turned to other matters and Edelgard was quite happy drinking the jug of wine.

In walked Naomi, "So this is where you're all hiding," said Naomi.

"Come, sit here on my knee!" beckoned Atticus. The next hour passed by rather quickly and it had come to the time for Atticus to return to the fort. Naomi and Atticus left the room and went to their bedroom to say their farewell in private which was quite painful for them both.

Atticus and Naomi went out into the courtyard where by now the whole household had come to say farewell. Little Alesandro was quickly picked up and hugged by Atticus.

"Are you going to chop some bad men's heads off?" the mood in the courtyard was very sombre but this made almost everyone laugh.

"Yes, if I have to but I will be home soon and it's your job to look after my Naomi while I'm away."

Atticus put Alesandro down, ruffled his hair, then kissed Naomi, and said his farewells to all, giving a kiss on the cheek to both Julia and Lydia. Atticus then mounted Fury. Without looking back due to the pain he now felt in his heart, a tear in his eye, he galloped down the road followed closely by Edelgard and Adelar in silence.

After riding hard for an hour Atticus finally broke the silence, "We leave in two days, and I have a meeting with Maximus as soon as he returns from Rome."

"Well, I hope the ships are carrying plenty of wine," replied Edelgard trying to lift Atticus's mood.

"Don't worry, if you hadn't noticed I've strapped two full wineskins of my father's finest to my saddle just for you."

"See Edelgard! Atticus won't send you into battle on an empty stomach," said Adelar, this seemed to do the trick as Atticus began laughing.

It wasn't long before they had returned to the fort at Ostia. As they rode down to the barracks, Atticus told Edelgard and Adelar he would see them later; he needed to visit the quartermaster to make sure everything had been provided for the mission.

When he arrived and walked into the quartermaster's warehouse the old man in charge saluted. He was wearing a tunic and sweat poured down his face as he stocked weapons neatly to one side. As soon as Atticus walked in, he could feel the heat take his breath away, "Greetings Publius, it's bloody warm in here!"

"Yes, sir, what can I do for you?"

"Just checking we have everything we need."

"You have, the last of your requirements were loaded on the ships this morning." replied Publius.

"Have you any caltrops stored here?"

"We have but they were not on the list for your mission."

"How much per case?"

"Fifty."

"Can you send six cases to be loaded aboard one of the ships straight away?"

Publius walked behind his counter and asked, "Have you got an order slip signed by your Tribune?"

"No, just do it. I will get the slip sent to you." Publius was about to protest but after seeing the look from Atticus decided he best get on with it.

"Yes sir! straight away let me have the slip at your earliest convenience." Atticus left and took hold of Fury's reins who'd been waiting outside chewing on some grass and led him to the livery.

When he got there, he put him in his stall and began stroking his neck and sunk his head into Fury's cheek who snorted lightly. Neither of them moved for several minutes. Atticus patted Fury before leaving his stall and making his way back to his quarters.

On his way, he met Edelgard and Adelar leaning on a fence, watching several of the Cilician archers firing arrows at targets over a hundred yards away.

Atticus lent on the fence beside them; he looked at some bows neatly piled up and admired one of them black in colour. It was decorated with gold markings painted down its length; the bow was curved outwards at each end.

One of the Cilician archers walked over, "Greetings, first Centurion sir," said the Cilician archer, saluting Atticus.

"I was just admiring the style of your bows," replied Atticus.

"May I introduce myself…I am Farrokh, commander of the Cilician archers. I understand we have been attached to your first cohort for the foreseeable future."

"You have," replied Atticus.

"I see you carry two swords; they must be your favoured weapon of choice. They look very highly crafted. May I look at one?" asked Farrokh.

Atticus drew one of his swords and handed it to Farrokh who had spoken in perfect Latin. As he examined the sword's quality, he read out loud the inscription etched in Latin down the blade.

"MORI QUAM FOEDARI," '*DEATH BEFORE DISHONOUR*', Farrokh handed it back tilting his head to the side and said, "Great words for a great warrior."

"Would you like to use the bow or is it a weapon you're not familiar with?" Adelar glanced over at Edelgard thinking he might be able to win some coin. Edelgard just shook his head knowing full well what was going through Adelar's mind.

Adelar turned to Farrokh, "Would you be interested in a small wager?" Farrokh smiled before replying.

"What would be the…small wager?"

"You Cilician archers are renowned as some of the best in the world are you not?"

"That is so!" replied Farrokh, stiffening his back and holding his head high with pride. Farrokh was a man usually quiet in manner and certainly not one to boast. But he was proud of his Cilician routes and traditions.

"I offer one of my sesterces to three of yours that Atticus could beat you with the bow aiming at those targets over there."

A couple of the Cilician archers listening to the conversation chuckled.

"Do you fancy the challenge, 1st Centurion?" enquired Farrokh.

Atticus wasn't too happy with the position Adelar had placed him in again and gave him a stern look.

"Go bring me my bow Adelar."

Now realising the honour of the Augusta 11 legion had been put at stake. "You may use one of these," said Farrokh pointing at the Cilician bows.

"I would prefer to use mine if it is alright with you," replied Atticus as Adelar ran off to get the bow.

"How do you want the competition to play out?" asked Atticus. "We place our targets side by side starting at say seventy-five paces. The first to miss the middle ring of the target loses. And after each shot, the targets will be moved a further twenty-five paces back until one of us misses the middle ring," answered Farrokh.

Edelgard gave Atticus a friendly nod as Adelar returned with Atticus's bow.

"How many sesterces do you wish to bet?" asked Farrokh, feeling very confident.

"Twenty that means if I win the bet, you owe me sixty, if that's not more than you can afford?" asked Adelar with a grin, clearly trying to upset the Cilician a little.

"That will be fine German!" clearly annoyed at Adelar's remark. The other Cilician archers set the two targets at seventy-five paces. Atticus strung his bow and stretched it slightly making sure he was happy with the bow's tension. He then walked to the line laid for them to stand behind next to Farrokh.

"I will give you the honour of going first," said Atticus. Farrokh knocked an arrow aimed and fired hitting the centre of the middle ring of the target.

Atticus then aimed and fired, hitting the centre of the middle ring. Farrokh looked over at Atticus and smiled as the targets were taken further away and placed. As soon as they were in place, Farrokh aimed and fired. The arrow took a little longer to reach its target but again hit it dead centre. Again, Atticus aimed and fired, hitting the target dead centre. Adelar smiled and wiped some sweat off his forehead, watching intently.

Farrokh shouted across to Atticus, "It appears you at least know how to use a bow. Now is the time for it to become a little harder."

The targets were now set at a hundred and twenty-five paces, Farrokh took a little longer at aiming his bow, then fired again hitting the dead centre of the middle ring to the applause of the other Cilician archers.

Edelgard looked at Adelar, clearly impressed with the shot. Adelar had begun to feel a little nervous and gripped the fence he was holding.

Atticus took aim and fired, everyone's eyes were fixed on the target as the arrow hit its dead centre, Farrokh looked over at Atticus clearly impressed with the shot and now realised he had a battle on his hands. Adelar punched the air with his fist and roared. Edelgard just laughed at his German friend and drank from his wineskin.

The targets were now at one hundred and fifty paces, and it was difficult to see the centre of the target, making it seemingly impossible to hit from that distance.

Farrokh took his time knocking the arrow and didn't take his eye off the target, he slowly aimed and fired the arrow. It seemed to be an eternity before the arrow embedded itself into the target. They all waited for one of the Cilician archers to shout back where it had struck. Adelar still gripped the fence, sweat pouring down his cheeks.

"Just outside the middle ring!" came the shout. Farrokh turned to Atticus and said, "You still have to hit the middle ring or nearer the centre my friend to win," trying to put a little extra pressure on Atticus.

There were many worried looks on the face of the Cilician archers watching, including the face of Adelar. Edelgard drank from his wineskin remembering that day in the forest when Atticus had saved their lives. He knew exactly how much skill Atticus had with the bow. Atticus aimed his bow at the target and fired the arrow, it flew fast, accurate, hitting the target dead centre with a thud. Everyone waited for the shout as to where it had hit, many holding their breath.

"Dead centre!" came the shout from the Cilician archer at the target. Farrokh walked to Atticus, bowed and clasped his forearm before saying.

"It is rare for a Roman to outshoot a Cilician archer; it is quite clear that me and my men will be in capable hands when we go into battle."

Farrokh then walked over to Adelar, took out his purse and paid the bet in full without saying a word. He then turned to his men and shouted, "Come, it is time to eat!" His men gathered up their bows, saluted Atticus and left.

Maximus and his escort had charged through the gates and rode down to where Atticus stood. He was telling Adelar he wasn't happy about being put in that position again. But the one good thing that had come out of it was that he had gained the trust of the Cilician archers.

"Greetings, Atticus. I need a meeting with you straight away and you Edelgard, and I suppose you better come as well Adelar," said Maximus.

"Yes sir!" replied Atticus, and all three of them followed Maximus to his quarters.

Tribune Matias was waiting for the General as they arrived.

"SIR!" shouted Atticus, and saluted.

"Good evening, Atticus, I trust your wife is happy to be home for the time being?" asked Matias.

"She is!" replied Atticus.

"Sit, gentlemen!" ordered Maximus.

"Would you be ready to leave at first light tomorrow? I know it's a day early, but speed is essential."

"Yes, I've already checked with the quartermaster, and he assured me everything we require has been loaded onto the ships." answered Atticus.

"Are you sure you don't need me to take charge of this mission and leave for Tadmor?" enquired Matias.

"No! Atticus had planned it. He has my full support, along with the emperor's. We both feel he is the best one to lead this mission."

"Yes, sir!" came the quick response from the Tribune.

"Sorry to have kept you in the dark but there have been many developments taking place over the last couple of days and now is not the time to discuss them," said Maximus.

"What I need you to do is round up all the officers of the first cohort including the officer in charge of the Cilician archers. They need to be at Atticus's quarters within the hour so he can issue his orders. Which will have to come from me so if you would please?"

"Yes, I will sir!" Matias saluted and left.

"Is there anything else you need, Atticus?" asked Maximus.

"Only a slip for the quartermaster for some cases of caltrops I've instructed him to put aboard," replied Atticus.

"Bloody quartermasters, anyone would think they owned all that equipment," said Maximus with a chuckle.

"Come on, Edelgard, pour some wine my throat is as dry as an ant's arse," Edelgard didn't need any further encouragement and quickly filled three glasses.

"After you have left, and that traitor Adrian has sent one of his spies or more confirming your departure. I will personally slit his throat or have him crucified and any other co-conspirators that still remain at that tavern!" growled Maximus with a face like thunder.

As soon as Maximus had drunk his wine, he instructed Edelgard to pour him another.

"I see you have taken to drinking wine as much as I have!" said Edelgard, drinking his and pouring himself another.

"That will be the day!" responded Maximus with a grin.

"Here before I forget, you may need this," Maximus passed Atticus a small narrow tube with the emperor's gold seal on the outside.

"What is this?" enquired Atticus.

"That gives you the full authority from Emperor Augustus and grants you all the power of Rome. If you require anything on this mission throughout the Roman empire show this and it will be given. As if the emperor was asking himself," replied Maximus.

Atticus exhaled from deep down in his lungs that seemed to go on forever.

"Don't worry when I arrive at Tadmor you can give me that back," said Maximus before draining his glass of wine and wiping his chin.

"What punishment have you decided for Sextus?" asked Atticus.

"Nothing at the moment, he may not survive the mission so if that's the case there will be no need. But we'll discuss that at Tadmor if necessary."

"Edelgard, make sure you and Adelar stay close to Atticus at all times and do his bidding."

"I will!" he replied.

"I better get back for that meeting with the officers and make my final preparations," said Atticus standing up. Maximus walked up to Atticus and clasped his forearm and said, "May the gods be with you, and I will see you at Tadmor in two months."

"Thank you!" answered Atticus.

Maximus then turned to Edelgard and patted him on his shoulder saying "Take care my old friend and good hunting," Edelgard just nodded his head and followed Atticus out of his office. All the officers including Farrokh were waiting outside Atticus's quarters talking amongst themselves as he arrived with Edelgard.

"I will leave you to it," said Tribune Matias and clasped his forearm before leaving. All the officers listened intently as Atticus gave them their orders and instructions for the men of the first cohort to be ready to leave at first light. After they had all left, Atticus retired to get a good night's sleep as he wasn't sure when he'd get another.

Chapter 5

Atticus hadn't long been a Roman soldier but had already dealt with the enemies of Rome, on more than one occasion.

Trained since the very young age of six, so he was more than capable for the tasks ahead and had the full confidence of his men.

Before daylight had broken, Atticus had collected Fury from his stable where he had met up with Edelgard and Adelar.

All three of them made their way on horseback to the parade ground as the men of the first cohort of the Augusta 11 legion were arriving with all their kit.

Atticus had made sure he wore his red jasper, which hung from his neck from a leather cord chain. His gold eagle was pinned to his tunic, and he wore the ring he'd been given for saving a man and boy several months previous.

Naomi had cut a small braid of her hair which he had placed in a pouch hanging from his belt. The Centurions rode horseback ahead of each of their centuries with the Optio walking proudly behind him. Centurions Decimus and Cyrus confirmed all the men were present and ready to leave; Farrokh had also confirmed his full complement of Cilician archers were ready to leave and saluted. Atticus rode Fury to the front along with Edelgard and Adelar and gave the order to leave the fort. The sound of hobnailed boots crunching the floor echoed off the fort's walls in the quiet of the early morning sunrise. The sound of the horses' hooves clattered the stone road. Maximus was standing with the guards at the gate saluting and smiling as Atticus and his men marched out.

Only the officers knew of their destination, the men would be told once they were at sea. Centurion Gaius had been given the honour of carrying one of the legions banners, which fluttered in the light sea breeze.

The men and horses were settled aboard the ships. Atticus went below deck with Fury, wanting to personally make sure he was comfortable with his new surroundings for the journey. Fury was always calm and well-behaved in his presence, and Atticus made sure Fury had ample food and water. He gave the cabin boy his instructions on how best to treat Fury while at sea. Atticus then introduced the cabin boy to Fury; he was a little apprehensive at first. Fury seemed quite at ease with the cabin boy, letting him reach up as far as he could to stroke Fury's neck.

"What is your name?" enquired Atticus.

"Marco Enzo Ricci, sir!"

"Well, Marco Enzo Ricci It looks like Fury is quite fond of you, so you won't have any problems with him!"

"Fury is a beautiful horse, sir; have you had him long if I am not being too bold to ask?" Atticus had also decided he liked the boy.

"I've been lucky to be acquainted with Fury from the age of 6. He is very precious to me!"

"I will make sure he has everything he needs on this voyage, sir!"

"I know you will…and when I am down here with you, Marco and Fury, it will not be necessary to call me sir! Atticus will do!" "Atticus, I have heard of your name…you are the great warrior who saved the life of our great General Maximus."

Atticus looked at the young boy's face full of life, smiled, and ruffled his blond hair. "Well, I have to go and carry out my duties. I will come and see you and Fury as soon as I am able."

Fury wasn't at all bothered by the ship's slight roll; and chomped on some carrots Marco had given him. Marco picked up a hand brush and began to groom Fury as he ate the carrots.

The sound of men running back and forth on the deck above them could be heard; orders were being shouted. Then the sound of the anchor being dragged aboard made the ship's timbers creek, and the ship now rolled more with the swell of the sea.

"I'll leave you to it; anything you need for Fury, let me know!" Atticus then stroked Fury's face and patted him on his neck and said, "I will see you soon, Fury."

Atticus climbed up the wooden stairs back on deck and made his way up onto the platform at the stern of the ship, where the captain stood barking out his orders. Edelgard and Adelar were there leaning on the ship's rail, looking over towards the Merry Sailor tavern, where Adrian stood with another man watching the two triremes leave the harbour.

The shout for the ores to be deployed came from below, and as soon as they hit the surface of the sea, the drumbeat rang out, dictating the speed.

Once they had left the harbour, the sails were dropped and were soon filled with a strong breeze, and the order for the ores to be hauled aboard sounded. Atticus was addressed by the ship's captain, a tall fat red faced man with a neatly trimmed beard, "Good day, sir. I'm Captain Appius Faustus at your service." The Roman navy captain said, senior in rank while at sea, but after his meetings with General Maximus, had been left in no doubt who was in charge.

"Good day to you, Captain this is Edelgard and Adelar, two of Maximus's most trusted bodyguards." replied Atticus.

"Have you been to sea before?" enquired Appius before shouting at one of the crew to tighten one of the sails.

"Sorry for the interruption, we have a good crew, but you need to keep on top of them."

"No, I haven't been to the sea, but I've been looking forward to it," answered Atticus.

"I suppose you two, being the General's bodyguards, have been to sea many times?" asked Appius.

"We have!" answered Adelar.

"I don't suppose you have any wine handy, Captain; the sea air always makes my throat a little dry?" enquired Edelgard.

Appius didn't answer but smiled, then shouted to his cabin boy to go below and fetch an amphora of wine from his cabin and bring it with all haste.

"Is everything to your liking in your cabin?" asked Appius.

"Yes, fine it should be interesting sleeping in that hammock hanging in there. It's a bit short and I've never had the pleasure of sleeping in one but I'm sure it won't take me long to adjust!" Edelgard smiled as the cabin boy arrived carrying the wine and some pot cups. The boy was about to hand it to his captain, but Edelgard quickly took them and filled the cups without spilling a drop as the ship rolled from front to stern.

"I can see you've done that before," said Appius with a chuckle.

"Once or twice, you might say," answered Edelgard. The captain struggled a little with Edelgard's thick German accent but thought it would be better not to upset him by asking him to repeat what he had said.

"Right, Appius, we will leave you to it. I need to check on my men and make sure they're all settled."

Many of the Cilician archers were already on deck looking back at the land, which was starting to disappear while the other Tyrime sailed about a thousand yards behind. The trireme had a bolt thrower positioned at the stern and also on a platform at the front; above the sails at the top of the masts were two platforms for the ship's archers and lookouts. At the front was a large, thick wooden ram to sink enemy ships, decorated with two large eyes. Atticus thought the ship seemed quite capable of fighting any pirate ships they might come across.

Atticus could see Farrokh leaning on the ship's rail, looking out to sea as several dolphins broke the surface of the water before disappearing again.

"Are all your men settled for the journey?" enquired Atticus.

"They are sir, one or two are feeling a little sick but that will pass." he replied.

"Good, tomorrow, I will let you know of our destination!" Farrokh bowed his head in response as Atticus and the two Germans walked further on, trying to find a quiet spot where they could talk in private, which wasn't easy due to the number of men aboard. Sextus came out from below deck.

"The men are becoming adjusted to their cramped sleeping quarters, but I've issued a rota as to how many on deck at once for fresh air and exercise, sir!"

"Good, we need to talk somewhere quiet," Edelgard walked to the bow of the ship and cleared any crew or soldiers in that area for them to speak in private; there were a couple of benches bolted to the floor, so they sat down. The occasional gust of wind blew a spray of sea water over the deck, not enough to drench them but enough for Adelar to moan. Edelgard passed Atticus and Adelar a cup each of the wine.

The sun was very strong, bearing down on them from high up in the sky. Sea birds squawked, flying high above the ship, returning to an island on the ship's starboard side.

"Sextus, you need to listen carefully to what I have to say," said Atticus. Sextus looked at Atticus, wondering what could be so important, feeling a subdued tone in Atticus's voice.

"Your so-called friend Adrian is a traitor and a spy for the enemies of Rome!" Atticus paused to allow his words to sink in.

"You must be mistaken, surely, he…he, couldn't be, I've…" Atticus held up his hand and cut him off in mid-speech.

"Sextus, you need to listen and not interrupt. Adrian has been filling you with wine, loosening your tongue. He'd arranged for Amaya to sexually please you in a way that not many men would have the willpower to resist. Adrian was befriending you solely for the purpose of gaining your trust."

The blood seemed to drain from Sextus's face as he tried to recall the events that had taken place at the Merry Sailor over the past few months. Sextus put his head in his hands, finally realising how stupid he'd been. He felt a bitter taste in his mouth, as he recalled the memories of the time he'd spent with Amaya. He'd been blinded by the strong feelings he'd had for her. But she was nothing more than a whore being paid to mislead him.

"It was the emperor Augustus's spies who found out about Adrian and his web of traitors and informed Maximus," Atticus took a drink of wine and paused before carrying on; he liked Sextus and wasn't enjoying the conversation one bit.

"Maximus and I came up with a plan to deceive Adrian. That last encounter you had with that whore Amaya and the information about this mission you divulged had been greatly distorted. So, the information she acquired while fucking you was false. Which in turn she passed on to Adrian. That information will have gone to benefit our mission so hopefully our whereabouts when we arrive in Mesopotamia, will not be common knowledge." Sextus felt a little better on hearing that news.

"But you realise that the attempt on Maximus's life came about through the information you gave them to his daily routine."

"And my life also!" growled Edelgard.

Sextus now understood the whole gravity of the situation he'd gotten himself into.

"What will become of me?" asked Sextus.

"That will be up to Maximus. If this mission is a total success it may go in your favour, but at least if you're lucky you will only be demoted."

"I'm not fit to be a Centurion, put me back in the ranks!"

"No! You're a good officer and a loyal soldier. Yes, you've been duped and foolish, but I need you to lead your men for now what will be will be, can I count on you?" asked Atticus.

"Yes, until my dying day SIR! I am grateful for the chance you have given me. I will fight the enemies of Rome with my last dying breath if the gods will it."

Atticus smiled and said, "I know you will."

"I wish I was in a position to kill that bastard, Adrian." growled Sextus.

"No need, Maximus will have probably done that already. Better get on with your duty for Rome my friend," Sextus stood up and saluted and walked along the ship feeling very angry with himself for being so easily duped.

Edelgard then stood up, "Come, let's get some exercise my legs are stiff," Atticus looked up at him with a grin, taking himself out of his black mood.

"Good idea, let's get something to eat I'm hungry."

The ship rolled again causing Adelar to sidestep a few paces, "Looks like Adelar's had too much wine!" joked Edelgard.

"Fuck off!" came the swift rebuke from Adelar.

Later that afternoon, Atticus went below deck to check on Fury. Marco was mucking out and the heat below the deck was quite stifling.

"See that wooden bucket, tie a rope to the handle, and fill it with sea water and bring it here! we have to keep the horses cool," said Atticus.

"Yes sir!" Marco picked it up and ran up the wooden stairs tying some rope to it as he went.

Atticus took a small brush and began to brush Fury's mane. It wasn't long before Marco returned with a full bucket of cold sea water.

"Pass it here!" As soon as Marco set the bucket down Atticus plunged the brush into it and began to brush Fury with the cold water. Which seemed to have an instant impact on Fury, Atticus could tell Fury was a lot happier.

"Let me do that sir," asked Marco.

"Go, get one of the other buckets and see to the other horses. I will see Fury! you need to do this several times a day, Marco, to help keep them cool."

"I will!" answered Marco. As soon as he returned with the water, he began brushing the other horses vigorously.

Atticus finished seeing to Fury's needs and returned to the main deck to seek the captain out, wanting to find their present position.

Appius was still at the stern of the ship making sure everything was to his liking. Mistakes could quite easily cause death while at sea.

Atticus approached Appius and enquired as to their present position. Appius shouted some orders to several members of his crew. Appius acknowledged Atticus and led the way below deck to his cabin. He would show their position on the map. But before he left, he instructed his second in command to keep everything running smoothly until his return.

The captain's cabin was quite big; it had a bed rather than a hammock under a window at the back, a desk positioned to one side with a bench behind it both secured to the floor. A bust of Augustus was also secured on a ledge under the window, and a map of the Mediterranean Sea was pinned up on the desk.

"All the comforts of home I see," Atticus said, having to remove his helmet and stoop under the beams of the ceiling.

"Yes, you could say that, but it also helps being a lot shorter than you." replied Appius with a grin.

"It is," answered Atticus, smiling.

They both looked down at the map. Appius pointed to a point on the map and said, "That land we could just make out was Carthage. We are now here. Tomorrow if we keep the wind blowing behind us in this direction, we will pass this piece of land far to our port side and then cut into Corinth here." Atticus took in every detail showing on the map.

"How long do you anticipate us reaching Corinth and that inlet where we board those merchant boats?"

"That depends if we run into any pirates, or if the wind changes direction. But so far everything seems to be going in our favour. If that continues, we should be there late afternoon two days from now," replied Appius.

He then took a jug of watered wine from one of his shelves and poured it into two cups passing one to Atticus.

"You could say we are in the hands of the gods so to speak," said Appius, before drinking the contents of his cup.

"Thank you!" Atticus swallowed his cup of wine and took a last look at the map.

"I need to check on my men before retiring to bed," said Atticus with a slight yawn. He then returned above deck; the sun was starting to set. Lanterns were being lit.

The sea was very calm; it resembled a pond rather than a vast ocean. Atticus met up with Edelgard who accompanied him down below deck to check on the men.

Chapter 6

Back in Ostia, General Maximus had arrived outside the Merry Sailor along with Tribune Tiberius. He had brought a squad of Praetorians to make sure his orders were carried out to the letter.

"I don't want anyone escaping Tiberius or there will be consequences; mark my words!" demanded Maximus. He was in no mood for mistakes. They immediately blocked all the exits from the tavern. All the surrounding streets and alleyways had been sealed off; nobody was allowed in or around the tavern.

"Where the fuck do you think you're going?" shouted one of the soldiers to a group of fishermen making their way down one of the alleyways near to the tavern.

"To our boats to go fishing sir!" replied one of them.

"Not this way you're not, find another way!" Quickly and without a further response the fishermen disappeared back up the alleyway and out of sight.

It was very early, and the sun had just risen. The only other people nearby were fishermen tending to their nets and getting their boats ready for the day's fishing.

Tiberius returned to Maximus, "The place is surrounded, sir!" said Tiberius saluting.

Maximus along with Almut, one of his German bodyguards entered the tavern followed by Tribune Tiberius. Centurion Metelus and half a dozen Praetorian soldiers blocked the exit behind them.

There was only a young girl cleaning behind the counter, and the smell of stale fish hung in the air. Maximus ordered the Praetorian soldiers and Metelus to search the whole building.

"Bring anyone regardless of who they are down to this room whether they are dressed or not!" The sound of boots running upstairs broke the silence. Voices shouted and screams could now be heard from above.

Maximus instructed the girl to come from behind the counter and sit on the floor. Optio Paulinus entered the tavern with two Praetorians dragging a man protesting.

"SIR! this man was trying to escape the tavern from the side door," shouted Paulinus.

Maximus kicked the man to the floor next to the frightened girl which made her flinch.

"Don't move or speak! unless you want my sword slitting your throat," shouted Maximus.

The man was small in stature, fat and bald. He sat gripped with fear in silence not wanting to provoke the Roman General.

The young girl began to cry, shaking with fear, "No need to be frightened girl get up please and sit on that stool."

As soon as she was seated, Maximus knelt down in front of her. "What is your name?" asked Maximus in a quiet, reassuring tone.

"My name is Livia sir," she whimpered in reply.

"Everything will be fine as soon as I have found Adrian and his accomplices," said Maximus.

"Optio go search the kitchen and any rooms back there behind that counter!"

"SIR…you two come with me!" Paulinus instructed the two other soldiers standing with him.

The soldiers from upstairs came back into the room dragging and pushing several men and women. They were forced to sit on the floor to await their fate. A soldier then walked into the room escorting a very good looking Persian woman dressed in a fine white toga.

She was clearly annoyed at being woken but stood in silence in the presence of the Roman General. Optio Paulinus returned from behind the counter dragging the tavern owner Adrian who, protesting at the treatment he'd received shouted, "What is the meaning of this? The magistrate will hear of this. He is a good friend of mine!" Adrian then stood in silence with a blank expression, pleading ignorance as to why his premises had become under siege.

"I found him hiding in a cellar back there," said Paulinus, with a smile of satisfaction.

"Did you now!" replied Maximus.

Centurion Metelus then walked into the room followed by one of the Roman senators, Metelus saluted. "Sir! The upstairs is clear, we have checked everywhere."

"Ah senator Rimus…I wouldn't have expected to bump into you in this establishment at such an early hour." Maximus enjoyed inflicting a little discomfort on the senator.

"How is your wife?" Maximus asked while slowly looking around the room at the faces of those found in the tavern.

"My wife…is fine, she is away in Brundisium visiting a sick relative. So, if it is alright with you Maximus I wish to leave and let you go about your business." Maximus regarded Rimus as a bit of a pompous arse. He gave Rimus a stern look but allowed him to leave. Which he did, and as fast as his chubby legs could get him out of there.

Adrian had been made to kneel on the floor, he hung his head deciding not to make eye contact with Maximus or say another word.

In walked one of Maximus's new bodyguards by the name of Diemo. The young girl sitting on a stool recognised him as someone who had been frequenting the tavern for the past several days. He had always given her a coin for serving him at his table. She had happily given him the names of people he enquired about thinking nothing of it.

Maximus turned and smiled at Diemo as he walked in.

"Sir!" said Diemo and bowed his head slightly, then he began to look around the room before speaking.

"That one is Jason," pointing to the one Paulinus had stopped from escaping. "He is one of Adrian's spies, the woman in the white toga is Amaya, his whore. She gets information from the likes of Sextus and maybe that senator Rimus that just left. She gives the information to him for a price. The rest you see before you are customers and whores making Adrian rich." Maximus slowly walked amongst them stroking his neatly trimmed beard and stopped in front of Amaya who promptly dropped her white toga to the floor revealing her naked body.

"Surely, General, I can be of service to you!" Amaya smiled, pouting and licking her painted lips with her long tongue and fluttering her long eyelashes. Maximus looked at her with disdain.

"Put your garment back on, I have no use for a well-used harlot!" retorted Maximus angrily. She slowly covered up her naked body, still hoping she could entice Maximus into changing his mind. Cupping her large breasts provocatively back underneath her white loose toga.

"Paulinus, if you please, fetch Aurelius the slave trader and have him bring his caged waggon here, immediately. Let him know he will gain a tidy profit for his service!"

"Yes, sir," replied Paulinus who saluted and left the tavern. Maximus lifted Amaya's chin forcing her to look directly at him.

"You…will be sold into slavery, but mark my words I will make sure no wealthy aristocrat purchases you to fuck. You will be sold many miles away from Rome and its trappings. Hopefully by a shepherd living in relative poverty in a shack somewhere in the mountains. Maybe I will have you sent to service the men at the salt mines. I hear in winter the temperature there drops far below freezing."

Finally, Amaya now realised her future would not be enjoyable.

"As for this tavern, the emperor Augustus has also decreed that it will be sold and the money will go to the legions death fund," Maximus went on to say.

On hearing this, Adrian finally raised his head looking up at Maximus.

"I'm glad you're paying attention you and that other traitor will be crucified outside these city walls," said Maximus glaring down at him.

Adrian screamed and begged for mercy; the other traitor knew full well there was no point in pleading and just accepted his fate.

"Centurion Metelus."

"SIR!"

"Take them outside the city gates and carry out the crucifixion immediately."

"Yes sir!" Metelus along with several of the Praetorians dragged them outside and out of the city's gates.

Large wooden crosses were being assembled. Adrian looked at the large wooden crosses laid before him and his fellow spy Jason. The horror that would soon befall him was now all too much for him to bear. He tried to pull himself away from the guards, kicking out, screaming out loud, begging for mercy. The large crowd that had now gathered shouted profanities, baying for his blood.

Jason knelt awaiting his death without uttering a word. Adrian was forced down and positioned onto the giant cross. Metelus took the hammer and several iron nails from one of the carpenters standing to one side. He smiled looking down at Adrian who was sobbing like a child. His eyes bulged as he looked up at Metelus holding the heavy hammer standing over him. Metelus placed the first nail by pressing it into the palm of one of Adrian's hands. He hammered the nail, crashing it through skin and bone.

Adrian's screams filled the air to the sound of cheers from the large crowd gathered to witness the proceedings. Metelus hammered another nail into Adrian's other hand, again Adrian's screams filled the air as the nail was hammered into his flesh, crunching bone and sinew, blood trickled out from both of his hands. Metelus then hammered a couple of nails into Adrian's feet. He then signalled for the large cross to be elevated and as it was done the reaction from the crowd was a great roar of approval.

Jason had been nailed to the cross and it too was elevated into the air to another roar of approval. Adrian's eyes bulged with pain as his screams rang out, making the crowd cheer even louder. Jason the other traitor had died almost immediately, his heart had stopped beating as soon as the nails were hammered home.

The crowd screamed in jubilation now the crucifixion had been completed.

The doors to the tavern were nailed shut. Everyone inside had been ordered to leave. Livia was standing near the harbour's edge, tears streaming down her face. She had nowhere to go, no money. Maximus walked over to her.

"Have you nowhere to stay?"

"No!" Livia replied, sobbing uncontrollably.

"Come with me!" Livia looked a little apprehensive but did as she was asked and followed Maximus.

The Praetorians then marched behind them as they headed along the quayside and the waggon with the caged Amaya trundled past. It was being escorted to Rome by Centurion Metelus who had returned from the execution of the two traitors to Rome and a dozen Praetorian soldiers. Her fate and final destination would be decided by Augustus himself.

Maximus approached a large building on the quayside which rented out rooms to merchants who'd arrived to sell their wares in the market of Ostia.

"Wait here!" Maximus instructed his men.

"Come with me, Livia!" instructed Maximus with a gentle tone.

Inside the building, a short hallway led to a counter at the end of it, where a tall, slender man wearing spectacles was standing behind it. He looked over the rim of his spectacles at the Roman General approaching him followed by the young slender girl. He swallowed deeply. It wasn't often a General of the Roman legions came calling, let alone the famous General Maximus.

"Who are you?" demanded Maximus.

"I am the proprietor Fastius, how can I be of service to you General?"

"This young lady requires a job, perhaps cleaning rooms or working in your kitchen. She also requires accommodation." responded Maximus.

Fastius looked towards the young girl, "What is your name?" he enquired.

She stepped forward sheepishly, "Livia sir!"

"Well, Livia, do you have any experience required to clean and work in my kitchen?" Livia turned and looked at Maximus before she answered.

Maximus smiled and encouraged her to answer Fastius.

"I have and I will work hard for you if you let me," replied Livia.

"Very well, you can work for me in return. I will be happy to house and feed you." Livia smiled and bowed her head slightly in response.

Maximus looked at Fastius, who returned his attention to Maximus.

"And?" enquired Maximus sternly.

Fastius clearly understood what Maximus meant, "You will also receive one sesterce a month for your hard work."

"Are you happy with that, Livia?" asked Maximus.

"Yes, thank you. It is more than I received from Adrian, and he beat me for no reason." replied Livia.

"That will not happen here…will it Fastius?" responded Maximus sternly.

"It will not, I assure you!" answered Fastius.

"I must go now, Livia, but I will call from time to time to check on you!" said Maximus.

Livia threw her small arms around Maximus's waist; this seemed to surprise Maximus.

"Thank you!" said Livia, Maximus patted Livia lightly on her head before returning outside to his men and returning to the fort.

Chapter 7

The following morning, the men were being exercised in groups by the Centurion Sextus on deck while Atticus and Edelgard were below, with Appius being shown their new position on the map. They were not far from approaching Corinth, and the inlet, deep enough for the triremes to unload on its beach. They would then transfer to the six merchant vessels, which were hopefully already there waiting for them.

"We'll be there sometime early evening, but I would have thought we'd have seen the sail of at least one of the pirate ships looking for merchant vessels to attack," said Appius.

"That could have something to do with the false information carried by Adrians spies to their Parthian pay masters," replied Atticus.

"What do you mean?"

"I gained some intel from them and the pirates were being paid a small fortune to intercept us somewhere in the ocean here," replied Atticus pointing at an area on the map.

"Very clever," said Appius, smiling.

"Not only that, once we have transferred to the merchant vessels, any ships looking to intercept the two triremes will not give us a second look. We will look like we're a group of merchant vessels travelling together," said Atticus.

Appius and the captain of the other trireme had not been told the course Atticus and the merchant boats would be taking once they had departed Corinth and the place of landing in Mesopotamia, just in case they were intercepted on the return journey from Corinth to Ostia. Atticus had also taken into account when discussing that the plan with Maximus the smaller boats would be able to navigate past all the numerous small islands and shallower water between Corinth and Tarsus.

"Time for some fresh air and breakfast," said Atticus, looking at Edelgard.

"Yes, good idea. My stomach is beginning to growl." answered Edelgard.

"I will inform you as soon as our destination comes into view," said Appius as he left to go back on deck.

As they walked along the deck, Atticus shouted for Sextus, who was instructing the soldiers to make sure their kit was in good order and ready for the transfer to the smaller boats.

"Sir!" replied Sextus.

"Have any men taken ill during our voyage and not fit for duty?"

"No, sir, everyone's fit and well."

"Good, later today, according to Appius we will be disembarking in Corinth, let all the officers know. Make sure the men are packed and ready. I don't want any delay when we disembark."

"Yes, sir!" replied Sextus.

"Also, have all the officers on deck at the stern in one hour for an update and have Optio Linus come to my cabin immediately."

Sextus went off to carry out his orders. Atticus and Edelgard reached Atticus's cabin as Adelar arrived carrying a tray of fresh fish and fruit, "Breakfast boys," he then placed the tray on the table as they all began to tuck in.

Moments later there was a knock on the door, "Come!" shouted Atticus. In walked Optio Linus.

"Sir!"

"I'm going to organise one of the small boats aboard to be lowered with you and a small crew to row to the other ship with this dispatch for the Centurion Decimus, detailing my instructions when we disembark on Corinth."

"Yes, sir!" replied Linus.

"Be ready in thirty minutes," Linus saluted and left.

Atticus met Linus and the captain ready to lower the boat the anchor had been dropped and the ship was at a virtual standstill the sea was very calm nothing more than a slight swell could be felt. The captain sent a signal to the other ship to follow suit with the use of small flags, the whole manoeuvre took just over an hour once Optio Linus had returned and the boat was retrieved, the ships then carried on their journey.

The coastline of Corinth was in full view only a few thousand yards to the ships port side so far, the weather and wind had been perfect, so they had made good time.

Appius shouted for the sails to be taken in. Once this was done, the order for the ores to be put in the water rang out and the drumbeat setting out the ships speed sounded. Atticus stood next to Appius and Edelgard on the platform at the front of the ship.

Atticus then shouted for Farrokh, the Cilician archer's commander. Farrokh quickly responded.

"Yes sir!"

"Have several of your archers make their way to the platforms at the top of the masts and keep a sharp eye for any trouble." Farrokh saluted and carried out the order and the archers began climbing the rope ladders.

"Appius have the bolt throwers manned and ready!" shouted Atticus.

The sun glinted off the clear blue water as the ship entered the inlet, the ores breaking the surface of the water transcending them nearer to the beach of pure white sand. The merchant vessels were moored on the far left, slightly hidden out of sight by the overhanging cliffs with nests of seabirds scattered above. The cliff went up by at least five hundred yards where Atticus could just make out a lookout positioned at the top of the cliff. Steps made of sandstone weathered from the many years they had laid there. The steps leading up the cliff side were at times hidden from view behind the jagged rock face and brush. The beach was about half a mile in length and the cliffs became a lot lower to the right leading down to a forest of palm trees, brush, and sand dunes.

Several men now appeared from the boats and were running along the beach. The water was very deep but crystal clear and all manner of fish could be seen swimming under the ship as it got closer to the beach. All of a sudden there was a loud scream followed by a splash. One of the ship's crew who'd been securing one of the sails had lost his footing and fell overboard, much to the amusement of a couple of his crew mates. But the amusement didn't last.

Out of nowhere, a large sea monster came up from below, crashing out of the water. It struck the sailor, taking the man out of the water in its large open mouth, its sharp teeth penetrating and biting into his flesh as they both went under the surface. Atticus grabbed one of the Pilum situated in a rack on the platform; it had a heavy ball at the top of its shaft. Atticus looked down into the clear water at the giant monster below, thrashing from side to side with the sailor still hanging from its mouth. Blood had started to cloud the water pouring out from the sailor's midriff. The monster let go of the sailor who then clawed at the water pulling himself up to the surface gasping for air and screaming with fear and pain as he broke the surface. Atticus could see the grey colour of the monster speeding towards the sailor to attack again.

As it was about to strike at the sailor's legs Atticus launched the Pilum aiming for its head. Some of the sailors tried to pull the man out of the water before he was attacked again. The Pilum hit the water and punched into the head of the monster of a fish it was at least twenty foot long. The spear embedded itself deep into its head, blood flushed out, The monster turned direction swimming away from the boat.

"What the fuck was that?" asked Atticus.

"That is what is known as a shark, a giant one I've never seen one that big in all my life at sea!" exclaimed Appius.

The sailor had been pulled back on board but was dead; one of his legs was missing and there was a large bite mark which had ripped open his midriff.

"Poor bastard!" said Adelar, looking down at what was left of the sailor, bleeding out the remainder of his blood.

"There is nothing we can do but throw him back overboard, he was a good sailor," remarked Appius with a deep sigh.

"Make a full report in your ship's log and make sure his family, if he has any, receives any money due," replied Atticus.

The ship was only a few yards from the beach, the beach had a deep drop descending only a few feet away from the edge of the beach where the waves slowly lapped ashore. The ship's anchor was dropped, and large gangplanks were run out onto the beach. These were quickly grabbed by the sailors of the merchant vessels being watched over by a Roman officer and four legionnaires.

Atticus was the first to disembark, quickly followed by Edelgard and Adelar. Appius was still on board, barking out orders as the other trireme pulled up at the beach, its gangplanks quickly secured to the beach. The Centurion and the four legionnaires stood to attention as Atticus and Edelgard approached, the Centurion saluted.

"My name is Sirius Centurion of the garrison of Corinth."

"Good day, I'm Atticus 1st Centurion of the Augusta 11 legion in charge of this mission. This is Edelgard and Adelar, two of General Maximus's bodyguards. Feel free to make your report in front of them."

While the Centurion relayed his report the ships were being unloaded onto the beach. The horses were first off. Marco walked over to Atticus leading Fury by his reins.

"Sir!" said Marco, while handing Fury's reins to Atticus.

"Fury, my boy!" Atticus said, stroking his neck and kissing him on his cheek, Fury seemed happy to be on firm ground shaking his mane vigorously.

Atticus took off his reins, "Go on then, Fury run along the beach and let some steam off." Fury didn't need a second command and charged off in the direction of the sand dunes kicking his legs wildly as he galloped. The other horses were being exercised by members of the ship's crew; Centurion Decimus saluted as he approached.

"How was everything on your ship, men behaving?"

"Yes, nothing too untoward, A couple had a fight over alleged cheating at dice. Many have been asking as to their destination!"

"The two who were fighting, what punishment have you dealt?" asked Atticus.

"They are digging our latrines as we speak sir." replied Decimus.

"Good …Once we have loaded everything onto the merchant boats, I will address the men and give them a full update," answered Atticus.

"Have the officers exercised all the men. I don't want them getting idle, we need to keep them fit and ready to fight!"

"Yes sir!" replied Decimus, and off he went to carry out his orders. The ship's crew's job was to unload the triremes and reload everything onto the smaller merchant vessels which was getting done at pace under the watchful eye of Captain Appius.

The captains of the merchant boats had walked over together to meet Atticus and receive any instructions. A stocky man in his mid-thirties, bald with a little hair, cut short above his ears, addressed Atticus.

"My name is Crassus. I'm the cousin of General Maximus and these are my boats and captains," he said with a smile.

"It's a pleasure to meet you!" replied Atticus and clasped his forearm.

"I wondered how Maximus had quickly acquired the boats and have you meet us here so fast." Atticus went on to say.

"Yes, it was a little short notice," replied Crassus with a chuckle.

"We'll head off at first light, we don't want to really navigate around those small islands in the dark. Some of the water around them can be shallow in places with reefs that will cut a hole in our boats if we are not careful…so if it will be alright with you, we should wait until tomorrow?" Atticus knew all haste was paramount but thought the risk to the boats at night was too great.

"I agree you know these waters, so daylight it is. We will give the men time to stretch their legs and eat, and a good night's sleep on firm ground," answered Atticus.

"Some of the crews are fishing so there will be plenty of fresh fish for all, the waters here are teeming with fish, and we have cut down plenty of coconuts from those palm trees. You may as well save as much of your dry rations as possible," said Crassus.

He clasped Atticus's forearm and returned to keep watch on the loading of the boats. The horses would be put last at first light. The men were being drilled on the beach by the Centurions, Fury was tied up alongside the other horses. Atticus rejoined Sirius, the garrison's Centurion, who was drinking some wine offered to him by Edelgard and sharing a joke.

"Sirius how far is your garrison from here?" enquired Atticus.

"A little over a mile from the top of those steps!"

"Show me the way I fancy a bit of exercise after being cooped up on that boat, Come on Edelgard you can walk off some of that fat you're gaining!"

"What fat?" responded Edelgard with a grin, knowing Atticus was just taking the piss. Atticus reached the top of the cliff taking two steps at a time without seemingly getting out of breath or breaking a sweat. Edelgard and the Centurion Sirius reached the top several minutes later gasping for air, sweat pouring down their faces.

"You're not fucking human Atticus my friend!" said Edelgard, sucking in air as his heart pounded inside his chest.

"I'm inclined to agree with you!" responded Sirius bending over with his hands on his knees struggling to control his breathing. Atticus laughed, "Which way now?" he asked.

"We follow that trail down there and along through those olive trees. We have plenty of time to get there and for you to return before dusk," replied Sirius, who was finally catching his breath.

It wasn't long before the small fort high up on a hill came into view. Its stone walls looked solid and in one corner of the battlements stood a high tower overlooking the sea at the far side of the island. This was manned by a contingent of archers. A large moat had been dug around the fort which was bone dry. But its bed was full of sharp steaks protruding in all directions along with caltrops scattered everywhere. Bolt throwers were placed on all four battlements, the fort's defences impressed Atticus.

"Your fort is well situated on that hill, and your defences look very capable of withstanding an attack!" said Atticus.

"It needs to be, we have no more than two hundred men to garrison it, and reinforcements are far away. The pirates operating in this area tried several years ago to capture it. They were dealt a heavy defeat and have left us alone since. The tower gives us a great view of the surrounding ocean that at times enables us to alert local merchant boats and fishermen to an impending attack."

"It must be quite lonely for the men stationed here?" said Edelgard as they entered the fort.

The guards saluted Sirius and Atticus, "If you mean the comfort of a woman…there is a small town down in the valley beyond. This houses several very lucrative brothels that seem to relieve our men of most of their pay!" replied Sirius with a grin.

"Who is in charge of the fort?" enquired Atticus.

"I am…as I have said, we are but a small force, and the powers that be don't think we need a senior officer above Centurion!" answered Sirius.

"Come, follow me to my quarters, and I will have one of my orderlies bring fresh fish and bread. You must be feeling hungry!" said Sirius.

After eating and spending over an hour touring the fort, Atticus and Edelgard returned to the beach.

Crassus returned and addressed Atticus, "The two bigger of the boats have been loaded with all the heavier equipment. My advice would be to separate your archers amongst all the boats in case we are attacked at sea." said Crassus.

"Yes, good idea, I will instruct their commander to make the arrangements," answered Atticus. I've made arrangements for you and Maximus's bodyguards, along with the horses and one hundred men, to sail on the lead boat with me.

"The remainder will comfortably be accommodated throughout the other boats," the boats had been filled with all the supplies and equipment, the drill had finished, and the men were lined up in their units ready for Atticus to address.

Appius smiled as he walked over to Atticus and said, "Sir, it is time for us to return to Ostia. I want to make good time while the weather is in our favour. The weather can turn on the flip of a coin."

Atticus clasped his forearm, "Thank you, and I wish you a safe return." Edelgard and Adelar bid him farewell.

They watched him and his crew board the ship. The gang planks were pulled aboard, the anchor was raised as the ores hit the surface and began to pull the ships slowly out of the inlet and back into the open sea. Atticus turned to face his men who were all still standing to attention in the glaring late evening sun, but it would soon be dark.

"At ease!" gentlemen shouted Atticus.

"I suppose now is the time to let you know of our destination and to our orders from General Maximus. Some of you, if not all, will have heard many rumours over the past few days, our destination is the fort at Tadmor in Mesopotamia." There was a slight noise of whispered chatter amongst the ranks which was quickly dealt with by the Centurions and Optio's.

Atticus paused and drank water from his canteen while silence returned.

"We will arrive at the port city of Tarsus in Cilicia, from there to Tadmor the exact route I will inform you when necessary. The fort is under attack; General Felix has already sent two thousand men and hopefully will reach the fort sooner rather than later. We have been sent in case they need extra forces, and to deliver these heavy weapons to strengthen their defences. So that is all for the moment so tonight eat well and rest we leave here at first light in the morning!"

"That was short and sweet," said Edelgard.

"No need to have them stand in this heat listening to me besides I'm still hungry with all that walking. That fish cooking on that fire smells nice," replied Atticus.

Atticus filled a plate with fish and cut a hole in the top of one of the coconuts and drank its milk and sat down on the sand. Edelgard filled a plate then pulled the stopper off a wine skin and drank.

"First things first…" said Adelar with a grin, "I've earned this drink, while you were sitting on your arse sunning yourself! I got dragged up those fucking steps," replied Edelgard with a chuckle. Atticus grinned at Edelgard's words.

Laughter filled the beach as the men sat around eating and drinking, the Centurion from the Corinth barracks had situated lookouts above on top of the cliffs just in case any ships came into view. Even when it became dark, they would be able to see any lights from boats out at sea.

The following morning, they left for Tarsus, navigating the many small islands, and lookouts climbed the boat's masts to keep a sharp eye. Large tarpaulins had been erected to keep the sun off the heads of the men and also to keep them out of sight. These boats didn't have any bolt throwers but had a platform front and back for archers if needed. Two days after leaving Corinth, one of the lookouts spotted a large boat on the horizon.

"Sails on the starboard side several thousand yards out!" came the shout from the mast directly above Atticus. He quickly climbed the mast, "Over their sir!" said the sailor pointing in its direction.

"What do you make of it?" asked Atticus, shielding his eyes from the glare of the sun.

"Looks like a pirate boat to me and she's seen us and heading our way!" replied the sailor. Atticus grabbed a rope and slid down to the deck. Atticus signalled to one of the other boats to come closer to Atticus's boat.

"I've seen the pirate boat, what do you want to do?" asked the captain.

"Lead the other boats away from our boat as if you're making a run for it, we will make them think we are taking on water and unable to escape," shouted Atticus to him, "What then?" asked the captain, looking a little surprised.

"Then we will give them a bit of a surprise, just do as I say! We don't have much time!" replied Atticus sternly.

The captain looked a little perplexed but carried out Atticus's instructions without further delay.

"Crassus, have several of your crew get buckets on ropes and drop them into the water as if we're emptying them rather than filling them." Crassus instantly knew what Atticus had in mind and smiled in response.

"Farrokh, have your archers ready to strike on my order out of sight down here!"

"SIR!" came his reply and carried out the order.

"Men arm yourselves, be ready for the fight as soon as I order …not a moment before!" demanded Atticus.

The pirate ship began to get closer, "Look Captain!" said one of the pirates, "That boat is falling behind; they are crippled and taking on water!" he went on to say with excitement at the prospect of gaining some booty.

"We are already late joining the other boats searching for the two Roman ships!" shouted another pirate who was second in command.

"We still have time to reach them; I cannot just leave that merchant boat and its booty. Get the men to board her," replied the captain, angrily. The pirate boat was gaining on Atticus's boat rapidly. Edelgard held his axe at the side of Atticus, eager for the fight.

"I can't wait to see the look on their faces when we surprise those buggers," said Edelgard with a grin. Many of the soldiers waiting with spears or swords in hand, hiding out of sight underneath the tarpaulin, laughed loudly.

73

"Quiet lads, let's not give the game away," said Atticus with a smile.

Crassus was standing at the boat's helm barking out orders pretending to be in fear of the pirates. who were now close and throwing grappling hooks towards Crassus's boat.

"NOW!" Atticus shouted the order for Farrokh and his archers to fire their arrows. The order was immediately carried out as the tarpaulin was pulled back by members of the boat's crew.

Arrows struck their targets killing many of the pirates waiting to jump aboard, many of whom fell into the ocean. The pirate boat sailed over the top of them as it came alongside, hooked to the merchant boat by grappling hooks. The shock and surprise were immediate, but the pirate boat couldn't pull away. Atticus leapt onto the pirate boat sword in hand, striking blows that killed instantly, his sword slicing through flesh and bone. Atticus had killed several pirates within seconds of leaping aboard, as he powered his way along the deck. He thundered his leg forward at the pirate captain, kicking him overboard. Edelgard and Adelar had now joined the fight, killing with impunity. One of the pirates leapt into the sea to avoid the blade of Adelar and began to swim frantically away from the boats.

"Where does he think he's going!" shouted Edelgard laughing.

"Not bloody far if there's any sharks around like that one yesterday," Thaddius bellowed looking over the side.

Most of the pirates had been killed, those that were bleeding out from their wounds were swiftly finished off.

"The boats ours!" said Edelgard, "Go below Thaddius, check for any valuables, maps, anything you can find of any value, take a couple of men with you."

"Sir!" came the swift reply.

"Edelgard as soon as Thaddius and those men have finished, strike a hole in her hull with your axe and scuttle her."

"It will be my pleasure," Edelgard replied. "The rest of you back on board our boat!" shouted Atticus.

It wasn't long before they were all back on board Crassus's merchant boat, the pirate boat filled with water and disappeared under the water.

Several days later, and without further incident, the Cilician port of Tarsus came into sight. The crew began preparing for disembarkation even though it was still a couple of hours away. It was midday when they moored the boats to the quayside, and many onlookers were surprised to see the many Roman soldiers running down their gang planks and assembling into their units. A squad of Cilician Auxiliaries being led by a Roman Centurion marched towards them from the port's garrison. Atticus had mounted Fury along with Edelgard and Adelar mounting their horses, and rode towards them, instructions had been left with the officers as to the unloading. Atticus wanted to seek out the garrison's legate to acquire waggons and mules for the heavy weapons, food, water, and equipment. The squad of soldiers came to an abrupt stop and stood to attention.

The Centurion saluted Atticus and said, "I am Centurion Thaddius of the Cilician port of Tarsus garrison," Atticus returned his salute.

"I am Atticus, first Centurion of the first cohort of Augusta 11 legion under the orders of General Maximus and Emperor Augustus."

Atticus didn't dismount; he asked the Centurion, "Who is in charge of the garrison?" the Centurion raised his eyebrows at the mention of the emperor's name.

Then quickly replied, "The legate in charge is Flavius Quintus Valerious sir!"

"Where can I find him?" asked Atticus. "He will be in his office at this time of day I should think."

Atticus thanked him and rode off down the side of the harbour and out towards the garrison gates. When they arrived, they were questioned by the gate's officer in charge before being allowed entry. As they rode into the garrison, Atticus noticed the poor condition of the fort's walls and defences and the lack of sentries on the battlements.

Edelgard had also noticed and shook his head, saying, "Are you thinking what I'm thinking Atticus?"

"I am very slack; things need to change, and change quickly, especially under the present circumstances," replied Atticus.

They arrived outside the legate's office, where two guards were standing at the entrance talking with each other, leaning against the wall. They were not paying much attention until Atticus towered over them, sitting on Fury. One of the soldiers looked up, shielding his eyes from the sunlight bouncing off Atticus's armour. Which in fact Atticus was doing on purpose to make the guard look up.

"How can I help you?" asked the soldier.

"I think you need to add sir to that," growled Edelgard.

"SIR!" shouted the soldier, finally standing to attention.

"Is the legate in his office?" enquired Atticus. "He is but has left orders not to be disturbed." replied the soldier.

"Has he now, well, you better go disturb him if you know what is good for you!" snapped Atticus.

The soldier looking at the three of them swallowed and looked across at his comrade for any sign of help, "I didn't ask you; I'm telling you bring him here."

The soldier turned and went inside the large building and down what looked like a long corridor. The other soldier looked straight ahead and did not want to make eye contact.

"At least somebody around here still believes in good soldering," said Adelar, who was looking up the road which led to a large courtyard.

A well-dressed Centurion was drilling a squad of men. Atticus looked over and prompted Fury to trot up there to see if he could gain any information while he waited for the legate.

"Good day, Centurion!" Atticus shouted.

The Centurion looked over at Atticus. He then ordered his men to carry on with the drill watched over by his Optio and marched towards Atticus and saluted.

"Good day, 1st Centurion," taking note of Atticus's uniform, "How can I be of service to you?"

"My name is Atticus. I'm waiting for your legate Flavius and wonder if you could enlighten me on one or two things."

Edelgard had ridden up to join Atticus as Adelar stayed waiting for the legate to appear.

"My name is Clictus, what things?"

"Why is this fort in such a poor state, discipline, seems to be very lax, to say the least, due to the incursion by the Parthians further east," Clictus was about to reply when his Optio who'd been listening, made a gesture to his Centurion, which Atticus took to be some sort of warning.

"Speak freely, I need to know," said Atticus, looking directly at Clictus.

"That would be wise," said Edelgard in support of Atticus.

Edelgard knew all too well that Atticus was in no mood for excuses and would one way or another get his answer. Clictus was in his early to mid-forties, clean-shaven, his uniform and armour that he wore was well kept and in good order. He was clearly a veteran of many years' service but still looked proud to serve in the army of Rome.

He in turn looked at Atticus and took into account that he was very young to be first Centurion. He also noted Atticus's armour gleamed and his uniform was well presented. Clictus felt an aura surrounding Atticus. Clictus could see that his German accomplice was obviously very proud to be riding at his side.

"In that case I will be frank, ask me what you will, and I will answer."

"Is your legate a competent leader and a good soldier of Rome?"

"He prefers the company of young boys rather than doing his duty to Rome!"

Edelgard coughed at the answer so freely given. Atticus didn't even stir in response and just asked his next question.

"And what of his Tribune? Hasn't he questioned his legate's lack of duty?"

"At this time of day, he probably can be found half pissed and shagging some whore in one of the city's brothels!"

"Sir!" shouted the Optio with some alarm at his candidness cutting in. Atticus looked at the Optio for a second and said.

"Don't worry, I asked him to speak freely. I want the truth so I can put things right before I leave."

"Maybe, but what happens when you leave?"

"Trust him, you don't need to worry." said Edelgard.

This seemed to embolden Clictus even more.

"If it wasn't for me and the other Centurion Thaddius, things would be even worse!"

"Go on!" said Atticus.

"We send out patrols daily, the harbour is regularly patrolled by Thaddius. We keep the two cohorts of Cilician Auxiliaries under our command well-trained."

"Why are the battlements in such poor repair and poorly managed? The gate is under manned and there are far too few sentries patrolling the battlements for such a large fort. With no one to escort us up to the legate's office we could be imposters sent here to assassinate the legate at the very least."

Clictus felt a little ashamed of Atticus's observations.

"There are too many who are pretending to be sick, shirking their duties. Many of these are the ones the Tribune always tends to take with him to the city to frequent the brothels. In my opinion none of them deserve to be soldiers of Rome and that includes the Tribune."

Back down outside the legate's office, a loud shriek could be heard followed by a bit of commotion. Atticus nudged Fury back down followed by Clictus and his Optio.

Edelgard rode at the side of Atticus grinning.

"Well, we'll soon find out how much trouble I've got myself into," said Clictus looking at his Optio as they walked down to Flavius's office.

As Atticus approached, he saw two young boys run off down towards the fort's gate half-naked.

"What is the meaning of this? I said I was not to be disturbed!" shouted Flavius. The legate Flavius looked in his early thirties, very short and fat, his cheeks flapping as he shouted to the amusement of Adelar who was the target of Flavius's anger. His face was bright red. He wore a tunic that was stained at the front; he was bald but had chosen to wear an orange-coloured wig.

"Fuck me!" said Edelgard chuckling to himself, Atticus was trying to keep a straight face realising he needed to get this situation dealt with.

Adelar just sat astride his horse and smiled looking down at Flavius. The sound of hobnailed boots crunching the road rang out as Cyrus carried the banner of the Augusta 11 marching proudly leading his century of men towards Atticus.

"Attention!" shouted Cyrus. They came to a standstill in front of where Atticus and the others were congregated. Flavius turned and watched them come to a standstill in perfect order.

"What's up, Flavius forgot what a properly organised, disciplined century looks like?" asked Atticus, still sitting on Fury angrily.

"How dare you speak to me like that…I am Flavius Quintus Valerious, legate of this garrison, and you appear to be a 1st Centurion. Have you gone completely mad and forgotten how the ranks in the Roman army work?"

Atticus slowly dismounted Fury; and stood towering over Flavius, who was trying not to feel intimidated by the tall, muscular young man standing over him.

"What is your name? so I can inform the powers that be in my next correspondence with Rome! And have you flogged for your impertinence."

"Atticus! is my name!"

"Atticus, Atticus!" Flavius said, adjusting his wig.

"Where have I heard that name before?" Then he suddenly realised who was standing in front of him. The colour of his face turned pale as if all the blood had drained from his body. Fear now gripped Flavius.

Edelgard, looking down at Flavius from his horse, also saw the look of realisation on his face, "Yes Flavius…Quintus…Valerious…Atticus, the one who saved the life of General Maximus along with me and Adelar here."

Flavius tried to deflect the situation, "But that doesn't change the fact that I out rank you and…" his words then failed him.

Flavius quickly shut his mouth as Atticus took out the golden tube with the emperor's crest and gold eagle at its top. He knew all too well what exactly that meant, and his fat cheeks began to tremble. The Tribune of the garrison walked up past Cyrus and his century. Those who were still standing to attention though, many of the men in the ranks were smiling and finding it hard to keep a straight face. Atticus looked at him with disdain.

He was clearly drunk and staggered slightly as he walked, "Ah, Flavius how are you today, and what's happening?" enquired Tribune Publius.

He followed his question with a yawn.

"This is Tribune Publius," said Flavius, introducing him to Atticus feeling totally deflated and sighed.

"Is he on duty?" demanded Atticus.

"He is!" replied Flavius.

"Who wants to know?" asked Publius, feeling a little cocky with all the drink inside him.

But before he could utter another word, Atticus spun around, raised his leg and kicked him to the ground. Publius fell hard onto his back with a thud and had the wind knocked out of himself. He struggled to get back onto his feet, having to crouch on his hands and knees for a while as everyone looked in his direction. Atticus then turned to the Centurion Clictus and his Optio, "Have this man locked up in the stockade until he can properly be dealt with."

Publius at last managed to get to his feet, breathing heavily, and asked, "What for?"

"Drunk on duty to start with, the other charges will follow!" growled Atticus.

"With pleasure!" shouted Clictus as he and the Optio grabbed his arms and led him away.

"Fuck me, I haven't had this much fun since I can remember," said the Optio as they left heading towards the stockade.

"You need to get behind your desk and have the full inventory of your command ready for me to go over with you as soon as I have had time to wash and freshen up. That is if you have a functioning bath house?"

Flavius started to come to his senses, "Yes, we have Atticus err, I will have these two guards escort you while I attend to your requirements." Atticus turned to Cyrus.

"Have a couple of the men organise feed and water for Fury and the horses!"

"Yes, sir!" he quickly replied.

"Come on, Edelgard, let's take a bath, last one for a while probably," said Atticus.

"You better come too Adelar! you smell," shouted Edelgard.

The two guards escorted them to the bath house, daring not to put a foot out of line.

"At least the bath house is in good order," stated Atticus after he had entered. In fact, it was quite elegant, the mosaic tiled floor was pure white with gold and blue patterns, the walls were tiled with pictures of sea serpents and dolphins. Steam drifted up to the ceiling and several servants were there to attend to their every need.

Word quickly spread around the fort. Many of those allegedly feeling too sick for duty made a quick recovery and left the infirmary and reported for duty. One of the guards left the fort and ran to the town's main street where most of the fort's soldiers frequented the taverns and brothels. He went straight to the town's most favoured brothel and as soon as he went in one of the legionnaires shouted.

"What's up, Brutus? You look as if somebody's taken a crap in your bed!" Other soldiers inside fell about half drunk, laughing.

"You'd better get yourself back to the fort pronto," replied Brutus.

"Why would I want to do that?" asked the legionnaire who had his arm around a half-naked girl.

"A couple of hundred men have arrived from the Augusta 11 legion led by some big bugger of a first Centurion!" said Brutus rather frantically.

"So why should we give a fuck?" asked the legionnaire.

"Put it this way. Flavius has just shit himself, and the Tribune has been kicked on his arse and been put in the stockade by that fucking first Centurion. So my advice is, unless you want to clean the shithouse out for the foreseeable future or worse. You better get the rest of the lads back to the fort," Brutus turned and ran back out before the legionnaire had time to answer.

Word spread fast amongst the men he found who quickly left and returned to the fort not wishing to end up with their Tribune in the stockade. Guards were doubled at the gates as the patrols returned to the fort. The soldiers returning from the brothels took to the battlements swiftly. The city gates were now properly guarded and people entering and leaving were being checked. Which hadn't gone unnoticed by a couple of Parthian spies lurking in the shadows. All the equipment and the rest of the men from the boats had entered the fort.

Centurion Clictus arranged for them all to have billets for the night's stay and were fed.

Atticus went to meet with Flavius along with Edelgard feeling very refreshed after their bath. This time the guards standing outside quickly stood to attention and saluted, one of them escorted them inside down the long corridor leading to Flavius's office and knocked on the door.

"Come!" shouted Flavius from within.

The guard opened the door and returned outside, "Ah, gentlemen, please sit," pointing at two comfortable couches, "Or would you prefer my chair Atticus?"

"No, the couches will be fine."

Flavius clapped his hands, and a servant immediately brought wine and glasses on a tray placing the tray on Flavius's desk. Flavius poured out three glasses of wine, passing one each to Edelgard and Atticus, then returned to his seat on the other side of the desk. Adelar had gone into the city to find the company of a good woman.

"May I offer my apologies for the err' let's say my misunderstanding earlier I err…"

"No, need!" Atticus cut in, "But I will not tolerate any dysfunction of Rome's Authority which reflects poorly on our Emperor Augustus," Atticus paused for the gravity of his words to sink in.

"The enemies of Rome are watching; they have spies everywhere and will seek to take advantage of any weaknesses."

"Yes, yes, I quite agree," then Flavius drank from his glass feeling very nervous and realising the young man sitting in front of him was wise way above his age. Flavius wondered what would become of him at the end of this meeting. He sat waiting patiently for Atticus to speak again.

"Your Tribune will be returning to Ostia tomorrow when the boats return. I have given the captain dispatches for General Maximus. The captain and owner of those boats is also Maximus's cousin Crassus. I will be blunt."

I found everything on arrival, but I realise I have a mission to complete and I'm leaving here tomorrow.

Edelgard shifted in his seat and took hold of the amphora of wine and filled his glass.

"Want some Atticus?"

"No thank you, my friend," he replied.

Flavius had taken a mental note, at the quiet tone in the voice of Atticus and was hoping for a reasonable outcome of the meeting. Atticus returned his attention to Flavius.

"The order of command here is important and must be upheld, you will remain in charge here until General Maximus arrives here. Probably no longer than a couple of months from now with his legions. So, my advice to you is to repair this fort, strengthen the battlements and dig that moat deeper and replace the spikes that have fallen into disrepair. Pay local tradesmen to work alongside the fort's engineers for speed. I have noted that your Centurion Clictus has already put out extra sentries and manned the city's gates."

"Yes, I will send for reputable tradesmen immediately," replied Flavius.

"My advice to you…would be to promote Clictus temporarily to Tribune; he is more than capable until at least Maximus can make a decision on who the permanent replacement should be when he arrives; it has all been explained in my dispatches."

"Yes, he is more than capable. Is there anything else I can help you with?"

"Our guides should arrive no later than tomorrow. We arrived here a day earlier than expected due to the favourable weather," at this point Atticus finally took a drink of wine before continuing.

"We need six waggons and six teams of mules! To transport our supplies and heavy weapons we carry."

"I will see to that personally at the conclusion of our meeting, anything else?"

"Just some extra provisions for my men that is all."

"Consider it done!"

"That is all then I need to check on my men."

Atticus then stood up as Edelgard finished off another glass of wine before leaving to follow Atticus out into the evening sunshine.

Adelar had returned from the town and was waiting outside with a smile on his face.

"You missed out on some fine wine my friend," said Edelgard with a grin.

"Don't worry my friend, I've had a little fun of my own," responded Adelar grinning.

Edelgard knew exactly what Adelar meant. He patted Adelar on his shoulder. "I'm pleased to know your cock still works," said Edelgard.

Atticus laughed loudly at Edelgard's comment and off they went to check on the men.

As they arrived at their temporary billets, the men who were sitting around began to stand at attention. "Sit down lads, just carry on," shouted Atticus.

Centurion Decimus and Sextus came out of their billet on hearing the voice of Atticus.

"Right, I want you to rotate the men to leave fifty at a time, two hours each, that's enough time for them to visit the town's taverns and brothels," said Atticus to wild cheers coming from his men as the news spread out among them.

"Yes sir!" replied Decimus with a smile.

"I don't want any trouble with the locals understand; carry on."

Sextus took Atticus and the two Germans and showed them to their quarters.

"These will do! I'm glad to be sleeping in a proper bed before we cross that dessert," said Adelar feeling a little tired from his excursions in one of the town's brothels.

"Open those shutters, it's bloody hot in here," said Edelgard.

"We better have a walk around town later and make sure the men are behaving," groaned Atticus. He too was feeling a little tired but wanted to make sure there was no trouble with the locals. Atticus laid down on his bed which had been covered with fresh hay and a blanket. His thoughts drifted to home and his wife Naomi.

After a couple of hours, the three of them set off for a walk around the town. Stalls were set up along the streets selling all manner of goods. Many of the buildings near the harbour front were very run down and filth filled many of the alleyways they passed. The stench was quite pungent, but didn't seem to bother the locals purchasing their goods at the stalls. All the locals wore long robes and headscarves protecting them from the sun. The women were covered from head to toe with the exception of a slit in their head dress to see where they were going.

"Do you think they are ugly and that is why they hide their faces?" commented Adelar. Up ahead they could see a tavern full of soldiers drinking and laughing, many standing in the street.

"It's good to see the men enjoying themselves. It won't be long before they will be fighting to keep each other alive," said Atticus.

"I agree so let us try some of the local wine and enjoy a short break from duty," replied Edelgard with a wide grin.

"A little wine, no more!" said Atticus with a smile.

"Yes, that is what I meant," answered Edelgard, still grinning.

"Your little is a lot more than what Atticus means," Adelar said loudly followed by a raucous laugh. Many of the men raised their cups of wine and some saluted as they walked in.

"Over there, a free table in the corner!" said Edelgard, nodding in its direction.

"Go, sit I will bring some wine and food," shouted Atticus above the din.

Atticus then sat with his back to the wall after placing a tray of fresh meat and fish on the table facing the door they had entered. He wanted to keep an eye on his men's behaviour. It wasn't long before his thoughts again turned to home, with Naomi picturing in his mind what they would be doing and lost track of time a little. Edelgard and Adelar also spoke to each other about home. Atticus's thoughts became distracted as two men approached the table. Atticus instinctively put his hand on the hilt of one of his swords in a flash. One of the men quickly held his palms in the air and bowed.

"Sorry to disturb you, my name is Abd-El-Kader and this is my cousin Abdul," he spoke in perfect Greek and as he did his cousin also bowed his head.

"We are in the employ of your General Maximus and are to guide you to the fort at Tadmor."

Atticus pointed to two empty stools and asked them to sit which was done under the watchful eyes of both Edelgard and Adelar. Atticus introduced them both to the guides and Abd-El-Kader then produced a small scroll from under his gown and handed it to Atticus. He opened it and read it just loud enough so Edelgard and Adelar could hear.

At the bottom was Maximus's seal to prove its authenticity, "Come with us to the fort where it is more private, and we can discuss matters further."

Once they had returned to the fort, Atticus used Flavius's office for privacy, which Flavius was quite happy with, and made his way to the bath house to relax until his office was returned to him. Atticus unrolled a map out on the desk showing the Roman empire in the east; all the forts were marked clearly on the map.

Abd-El-Kader quickly pointed and marked out their route to Tadmor. The map also showed two oases on their route for water but there was still over one hundred miles to the fort after they had left the last oasis. Atticus then pointed at the map to a small mountain range about fifty miles from Tadmor, "There is a well dug deep in those mountains not shown on this map if I am not mistaken."

Abd-El-Kader looked over at his cousin Abdul, then at Atticus, "Yes, there is you are well informed not many know of it. How may I ask, have you come across this information?"

Abd-El-Kader also noticed when Atticus had pointed on the map the fine ring he wore on his finger.

"My father and his friend served in the legions of Rome and fought here many years ago, and wherever he went he would make small maps of the region. He'd fought in those mountains against a local tribal leader who didn't like paying taxes to Rome. The man he was on patrol with came across it and, knowing of its value, drew a map as to its whereabouts. He'd made me look at his maps over and over again during my upbringing and drilled them into my head. Knowing full well one day some of those maps would be of great use to me." replied Atticus.

"Why did you not disclose that well?" asked Edelgard.

"As I said it is not well announced, it is used in the area by local villages and by some nomadic tribes. We would not want our enemies to know its whereabouts." answered Abd-El-Kader.

"Where not your enemy or are we?" asked Atticus.

"You are not, we are servants of Rome and gladly serve if we had needed water for whatever reason when we reached that area, I would have gladly notified you."

Atticus looked closely at Abd-El-Kader which made him feel a little uncomfortable.

"Maximus trusts you and I trust his judgement," replied Atticus.

Abd-El-Kader bowed towards Atticus and said, "Thank you, sir. I will serve you well, may I ask how you came about such a fine ring?"

Atticus relayed the events of that day on his return from Ostia and how he'd been given the ring in return for saving the life of its former owner along with his son.

"You may not know but the former owner of that ring is one of the kings in Mesopotamia who I had met while in his service as a young man. I was only fourteen at the time," said Abd-El-Kader.

Abdul also said, "Yes, it is the same ring, and it is of great value. You saved his life so he will always be in your debt and will not take that lightly. He will be honour bound to you for the rest of his life."

Atticus returned his attention to the map for several more minutes in silence.

"We will leave at dawn and meet us at the gate," said Atticus. The two guides bowed and left.

"What do you make of that? They both recognised the ring you wear," asked Adelar.

"It's of no relevance to our mission," answered Atticus dismissing their revelation, shrugging his shoulders.

"Better go make sure all the men have now returned, and the waggons have been loaded ready to leave and I need to go check on Fury before we rest for the night." said Atticus.

Chapter 8

They left the fort at Tarsus in the capable hands of the now-Tribune Clictus and had left clear instructions for the legate Flavius not to get in his way. The road through the dessert they travelled was a well-used caravan trail, and it wasn't long before they passed one travelling to Tarsus. With many fully laden camels and waggons being pulled by mules and protected by men riding camels carrying long, curved swords probably hired from a local tribe. Atticus rode Fury at the front, as his men marched behind in good spirits, talking amongst themselves about the beautiful whores; they had come across in the brothels in Tarsus the previous day. Which helped them forget about the heat as they marched in the strong sunshine.

Abd-El-Kader rode alongside Atticus with Edelgard at his left as the guide talked of the days toil and how far he estimated they would travel before sundown and leaving enough time for a marching camp to be erected before the dark, cold night would descend. Abdul had ridden ahead to scout, but would return well before nightfall. The days would be extremely hot, but the nights would be extremely cold. Atticus was interested to find out as much as he could about the tribes who roamed the region, the history of its cities and rulers. Atticus learned there were two main kings living under Roman law in Mesopotamia, one in Babylon and the other in the far south of its region.

He also learned they both had different views about their land being occupied by the Romans. Abd-El-Kader had explained why it had been easy for Rome to conquer the region; the tribes would just as easily fight each other, let alone the Romans.

The rulers and kings didn't trust each other. Atticus had decided after a couple of days into their journey that he quite liked Abd-El-Kader and grew to trust him along with his cousin Abdul.

Back at Atticus's home, life carried on as normal in the early evening. Naomi would stand gazing at the stars in the clear sky thinking of Atticus, hoping he was safe and well. She often felt a pain in her chest while thinking of him, longing to be with him and couldn't wait to tell him the news that she was pregnant. She hadn't told anyone, it was very early and there weren't any outward signs of sickness in the morning, but she knew her own body and placed her hands on her stomach and wondered about the life growing inside her. The gods were watching from above, smiling down on Naomi. They knew what she didn't: she was to give birth to twin boys.

"Hello Naomi!" came the quiet voice of Lydia from behind her, which startled her a little and took her away from her thoughts.

"Oh, sorry, did I startle you?"

"Only a little!" smiled Naomi.

"Were you thinking about Atticus, or is that a stupid question?" Lydia then put her arm around Naomi; and looked up at the stars above, which Naomi returned her gaze to.

"Well, are you not going to share your news with me?"

Naomi didn't answer and carried on gazing at the sky and was wondering how to answer Lydia.

"If you tell me your news, I will tell you mine."

Naomi turned to face Lydia.

"You mean you're with child?"

"Yes!"

"How far?"

"Seven weeks I think?"

"Does Zuma know yet?"

"Not yet, but I will tell him tomorrow."

"And?"

"Yes, I am! probably from our wedding night by the looks of things."

"So, he will not know. Which is a good thing, one less thing on his mind."

"Yes, I suppose it is," replied Naomi, feeling the pain return in her chest as she returned her gaze up to the stars again.

"I can't wait to see the look on Zuma's face when he finds out," said Lydia which made them both giggle.

Back at the fort in Ostia, preparations for Maximus's legions to go east were well on their way, recruits were filling the ranks, some new but many were veterans being called back to serve Rome from retirement. It was now only a matter of days away from Maximus's departure. The harbour was full of Roman war ships preparing to take the legions to confront the Parthian incursions into Mesopotamia.

Chapter 9

On the third day Atticus and his men arrived at the first of the two oasis's late in the afternoon. Atticus had chosen to build his camp high up above the oasis in the middle of a clump of rocks with sand dunes rolling down the other side. The oasis itself was quite large and had many palm trees sprawling around it and large reeds protruding out of the water at one end. Several large tarpaulin tents had been erected amongst some dunes on its far side, and goats roamed free under the watchful eye of a couple of shepherds. Atticus ordered the men to build the camp straight away for their protection before allowing anyone to approach the oasis and collect water.

Women could be seen preparing food in small groups together, while several children were playing games, and the sound of laughter could be heard from across the water. Sentries were placed all over the high ground, keeping watch. Abdul and Abd-El-Kader had scouted ahead to the oasis. They could be seen leaving a large tent set up in the middle of the camp at the far side and mounted their horses and trotted around the water towards Atticus, kicking up dust as they came.

Edelgard and Adelar stood with Atticus awaiting their return; Decimus and Sextus, along with the other officers, were instructing the men, keeping them hard at work constructing the marching camp; Atticus never cut any corners, putting his men at risk. Several men could be seen leaving the tent from which Abd-El-Kader had previously left.

"Looks like they've been having a bit of a meeting," said Adelar.

"We will know soon enough!" replied Atticus, who now drank from his canteen, then tipped it upside down. No drops came out, it was completely empty. Abd-El-Kader dismounted along with Abdul, both of them bowing their heads slightly as they did so.

"What have you found out?" asked Atticus. "They appear to be a nomadic tribe from far south and have come here for water for themselves and that flock of goats over there." answered Abdul.

"How far south have they travelled from?" asked Atticus, feeling it was a little strange that they would venture so far.

"They were a little vague to say the least, but I would say over one hundred miles or more." answered Abd-El-Kader.

Atticus looked at Edelgard and paused while thinking, "Is there no other water in the direction they say they come from?" asked Atticus, "There is indeed to my recollection a small village not more than fifty miles back from whence they say they came. It is called Arim and has two wells, which provide plenty of water," answered Abdul.

"What are you thinking?" asked Abd-El-Kader.

"How trustworthy are these nomadic tribes?" asked Atticus.

Abdul grinned "I wouldn't trust them as far as I can piss," replied Abdul.

"That is what I'm thinking," said Atticus.

"What do you make of it?" asked Edelgard.

"I think they have been paid to look out for any Roman soldiers heading towards Tadmor," replied Atticus.

Atticus walked a bit further towards the camp of nomads, "Obviously, our whereabouts after leaving Ostia are still not known. The pirates sitting in wait will have expected to see us by now and will have sent messengers to inform their paymasters they have not yet encountered us. What did they ask you?" asked Atticus.

"Why were we here and where were we travelling?" answered Abd-El-Kader.

"We told them exactly what you had instructed us to say if we came across anyone asking questions!"

"What was that?" enquired Adelar.

"We are travelling to the fort at Niblis from the barracks at Tarsus to collect prisoners for interrogation and we are paid to guide you there!"

"Very clever!" said Adelar in response.

"Do you think they believed you?" asked Edelgard.

"We will know soon enough, if they haven't, they will send riders to inform their paymasters of our presence," answered Atticus.

Sextus interrupted, "The camp is finished sir, what are your further orders?"

"Send a party of men to refill all the canteens and water barrels on the waggons and take the horses and mules to the water to drink."

"Yes, sir!" replied Sextus and went off to carry out the orders.

"Let's make them think we suspect nothing and we're going about our business," said Atticus.

"If it is as I suspect they will send riders as soon as it's dark, I want you four to be ready to leave with me and intercept them," said Atticus.

"I know which way they will go if your suspicions are correct and where we can wait. They will most definitely leave tonight." replied Abd-El-Kader.

Chapter 10

Atticus and the others left from the rear of the camp, skirting around the rocks out of view from the nomads camped at the far side of the oasis. Atticus had left instructions with the Centurions Decimus and Sextus. They had asked if it was wise for him to go under the circumstances. Decimus had pointed out that the successful outcome of the mission was paramount. He was a little worried that Atticus could be killed chasing a few bandits and thought he should go instead of Atticus. Which made Edelgard burst out into a fit of laughter. Edelgard stated to Decimus, "You clearly have not seen Atticus fight and should not worry!" Atticus smiled at Decimus, patting him on the shoulder, and assured him he would be back before dawn.

They had left early to travel slowly and not have the horses kick up a sand cloud. It had only taken thirty minutes or so to reach the place where Abd-El-Kader had picked. It was high up on a small mountain range and had a good view of the surrounding area, and far in the distance they could just make out the oasis surrounded by the palm trees. It was, in Atticus's opinion, the perfect place for an ambush.

"Right, let's see if any rats leave the den," said Atticus. After an hour or so the heat of the day had given way to a deep chill.

"I'm glad we took your advice, Abdul, bringing these capes to keep the chill out!" said Edelgard.

"Look there!" said Atticus who pointed in the direction of the oasis.

They could just make out three riders leaving the camp, making their way slowly along the trail towards Atticus, and the others hiding above the trail leading south.

"We take one alive!" said Atticus. Who then knocked an arrow to his bow and waited.

Edelgard and Adelar had made their way down and mounted their horses, hidden out of view. As soon as the riders who were now travelling at speed below appeared on the trail, Atticus fired, hitting the rider in front of the other two. The arrow punched through his cheekbone and knocked him off his horse as he screamed in pain, hitting the floor. Edelgard, along with Adelar, charged at the remaining two riders who had swung their horses away from the dead rider but were soon overcome by Edelgard and Adelar.

Edelgard punched one of the riders, knocking him off his horse unconscious, as Adelar sliced his sword into the other rider's chest, and the sucking noise of his sword could be heard as he pulled it back out slowly. The rider slid off his horse; he laid there bleeding out, his blood-soaked the ground from the gaping wound in his chest. Edelgard dismounted and stood over the surviving rider, who was still unconscious with his face half buried in the sand.

"Is he still alive?" asked Atticus as he dismounted Fury.

"He is, I can see him breathing!" replied Edelgard.

Atticus pulled him up and shook him slowly, his eyes opened, and he began to cough while rubbing the lump on the side of his head. Abd-El-Kader spoke to him in a language Atticus couldn't understand so he and the two Germans stood waiting patiently while the conversation took place. Abd-El-Kader then turned to face Atticus.

"He says they were paid by the Parthians to watch out for any columns of Roman soldiers heading this way." said Abd-El-Kader.

"It didn't take much for him to squeal like a wild boar!" said Adelar. "He knows who I am and what torture my tribe does to gain information," smiled Abd-El-Kader in response.

Abdul returned with the riders' horses he'd rounded up. "What now?" asked Edelgard.

"We head back to camp, and in the morning, we'll pay the leader of that camp a visit, tie him up, and let's get back." answered Atticus.

Back at camp, Atticus summoned all his officers to a meeting and discussed his plans for the following day. After the meeting had finished, Atticus and Edelgard walked amongst his men, joking and chatting with them, making sure their morale was high. Many of his men, young new recruits, or veterans of many battles with scars to prove it felt Atticus, even though he was so young to lead them, had an aura about him. Many felt he was blessed by the gods. But apart from that he was a very skilled fighter and a cunning leader. They knew all too well that when the fighting started, Atticus would lead from the front and wouldn't let them get killed needlessly. Men die in battle, but a foolish leader would get you killed far too easily while sitting back out of the way without a care for his men.

As soon as dawn broke, Atticus Edelgard and Abd-El-Kader, followed by thirty soldiers, including Sextus, marched to the other side of the oasis and into the camp. The leader of the tribe of nomads came out of his tent with a big smile on his face and bowed; he was in his sixties, very fat with a long grey beard.

He was about to speak then, noticed one of his riders sent to meet with the Parthian spies in the south, with a rope tied around his neck being dragged towards him by Edelgard. The leader's face changed from a smile to instant fear. He immediately fell to the floor and began to plead for forgiveness. Several women began to fall to their knees crying, they began slapping themselves, rocking back and forth.

Atticus turned to Abd-El-Kader, "Who are they?" gesturing to the women. "They are his wives!" replied Abd-El-Kader.

"What all of them?" asked Atticus.

"Yes," replied Abd-El-Kader.

"Sextus!"

"Sir!"

"Search the tents, and the camp, bring everyone here!" shouted Atticus.

"Quick men search the tents and follow me!" shouted Sextus. The soldiers drew their swords and began to carry out the order. Anyone they found cowering in the tents was quickly rounded up and made to sit alongside the women who were still crying and rocking back and forth. One of the men dashed out from behind a tent and ran towards a row of horses tied up but before he could mount one Atticus spun on the balls of his feet. Quickly drawing one of his swords and at the same time launching it spinning through the air straight at him. The sword punched him in his spine, the sound of bone shattering as it entered his body and his scream of death pierced the camp, as he fell headfirst into the sand.

"Camp is clear sir!" shouted Sextus, as he returned looking over at the dead man. There was now a large group all sitting on the sand. There were a dozen children, over twenty men and as many women. Several of them hung their heads, staring at the ground, seemingly awaiting their fate.

Atticus turned his attention to their leader, "So you take gold from the enemies of Rome!" shouted Atticus. A voice from within the group sitting on the floor pleaded for mercy to be shown. Atticus looked at the group, the young man who had shouted was about sixteen, clean-shaven with curly brown hair. The soldiers had removed all the headscarves from all the men and women so their faces could be seen.

"Who is he to you?" enquired Atticus, the leader spoke fluent Greek.

"He is my eldest son," replied the leader.

"What did the Parthian spies instruct you to do and who to look out for?" asked Atticus.

The leader looked up at Atticus, sighed and asked, "What will become of us?"

He looked across at his family and other people sitting sobbing in a circle.

"That all depends on how truthful you are," replied Atticus.

"The Parthians have been raiding and attacking your eastern border; most of the Roman garrisons are held up in their forts awaiting the arrival of your General Maximus and his legions."

Atticus knew most of what he was saying and let him carry on, "The Parthians have many spies and had heard of reinforcements and heavy artillery being escorted from Ostia to the main fort at Tadmor. But having known the idea of their whereabouts, they were expected to take a certain route and were to be ambushed by pirates paid in gold by the Parthians. May I have a drink of water please?" asked the leader as he sat with the sun glaring into his eyes.

Beads of sweat running off his forehead began to drip from his long nose. Several flies buzzed around his chin making him feel very uncomfortable. Atticus picked up a canteen of water which laid on a carpet outside the leader's tent and passed it to him. He swallowed a large mouthful and thanked Atticus.

"Carry on!" said Atticus.

"We were camped outside a settlement called Isin when I was approached by two Parthian spies. They paid me to come here and alert them if any large force of Romans travelled this way," Atticus walked off and beckoned Edelgard to follow him.

"What are you going to do with them?" asked Edelgard. But before he answered the leader shouted.

"I have information that may help you before you make your decision!" pleaded the leader.

Atticus walked back with Edelgard, "Go on, tell me!" demanded Atticus.

"The two spies are waiting in a tavern called the camel's hump. They have hired a room on the first floor and await any information we might gain for them. Also, two miles out of the settlement there is a small group of rocks set up on a hill. Which hides a camp of Parthian soldiers who have been attacking any Roman patrols in the area."

"How do you know this?" snarled Edelgard.

"Because I got them drunk and loosened their tongues it is always an advantage to have as much information as one can get for times like this."

"I know where that place is," said Abd-El-Kader, "Take all their horses and weapons!" shouted Atticus to his men.

"But sir how can we?" Atticus cut in "be thankful I am letting you live! But if I find out you're lying, this country won't be big enough for you to hide in" retorted Atticus.

"Is it wise not to kill them?" asked Abdul.

"I don't kill women and children, he won't say a word to our enemies and besides that we will be long gone," replied Atticus.

Abdul bowed his head to Atticus. Once they were back with the rest of the men who were already waiting in line with the waggons at the rear. Atticus led them out of the oasis riding Fury with Edelgard, Adelar, and the two guides. Atticus had also taken the leader's son as hostage and if everything the leader had told him turned out to be true, he would be released unharmed and given a horse to return to the oasis.

Atticus had asked Abd-El-Kader how long it would take to reach Isin, how big a settlement it was and gain as much information as possible.

Two days later, Atticus made his marching camp, hidden from the trail several miles short of Isin and the Parthian raiders' camp in the hills. Abd-El-Kader had drawn a map in the sand of Isin. He had also given a full description of the hills with the Parthian camp hidden amongst them.

"What is your plan, Atticus?" enquired Edelgard, Atticus knelt looking at the map drawn in the sand taking a drink of water as he pondered over his plan of action.

"First, we need to kill those spies and anyone else with them, we have been lucky not to come into contact with anyone on this trail after leaving that oasis," Atticus wiped some sweat from his forehead, it was early evening and was still very warm.

Atticus turned to Abd-El-Kader, "How long will it take you to enter Isin, find that tavern and kill those spies?"

"If all goes well two hours will do."

"How long will it take to march enough men to the Parthian camp?" asked Atticus.

"Again, it will take only about two hours, maybe a little more. It's nearer but we are on horseback and your men will be on foot," answered Abd-El-Kader.

"Abdul can lead us to those hills, and a dozen of my Cilician archers can ride to Isin with you and if all is well kill those spies. Then head back towards the Parthian camp and cut off and kill any Parthians that manage to escape our attack. They will head straight for Isin to warn of our presence," said Atticus.

Abd-El-Kader bowed and went to make his preparations, Atticus and Edelgard went and found Farrokh who was in charge of the Cilician archers and gave him his instructions for a dozen of his archers to accompany Abd-El-Kader to Isin. He also gave him his orders to have the rest of his archers ready to travel with him and his legionnaires along with Edelgard, Adelar and Centurion Sextus to attack the Parthian camp.

Chapter 11

Centurion Decimus had been left in charge of the Roman camp. Abd-El-Kader had left for Isin with the Cilician archers. Atticus had set off, riding Fury, leading his men guided by Abdul, and headed off to find and kill the Parthians camped high up in the hills. The men had been instructed to use woollen cloth to wrap up any loose weapons and metal armour to cut down on any noise that could alert the enemy. Atticus was hoping the Parthians, having not received any information regarding Roman soldiers in the area, would make them feel safe. And not expecting an attack would hopefully not bother them to take many precautions for a fight. He hoped the lookouts might be sparse or even asleep.

It was quite dark when Atticus and his men approached the outskirts of the hills, Abdul had gone with Adelar ahead to scout out the Parthian camp and would return shortly. Abd-El-Kader and the Cilician archers had snuck into Isin unnoticed and found the Parthian spies without any trouble. They were asleep when Abd-El-Kader sneaked into their room and slit their throats as they slept snoring. He'd slit the throat of a third who was sleeping on the floor outside their room while supposedly on guard. He quickly returned to the archers who were hiding in the shadows.

Quietly, they left Isin totally undiscovered and headed towards the Parthian camp, happy with the total success of his mission. They had carried off the bodies and buried them in the desert so the locals would think they had ridden out at night.

Abdul and Adelar returned and quickly reported their findings; there was an entrance or exit at either end of the camp; one end had a trail leading to Isin.

The number of tents suggested there were about four hundred Parthians within the camp; they had been able to get close due to the lack of lookouts. Adelar explained he had nearly tripped over one sleeping where he was supposed to be on lookout duty, quickly sending him to the afterlife.

At the base of the hills and made their way to the far exit and trail to Isin; they had found three lookouts at the base of the hills. Without hesitation, they slit their throats and hid the bodies well out of sight. Most of the Parthians were asleep in their tents, but there were some sitting around small fires drinking what Abdul had described as goats piss but quite potent.

"Sextus over here," beckoned Atticus quietly.

"Sir!"

"Take half the men and half the archers with Abdul to the far side of the camp to form shields. Block their retreat and kill anyone trying to escape. No prisoners, kill them all. I don't want any escaping to warn our enemies of our presence, have the archers form up behind the shield wall."

"Yes, sir!"

"Hopefully, it won't be long before Abd-El-Kader and the other archers arrive at your back to help you."

"Farrokh!"

"Sir, get your archers split into two, you come with me," quickly the Roman force split into two and made their way quietly to their positions.

Atticus wanted to make haste just in case the three lookouts who had been killed were missed.

Atticus left several men to look after the horses. Fury was quite restless letting Atticus know he wanted to come but for this battle Atticus needed to lead his men on foot with Edelgard at his side.

Quickly they marched to the Parthian camp and as soon as they arrived Atticus got Farrokh to place his archers high up amongst the rocks to cover Atticus and his men. Atticus formed two lines of men with himself and Edelgard in the centre of the first rank. Optio Linus was at Atticus's left shoulder.

Linus was a foot shorter than Atticus; he held his shield tight and was gripping his spear, Atticus had noticed a slight tremble in Linus's hand holding his spear.

Linus was in his early twenties, a few years older than Atticus who was only eighteen.

"Linus!"

"Yes, sir!"

"Is this your first time facing the enemy in battle?" asked Atticus.

"No, but it's the first time in the front rank," replied Linus.

"Protect the man on either side of you, they in turn will fight to protect you. It's fine to be nervous, we all get nervous."

Linus looked up at Atticus in awe of his size and presence. He then returned his gaze to the front, feeling a little more at ease. Farrokh and his archers were well placed ready for the battle to begin.

The Parthians below had no idea what was about to be leashed upon them as most of them slept in their tents.

The two lines of Romans were a hundred men abreast.

"Forward!" came the order from Atticus, and down into the camp they marched in perfect formation.

As prearranged with Farrokh, the archers let loose a volley of flaming arrows which soon set fire to many of the tents; some of the arrows impaled the men sitting around the fires. Screams rang out as men clambered out of their tents, some with their clothing set alight. The men hit by arrows fell, dying as their bodies were engulfed in flames. The smell of burning flesh filled the air. Panic had now overcome the camp as Atticus and his men arrived.

"Now!" shouted Atticus. The lines of Roman soldiers responding to his order launched their spears into the Parthians, killing many. More screams of dying men rang out filling the air.

Then again, Atticus and his men threw their second spear, more Parthians fell, bodies littered the ground. Atticus and his men punched their shields into the throng of Parthians who were totally unorganised. Atticus punched his sword into the flesh of a Parthian in front as did all the front rank, slicing bare flesh with their short swords. The Roman line punched its way forward at pace, killing the enemy. Their swords flashed back and forth, slipping swiftly between their wall of shields. Edelgard thrust his sword into the face of a Parthian, splitting it wide open. Blood and entrails now covered the sandy floor, the blood looked dark in the moonlit sky.

As they drove their shields and swords into the enemy, men died with their limbs hacked off. Legs and arms littered the floor. The dismembered bodies twitched as Atticus strode over them with his line of men. The second rank of Romans quickly killed any Parthian still alive, in pain, crawling and screaming, trying to get out of the way. The second rank automatically raised and locked their shields with the front rank as arrows were fired down at them from some rocks above their front. The Parthian archers, who had been formed by a tall, slim, dark-haired officer, were clearly aiming for Atticus.

He wanted the Roman officer dead at all costs.

"I see they are wanting to kill you my friend," shouted Edelgard as he punched his sword into the neck of a Parthian.

"It comes with the task of being in charge," Atticus smiled, shouting his reply.

Many of the Parthians were now retreating and running to the exit at the far side of the camp but as soon as they reached the brow of the hill they were cut down by arrows and spears launched by Sextus and his men. They had been joined by Abd-El-Kader and the other Cilician archers who'd returned from Isin.

The Parthians were trapped between the two forces of Romans who were relentless in their killing of the enemies of Rome. The small force of Parthians who'd formed up to fire arrows trying to kill the Roman officers were now under a barrage of arrows being fired by Farrokh and his men. Many fell dying, not wearing any armour of much description. As Atticus and the line of Romans approached them, the officer charged at the centre of the Roman line to attack Atticus.

"He's mine!" shouted Atticus as he stepped forward out of line, dropping his shield and taking his stance. Atticus held both his swords out in front of him with the inscription 'MORI QUAM FOEDARI' for all to see. His attacker charged at him with his sword above his head screaming.

"Die, you, Roman pig!" but as his last words were uttered Atticus punched both swords into his chest. Pushing him back several yards, the Parthian fell heavily falling onto his back, his eyes bulging out from their sockets with the shock of death. The battle was now over, for what remained of the Parthian force had thrown down their weapons and knelt, hands raised, begging for mercy.

Optio Linus approached Atticus and said, "Sir, you need to come with me over there to the rear of those tents." Linus had his head hung slightly low; he had the look of shock on his face as he spoke.

As they walked over Sextus arrived, "Sir we have taken twenty-three prisoners, we have only six dead and a further seven injured."

"That's quite remarkable!" answered Edelgard.

"How many Parthians have we killed?" asked Atticus.

"Still counting!" replied Sextus. Moments later, Atticus and the others gathered at the rear of the tents. Anger and shock gripped their faces, Abd-El-Kader arrived and stood behind Atticus looking down at the floor. Tied and staked out in the sand were four Roman soldiers who'd had their eyes eaten out by large ants which were crawling in and out of their eyes and mouths. Linus promptly threw up.

Edelgard looked down in horror and said, "That is no way for a man to die!"

"The ants eat their way in through the eye sockets and eat their way inside, killing them slowly and eating them from the inside out," said Abd-El-Kader.

Atticus quickly turned and walked over to the prisoners and looked down at an officer who sat there smiling knowing full well what Atticus had seen.

Atticus slowly drew one of his swords out of its scabbard, the smile soon leaving the Parthian officer's face as Atticus swung his sword, chopping his head clean off with ease.

"Kill the prisoners, they have no honour!" shouted Atticus.

Immediately the Roman soldiers standing near drew their swords and carried out the order. Atticus then shouted for his men to form up. The Roman dead had been buried; the Parthians however were left to feed the vultures flying high above. Atticus led his men back to their marching camp, collecting Fury and the other horses on the way.

Chapter 12

Atticus rested the men for several hours before carrying on their journey. The hostage was released to return to his father at the oasis. Abd-El-Kader, along with Abdul and Adelar, rode ahead to scout the trail; Atticus and Edelgard discussed the events of the previous night; they had killed over four hundred and eighty Parthians and several Mesopotamian scouts.

"According to Abdul, we will be at the second oasis by nightfall; we can make camp, then head through the mountains and should reach Tadmor in three days," said Atticus.

"Good, I'm sick of sand getting in my mouth spoiling the taste of my wine," replied Edelgard with a smile.

"Keep the pace going. I want to check on the men and waggons," said Atticus, and turned Fury around and trotted along his lines of men, slowly chatting and offering encouragement to those that struggled a little in the scorching sun.

There was a grim determination amongst the men to complete their mission and kill as many of the enemy as possible. The discovery of the Roman prisoners eaten alive by the ants had fuelled the men with anger and a newfound resolution to avenge them.

Centurion Cyrus carried the Augusta banner with pride, "How are you today, Cyrus?" asked Atticus as he rode at his side.

"Very well, thank you sir!"

"Good, we will arrive at the next oasis before nightfall, get fresh water and rest," answered Atticus. Cyrus smiled in response. Atticus rode Fury to the waggons and checked on the wounded. The medic was a veteran of many battles in his early fifties, stout with a neatly cut beard.

"Spurius!"

"Yes sir!" he replied while sitting in the back of one of the waggons, changing a dressing on the arm of one of the wounded.

"How are the casualties fairing?"

"Very well, all the wounds are relatively superficial; all but one will be fit for duty within a week. I would say, as long as the wounds are kept clean sir."

"Good, carry on, I will leave you to it," Atticus then rode fast back to join Edelgard at the front.

"Is everything well back there with the wounded?" asked Edelgard.

"Yes, and the men are coping well with the heat."

A cloud of dust could be seen ahead being kicked up, "Looks like Adelar and the others are returning," said Edelgard.

"HALT!" shouted Atticus and the column came to a standstill.

"Everything fine ahead?" asked Atticus.

"Yes, the trail ahead is clear, a small caravan of traders heading west. Other than that all is clear," replied Adelar.

Several hours later they arrived at the second oasis without incident and quickly a marching camp was erected high above the oasis which was a lot smaller than the first but there was plenty of water.

Atticus and Edelgard had finished erecting their tent just as Abdul approached returning from a scouting mission.

"Is everything fine?" enquired Atticus noting a look of trepidation on the face of Abdul.

"A sandstorm is making its way in our direction. We need to prepare immediately. You can just make out the cloud of sand far on the horizon over there." Abdul pointed Atticus looked at the grey haze becoming more apparent heading in their direction.

The horses now sensed something was wrong and had become rather restless.

"How long do you think we have before it hits us?" asked Edelgard.

"We have less than thirty minutes I would estimate."

"Decimus! Cyrus! On me!" shouted Atticus, Abd-El-Kader had already begun to cover the heads of the horses with sacks to keep the sand out of their eyes. He'd been caught in many sandstorms over the years and knew exactly what was needed before it hit them. Assist Abd-El-Kader and Abdul prepare for that coming storm.

"I wondered what those clouds were," said Decimus.

"No time to waste, get to it!" shouted Atticus. He secured Fury's head and covered it. Fury didn't seem to be overly bothered; he trusted Atticus.

The camp became a hive of activity as soon as the men became aware of the coming storm. Several of the older veterans had been caught in these storms in the past. One of them, Rimus, barked out instructions to his comrades; he knew all too well how deadly sandstorms could be. One of the mules began to panic, rearing up and kicking out with its hind legs and shaking its head vigorously. Thadius took charge of the situation before the mule could spook the others. Holding on to the rope it was tied to him whispered in its ear while stroking its neck, which seemed to have the desired effect, and it wasn't long before the mule settled.

"Well done, Thaddius!" said Atticus who had brought a hood to put over the mule's head.

"Thank you, sir," replied Thaddius. The mule didn't seem to mind the hood.

"Make sure everything is secured!" shouted Atticus.

The clouds of sand being blown ferociously towards them now blotted out the sun. Darkness hung over them as the sand lashed everything it came into contact with.

"Fuck me, that stings!" shouted Adelar as the sand covered them all.

Atticus had pulled a blanket over himself as he held Fury's reins tightly. The only sound that could be heard now was the gale-force wind whipping up the sand blowing through their camp. Atticus kept his eyes firmly shut under the large blanket doing his best to hold onto the blanket preventing it from being ripped from his grasp. Fury snorted at Atticus's side, feeling the sand harshly peppering his body as it blew past. It took well over an hour for the sandstorm to pass leaving Atticus his men and horses covered with sand.

As the wind died down, the camp came back to life, men coughing and spitting out the sand that seemed to fill every orifice of their bodies. Edelgard began running his hands through his hair to get rid of the thick blanket of sand covering his head. Atticus had decided to stay at the oasis for the remainder of the night and the following day to give everyone plenty of time to rest and clean all their equipment. Atticus polished his armour and weapons as did his men under the watchful eyes of the officers. Atticus also brushed Fury, making him feel more comfortable.

The following evening Atticus and his men left the oasis behind and headed towards some hills high above the main trail below. Several hours later a large group of vultures could be seen circling in the sky about six miles ahead on their left.

"HALT!" came the order from Atticus, and Abdul and Adelar came charging back, kicking up a sand cloud as they rode. The sun beat down relentlessly from a cloudless sky. Sweat poured down Atticus's face as he waited for them to arrive.

"What have you discovered?" asked Atticus.

"There's a valley past those hills to our left which looks like where the main concentration of vultures are above but we were still a few miles away and couldn't see why."

"What are you thinking, Atticus?" asked Edelgard, while wiping beads of sweat off his face with a small cloth.

"We need to find out what it is."

"Could just be an animal carcass," said Optio Linus, who was standing listening just behind Edelgard.

"Too many vultures," answered Atticus.

"Forward!" shouted Atticus.

"Sextus!"

"SIR," keeps a good pace, we will scout ahead.

"We will scout ahead and reach that valley as quickly as possible and if it's nothing we will return but follow our tracks, Abdul will guide us."

"Yes sir!" replied Sextus.

Atticus, along with Edelgard, Abd-El-Kader and Adelar, rode forward at a gallop towards the vultures circling high above the valley.

It didn't take long to reach the valley, arriving high above the valley below amongst some rocks and brush. Atticus did not expect to see the devastation unfold before him.

"Fuck me!" said Edelgard out loud, staring at the scene below. Down in the valley were the dead bodies of hundreds of Roman soldiers littered as far as they could see.

The vultures and many other scavengers were feasting on their bodies, burnt tents and waggons were evident to one end.

"Do you see what I see, Edelgard?" asked Atticus, as they rode cautiously down into the valley, looking all around to make sure they wouldn't be ambushed.

"What do you mean?" enquired Edelgard.

"That looks like the remains of Titus's force sent to Tadmor by General Felix. But it looks like Titus has been lazy, there hasn't been any marching camp defences erected," replied Atticus.

Edelgard scanned the valley below, taking in the position of the burnt-out waggons and tents. Some tents had survived and flapped in the strong breeze.

"I see what you mean but how can any officer of the Roman army be so stupid?" shouted Edelgard in anger.

"Arrogance!" replied Atticus.

They had now reached the valley floor and began to ride very slowly amongst the bodies of the fallen dead Roman soldiers. Many of them with their insides being eaten and ripped apart by the many scavengers and vultures. Many of the rocks on the other side of the valley had vultures sitting with their bellies full preening themselves. Atticus had drawn his bow in anger and fired arrow after arrow killing many of the scavengers ripping at the dead bodies which made many more run or fly off hiding out of sight amongst the rocks and brush.

"Not only is it a stupid thing not to erect adequate defences, who in their right mind would set up camp in the bottom of a valley wide open to attack on all sides," said Atticus.

"Over there!" shouted Adelar, who pointed to the far end of the valley.

A lone rider was charging towards them as fast as his horse could run. Edelgard and the others quickly drew their swords, "WAIT!" shouted Abd-El-Kader.

He recognised the horse and rider.

"Do you know who it is?" asked Atticus.

"It is my cousin he was scouting for Titus and his men," replied Abd-El-Kader.

When he arrived, pulling his horse to a standstill, Atticus noticed dried blood on his clothing and a cut above his left eye where the blood had dried in the sun, forming a scab.

"I'm glad to see you safe Abd."

"This is the first Centurion Atticus in charge of our mission."

"This is my cousin Yassur," said Abd-El-Kader, introducing them both.

Yasser bowed his head, "It is an honour to meet you Atticus, but it is a pity it is not under a more pleasant situation," said Yassur.

Atticus nodded his head in reply as he looked around at the multitude of dead Roman soldiers with a sombre look on his face. But Atticus also had a burning anger deep inside.

"When did this happen?" asked Atticus.

"Two nights ago."

"I can't understand why Titus hadn't reached Tadmor. He should have been there over a week ago at least." stated Atticus angrily.

"Titus moved his men very slowly and when he bothered to erect a marching camp, he would stay in camp for several days eating and drinking," replied Yassur.

Carefully choosing his words due to Titus being a legate of Rome and not wanting to provoke any kind of rebuke from the young Roman officer.

"I have sent word back to Maximus in Ostia about this terrible defeat with two of my fellow scouts!" Yassur went on to say.

"Sounds like he was hoping for another Roman force to reach Tadmor first if you ask me!" snarled Edelgard responding to what Yassur had said.

"The Parthians have taken Titus and over one hundred Roman soldiers as hostages; they have also raided several villages between here and the fort at Tadmor taking many hostages." said Yassur.

"What kind of hostages and why? Surely they will only slow the Parthians down?" asked Edelgard.

"Women and children." answered Yassur.

"There is a large auxiliary force of men from the surrounding towns and villages which have been conscripted into the Roman army at the fort at Tadmor," interrupted Abd-El-Kader.

"They will display them alongside the Roman legate Titus and his men outside the fort and tell them to surrender the fort or they will kill all the hostages." said Yassur.

Atticus now completely understood the Parthian plan; he knew that the women and children would be wives, sons and daughters, sisters of the auxiliaries. This could cause them to rise up if Commander Marcellus refused to surrender the fort; he needed to get his men there as quickly as possible and stop the Parthians' plan.

"Adelar return to the main force and get them to get here as fast as possible," shouted Atticus, Adelar saluted, dug his heels into the side of his horse and galloped back over the hills.

"We can catch them and cut them off before they reach the fort. The hostages will slow them down and the trail they travel is long."

Abd-El-Kader drew a map in the sand at Atticus's feet, "This is where we are, this is the trail they travel and here is a mountain trail only wide enough for men on foot or horseback. The waggons will have to follow their trail but will be quicker than women and children walking in this heat but that won't worry the Parthians. As long as they know they have killed the reinforcements heading to the fort, they don't know we're not too far behind," said Abd-El-Kader.

Atticus looked at Yassur, "How many men have the Parthian force got?"

"At least fifteen hundred hostages are travelling at the rear, and they are well strung out."

"Edelgard come walk with me," Atticus began to walk amongst the dead as the vultures carried on circling them above awaiting the chance to feed.

"You have a plan, I can see it on your face," said Edelgard.

"Yes, I will have to split the men up again. We will go across the mountain trail to cut them off and free the hostages. We return to the main force at the far side of that mountain range. The Parthians will attack us as we retreat with the hostages to the main force, but we will counter them. We will kill the remaining Parthians, then head straight for the fort!"

"You make it sound so easy," replied Edelgard.

"It won't, I know but with the will of the gods and a little luck on our side we might just pull it off."

The sound of the main body of men and waggons entering the valley rang out, making Atticus and Edelgard look to their rear.

As the men marched into the valley, the faces of many were filled with horror at the sight that greeted them but also there was a look of anger and vengeance. The bodies had been stripped of all armour, weapons and anything of value. The bodies and remains of the fallen were piled up and set alight before Atticus marched his men out of the valley.

Chapter 13

Atticus had quickly informed his officers of his plan along with his scouts, the force split into two once again. Atticus, along with Yassur, Abdul, and Edelgard, lead their horses up along the mountain pass. There were no complaints from the men about fatigue or the heat; they had only one thing on their minds at that time, *VENGEANCE.*

"We have only a few hours of daylight left; it will be a full moon tonight." said Yassur.

Atticus wiped sweat off his face, which was pouring down his cheeks from under his helmet straps. "If we stop here and refresh the men, we can travel through the night when it's cooler and, with the moonlight, still see where we're going. and up here on this mountain trail we don't need to erect a defensive camp," replied Atticus.

"HALT!" shouted Atticus; he quickly informed his officers and men of his plan to travel at night.

The men laid down amongst the rocks and erected some screens above their heads to block out the blinding sun; guards were placed at either end of the camp high up so they could see the whole surrounding area. The men ate some of their rations; most of their conversation was about what they had witnessed in the valley earlier and what they would do to the Parthians when they caught up with them.

Atticus sat with Edelgard in quiet reflection, Edelgard broke the silence after drinking a large cup of wine.

"Well, Atticus, my friend, are you thinking of home and that beautiful wife of yours?" Atticus smiled at his friend and replied.

"Naomi is never far from my thoughts, but I know she is safe and being looked after at home. She will be happy amongst her family and friends. She will have plenty of chores to do to keep her mind occupied."

Edelgard filled his cup with wine and another for Atticus, and as they drank, Edelgard told Atticus of his family back in Germanica. It wasn't long before they were both asleep, needing to be fully awake for the night's travel.

It didn't seem long before Abdul woke them up, the moonlight shone and visibility was good, most of the men had already formed ranks three abreast. Filling the width of the mountain trail. On one side of the trail was a drop of over a hundred feet leading down to a valley of sand and dried brush below. The terrain was quite barren. It was cold at night, but with a steady march, the men kept warm. The only thing on their minds was to wreak revenge on their enemy. Wanting nothing more than to catch up to the Parthians and kill them. With it being cooler, it was a lot easier for them to march at a fast pace. Atticus rode Fury, chomping at the bit, wanting to reach the enemy as quickly as possible. Abdul and Yassur had ridden ahead, scouting the mountain trail, and after several hours returned with the news that they had sighted the Parthians.

"They have made camp several miles ahead in the valley below," said Yassur.

"Could you see the prisoners?" asked Atticus eagerly.

"Yes, they are situated at the rear of the main Parthian army."

"How many guards?"

"They are guarded by at least fifty sat around the edges in groups of five or six; the Roman soldiers are in the middle tied and bound together and the women and children are scattered about tied in groups, but I know by nightfall tomorrow many of the soldiers not on guard duty will be drunk." replied Yassur.

"How long will it take us to get there?" asked Atticus, "About three hours at a brisk march," said Abdul.

"That means it will be late evening when we reach them. We can then rest the men for a couple of hours while we scout the enemy's camp and put a plan of action together," said Atticus.

"Forward men at the double," shouted Atticus.

The men needed no encouragement as they set off through the mountains, getting higher above the trail below.

They arrived high above the Parthian camp, well out of sight and could not be seen from below; it had taken only two hours to get there, such was the eagerness of the men. Atticus had the men eat and rest, while he walked amongst them talking with them and making light of the battle ahead. Atticus had grown the full respect already from his men and also knew many of them by name.

Thaddius, the new recruit Atticus had spoken to on the training march, had been chosen by Atticus to join the first cohort as Atticus had seen something in him he liked.

Atticus was only eighteen and was the youngest ever first Centurion, but commanded respect of everyone no matter what their age. Atticus was taller than most by a good few inches and his body was a slab of pure muscle, and his strength was second to no other not to mention his fighting skills with all manner of weapons.

As Atticus approached the group of men sitting with Thaddius, who was about to stand and salute.

"No need Thaddius, sit and rest. How are you men coping with this heat and the march?" Appius, one of the oldest veterans, answered.

"We are well thanking you, just can't wait to get amongst those Parthians and give them a taste of Roman steel and justice."

This made the others smile and respond in agreement, "Good!" replied Atticus.

"Don't forget your training, Thaddius. Hold that spear firmly and stand in line with your brothers in arms," said Atticus.

"I will!" replied Thaddius feeling proud to be spoken to and remembered by Atticus, "carry on then lads."

As he walked off, many of the men thanked him for his words of encouragement, "How are your men?" asked Edelgard on Atticus's return. "Good and rearing to get at those Parthians!" replied Atticus with a grin.

"Abdul, I want you to make your way down back there and reach the rest of the men and waggons. I want them ready and formed in battle lines here," as Atticus drew a map in the sand of the surrounding terrain.

"Centurion Cyrus Is to be in charge, here are his orders I have written them down and he has to follow them to the letter."

"Yes!" replied Abdul.

"Take these two archers with you," as two of the Cilician archers stood waiting having already received their orders and had been given a letter of instructions for Farrokh the Cilician archers commander.

After they had left Atticus, along with Edelgard and Yasser, made their way quietly down amongst the rocks and brush to get a closer look for Atticus to make his plan of action. It took Atticus an hour to check the prisoners camp situated at the rear of the Parthians main camp which was spread out along the trail with several makeshift tents scattered between the prisoner's camp and the main camp separating the two with a gap of about one hundred yards. There were many fires lit around the camp with men drinking and laughing. Atticus had sent all his archers under the leadership of Adelar accompanied by Yasser down to where the prisoners were camped. Their job was to kill the guards as quickly and quietly as possible, release the prisoners and make their way back down the trail to where Cyrus and his men would be waiting to cover their retreat.

Atticus and his three hundred men would form battle lines and hold off the Parthians, they would be outnumbered by at least five to one, but Atticus thought this to be reasonably good odds. Atticus and his men had made their way down to the edge of the gap between the prisoners and the Parthian main encampment.

"Why do you think they have left such a gap between the prisoners and the main camp?" asked Edelgard.

"The Parthian officers would have been aware that so many women prisoners would distract the men, and rape would be rife, that's my guess," replied Atticus.

Sextus, Linus and the other officers waited in their sections crouched down awaiting Atticus's order to form lines and block the trail. Edelgard crouched at the side of Atticus as they looked across at the prisoners and their guards camped around the edges.

"Shouldn't be long now," whispered Atticus. "Good I'm getting cramps squatting here and my swords are wanting to kill." replied Edelgard with a grin.

Hiss was the sound of the arrows cutting through the air as they flew towards the guards and the muffled sound of Parthians being struck and killed around their campfires.

So far, no alarms have been raised. Atticus could hear the sound of his heart thumping in his chest.

More and more arrows flew through the night sky finding their targets, the killing had begun in earnest. Adelar and his men sprang out from their hidden positions and began to cut the Roman soldiers free of their bonds. Others rounded up the women and children and herded them up the trail. A shout of alarm rang out as one of the remaining guards then fell dying with an arrow striking his throat. But the surprise was now over as Parthians came from the main camp to see what was happening.

"NOW!" shouted Atticus as he sprang to his feet, charging forward followed by Edelgard and the men, all their training and natural instincts coming to bear.

Atticus launched one of his spears with such force it struck and pinned two Parthians together killing them in an instant. The Parthians wore no armour having been asleep moments before the attack had started. Some hadn't even picked up a weapon in their eagerness and under the influence of drink rushing to see what the alarm was.

Many died as Atticus and his men had quickly formed a battle line across the trail and began to step back one pace at a time as the Parthians charged past the tents to attack the Roman lines.

Atticus shouted, "Stand firm front row launch spears!"

In seconds spears flew at the Parthians, screams of death rang out as the spears hit their targets.

"Second row, launch spears," came the order from Atticus again as more Parthians fell. There was no order in the Parthian assault on the two Roman lines with Atticus and Edelgard in the centre of the front rank.

Parthians at the rear stumbled and fell over the bodies of their comrades dead and dying on the ground, fear and screams filled the air.

"Take five steps back in formation!" shouted Atticus. Immediately and as one the two ranks of Roman soldiers moved then became stationary, "Second row shields aloft." ordered Atticus as the Parthians now started firing arrows at Atticus and his men.

Arrows hit the shields but hadn't managed to penetrate the tightly formed shields. The Parthians grew in number and were now clearly being led more organised in their attack. The two lines of Romans were clearly now vastly outnumbered. Atticus and his men grounded their feet into the sand, ready for the Parthian assault. Their short swords in hand, ready to punch into the flesh of the enemy.

Crunch and the clash of steel from the Parthians swords and spears crashing against the Roman shields echoed in the valley. The line held and the killing started.

Swords punched through the narrow gaps between the shields, striking the soft flesh of the Parthians, crushed from their own men from behind into the Roman shields.

Blood and the insides of men's guts splashed to the floor as the screams of the dying rang out; men died with their lungs punctured, their eyes cut out as swords struck them in the face. Throats were slit open, the carnage of close combat was everywhere, limbs were hacked off. Any gap in the front row from a Roman soldier dying was quickly filled from the rear and the killing spree carried on. Atticus killed the enemy to his front left and right with no mercy. Edelgard screamed his battle cry as he killed the enemy with his double-headed axe.

The dead Parthians piled up in front of the Roman line. Disarray and fear now gripped the Parthians; many began to turn and push their way back out in fear of being the next to die. The Roman shields and swords were plastered with the enemy's blood. The Parthians retreat became a rout, many in fear of Atticus and his Roman line died trying to flee. The Roman line was a perfect killing machine, Atticus shouted out an order.

"Take ten paces back and reform your line tight."

The Roman line retreated in perfect order and came to a standstill, the mound of Parthian dead and dying had piled up across the valley floor. Atticus estimated they had killed hundreds.

The Parthians who had retreated were slightly out of view way back in their camp out of sight of the Roman archers. Loud voices could be heard, and an argument was obviously taking place.

"Quick men at the double turn let's make some ground between us and them before they organise another charge at us." ordered Atticus.

The order was carried out, his lines turned and ran through the prisoners' camp but still in formation.

Bodies of the dead guards were strewn about with multiple arrows embedded in their bodies.

The body of a woman lay dead, stripped naked by one of the fires, with her throat cut. Two Parthians had died by her side. It was obvious they had raped and killed her. The Parthians still hadn't yet organised another charge, so Atticus and his men gained more distance and hoped he had plenty of time to implement the second part of his plan. Edelgard was breathing heavily as they made their way with the rest of Atticus's men, "How long do you think we have before they attack again?" asked Edelgard, between long gulps of air filling his lungs.

"Not long as soon as some officer gets to grips with the situation, I would say, but they won't like climbing over their dead companions so maybe we have ten minutes if we're lucky," replied Atticus.

He could now see the retreating Roman prisoners along with the women and children a few hundred yards ahead. Several were carrying someone on a makeshift stretcher Atticus knew he needed to gain more time.

Many of the women carried small children in their arms as the older children ran alongside.

As ordered, half the Cilician archers, led by Yassur, rejoined Atticus.

Then the soldiers left up on the mountain trail came down through the rocks with the horses. Atticus quickly mounted Fury and took his bow in hand; it also gave him a better view back down the valley in the moonlight.

Abdul then arrived back pulling two mules carrying long wooden boxes, the men and waggons are ready as you ordered.

"Good!" shouted Atticus as he sat on Fury.

"What's in the boxes?" asked Sextus.

"A little surprise for our Parthian guests. Caltrops get them dispersed quickly before they arrive. I want them strewn the full width of the trail a hundred yards in front of us," shouted Atticus.

"Yassur, I want you and the archers to make your way up above the trail to the far side. I don't want any Parthians to be able to reach their force at Tadmor and warn them about us!"

"Yes, come follow me!" shouted Yasser as he ran back up the mountain trail quickly followed by the Cilician archers.

The caltrops were dispersed in the sand and amongst the brush and small rocks. Sextus and his men returned and joined the Roman lines. Atticus sat above Fury and could see the Parthians dragging their dead and wounded out of the way. The Parthians then formed neat lines of men this time with shields and armour.

"Looks like they mean business this time!" shouted Atticus. A tall Parthian officer was standing in the centre of his line of men. The Parthian and Roman lines were at least two hundred and fifty yards apart from each other.

"Let me see if I can give our Parthian friends something else to think about," shouted Atticus.

He then drew his bow to its full stretch, his large biceps bulging the size of coconuts as he pulled the bow back. The veins pumping blood and oxygen down his arms bulged as he took aim.

He quickly fired the arrow, the speed and accuracy of it hissing as it flew through the air, moments later which seemed like an eternity, it struck the Parthian officer dead centre in his head, killing him. The Parthians on either side stepped back in fear as he fell to the ground. Blood and bone fragments dribbled down his face as he lay staring lifelessly up at the blue sky. Many of the Parthians had never seen such a shot from that distance. The cries of Atticus rang out from the Roman lines as his men chanted his name and banged their swords against their shields as they chanted which filled the night air. Striking fear into their Parthian enemies.

Centurion Cyrus Carrying the banner of the Augusta 11 arrived with two ranks of men shouting Augusta and smashing their shields with their spears and quickly joined the two lines of men in front.

The Roman lines were now four deep, and the Parthians still outnumbered them, but only by two to one. Fear had filled them at the sight of the Roman lines chanting loudly and the crash of weapons against shields.

The Parthians stood motionless awaiting someone to take charge. Another officer had finally joined the front line of the Parthians. He stood holding a large shield in front of himself, not wanting to end up like his predecessor.

Men at the back of the Parthians had started to lash out with whips forcing the reluctant Parthians to attack the Roman lines fearing for their lives. It wasn't long before screams rang out as the Parthians trod on the sharp edges of the caltrops; many fell to the floor grabbing the torn flesh of their feet as the caltrops ripped through their sandals. Some of the poorer Parthians walked barefoot, not able to afford sandals.

The men with the whips lashed out ferociously forcing them to carry on with the attack towards the Roman lines. They did not realise their comrades were being felled by the scattered caltrops. Atticus shouted for the rear ranks of Roman soldiers to launch their spears at the attacking Parthians.

The neatly lined Parthians had now descended into a rabble of dying men felled by spears and the deadly caltrops. Many began turning from their Roman enemies and ran past those whipping them to attack.

Some Parthians retreating killed their own men as they lashed out with the whips as the Parthian survivors ran back through their camp in fear. But were now slain by the Cilician archers from above.

It wasn't long before silence descended on the valley, the rout of the Parthians had finished. Young Thaddius, standing in the front rank, looking at the dead and dying only yards away in front, felt no emotion; they were the enemy of Rome; they had slaughtered his countrymen in the valley days earlier without mercy. He also remembered seeing Roman prisoners who had been staked out and left to be eaten alive by ants.

Atticus shouted for Sextus but there was no reply, Atticus turned and looked along the lines of his men. Linus, the young Optio, came up to Atticus and saluted. "Sir I regret to inform you that Sextus has been killed!" Atticus swallowed hard before replying.

"Show me where his body lies," Linus saluted and turned walking forward towards the dead strewn ahead all across the valley trail. Atticus and Edelgard followed close behind; he sent men forward to retrieve the caltrops and make the area safe for them to go forward; any dying Parthians were quickly put to death.

Linus pointed, "there he is!" Sextus had a spear plunged into his chest, still with his sword in his hand. His lifeless body was surrounded by the dead Parthians he'd killed before he fell. Atticus knelt down beside Sextus's body and placed his hand on his dead friend's shoulder and whispered a few words to his gods. Atticus then kissed the red jasper stone hanging around his neck which now glowed bright and felt warm in his hand.

"Linus form a burial party and bury our dead and place Sextus in the middle," said Atticus.

"Yes sir," replied Linus who then left to carry out the order.

"Cyrus!" shouted Atticus.

"Sir!" came his reply.

"Make a full report of today's action, and I want an inventory of our dead and wounded as soon as possible."

Yassur returned with the archers, "The Parthians are all dead Atticus, nobody escaped."

"Good," replied Atticus.

The waggons and the released prisoners had now joined Atticus and his men, and one of the Roman officers they'd rescued approached Atticus and saluted.

"My name is Flavius Tribune of the Felix 1V legion sent to reinforce the garrison under siege at Tadmor," Flavius was a tall thin man with a very pointed nose. He was in his late forties with a thin crop of hair that was brushed across trying to cover up his bald head. Flavius had an air of arrogance that befitted many from the senatorial class.

"Who is in command of your force?" asked Flavius, addressing his question to Atticus looking at Atticus's first Centurion's uniform.

Atticus didn't answer straight away, still pondering over the death of his friend Sextus and looking towards the women and children they'd freed.

"First Centurion, I ask you a question!" barked the Tribune Flavius, and Edelgard raised his voice and answered.

"This is the first Centurion Atticus of the legion Augusta 11 in charge of this mission and your rescue."

Flavius turned his attention to the large German addressing him with disdain, but before he could speak Atticus intervened, "How is the legate, Titus? And what ailment befalls him?" asked Atticus, in a low voice.

"He has succumbed to some form of heat or sun stroke and is delirious," replied Flavius.

"Spurius!" shouted Atticus.

"Sir!"

"Go, tend to the legate Titus and when you have finished report to me of his condition." asked Atticus.

"Yes sir."

Flavius was trying to figure out how someone as young as Atticus was 1st Centurion thinking he must have a wealthy benefactor in Rome.

"Well, 1st Centurion I thank you for our rescue, but due to the legate being unwell and not fit for duty as senior officer I now take command of this force," said Flavius raising his head looking up at Atticus. Even though Flavius was quite tall, Atticus still stood a foot taller and looked down at Flavius.

He swallowed hard after speaking to Atticus, now looking up into Atticus's dark eyes.

"What makes you think you are fit to take command?" asked Atticus, Edelgard had laughed on hearing Flavius's demand that he was now in charge.

Flavius gave Edelgard a stern look but was feeling a little unsure of himself as Edelgard also towered over Flavius and was still grinning at Flavius.

"Who was in charge in the valley when you were attacked at night by the Parthians?" demanded Atticus.

"I was, Titus was unwell and…" but before he could finish, "Why did you not erect a defensive camp?"

"It was late, and my scouts informed me there was no enemy insight."

"Well, due to your incompetence almost two thousand Roman soldiers lay dead in that valley!" shouted Atticus.

"But…" replied Flavius, "But nothing, you are a disgrace to that uniform," retorted Atticus.

"How dare you talk to me in that manner, I will have you flogged," shrieked Flavius.

"I have been put in charge of this mission by General Maximus of the Agusta legions with the authority of the Emperor Augustus himself."

The blood now drained from the face of Flavius as Atticus produced the gold sceptre indicating the power of the emperor with its bearer.

"You will be dealt with in due course now get out of my sight," growled Atticus. Flavius now hung his head and returned to the stretcher where Titus lay. He was being attended by Spurius.

Cyrus returned carrying a wax tablet with his report for Atticus, "Sir, we have twenty-three dead and eleven injured, four of which will not be fit to fight for several weeks."

Under the circumstances and the overwhelming odds, Edelgard regarded it as quite amazing and patted Atticus on his shoulder and said.

"Well done, Atticus my friend many men here are alive today due to your plan of action. Look at the men's faces," Atticus turned to face his men who were all standing to attention in line, many smeared with the blood of their enemy due to the ferocity of the battle. But many standing there, young and old, had smiles on their faces as the sweat of battle ran down from under their helmets.

Centurion Decimus then shouted, raising his sword, "ATTICUS!" This was quickly reciprocated by all the ranks of men including Farrokh and the Cilician archers who cheered and responded shouting his name over again.

The rescued women and children smiled with delight at being freed and the Roman soldiers of the rescued Felix legion stood to attention and saluted.

Flavius, sitting next to Titus, was pondering over his fate on his return to Rome and looked over at Atticus, now realising the young Roman officer had the total respect of the men under his command. This was something he and Titus never had due to their incompetence.

A young woman in her mid-twenties ran towards Atticus. She fell to her knees and grabbed Atticus's hand and kissed it with tears rolling down her cheeks looking up into Atticus's face.

"Thank you! The gods have blessed us and brought you as our saviour," said the woman.

Atticus pulled her up gently. I am just happy we were able to save you.

"Please return to your friends. We still have much to do," replied Atticus. The woman smiled and returned to the others.

Chapter 14

Several hours later after the men had finished preparing to leave and had some of their rations. The horses were watered and the wounded had been placed on the waggons with the smaller children. The column began to march down the trail towards Tadmor. Which, according to Abd-El-Kader, was only a couple of days' march away.

Abdul and Yassur, again with several of the Cilician archers now on horseback from captured Parthian horses, rode ahead, scouting.

Back at the fort in Ostia, Maximus's legions were ready to leave for Tadmor, and the port at Ostia was full of Roman warships ready to take them. Ships of all sizes were being loaded with both men and equipment.

It made a formidable sight, and the port was full of locals gazing at the Roman fleet stretching the full extent of its harbour and beyond.

General Maximus had gone to the emperor's palace in Rome, Maximus was taken to the emperor's private quarters.

"Come Maximus, sit!" as Augustus pointed to a lavish couch, then he ordered one of his servants to pour wine for them. Once the wine had been poured, Augustus ordered all the servants and guards to leave the room, and the large golden doors were closed behind them as they left.

"Well, Maximus, my friend, what news do you have for me before you leave for Tadmor?" Augustus now sat behind his desk and took a large drink of his fine wine placing the golden goblet down in front of him.

Maximus pulled out several scrolls from a satchel he'd placed on the couch at his side, "I have received these dispatches from Atticus. They arrived here this morning with my cousin, the owner of the merchant boats that transported them from Corinth to Tarsus."

"Wonderful, I hope all goes well?"

"Yes, so far, they have landed at Tarsus without incident. He has dealt with a problem regarding the port garrison at Tarsus."

"I see. What was the problem?" enquired Augustus.

"Lack of leadership and discipline which I will with your consent further deal with when I arrive there."

"You have my full authority to do anything necessary that goes without saying."

"Atticus has met with our scouts and left Tarsus for Tadmor. If all has gone well, he should be almost there as we speak."

"Good," replied Augustus before taking another sip of his wine.

"But I also have grave news from our spies in Mesopotamia regarding the legate Titus and his force heading for Tadmor," Maximus now drank his wine before divulging the bad news.

"Well," demanded Augustus.

"His forces have been attacked and destroyed."

"WHAT!" screamed Augustus.

"It seems his and his tribunes' incompetence has got them killed. Some have been captured, including Titus, by all accounts, but at this moment that is all we know."

"When did this happen?"

"As far as I am aware, about a week ago the messengers travelled night and day with this news."

"JUPITER!" shouted Augustus.

"This makes it more imperative that Atticus and his force succeeds with his mission."

Augustus sprang to his feet and began pacing the room back and forth, Maximus decided to let Augustus think for a while without interrupting him. Augustus then refilled his goblet with wine and sat down again, drumming his fingers on his desk.

"When do you and your legions leave for Tadmor?"

"Today, as soon as I return to Ostia the men are boarding as we speak," answered Maximus.

"Good I will keep you no longer, let's hope the gods still walk with Atticus!" Maximus got to his feet and saluted.

"They do, I have no doubt about that," responded Maximus as he left to return to Ostia.

At the Romulus homestead, Marcus and his wife Aurelia and escort arrived with letters for Romulus and Zuma, also a private one for Naomi from Atticus.

On arrival, Romulus and Marcus clasped forearms while Aurelia, Julia and Lydia hugged, Naomi came into the courtyard with young Alesandro skipping at her side with a big smile.

"You look wonderful Naomi and I've not seen that boy happier," said Aurelia with a smile.

"Come, Naomi, take a walk with me. I have a letter here for you from that handsome husband of yours."

"Really quick give it to me," responded Naomi as her face lit up with glee.

She quickly rolled open the sealed scroll and read it intently.

Little Alesandro shouted, "Has he chopped any bad men's heads off yet!" Aurelia laughed out loud.

"My, my, what goes on in the little ones' heads these days."

"That's partly my fault I'll tell you later," said Naomi with a smile.

Aramea had brought a tray of wine and figs out into the courtyard and placed it on the stone table.

"Thank you!" said Romulus who poured the wine into cups for himself, Zuma and Marcus.

Doukasi walked down from the stable into the courtyard and bowed.

"Come Doukasi, join us here, have a cup of wine and sit with us," said Romulus.

"We have received news from my son Atticus."

"He has arrived in Tarsus safely, sends his regards and also hopes you Doukasi have settled in your new surroundings. But ask you not to make too many of your fine oatcakes, making your father fat." This made Doukasi smile and Zuma laugh.

"When do you leave for Tadmor?" Romulus asked Marcus.

"Later today, I won't be able to stay long but I thought you and Naomi would want his letters promptly and I wanted to see you all before leaving. Aurelia will be staying at our quarters in Ostia, and I would be pleased if Julia and the ladies would visit her."

"We all will, and she is more than welcome to stay here now and again until your safe return."

"That is very kind of you my friend."

Aurelia and Naomi returned to the courtyard with young Alesandro who was jumping around all excited.

Romulus put his arm around Naomi and said, "Don't worry, Atticus, will be fine doing what his destiny calls and before long he will be home in your arms once more."

"I hope so!" replied Naomi with a tear in her eye.

"Come, Aurelia, we need to go," Their escort still sat mounted outside the gate ready for the order to leave.

As everyone bids their farewells, Romulus and Naomi pass some letters for Marcus to give to Atticus as soon as he arrived at Tadmor.

Maximus, Marcus and the Augusta legions had now boarded the Roman warships which sailed out of the port and began their journey east. The harbour was full of people waving from the dockside, screaming and shouting good wishes. Some openly pray, asking the gods Mars and Jupiter to watch over them and grant them a great victory.

Chapter 15

Atticus and his force were making progress towards the fort at Tadmor slowly due to the women and children they'd rescued.

Atticus and Edelgard, along with Adelar and Abd-El-Kader, rode in front of the long column as they left the valley, full of dead Parthians behind, with the vultures circling above. Wild dogs had arrived sitting amongst the rocks above waiting to feed as soon as the living had left. They panted in the heat, saliva dripping from their open jaws. Sextus and the other dead Roman soldiers had been given a proper burial too deep for the wild animals to get at. While their enemy had been left for the vultures to feed on.

"What is your plan to get the women and children into the fort safely?" enquired Abd-El-Kader.

"It won't be easy," said Adelar. Fury raised his head and snorted loudly.

"What does Fury think, Atticus?" asked Edelgard with a grin. Atticus laughed loudly and spoke.

"You seem to be getting used to Fury's ways; he thinks we should charge through the Parthians to the fort's gates. Kill as many of them as we can!"

Fury immediately nodded his head vigorously, chomping on his bit. Abd-El-Kader looked at Adelar with an expression of bewilderment. Adelar shrugged his shoulders in response with a grin.

It was now early evening, and the sun began to go down on the horizon. "How much further?" Atticus asked Abd-El-Kader.

"At this pace at least several hours still," he replied.

"Better start looking for a safe place to build a camp. The Parthians might send out scouts looking for their comrades we have killed," said Atticus.

Abdul and Yassur returned with the archers, "HALT!" shouted Atticus and the column came to a standstill.

"What do you have to report?" asked Atticus.

"The trail ahead is clear, further on about a mile there is a range of mountains to the left. It will be hard but a few of us could make a climb to the top of one. We should be able to see the fort and our enemy surrounding it from there before dark," replied Abdul.

"Is there anywhere nearby where we can make a camp?" asked Atticus.

"Yes, this side at the base of the mountains is a gully large enough and out of sight we can build a camp and fortify it quite easily," replied Abdul.

"That is good we can climb that mountain while the camp is built and see what we are up against," said Atticus.

As soon as they arrived in the gully preparations for the camp were started and lookouts were placed above amongst the brush and rocks.

"Come Abdul, show me where we climb and let's get started,"

"I will come also!" shouted Edelgard.

The climb was hard, dust was blown into their faces from a strong evening breeze that had picked up. Atticus was almost bitten by a snake he'd disturbed coiled up behind some brush, but he was quick enough to grab the snake's neck and hurl it down the rock face they were climbing. Many times, they lost their footing slightly on the loose rocks beneath their feet, sending small stones tumbling to the ground below.

Edelgard slid, cursing, cutting his knee. Abdul grabbed his hand to prevent him falling further. Finally, they arrived at the summit. It had taken them just over an hour.

"I can see what you mean Abdul, it is a fantastic view of the fort, and the enemy camped around it," said Atticus.

All three of them were covered in dirt and sweat which ran down their whole bodies.

"Pass me that canteen of yours Edelgard," asked Atticus, who then opened it and drank he then passed it to Abdul who swallowed most of what was left before returning it to Edelgard.

"Fuck me, it's still hot even with that breeze," said Edelgard, who was still breathing heavily from the climb.

The fort standing at the top of a hill looked magnificent in the evening glow of the sun. Its walls were twice the size of the fort in Ostia; there were two gates, a large one at the front facing down hill and a smaller one in the wall facing them.

There was a tower in each corner and three more evenly placed along each of the fort's thick stone walls between its corners. The fort had been built decades before Atticus was born. The deep cavern below it had been discovered many hundreds of years before the Roman empire existed. Nomadic tribes that had roamed the land had first discovered it. When the Romans had invaded Mesopotamia and discovered the deep cavern, they had decided to build a fort above and around the deep-water cavern system. A large reservoir of water deep below ground was fed by the Tigris-Euphrates river system. Thousands of slaves from around the Roman empire were transported there.

Roman engineering and ingenuity were second to none throughout the civilised world. It took them over many years to build the fort and put in a system to have the water pumped to the surface within the fort. Deep stone wells were dug to store the water which was housed in a huge stone building situated behind the fort's bathhouse. Hundreds upon hundreds of slaves died building the fort, many of whom died below ground excavating the cavern.

The Parthians had erected thousands of tents all around the fort just out of range of the catapults and heavy weapons on the fort's battlements.

Cooking fires had been lit and the glow from them could be seen quite easily in the sunset now descending.

A large tent had been erected in the centre, far back, facing the front wall with the large gate. "That must be their General's tent," said Edelgard.

"It will be their king's," replied Abdul.

Edelgard raised an eyebrow.

"The Parthians must mean business if the king's here!" answered Edelgard, laughing at the same time.

"Right, I've seen enough, let's get down before it gets dark," said Atticus.

"Got a plan then?" asked Edelgard with a grin, knowing full well by the look on Atticus's face he had.

"You will know soon enough my friend but let's get down off this mountain," shouted Atticus as he began his descent.

By the time they had finished their descent the camp had been erected, the women had lit fires and began cooking what looked like a broth which smelt quite delicious. The woman that had thanked Atticus earlier quickly ran over to Atticus and bowed.

"No need to bow, I'm just a soldier of Rome," said Atticus.

"We have made hot food for you and all your fine soldiers," she replied with a smile.

"What is your name?" enquired Atticus.

"My name is Aisha," replied the woman.

"I'm Atticus, you speak Latin very well, where did you learn?"

"My father fought in Rome's legions with the auxiliaries and taught me as a child, now my husband fights in Rome's legions with the auxiliaries at Tadmor."

"Then may I thank you on behalf of my men for the food. It's been a while since we have eaten hot food. But let your women and children eat first then we shall eat." Aisha smiled at Atticus's response and returned to the others, stirring the large pots on the cooking fires.

After everyone had eaten, Atticus called his men to assemble in the centre of the camp with the officers at the front. Edelgard and Adelar stood at his side.

"You will all be wondering no doubt how we are going to get inside the fort with the women and children safely through the enemy's forces," muttered voices could be heard from the men in anticipation.

"Well, we're going to march right up the road through them and in through the gate," Atticus shouted with a grin. Many of his men began to laugh.

"How?" asked Linus the Optio.

"The wounded and the smallest children will be put on a waggon in the middle of our force. We will form a marching square the width of the road Centurions Decimus Cyrus and Gaius will form the wedge at the front. Behind them will be our first waggon shields strapped around both sides. The square will be filled with archers who will fire upon the enemy from above the heads of their men marching in square formation protected by shields. aiming to the right." Atticus paused and waited for any questions; none came.

"Apart from the waggon carrying the wounded and children, we will do the same with the other waggons. That's four in total so the convoy will be two waggons of archers then the wounded then the other two filled with archers. We have sixty horses, most of which were taken from the battle with the Parthians."

"I want our best riders from our ranks to act as cavalry support. Then along with me Edelgard, Adelar the scouts and remaining Cilician archers will charge and attack the enemy to the left of the column. The women and older children will walk in the centre between the waggons. It is imperative we keep the same pace. I don't want anyone getting trampled on," Atticus paused again.

"We have ten excellent riders!" shouted the Centurion of the 111 Gallicia Raphanea.

"We have also sixty men fit and ready to join the fight, what do you want us to do?" The Centurion enquired.

"Good, I was just coming to that, your men fit enough to fight will plug the gaps in the square if any of our men are killed."

"You will all know what to do with the enemy if they crush against our shields."

"Stick our swords between their bollocks!" shouted a burley veteran which caused fits of laughter.

"Right, get some rest men, we leave at dusk tomorrow," shouted Atticus.

"Well, that seemed to go down well," said Centurion Decimus.

"Centurions follow me, let's get the waggons ready with those shields," shouted Atticus.

"Yassur!"

"Yes Atticus, what can I do?"

"I want you and Abd-El-Kader to sneak through the enemy lines tonight and deliver this dispatch to the legate Marcellus in the fort and give it to him personally."

"Yes, but I am not a Roman; they might not listen to me," answered Yassur.

"I know but you two will be able to disguise yourselves and go unnoticed by the enemy. Take this, show it to him and tell him it belongs to me, and he must carry out my instructions without question."

Atticus passed him the gold sceptre, "Both of you leave now we have much to do before dusk tomorrow."

Yassur bowed and they both left. It took only a couple of hours for the shields to be secured in place and the tarpaulin sides were rolled up to the roof, which left a gap just wide enough for the archers to fire through.

"Very clever, sir, and the heavy weapons we carry will act as a platform for them to stand on," said Centurion Cyrus.

"Now, I fully understand your train of thought," said Decimus.

Darkness fell, and the cooking fires had been extinguished so they didn't glow at night in case they were seen by the enemy. The heat of the day had given way to the cold of the night. The women and children all huddled together for warmth, guards kept a lookout from the rocks above and were changed every two hours.

Atticus and the Centurions finished preparing the waggons for the following night. Once they were finished, Atticus went to see Spurius the medic.

"Well, Spurius, how are the wounded? We have only six remaining not fit for duty; several others in my opinion are still not fit to fight but they have returned to duty and wouldn't listen to me. They want to do their duty in the attempt to get inside the fort all wishing to play their part." Spurius sighed and rubbed his eyes feeling tired.

"What about the legate Titus?" asked Atticus, he's improved slightly and is being attended to by his Tribune Flavius.

"Fine, get some rest and let one of the orderlies watch over the wounded for a while."

"Yes, I will do that," answered Spurius.

Atticus then left and made his way to Edelgard and sat down.

"Pass that canteen of watered wine, my friend," asked Atticus.

"Here you are…everything ready for tomorrow night?"

"It is!"

"And the wounded?"

"Good, some have decided to return to duty a little early according to Spurius." Atticus then drank a large mouthful of wine and wiped his chin.

"Save some for me," said Adelar as he joined them and sat down.

"I knew you were on your way to us," said Edelgard.

"How?" asked Adelar.

"I could smell pig shit!" teased Edelgard grinning.

Atticus laughed loudly, quickly followed by both Edelgard and Adelar. Atticus passed him a canteen of wine.

"We'd better get some sleep; the sun will rise shortly," said Atticus as he laid down and pulled his cloak around his body tightly feeling the night chill.

Within moments began snoring in a deep sleep, dreaming of home and his wife Naomi.

"Fuck me! He snores as loud as Fury snorts," said Adelar, while lying down and trying to make himself more comfortable.

Meanwhile Yassur and Abd-el-Kader strolled through the Parthian camp chatting to each other in Arabic. Saying what they would do to the Romans once they had captured the fort. The Parthians were still awake, sitting around their fires, drinking and laughing, other than the occasional glance they took no real notice of them.

It was pitch black when they reached the base of the fort's wall. Abd-El-Kader shouted up to one of the guards patrolling above on the battlements.

The legionnaire grabbed a torch, held it aloft and looked down; he could see the two men below in the flickers of the torch's light.

"Who are you?" he demanded.

"We have been sent by Atticus, first Centurion of the Legion 11 Augusta with a dispatch for the legate Marcellus,"

"Wait there!" The legionnaire disappeared but they could hear him shout for the officer in charge of the watch who promptly appeared above looking down at them in the torchlight.

"I will drop a rope down for you to climb up but be warned if you are not who you propose to be I personally will slice you both in two."

Abd-El-Kader nodded to the officer and the rope was dropped, and Abd-El-Kader climbed up first, quickly followed by Yassur. As soon as they dropped over the wall onto the battlement walkway they were quickly grabbed and their weapons removed.

"Give me that dispatch!" demanded the officer in charge.

"Sorry sir, I cannot. I have strict instructions from the first Centurion Atticus to personally place it in the hands of the legate Marcellus without delay."

The officer, a Centurion of the 111 Gallicia Raphanea, glared at Abd-El-Kader for a few moments. He then turned and shouted to his men, "Bring them and follow me. If this turns out not to be important and I awake the legate, you will pay with your lives." They quickly descended down a stone stairway inside one of the towers to the ground below and escorted across the large stone courtyard. There were guards at every corner.

They walked up a large street lined with billets on either side, they then passed a large bathhouse. As they turned a corner, a tavern full of off-duty soldiers were laughing and joking, some standing outside saluted the Centurion as they passed.

They arrived at a large stone building in the centre. It had six stone pillars and above the large doors sculptured into the stonework was a large chariot. It was being driven by a Roman soldier carrying a banner with the letters S-P-Q-R at its top.

Outside the doors stood four Praetorian guards barring their way.

"Good evening, Centurion Grasus, the legate Marcellus is asleep, and we have orders he's not to be disturbed," said the Praetorian in charge while he saluted Grasus.

"I understand, but according to these two shall we say gentlemen, who have managed to get through those Parthian boy fuckers." Grasus then turned and looked at them.

"And with our help climbed over our walls demanding an immediate audience with the legate."

"Well, they will have to wait until morning," responded the Praetorian.

Abd-El-Kader stepped forward and bowed.

"Sir, if I may, I am Abd-El-Kader, in service to the General Maximus of the Augusta legions," Centurion Grasus stood to one side and said, "Carry on, don't let me stop you." Abd-El-Kader smiled before carrying on.

"I am scouting for the first Centurion Atticus of the First cohort of the 11 Augusta sent here with some reinforcements and heavy weapons from Ostia," The Praetorian rubbed his chin and said, "Well, you will still have to wait until morning. It is more than my life's worth to awaken the legate!"

"It will be more than your life's worth if you don't," replied Abd-El-Kader rather forcibly.

"Why, you cheeky bugger!" But before he could utter another word, Abd-El-Kader produced the gold sceptre and held it out at arm's length for all to see.

"Fuck me!" shouted Grasus.

"Where did you get that?" asked the Praetorian. "It belongs to Atticus, given to him by General Maximus on behalf of the Emperor Augustus. Atticus gave it to me in case I wasn't taken seriously. Now, wake the legate, Marcellus."

Grasus and the Praetorian looked at each other before the Praetorian opened the door and shouted, "Follow me!"

Praetorian followed by Grasus led them down a great hallway with a bust of the Emperor Augustus situated in the middle at the end of the marbled hallway. On the left wall, like most buildings in Roman forts, belonged to the legate. Fine artwork hung from the walls. There were two large golden gilt doors situated on the right leading to the legate's private quarters.

Two Praetorian guards were standing to attention at either side of them who both saluted, "Wait here!" said the Praetorian officer in charge.

Who then glanced at Grasus and took a deep breath before entering and walking through the doors. Inside was Marcellus's splendid office and at the far end was a door leading to Marcellus's sleeping quarters. Outside the door was a Praetorian guard who saluted and was about to speak when the officer shook his head, so the guard quickly shut his mouth. The Praetorian officer hesitated for a moment, before banging loudly on the door and waiting. He could hear Marcellus cough loudly and curse as he awoke. The sound of footsteps echoed towards the door; it was then opened and pulled inwards.

"What's up! Are the Parthians attacking the fort? Demanded the legate while rubbing his eyes trying to wake himself up properly."

"No sir!" replied the Praetorian officer while saluting.

"Then by the gods why have you got me out of bed? What part of you doesn't understand do not wake me up for any other reason!" shouted Marcellus.

"I had no choice sir, you need to come with me, you have visitors."

"VISITORS! At this hour," Marcellus marched out and sat behind his desk and adjusted his gown.

"Well, bring them in!" The Praetorian quickly marched to the opened door and shouted, "The legate Marcellus will see you now!"

Abd-El-Kader and Yassur walked in and bowed, "Sit, sit!" Marcellus hissed still not fully awake.

"And what is so important that I need to be disturbed at this unearthly hour?" demanded Marcellus rather angrily.

"If I may, I am Abd-El-Kader, and this is my fellow scout Yassur. We are currently in the employ of your General Maximus. Our current mission has been to scout and escort the first Centurion Atticus of the 11 Augusta legion and his men along with the heavy weapons you require. I have an urgent dispatch here for you from Atticus and was instructed to give it to you personally."

Abd-El-Kader then passed the dispatch to Marcellus and also placed the gold sceptre on his desk, so he understood its importance. Marcellus's eyes widened upon seeing the golden sceptre, knowing full well the power bestowed on its holder.

"This belongs to Atticus," said Abd-El-Kader as he put it down. Marcellus instructed the Praetorian officer to go and get one of the orderlies to bring food and wine and to be quick about it.

Marcellus's tone changed and his frown became a smile, silence ensued while Marcellus read the dispatch very carefully.

Even when a servant brought the food and wine, he didn't lift his head from the parchment. The servant placed the tray on the desk, bowed and left.

Marcellus finally lifted his head and looked over at Centurion Grasus and ordered him to awake his Tribune and first Centurion and bring them to his office without delay. The dispatch fully informed Marcellus of the demise of the reinforcements sent by General Felix.

"Did you two see the devastation and bodies of the slain Roman soldiers coming to our aid?"

"We did," replied Abd-El-Kader.

"I was scouting for them," said Yassur, then Marcellus stood and poured out the wine into three cups.

"Please help yourselves to some of these fine pastries," while they ate and drank the wine Marcellus enquired as to Atticus's position as he rolled out a map on his desk. Abd-El-Kader pointed to Atticus's position and explained the Parthian's reason for taking the hostages and keeping the Roman prisoners alive.

Marcellus now realised the actions taken by Atticus in killing the Parthians and rescuing the women, children and the legate Titus along with the surviving soldiers had probably saved the fort from being captured.

If the auxiliaries had risen up thinking they could save their family members from execution, this would no doubt have allowed the Parthians to take the fort. Not that the Parthians wouldn't have killed the prisoners anyway.

A loud knock on the door made all three of them lift their heads from the map laid out on the desk.

"ENTER!" shouted Marcellus and the door opened. In walked the fort's Tribune, along with the first Centurion, followed by Grasus.

The door was closed by the Praetorian guards on duty behind them.

"This is my Tribune Justus," who saluted, "And this is my first Centurion, Publius."

"May I introduce our guests Abd-El-Kader and Yassur, scouts from General Maximus bringing reinforcements led by first Centurion Atticus of the Legion 11 Augusta."

Everyone acknowledged one another and Marcellus beckoned them all to be seated.

For the next two hours plans were made as to per instructions in the dispatch from Atticus. When they had finished, Abd-El-Kader and Yassur were shown to some sleeping quarters that were quite lavish and were soon fast asleep.

Chapter 16

Atticus and Edelgard spent the following day finalising the preparations for the attempt to get into the fort as soon as the darkness of night had descended.

Fury was, as usual, excited at the prospect, "I'm not getting too close to Fury today," said Edelgard, laughing loudly as he and Atticus strode around the camp talking to the men. He was also making sure their weapons were sharpened, cleaned and ready for the night's action ahead.

Aisha was with the children singing to them in a quiet voice, helping them keep their minds occupied. They were young but knew of the perils ahead before they would be safe inside the fort.

As Atticus and Edelgard stood and watched, Atticus noticed one of the young girls staring up at him. She had bright blue eyes and blond hair trailing all the way down her back. She looked so much like his friend Julia from his early years living in the Aventine slums. It brought back vividly the memory of the day he found her lifeless body being eaten by rats. Immediately he could feel anger, and a grim determination that these children would reach the fort safely.

The little girl got to her feet and ran up to Atticus and placed her arms around one of his legs. That was as far as she could reach and gazed up at Atticus with a beautiful smile on her face.

Aisha stopped singing and turned to see why the child had got up and ran not knowing Atticus and Edelgard had been standing there watching.

Atticus bent down and picked the young child up and kissed her on her head and asked, "What is your name, little one?"

"Ava," she replied with a giggle followed by a cute smile. Atticus also noted a warmth and a sparkle in her eyes.

Atticus instantly felt an affection for Ava. Atticus returned her smile, which was a bit like Zuma's, from ear to ear.

"I am Atticus," he replied, still smiling.

"I know," she quipped with a giggle. Edelgard laughed out loud and said, "You have a beautiful face, my little one."

"You will have nothing to fear tonight, Ava, I and my men will keep you all safe and tomorrow we will play games safely inside that fort," said Atticus.

He gave her another kiss on her forehead before putting her down.

"I know you will," Ava replied smiling. Then she skipped back to the other children. Aisha looked up at Atticus and said, "I don't believe it."

"Believe what?" asked Atticus.

"Ava has not spoken a word since we were captured the poor little thing witnessed the rape and murder of her mother at the hands of those Parthian devils!" Aisha looked over at Ava happily now playing with some of the smaller children.

Edelgard put his hand on Aisha's shoulder saying, "Since I met young Atticus on the day he saved my life and that of my General Maximus. Atticus has a way with people young and old who feel safe in his presence."

"Yes, I understand, I felt that same sort of trust and a belief that no further harm would come to us," replied Aisha.

"Don't be silly you two you're making me blush," said Atticus.

"Well, young man, my people have a name for you 'sāvyər' which in your language means saviour. Like it or not, without you we would probably have been executed outside that fort as soon as the Parthians had no further use for us."

Aisha then smiled, reached up and placed her hand on his cheek before returning to the children. Atticus and Edelgard looked at each other before walking off to carry out the rest of the preparations.

Nightfall came, the small children and wounded were placed on the waggon in the middle, Atticus had placed some of his best men all around it. They had only one instruction, to protect them with their lives. The archers climbed onto the other waggons and took their positions with arrows piled at their feet.

Decimus and the other Centurions formed up at the front. Atticus, Edelgard and the newly formed cavalry mounted up on the left. Optio Linus stood proud in the centre, just behind his Centurions carrying the banner of the Legion 11 Agusta fluttering in the slight breeze. The night was cold, but nobody seemed to notice, the faces of the soldiers showed no emotion. They were ready to fight and die if need be, shields gripped in one hand and a spear in the other. Many wanted nothing more than to get into the fort and kill as many Parthians as possible on the way.

Atticus noticed the new recruit Thaddius had mounted one of the horses. "Didn't know you could ride, Thaddius," said Atticus wanting to break the silence.

"My family breeds horses for the legions, and as soon as I could walk my father taught me to ride sir," answered Thaddius.

Atticus smiled and turned Fury to face his men, all formed and ready to go.

"Tonight, we do our duty for Rome…we get these women and children into Tadmor safely. Any Parthian goat fucker who stands in our way dies!" The soldiers banged their shields with their spears and shouted, "For the glory of Rome, the emperor! And death to the Parthians!"

When silence fell, Atticus shouted the order to march and in perfect formation, they headed down the road leading to the fort. The mules took the strain of the heavy waggon's six pulling each waggon. Their hooves pounded the ground as if to claw their way forward until they gained momentum.

"Keep those waggons steady, hold the pace!" Atticus shouted to the drivers.

The Parthian fires came into view and could be seen all around the fort just out of range of its heavy artillery. As the column passed the other side of the mountain range, Atticus and his cavalry peeled off and formed two lines facing the Parthians camped in a ravine facing the wall with the gate Atticus intended to use to gain access to the fort.

Atticus, along with Edelgard and Adelar, formed a line in front of the two The archers faced the Parthians to the right of the road and knocked their arrows ready to fire. The column began its march towards the fort. The nights were short, and it would be light again soon. Atticus turned and nodded to Farrockh to give the prearranged signal to the fort. He ignited an arrow and launched the flaming arrow high into the night sky.

"What if Yassur and Abd-el-Kader didn't make it to the fort?" asked Adelar.

"We will know soon enough," replied Atticus.

Atticus quickly drew his two swords, pressed his knees into Fury's flanks and dug his heels into his stirrups. Atticus had tied the reins to his saddle so he could fight with two swords.

"Atticus! I see you and Edelgard I see have both polished your armour and helmets! Looks nice but the Parthians will want to kill officers first. Good luck to you both!" teased Adelar laughing loudly.

"Well, you won't have to worry! you look like shit! and the smell of rats piss!" retorted Edelgard with a grin.

Most of the men lined up behind laughed out loudly, Atticus nudged Fury forward and shouted, "Hold the line and keep formation."

Down towards the Parthians they rode in the moonlight, men's shadows below could be seen in the glow of their fires.

Fury was chomping at his bit, foaming at the mouth and snorting loudly. "Easy, Fury won't be long now." An alarm was shouted as the Parthians became aware of the impending attack.

The sound of trumpets filled the air calling the Parthians to action. "CHARGE!" shouted Atticus as Fury bolted down the ravine in line with Edelgard and Adelar who both roared their Germanic battle cry.

They were soon amongst their prey and the killing started. No quarter was to be given, the Parthians had brought war to the Roman borders. Many of them would now pay with their lives.

Atticus plunged one of his swords in his left hand, into an enemy's chest, blood spraying Fury's flanks. While at the same time decapitating another with the sword in his right hand. The head flew and hit the face of another Parthian who screamed with fright. But before he finished screaming, Edelgard punched his sword into his gut, killing him in an instant. The killing had begun in earnest as Atticus and his cavalry charged through the Parthians. With their horses trampling over the dead, hooves cracking skulls, Atticus kept his cavalry in almost perfect formation as they pressed forward. Atticus's blades thrust indiscriminately into the foe. Disarray and fear grew amongst the Parthians.

Decimus and the other two Centurions at the head of the column marched on at the same pace and as soon as they encountered the Parthians blocking the road they thrust their shields and short swords into them. Bodies fell to the floor; the Roman column kept its pace and strode over the dead and dying Parthians.

The Parthians were shoved back with ease as the Roman column pushed its way towards the gate of the fort. The Parthians regrouped and again attacked the column on all sides. When they attacked the front of the column Decimus, and the others punched their short swords through the small gaps between their shields and into the flesh of their enemy.

Entrails slid to the ground as stomachs were ripped open.

Blood, guts and the dying Parthians were trampled over as the Roman column pushed on towards the fort's gate. The archers fired repeatedly from the waggons, finding their targets with ease. The children coward in the waggon, some whimpering, covering their ears to try to block out the sound of battle. Aisha and several other women were doing their best to calm them.

Bodies fell at the feet of the Roman soldiers over and over again, their screams piercing the night sky. The column continued its relentless march forward over them; many still alive were quickly put to death by the ranks behind.

The wheels of the waggons crushed their bones as they drove over them; the screams of the dying Parthians kept filling the air. They marched, punching their way through the ranks of the Parthians relentlessly.

Up on the fort's battlements, the legate Marcellus and his Tribune Justus watched the battle unfold, ready to implement Atticus's instructions.

Down in the courtyard, waiting was the cavalry of 111 Gallica Raphanea, hungry for the order to join the action. Three hundred men and horses, their armour glinting in the moonlight. The sound of the horses' hooves clattering the stone floor, being held back by their riders eager to charge out of the fort.

"Open the gates!" ordered Marcellus.

As soon as the wooden bars were removed and the gates were dragged inwards by six Roman auxiliaries, straight away the cavalry charged out to join up with Atticus, led by Grasus the Centurion.

All along the battlements of the wall facing the Parthians, charging the column's right flank from their main camp. Marcellus had placed the forts' heavy weapons primed and ready to fire as soon as the enemy came within range.

Down below, large catapults were loaded with clay pots filled with inflammable liquid, with tapers attached to the tops, as soldiers stood ready with torches, awaiting the order to ignite and fire. These had the longest range and would be fired first, well away from the Roman column.

The archers on the waggons were firing arrows as fast as they could, killing scores of Parthians attacking their right side.

The column was now within a few hundred yards of the fort's gate and safety. Marcellus raised his hand; hundreds of Parthians were now in range of the catapults unaware of what was about to be unleashed on them.

His hand descended as he shouted, igniting the pots and firing the catapults. Thwack came the sound as four large catapults unleashed their projectiles.

Balls of fire streaked through the night sky, illuminating the ground below. Immediately the catapults were rewound and loaded as the first wave of fire balls crashed into the Parthians. The burning clay pots exploded on impact, showering the Parthian hordes with burning liquid. Flames spit into the night sky, screams filled the air as the burning bodies of men fell to the floor engulfed in flames being burned alive.

Another volley of flaming pots lit up the night sky and crashed down onto the Parthians who were running in all directions trying to flee the devastation. But for many it was futile; they fell burnt to a crisp.

Marcellus gave the order for the ballistae to fire, their large bolts launched into the Parthians from the fort's battlements, ripping into their flesh. The vipers fired their large arrows one after another from the battlements killing scores of Parthians.

"Bloody hell!" shouted Abd-el-Kader. "I've never seen anything like it" responded Yasser, as more burning clay pots fired by the catapults exploded amongst the retreating Parthians.

The smell of burning flesh now filled their nostrils. Marcellus turned to face Yassur and Abd-el-Kader and said with a smile. "When you challenge the might of Rome that is the outcome. Your first Centurion Atticus certainly knows how to plan a battle."

Back down in the ravine, Atticus had now been joined by the cavalry from the fort. Fury reared up and crashed his hooves onto the head of a Parthian, crushing his skull, as Atticus punched one of his swords into the face of another. Both Fury and Atticus were covered with the blood of their enemy.

The Parthians in the ravine had started to retreat up into the rocks to escape the death below fear had taken hold of them. A Parthian archer hiding behind a rock fired an arrow straight at Atticus, the arrow bounced off Atticus's helmet to the Parthians' disbelief. He quickly fired again, this time it bounced off Atticus's breast plate. Adelar seeing it shouted, "Told you Atticus they want to kill you, my friend!"

"Hadn't noticed!" answered Atticus grinning at Adelar's remark as he plunged one of his swords into the chest of a Parthian trying to stick him with a spear.

Atticus could see hundreds of Parthians charging towards them from the far side of the fort.

Atticus charged out of the ravine and rode Fury straight at them, "ON ME!" he shouted to his men.

Thaddius was the first to respond and charged his horse out of the ravine after Atticus Edelgard growled, "Fuck me, come on, Adelar we need to catch up with those two!" Many others now heeded the call and charged after Atticus and Thaddius heading towards the charging Parthians. They were being led by a giant of a man wearing golden armour from head to toe.

As Atticus charged at them, a line of Parthians bent down on one knee and thrust a wall of spears in his direction. Thaddius was catching up close behind and the rest of the Roman cavalry led by Edelgard screamed their battle cry trying to catch up to Atticus.

Fury without hesitation leaped over the Parthians with ease, kicking one of them in the head as he did Killing him. Fury landed at their rear directly in front of the giant warrior wearing the golden armour.

He had been taken by surprise; Atticus struck him with the pommel of his sword knocking him unconscious. The warrior hit the ground hard, falling on his back. Atticus leapt from Fury and before anyone could respond held his sword at the throat of the unconscious Parthian leader. Atticus had gambled on the importance of this Parthian wearing gold from head to toe.

"Drop your weapons or he dies!" shouted Atticus pointing his other sword at them.

A golden eagle descended from the sky and landed on Fury's saddle. The eagle flapped its wingspan of over two metres and its large talons gripped Fury's saddle. The eagle screeched, flicking its head from side to side. Many of the Parthians, believing it to be an omen, threw down their weapons in fear and fell to their knees.

Any Parthians still holding a weapon were quickly killed by Edelgard and the other Roman cavalry who'd arrived. Thaddius couldn't believe what he had just witnessed, sitting on his horse, sweat pouring down his face. He stared down at the Parthians, now begging for mercy. Edelgard forced his mount through the throng of kneeling Parthians and joined Atticus.

"Fuck me, who's that big turd in gold flat on his back?" asked Edelgard, looking down at the still unconscious Parthian.

"No idea, but I guess he might be rather important judging the response from his men." answered Atticus.

"And what's that giant eagle doing sitting on Fury?"

"Not sure about that either, but where eagles are, the gods are not far away. The Parthians shit themselves and surrendered straight away. Mind you I also had my sword at the golden warriors throat I think that helped persuade them a little," said Atticus with a grin.

Atticus then walked over to Fury and the eagle perched on his saddle. The Parthians hung their heads while kneeling in the sand not wanting to look up as Atticus strode past them. When he approached Fury, the golden eagle twitched its head from side to side with its brown eyes flickering as it looked at Atticus.

Atticus spoke in a low voice as he stroked the breast of the eagle. "You are a magnificent bird my friend."

As he placed his hand on the eagle, Atticus felt his mind had been transported to a place beyond. Clouds and a strange mist swirled all around inside his head, and eagles flew back and forth amongst the clouds above.

A voice of a woman spoke, "Atticus" the voice hissed.

"Your gods are pleased with your strength and valour in the service of Rome! When you return home you will be blessed with a wonderful reward."

The vision disappeared from Atticus's mind as he felt a hand on his shoulder. The eagle launched itself up from Fury's saddle into the sky high above. The sunrise began breaking above the mountains.

"Atticus, my friend, are you alright?" enquired Edelgard.

He still had his hand on Atticus's shoulder.

"Yes, fine, why do you ask?" Atticus replied.

"I've been talking to you for several minutes without you responding, your eyes were pure white my friend," he whispered into Atticus's ear.

"I'm fine. We need to get these prisoners inside the fort before the Parthians can counterattack!"

"Agreed," replied Edelgard.

"Thaddius!"

"SIR!" organise the prisoners into two lines and escort them into the fort now quickly. Thaddius saluted, "Grasus have half your men join Thaddius to take them while the rest of the men can join me and protect the rear of the column."

The golden warrior had sat up and taken his helmet off, shaking his head and groaning. Abdul nudged his horse forward and approached Atticus; he could now see the face of the golden warrior.

"Do you know who you have captured?" asked Abdul.

"No!" replied Atticus.

"He is Prince Mithridate son of the Parthian king Artabanus11."

"No wonder the Parthians surrendered not wanting their prince to die at your hands," said Edelgard.

Atticus mounted Fury as the Parthian prince looked up at Atticus with disdain. Mithridate was feeling angry with himself for being captured so easily. The prince was young, in his early twenties, as tall as Zuma but slender; his armour made him look a lot broader than he was.

"Bind his hands and put him on a horse," shouted Atticus. Centurion Grasus stepped forward and gave him his horse then saluted Atticus.

"Get them into the fort!" ordered Atticus. "Edelgard, Adelar! Bring the men, follow me, we need to get the column in!"

Atticus rode Fury fast towards the rear of the column leading the cavalry. The Parthians were regrouping to attack the column. The archers on the waggons had ceased firing arrows to their right; the bombardment from the fort's heavy weapons had forced them to retreat out of range. The ground was scorched black where the fireballs had struck. Many bodies were Still burning; the stench of death filled the air with hundreds of dead Parthians littering the battlefield. The main threat now to Atticus's column was from the Parthians regrouping from the ravine and hills above to its left. They were moving at speed to attack the column's rear, according to an officer on horseback. Atticus lined his cavalry up, cutting across the trail directly in front of the charging Parthians.

"Ready your spears men!" ordered Atticus. Atticus took his bow from Fury's saddle and placed two arrows ready to fire.

"Why two arrows?" enquired Adelar.

"I want to put the shits up them and gain a little more time for the waggons to reach the fort." Edelgard smiled looking towards the Parthians charging them. Atticus drew back his bow, aimed and fired both arrows at once they flew with speed cutting through the air.

They struck the officer on horseback charging towards Atticus and his cavalry. His men were all on foot, running behind most of whom were conscripts who had been poorly trained for battle. The arrows were embedded in his skull through his eye sockets. He fell to the ground lying on his back and his men following on foot came to a standstill. Many looked down seeing the arrows protruding from his eye socket's blood trickling down his lifeless cheeks. Panic was beginning to grow within the Parthian ranks.

One of the other Parthian officers realising quickly now took charge shouting his men to carry on with the attack. Many of them still hesitated. Atticus nudged

Fury forward out of the line of Roman cavalry. Edelgard and Adelar followed suit.

"You have definitely put the shits up them my friend," said Edelgard grinning.

Atticus unsheathed one of his swords and pointed it towards the Parthian's and beckoned them to attack. The Parthian officer again repeated the order angrily to his men to attack and ran towards Atticus; several of his men refused to move but most charged at the Roman line. As soon as they were in range of the Roman cavalry's spears Atticus gave the order to launch them. It wasn't long before the spears struck the Parthians, killing many, including the officer leading them.

This took out the remaining will of the Parthians to fight; they turned and ran. The Roman column had now reached and entered the fort. Atticus turned Fury and led his men into the fort to cheers from its battlements.

The Parthian prince and the other captured Parthians were all lined up in the courtyard just inside the fort's gates which had now been closed.

Atticus rode Fury to a standstill just in front of Mithridate, looking down at him.

"My father will kill your Roman pig," he snarled at Atticus.

"Not today, he won't and if you wish to live. I suggest you close your mouth," replied Atticus.

Fury stamped one of his hooves into the stone floor which made Mithridate flinch.

"Are you going to melt that golden armour down Atticus and give it to the poor?" shouted Adelar from just behind Atticus. The prince spat towards him in defiance.

"Someone seems a bit upset," shouted Edelgard.

The Augusta 11 cohort were all now standing in three lines to attention facing Atticus. Over five hundred men, many breathing heavily from their fight to gain access to the fort. The Centurions stood proudly in front of them with Optio Linus holding the legions banner.

Women and children were being hugged by family members who had waited with bated breath while the battle raged. Many of whom served Rome in the fort's auxiliary cohort. Some of them openly cried with joy.

Smoke still bellowed into the air far outside the fort; the Parthian dead littering the landscape outside the fort could now clearly be seen from the battlements in the early morning sun.

The lines of Roman soldiers began to bang their shields with their swords and chant Atticus! Atticus! Over and over again this was then taken up by the Centurion Grasus and his cavalry.

The legate Marcellus and his Tribune Justus stood above on the ramparts looking down into the courtyard below.

"Bloody hell, he's captured the Parthian prince," said Justus.

Marcellus grinned and looked over the battlements in the direction of the large tent housing the Parthian king.

"I bet someone will pay with their lives after this, we just gave them a very bloody nose. That prince's father will not be happy…I can now see why Maximus and the emperor have picked this young man for the job!" said Marcellus.

"It is time we met Atticus!" Marcellus went on to say before descending down the stone steps from the battlements followed closely by Abd-El-Kader and Justus.

The Parthian prince was standing holding his head high with a glare of hatred in his eyes for his Roman captures. Gritting his teeth still feeling angry with himself for being taken prisoner so easily.

Atticus dismounted Fury and saluted Marcellus, "Sir!" Atticus shouted, and stood to attention.

Marcellus returned his salute; silence had descended in the courtyard.

"It is good to finally meet you Atticus, but I must admit I expected to meet someone shall I say with respect, somewhat a little older."

Atticus smiled in response, "I will take that as a compliment." replied Atticus.

"You certainly can," answered Marcellus.

He then clasped forearms with Atticus who quickly introduced Edelgard and Adelar, also adding that they were part of General Maximus's bodyguards sent to assist Atticus.

"Well done, Abd-El-Kader and to you too Yassur the success today was due to you both reaching the fort with my order's. At great risk to your lives, you have done Rome a great service and it will not be forgotten," said Atticus. Both of them bowed their heads and smiled in acknowledgement.

Atticus turned to the legate Marcellus and asked, "If I may?"

"Carry on!" came the reply.

Atticus turned to face his men with a broad smile, and shouted, "Men! I could not be prouder of you for the way you have conducted yourselves since we left Ostia. Your skill and dedication to duty for Rome is second to none."

Many of the men banged their shields again with their swords, when the noise died down Atticus continued.

"We have lost some very fine men on the way, but they will not be forgotten, and will be remembered in my dispatches for General Maximus when he arrives here soon." The men cheered in response.

"Get some rest, the legate will of no doubt already have organised our billets."

"I have!" shouted Marcellus from behind Atticus.

"Dismiss!" shouted Atticus who then turned to face Marcellus, "Thankyou sir!" said Atticus.

"Here you are, you will be needing this back," Marcellus said as he passed him the golden sceptre.

"Tribune Justus will show you to the bathhouse and then to your accommodation."

"You will want to refresh no doubt and clean all that blood off you."

"We do," replied Atticus ``In that case I am going to rest awhile and will meet with you later.

Justus makes sure the guard on the wall is doubled and only wakes me if we're being attacked.

"Yes sir!" replied Justus.

Marcellus strode off back to his quarters.

"Centurion Cyrus!" shouted Atticus.

"SIR! have the wounded taken to the infirmary. Put the legate Titus in a room of his own and have Spurius attend to him but have him under house arrest until General Maximus arrives to deal with him if he recovers."

"Yes sir!"

"Adelar, are you coming to bathe or are you happy smelling like shit!" shouted Edelgard.

"I hope there might be fun with the ladies in one of the forts' taverns tonight."

"Don't worry Justus, you will soon get used to my friends here," said Atticus. Justus laughed loudly. Centurion Grasus and his men had taken all the prisoners away and locked them in the stockade. The prince was locked up on his own in a cell and given bread and water.

He'd protested but the guards just laughed and said, "You're lucky to get that."

Aisha walked over to Atticus, along with Ava and one of the fort's Mesopotamian auxiliaries.

"Atticus, I would like to introduce my husband if I may? His name is Abbas which means Lion in my homeland." Atticus lifted Ava up into his arms and pinched her nose which made her giggle.

Atticus smiled at Aisha then looked at Abbas, "It is a pleasure to meet you Abbas."

"It is I who is thankful to you for saving my wife and the people of our villages."

"It was my duty, and I am only too happy we are all safe for the moment."

"Yes, sir but I am honoured to be in your debt for life."

"Nonsense, you owe me nothing."

"It is the way of my people, sir."

Atticus smiled and replied, "Then I will not dishonour your tradition."

"You promised we could play games when we got here," said Ava.

"We will as soon as we are all rested and the little one is cleaned up," answered Atticus, smiling at little Ava.

"Come, Ava, we will go with my husband and eat, we will see Atticus later."

"You will," responded Atticus who then followed Justus to the bathhouse.

Chapter 17

General Maximus and his legions had now disembarked from their Roman warships at Tarsus, and the legions were camped on the hills outside the city walls.

Meanwhile, many of the local population had locked themselves in their homes, keeping out of sight of the vast Roman army. Many others had lined the harbour to cheer.

Maximus and his German bodyguards along with Tribune Marcus and several of his Praetorians had entered the quarters of the legate Flavius, who was cowering behind his desk.

As they entered, Flavius stood up and saluted, trying his best to stop shaking.

"Welcome General, may I introduce myself? I am…"

Flavius was cut off abruptly in mid-speech, "I know who you are, Flavius, you are now relieved of your command." Flavius sunk back down into his chair; his face gripped with fear as the realisation of what would become of him when he returned to Rome.

"You will be returning to Rome on one of those ships tomorrow, then on arrival in Ostia you will be escorted straight away to the Emperor Augustus. Where you will answer for the charge of dereliction of duty to Rome. Do you understand?" Flavius could no longer stop himself from trembling and couldn't utter a reply.

"Tribune Marcus, if you will have two of your Praetorians escort him to the flagship and lock him up in the brig!"

"Metelus, Paulinus, if you would kindly take Flavius away!"

"Sir, yes, sir!" came the swift reply.

When Flavius had left the room Maximus sat down behind the desk, "Almut get one of the servants standing outside to bring wine and food if you will please, and fetch Tribune Tiberius."

"Yes, General."

"Sit, Marcus, and have the rest of your Praetorians wait outside," without having to be asked, the soldiers all left the room. Marcus sat down on a comfortable couch. Shortly after, the food and wine were placed on the desk by a young servant girl who quickly bowed and left. Marcus poured the wine into two cups and helped himself to some fresh fish, Maximus drank the whole cup and poured himself another.

"Looks like you needed that," said Marcus.

"I did this heat, and that sea doesn't always agree with me," replied Maximus.

It wasn't long before there was a knock on the door. "ENTER!" shouted Maximus, and in walked the Tribune Tiberius.

"Help yourself to a cup of wine, it's reasonable stuff, have a seat," said Maximus.

"Thank you, sir," replied Tiberius, he then sat down on a stool by the window. "Here are your orders from the emperor and your promotion to legate of the garrison of Tarsus active immediately."

Tiberius beamed with delight, "You deserve it you are a good soldier of Rome, Tiberius; the emperor needs good officers in this region, and you have earned it."

"Thank you, sir!"

"Your Tribune here goes by the name of Clictus who was temporarily promoted by Flavius on the advice of Atticus. Looking at how well he has repaired the fort's defences and posted extra guards, Atticus chose well. I also noted plenty of well-dressed units looking sharp patrolling the harbour as we disembarked."

Maximus drank another cup of wine before continuing, "So I will make his promotion permanent, and all the relevant documents will be sent to Rome. Do you have any questions?" enquired Maximus.

"No sir!" replied Tiberius, still beaming with pride.

"I want a meeting here with all the senior officers at seven this evening. We need to be ready to march to Tadmor within two days…I want a full list of any men too sick for duty and they will remain here. I want nothing to slow us down!" demanded Maximus.

Back at the fort in Tadmor it was early morning the day after Atticus had arrived, the legate Marcellus and his Tribune Justus walked along the battlements watching the Parthians removing their dead.

Marcellus had sent out burial details and had earlier retrieved the bodies of the dead Romans.

Both sides had agreed to allow this to take place, not wanting disease to spread. The sound of screams and laughter could be heard from within the fort as Atticus and several of his men along with Edelgard played games as promised with the children. "Listening to you, you wouldn't think we were surrounded by an army of boy fuckers wanting to send us to the afterlife!" said Justus with a grin.

A shout rang out from up above from a guard in one of the watchtowers "SIR! three riders are approaching under a flag of truce."

Marcellus and Justus quickly climbed the stone steps leading up to the tower. They could see the three riders slowly trotting towards the main gate down below the watchtower.

As they approached the gate Marcellus shouted to them, "That's far enough."

The riders halted their horses and a Parthian officer in the middle holding the flag of truce bowed his head.

"What do you want? Make it quick, I have things to attend to!" shouted Marcellus.

"My king, the ruler of all Parthia, Artabanus, bids you greetings. He would like to hold a parlay with you at his tent." replied the Parthian officer.

"I bet he does now that we have his son," whispered Justus in Marcellus's ear who smiled in response to Justus.

"My king grants your safe passage for you and a guard of honour of fifty of your men to attend the parlay if it pleases you?"

"Very polite, isn't he?" whispered Justus with a grin.

"When does your king wish this parlay to take place?" shouted Marcellus.

"At the beginning of sunset today if it pleases you?" replied the officer with a smile. But inside he was thinking to himself, "You Roman dogs will pay with your lives," he then sat up straight on his horse looking up at Marcellus awaiting the reply with a forced smile.

"Wait there while I speak with my officers," shouted Marcellus.

"As you wish!" replied the Parthian officer, before bowing his head slightly again. The Parthian officer in reality felt nothing but hatred towards the Romans as he bowed. He was only following protocol, wishing not to antagonise the Roman officer into refusing the offer of parlay. He knew if he didn't get the Romans to come, he would be executed for failing Artabanus.

Marcellus and Justus descended the steps and were met by Atticus and Edelgard who had finished playing games with the children.

Atticus saluted and asked, "What do they want, sir?"

"It appears the Parthian king wishes to parlay now that we have his son prisoner!"

"When?"

"At sunset today…What do you think Atticus, should we go?" asked Marcellus.

"Let's play for a little while, Maximus must have landed at Tarsus by now and will be making his way here hopefully. Let them know that any attempt to kill you or the escort, his son will die. The king knows he needs to capture this fort before Rome's legions arrive. If he hadn't captured this fort, his army could have suffered huge losses, forcing him to return to Parthia without a victory. He needs the water reservoir under this fort. His supply lines stretched all the way back to the river Euphrates for water and Parthia for grain. No doubt he will have exhausted any supplies from the towns and villages nearby and this barren land has little to offer his vast army."

"Come with me, Atticus, let's go and give them an answer. Open the gates!" shouted Marcellus. The huge wooden gates were slowly pulled open, creaking as they did. A dozen Roman soldiers toiled with the task. Atticus, Marcellus, along with Justus and Edelgard walked out towards the three riders.

Up above on the battlements, the Roman archers pointed their bows, arrows notched ready to fire at the first hint of treachery by the Parthians on horseback.

The sight of them made the Parthians feel a little uneasy.

"I will meet with your king, but tomorrow at sunrise, not today. And the first hint of treachery towards me or my men will result in Prince Mithridate being crucified straight away. Along with the four hundred Parthian soldiers captured with him by this young officer will be killed! Their bodies will then be thrown from these walls for all to see, mark my words Parthian."

Marcellus looked at Atticus with a broad smile before returning his attention to the Parthians, "Their bodies will feed the vultures," said Marcellus with a stern look.

"Yes, I will tell my king," replied the Parthian officer, who looked at Atticus with a deep anger burning in his chest. He then turned his horse, gave a further look towards Atticus before riding off at a gallop followed by his two companions kicking up a dust trail into the air.

Atticus looked at the Parthians riding away with a smile.

Marcellus and Atticus walked back into the fort, followed by Edelgard who was laughing.

"I see you have made another friend!" shouted Edelgard, as soon as he'd stopped laughing.

Justus stood a while watching them ride away before making his way back inside the fort. He wasn't too happy about the meeting with the Parthians taking place the following day.

He still thought it was some sort of trap.

"Let's go to my office so we can discuss matters further in private," said Marcellus. When they had all sat down Marcellus began the conversation.

"I don't think the Parthian king would be so stupid to give us any reason to kill his son."

"He won't," replied Atticus.

"I hope you are correct otherwise we might be on our way to the afterlife a little sooner than I had anticipated that," replied Marcellus grinning.

"I'm hoping I can anger the king so much tomorrow that he will attack the fort as soon as we have returned his son to him."

Marcellus raised his eyebrows and looked a little bewildered.

"Why would we return our son?"

"My guess is the prince will only serve a purpose to us if the king thinks he can bargain for his son's release."

"Go on!" said Marcellus, while stroking his chin.

"The king knows Maximus and his legions will arrive here soon," Atticus said with a smile.

"He won't want to be caught between Maximus, and us in the fort. His sole plan was to capture this fort as quickly as possible. But we scuppered that by rescuing the hostages on our way here. So, if he is forced to attack the fort and try to overwhelm us with his vast army his son will be of no advantage to us anymore. He will not want to attack the fort while his son lives until he has no other option. I want him to attack sooner rather than later."

"I know that look; you have a plan my young friend?" said Edelgard.

"I do!" grinned Atticus in response.

"But first it will only work if I can anger their king tomorrow."

"And how do you propose to do that?" asked Marcellus, "I have one or two ideas, but I don't want the meeting tomorrow to look like we are pushing him in a certain direction of our choosing. So, I will keep matters close to my chest."

"Have we no wine to taste?" asked Edelgard, rubbing his throat feeling parched.

"I have, Justus please do us the honours and pour that amphora of wine into those cups!"

"Yes, sir," he replied.

"I need to put some things into action with your permission sir! And will let you know as soon as I have done so," said Atticus.

Marcellus looked deep in thought for a while before he answered.

"Yes, but let me know as soon as it's done."

After they had drunk the wine, Atticus stood up, saluted, and left the room, followed by Edelgard.

"Is it wise to let him take the lead?" enquired Justus, as soon as they were alone.

"You forget he holds that sceptre. If his plan fails and the fort is captured, or Maximus is defeated," Marcellus paused and drank some wine.

Marcellus then with a smile carried on saying, "My family's name, along with my wealth and property back in Rome will not be forfeited. I will be exonerated of any blame for the defeat. My family is very wealthy and there are many in Rome that would love to get their greedy hands on it. The blame for any defeat will befall Atticus. As you know, Rome always wants a scapegoat for any defeat!"

"Very clever," replied Justus.

"Don't get me wrong…I hope his plan succeeds and I like him. He is without doubt a warrior with exceptional fighting skills. Not only that, honour and a love for the legions run through his veins. The likes I've never seen for a long time."

Marcellus paused again and drank the rest of his wine; "Mark my words I would not want him as an enemy even though he is so young. But the way Rome treats those that fail it…one must cover one's arse!"

Atticus wrote dispatches for Maximus in his private quarters while Edelgard snoozed sitting in a chair. "Come Edelgard, let's go find Abd-El-Kader and the others." Edelgard stretched and rubbed his eyes as he stood up.

"When do I get to know what you're up to?" asked Edelgard.

"Soon!" replied Atticus, as they walked outside.

The sun shone burning high up in a bright blue sky. Adelar came down from the battlements and joined them.

"That Parthian army out there seems to be getting bigger by the hour," shouted Adelar.

"More for us to kill then" grinned Edelgard.

"SIR!" shouted Centurion Cyrus.

"Yes," replied Atticus, turning to face him.

"I have the men at the training ground working out, keeping them ready for battle. Farrokh has his Cilician archers training with the bow, any further orders?"

"I want fifty of our best men, have them clean their armour and sharpen their weapons and be ready for duty one hour before sunrise tomorrow. Have them assembled to meet me at the main gate."

"Where are we going?" enquired Cyrus.

"We are going to meet with the king of Parthia," replied Atticus with a grin.

Cyrus, a veteran of many campaigns, couldn't believe what he had just heard, he stood still with his mouth wide open for a moment.

"Oh…l will make sure your instructions are followed to the letter sir." Cyrus then saluted, turned and marched off in bewilderment.

"He looked a little surprised to say the least," said Adelar. They made their way past the bathhouse and up towards the building where Abd-El-Kader and the others were sitting outside, shading themselves from the burning sun.

There were many civilians talking amongst themselves along the streets, many smiled and bowed their heads, some even cheered as they walked past.

"You have become very popular since you have arrived!" shouted Abd-El-Kader as they approached. Atticus felt a little embarrassed with all the fuss.

"Greetings!" said Yassur standing up, bowing his head slightly towards Atticus.

"Let's go inside, we need privacy."

"Sounds like you have a job for us?" asked Abdul. Once inside Abd-El-Kader's room they sat down on several stools that had been placed along one of the walls. It was quite a long, large room with several beds at the far end. The rooms were clean and basic, but the beds had fresh hay strewn on them, partly covered with animal skins.

"What do you have for us?" enquired Abd-El-Kader, Adelar had closed the door and lent against it so nobody could walk in and interrupt them.

"I need you to get these dispatches to General Maximus. I know it is dangerous and you will need to get through the Parthians again at night."

"It won't be as easy this time as they will have guards everywhere. They won't want to make the same mistake twice," said Abdul, looking a little apprehensive.

"Yes, I know I wouldn't have asked but it is imperative he gets this information, and tonight will probably be the last time you will have a chance to get through for a while," said Atticus in a low voice.

"Why is that?" asked Yassur. "We meet with the Parthian king tomorrow and if my plan works, he will be attacking this fort a day or so after."

"Bloody hell, is it prudent to poke the bear and anger it? I thought we were playing for longer?" asked Adelar.

"If King Artabanus has over forty thousand men out there and maybe a lot more, as more seem to arrive every hour. I need to force his hand into a rash attack on our walls. I want to kill as many Parthians as possible before General Maximus and his legions arrive!"

"What if he overwhelms the fort with sheer numbers?" enquired Abdul.

"It is a gamble I need to take," replied Atticus, who then stood up and paced the room.

"We have built all the heavy weapons we transported here and placed them on the battlements, with our men and the forts legion, the Mesapatamian auxiliaries, and Cilician archers we have just over seven thousand men, more than enough to defend these walls," said Atticus.

"We will do as you ask," replied Abd-El-Kader.

"Thank you!" answered Atticus.

He then gave him the dispatches and placed his hand on Abd's shoulder and said, "Take care, my friend, and that goes for you two also," Atticus looked over at Abdul and Yassur. They both bowed their heads slightly and smiled, "We will leave as soon as it's dark," said Abd-EL-Kader.

Atticus and Edelgard left the room followed by Adelar and walked out into the burning sun.

"What now?"

"I need to speak with Abbas the Roman auxiliary Centurion."

"You are setting your plan in motion, I see?" grinned Edelgard.

"I am!" replied Atticus, "Come, you two, follow me!" said Atticus taking off his helmet and wiping his brow as he walked.

The fort's side streets went off the main street in all directions, many of them had the married quarters of the officers' families. Children played among them as they walked on. The fort's walls towered above all around filled with soldiers. They passed the large granaries, then the armoury, as a unit of soldiers marched past, saluting them.

Atticus turned left down a wide street, talking with Edelgard and Adelar. Their words and laughter echoed off the stone buildings. They then passed the stables, "I will go see Fury and make sure he's behaving as soon as we have finished with Abbas," said Atticus.

It wasn't long before they arrived at his quarters, the door was open, Aisha was sweeping out the dust from inside covering Atticus as he approached the door. He coughed loudly, choking on the dust.

"Oh sorry!" shouted Aisha, all embarrassed, dropping the broom.

"Don't worry, my tunic is already quite dirty with all this sand blowing about," replied Atticus, laughing as he spoke. Aisha quickly started to brush the dust off Atticus's tunic, still frantically apologising.

"Stop, no need, Aisha, I need a bath anyway," grinned Atticus in reply.

"Is Abbas here?"

"He is inside putting on his uniform, he is going on duty shortly," answered Aisha.

"May I speak with him?" asked Atticus.

"Yes, please come in, would you like something to eat or drink?"

"A cup of water would be nice in this heat," replied Atticus.

"What about you two, some water perhaps?"

"Yes, that would be fine thank you." replied Adelar.

"Any wine?" asked Edelgard, wiping his forehead with a smile.

"I don't think Edelgard drinks anything else," said Atticus with a grin, which made Aisha smile.

"We have wine, come sit down." As they sat down on a wooden bench placed along a large table little Ava came running out of a small room carrying a small wooden box. Her face lit up at the sight of Atticus and quickly jumped on his lap almost dropping the box.

"What have you got here Ava?" asked Atticus as he gripped the box to prevent its contents falling out onto the stone floor.

"Look, look!" screamed Ava all excited.

"Abbas has made me these animals to play with." Ava took one of the small wooden carvings out of the box and gave it to Atticus.

"What animal is this?" enquired Atticus.

"It's a camel, have you not seen one before?" giggled Ava, "Yes, I was just testing you…What else have you got?"

"This is a pig, this one is a goat, and this one is Fury!" said Ava proudly holding the wooden horse.

Atticus held the carving of Fury which looked tiny in his big hand, "Abbas is very clever," said Atticus, as he ruffled Ava's curly hair.

Abbas walked in from another room which had a cloth sheet hanging down acting as a door.

"Good day, sir! And welcome gentlemen." He bowed his head slightly towards Edelgard and Adelar.

"No need to call me sir, we're all friends here," answered Atticus, Aisha passed out the drinks giving one to her husband who promptly kissed her cheek and smiled.

"What can I do for you?" asked Abbas, Ava climbed down off Atticus's knee and asked.

"Can I play outside with my toys?"

"Yes, but don't go too far, and keep out of the way of the soldiers patrolling the streets!"

"I will!" she shouted as she skipped outside.

"I need one of your most trusted and able men to dress up as a Parthian soldier. My men would stand out, but your men being Mesopotamian would fit in hopefully undetected. Slip into their main camp and get as much information about their strength and anything that would be of importance to us."

"When do you need him?" asked Abbas, while running one of his hands through his hair, and looking at his wife.

"Tonight, as soon as it's dark, I need him in place before tomorrow when I have a meeting with the Parthian king." replied Atticus.

"Yes, I have heard about the meeting," answered Abbas.

"Do you have anyone in mind?" enquired Atticus.

"I have…me!" Aisha looked at her husband proudly.

"It will be very dangerous if you're caught, you know the outcome,"

"I do, but you need the most trustworthy and capable, it will be my honour to serve you." answered Abbas.

For the next hour they sat drinking, talking amongst themselves, laughter filled the room.

Ava came back inside all smiles.

"Would you like to come and see Fury with me Ava?" asked Atticus.

"Oh yes, please! May I go to see Fury Aisha?"

"Yes, of course you can," replied Aisha.

"I will meet you at my quarters later Abbas an hour before sunset," said Atticus as he stood up taking hold of Ava's tiny hand.

"I will find a Parthian uniform to fit my size from one of the prisoners, and collect some captured weapons, must look the part." said Abbas grinning.

"I will bring Ava back shortly as soon as we have been to see Fury."

"Thank you," said Aisha, Atticus lifted Ava onto his broad shoulders and headed off in the direction of the stables followed by Edelgard and Adelar.

As they entered the stable the sound of hooves being kicked against a gate and shouts could be heard.

"What's all the commotion?" asked Atticus.

One of the soldiers was trying to calm Fury, another turned and saluted.

"Sir, I don't think your horse Fury likes us. We are just trying to clean his stall and groom him, but he's not having any of it, sir!" Edelgard laughed loudly.

As Atticus approached Fury's stall, Fury nodded his head and shook his main vigorously. Fury was happy to see Atticus and little Ava. One of his big brown eyes seemed to gaze at Ava sitting on Atticus's shoulder.

"See, Ava, Fury's looking at you, he really likes you, I can tell." The two soldiers were very happy that Fury had calmed down. Atticus, still with Ava on his shoulders, unlocked Fury's stall and led him outside.

"Would you like to sit on Fury Ava?" asked Atticus.

"Can I?"

"Yes," Atticus passed Ava to Edelgard, "Lift her up for me," said Atticus who promptly jumped up onto Fury.

As soon as Ava was sitting comfortably on Fury's saddle with her tiny legs sideways, Fury gently set off and trotted around the paddock. Ava screamed with delight and shouted, "This is wonderful!" Ava laughed as Fury snorted and shook his head. He was happy to be out in the fresh air after being cooped up in his stall.

After a while Atticus lowered Ava down into the arms of Edelgard, Atticus jumped down and kissed Fury on his nose.

"Ava, sees that bucket of apples over there, would you like to give one to Fury?" without answering Ava ran to the bucket and pulled two apples out and lifted one towards Fury's mouth.

"Hear you are, Fury!" she shouted all excited, Fury took two steps forward and gently lowered his head and took it out of Ava's hand.

"You're braver than me! there is no way I would put my hand anywhere near his mouth," said Adelar, watching from outside the paddock.

Ava then lifted the second apple up for Fury to eat. Atticus grabbed a bucket and sunk it into the water trough and poured its contents over Fury's back to cool him down. Atticus did this several times then locked the paddock's gate. Fury lifted his head over the paddock's wooden fence resting it on Atticus's shoulder. Atticus kissed Fury and gently patted his neck. He whispered several words into Fury's ear before leaving.

"Did you enjoy that?" asked Atticus, as he walked Ava home.

"Fury is lovely, can I ride him again?"

"Yes, when I have some spare time Fury would love it."

Atticus returned Ava home and went back to his quarters. The fort was busy with soldiers and civilians going about their business. There was a sense of urgency in the air all around. Many of the civilians had worried looks on their faces, knowing all too well that the enemy force outside was getting larger by the hour.

Chapter 18

An hour before sunset, Abbas arrived at Atticus's quarters and knocked on the door. Edelgard opened it and grinned, "Well, you certainly look the part, I nearly didn't recognise you."

Atticus then stepped outside and clasped his forearm, "I agree you do look like the enemy, follow me we need to get you out of the fort unnoticed." Atticus plucked up a roll of rope from the side of his quarters and passed it to Edelgard. They then made their way to the fort's wall and climbed up some stone steps leading up to the battlements. Two guards at the top of the steps stood back and saluted Atticus. when Abbas came into view, one of the guards grabbed the hilt of his short sword in a panic.

"Easy soldier, he's one of us!" said Edelgard, grinning.

The soldier then let out a sigh of relief, letting go of his sword. It was getting quite dark. Atticus looked out from the battlements and could easily see the many campfires of the enemy lighting up the sky far in the distance, well out of range of the fort's catapults.

Edelgard lowered the rope down the outside of the fort's stone wall and soon it reached the bottom. Atticus turned to face Abbas, "Take care, my friend, return to this part of the wall two nights from now regardless of what you have found out! don't stay any longer. I will be here waiting for you. Make the sound of an eagle twice so we know it is you and I will lower the rope and pull you back inside."

"Yes, sir!" replied Abbas.

"Quick, go now, and look luck," said Atticus.

Abbas descended down the rope and disappeared into the night.

Abd-El-Kader and the others left through the side gate, leading their horses quietly into the darkness. The torches at the gate had not been lit until they were well out of sight of the fort. The large fire pits were then set alight after Abd-El-Kader and his two companions were well out of sight of the fort. They quickly

160

illuminated the area outside the walls so any attempt by the Parthians to attack at night would be discovered.

"We better let Marcellus know what we've been up to!" said Atticus grinning.

"That would be a good idea," replied Edelgard. He was feeling a little worried for Abd-El-Kader, Yassur and Abdul knowing their task was very dangerous. Not only that, he was afraid for Abbas, knowing his mission was also not without great danger.

Abbas crept through the dark, moving along a shallow ravine, stopping and listening for any sound every few minutes. It was hard to see in the dark because the light from the stars above was very little. Clouds drifted across the night sky blotting out the stars most of the time. He almost stepped on a rattlesnake coiled up but calmly stepped back away as the snake hissed and rattled its tail in warning. When he got closer to the Parthian campfires he could see shadows of men guarding the Parthian lines of makeshift tents. He could see many more lying asleep wrapped in animal skins around the fires keeping warm from the night's chill. Abbas slipped past a guard who was taking a piss and moaning to himself about having to do guard duty at night in the cold.

Abbas smiled to himself and hid behind some bushes before making his way further into the camp. "Hey! You!" a voice shouted from the shadows of some rocks. Abbas felt the hairs on the back of his neck prick up.

He turned to face the direction where the voice came from. A tall thin man came into view and approached him; he hadn't drawn his weapon, so Abbas felt he wasn't seen as a threat.

"Who are you?" asked the man.

"My name is Fisal. I arrived here this morning with many others sent from Parthia to help kill many Romans," Abbas spoke as if he was a little simple and twitched as he spoke.

"What are you doing wandering around out here?" demanded the man,

"I was looking for somewhere to take a shit my belly hurts, I ate some goat earlier, but it smelt and…"

He was cut off by a man who shouted angrily at him. "Go up there far out behind those rocks. I don't want the smell of shit around my tent, go don't just stand there, do as I say!" Abbas was still pretending to be a little simple in the head.

"Yes, I will straight away!"

Abbas turned and quickly ran amongst the rocks grinning to himself while gripping his backside making it look like he'd already started to shit himself.

"Fuck me, if that's all Parthia has to send us to fight the Romans were fucked!" said the man shaking his head as he walked back to his tent.

Abbas waited awhile before descending down the slope from behind some rocks and walking on until he came to a campfire where several men sat drinking and talking.

When one of them saw Abbas approaching, he shouted, "Who the fuck are you? what do you want here?"

"My name is Fisal. I arrived today, and seemed to have lost my way in the dark from the rest of my unit. Some soldier, further back there, said I had to shit far up there, far out behind those rocks. The rocks could be seen from the flickering light of the fire. The burning wood snapped and crackled, shooting sparks into the dark night. May I sit at your fire to keep warm?"

The Parthians looked at each other before answering…one of them, quite older than the others, in his mid-fifties with a bald head and a thick black beard, smiled and gestured for him to sit.

Abbas sat between two others and bowed saying, "Thank you, my friend, for your gracious hospitality it has been a long day," Abbas sighed deeply as he sat down trying to emphasise his fatigue.

Abd-El-Kader and his two companions gently trotted their horses through the dark trying to make their way past the Parthians to the trail which hopefully would take them to General Maximus and his legions. They tried to avoid the many campfires burning. It was painstakingly slow work. Most of the time they travel on foot leading their horses due to the harsh terrain. The darkness helped conceal them but also hindered their progress. At times they had to double back on themselves and go further around doing their best not to be detected. They finally made their way up the other side of the ravine negotiating amongst the rocks and brush. Quietly edging further away from the Parthian campfires in the dark. A shout of alarm suddenly broke the silence and rang out from one of the Parthian centuries on guard hidden behind a boulder in the dark. The Parthian stepped out pointing his spear towards them.

"SHIT! Mount up! Ride ride! No time to waste!" shouted Abd-El-Kader.

The guard threw his spear at them but it fell to the ground well short of them, hitting and bouncing off one of the many rocks jutting out from the ground. As soon as Abdul had mounted, he drew his bow and fired an arrow at the guard, it struck the Parthian in the face killing him.

They frantically pressed their horses up the slope zig zagging around the many rocks; many more shouts could be heard behind them as arrows now zipped through the air around them. Some flew so close above their heads they could feel the draft as they flew past. Horses' hooves could be heard clattering the ground further back down the hill making their way towards them.

"We must make that ridge!" shouted Yasser who was out in front. Dawn was now breaking above the mountains to their right. Abdul was close behind Yassur, Abd-El-Kader who was at the rear turned in his saddle and fired an arrow killing one of the Parthians on horseback giving chase.

His scream rang out as he fell from his horse, momentarily his body and riderless horse got in the way of his companions giving chase. Which gave them a little extra time to create more of a gap between themselves and their pursuers.

As they rode up towards the ridge more arrows flew in their direction, Abd-El-Kader turned again and fired several arrows killing another of their pursuers. One of his arrows also hit a horse in its chest, causing it to rear up and fall backwards, crushing its rider as it died. But as he turned to ride on, he was struck in the back with an arrow, lurched forward and only just managed to stay on his horse. The searing pain he felt gripped his chest like a vise. His heart pounded fast, thumping inside his chest as blood poured from his wound.

He knew he was dying but drew enough strength to dig his heels into his horse, spurring it on towards the ridge.

Yassur and Abdul had reached the ridge and were waiting for Abd-El-Kader. As soon as he reached the others, he slipped sideways and fell to the ground.

Yassur jumped down from his horse and he could see the arrow protruding out from Abd's back.

Abd-El-Kader was gasping for air and blood was trickling out of the side of his mouth. Yassur panicked as he sat his cousin up and a tear ran down his cheek.

"You need to go, I have not long left in this life," muttered Abd. Abdul was sitting on his horse looking down the hill and could see a dozen Parthians on horseback scrambling their way up amongst the rocks. He drew his bow and began to fire arrows down at them causing them to temporarily take cover and fire back at Abdul.

"We haven't got long," shouted Abdul, as an arrow flew past him, only missing by inches. He could see more Parthians on foot carrying spears climbing up over the top of the hill in the light of the morning sun.

"Yassur go! go!" said Abd, spitting out blood.

"Prop me up here, pass me my bow, I will hold them off as long as I have air in my lungs. But you need to go ride fast, take my horse in case one of yours becomes lame." Abd-El-Kader now coughed again, spitting out more blood.

Yassur kissed his cousin on his forehead, and passed him his bow and quiver of arrows.

"I will see you in the afterlife, my cousin," said Yassur. Tears now streaming down his face.

"We need to go!" Abdul shouted frantically.

"Or we die!"

Yassur jumped on his horse, grabbed the reins of Abd's horse, bowed to his cousin and charged down the trail followed quickly by Abdul.

As soon as the Parthians appeared over the ridges, Sumit Abd-El-Kader sucked in as much air as his lungs would take. Mustering all the energy he had left began firing arrows repeatedly, killing several more Parthians.

This made the others take any cover they could find. Abd-El-Kader sucked in air and began to shout insults at the Parthians. Abd-El-Kader knew he had not long left his strength had gone and was not able to raise his bow. Arrows now hit the rocks where Abd was propped up behind, this was giving more valuable time for Yassur and Abdul to escape.

The Parthians on foot with their spears began to flank Abd, as the Parthian horse archers fired their arrows towards the rocks where Abd hid.

Two Parthians with spears charged at the rock. One punched his spear into Abd's chest, but he was already dead. A Parthian officer on horseback trotted over to the body of Abd-El-Kader, looked down at him and spat. He then looked down the trail, the sun had fully come up; he could only just see the dust trail being kicked by the horse's far off in the distance; he knew there was no way they would now catch up to them.

"What do we do now?" asked one of the Parthian foot soldiers standing holding his spear.

The Parthian officer looked around himself at his men numbering about twenty. He sighed and wiped sweat off his forehead before answering. "What we do Now! is to keep our bloody mouths shut about those who escaped!"

Some of the soldiers looked at each other in bewilderment but did not dare to question their officer. He could see their confusion. He sighed again and said, "Do you want to keep your heads! On your shoulders…or like the others when those Roman dogs broke through to the fort. Stuck on those spikes outside the king's tent being eaten by insects." The officer sat on his horse quietly letting his words sink in.

His men quickly realised their dilemma and now voiced their agreement. "We have captured and killed the one trying to escape our lines, understand?" shouted the officer.

"Yes sir!" They all shouted in reply, "Now bring that body and we will take it to our General showing him we did our duty." Abd-El-Kader's body was dragged and thrown over one of the riderless horses. The Parthians now returned down the hill back to their camp.

Yassur and Abdul sat on their horses looking back for any sign of their pursuers.

"It looks like our enemy has given up the chase," muttered Yassur still feeling the pain of the loss of his cousin.

They now rode at a steady pace, resting their horses a little. They were out in the open now, sand dunes as far as the eye could see. Further in the distance a mountain range could also be seen.

They encouraged their mounts to quicken the pace a little and headed towards Maximus's legions. Both Yassur and Abdul knew this land well and it would only be a matter of time before they would find Maximus if the gods willed it.

Chapter 19

Atticus had fully made Marcellus aware of the night's actions and was sitting on Fury at the side of Marcellus riding out of the fort. At the head of their column. Edelgard and Adelar riding just behind them, the column consisted of Centurion Cyrus marching at the front with young Thaddius at his side, carrying the banner of the Augusta 11 legion fluttering in the gentle breeze. Behind them marched the rest of the fifty men assembled by Cyrus, their armour gleaming in the sunshine.

"You don't appear to be phased in any way about this meeting with the Parthian king?" asked Marcellus as they rode towards the Parthian lines.

"I am not, even if it's not every day you get to meet the king of our enemy," replied Atticus smiling.

Marcellus still couldn't get over Atticus's skill and bravery for one so young. Wondering to himself what was going on inside Atticus's head as they rode out to meet the Parthian king.

"Do you fancy a wager Marcellus sir!" enquired Adelar, "Behave Adelar, now is not the time," said Atticus.

"Let him speak. I have been known to have the odd wager now and then," replied Marcellus.

"Two gold coins says Atticus can piss that king off rather quickly."

Marcellus laughed and replied, "That's not a wager...that's a foregone conclusion!" many of the soldiers marching behind, including Thaddius, started laughing loudly.

The lines of Parthian's standing to attention now came into full view.

"They look pretty," said Edelgard sarcastically with a grin.

"Well let's hope we are able to return to the fort alive!" said Marcellus, as they drew closer to the Parthian lines. Atticus could see a gap wide enough to allow a Roman column through.

"Look straight ahead men, ignore any insults, don't let these goat fuckers get inside your heads," said Atticus.

He didn't want anyone to give their enemy any excuse for a fight. Atticus and Marcellus kept their heads high and looked straight ahead, not making eye contact with the Parthian soldiers lined up.

Many of the Parthians spat on the floor and muttered insults at their Roman enemy, but many stood with fear etched into their faces as they looked at the giant figure of Atticus riding his great black stallion.

Many of the Parthians had been told of the story of a young giant Roman soldier killing their comrades without mercy. They also knew it was him who captured their Prince Mithridate, forcing his men to surrender almost single handedly. Jumping over the lines of attacking Parthians riding a great black stallion.

Some even believed him to be a demon sent by the Roman gods to punish the enemies of Rome. Hearing the story of a giant eagle descending to his side and sitting on the saddle of his horse. There was no doubt the story as it was passed on would have been exaggerated. Atticus and his men kept a steady pace making their way through the multitude of Parthians row after row. This had been well orchestrated by Artabanus, wanting to strike fear into the Romans. Atticus could now see the great splendid tent of the Parthian king Artabanus; it was decorated with gold silk curtains.

A large wooden floor outside its front was at least fifty yards in width and in the middle a golden throne had been placed where the king sat waiting. On either side, royal bodyguards stood holding spears. Behind the throne, under the tent's canopy shading them from the sun, stood a dozen finely dressed old men. They were all dressed in identical white robes with scarves wrapped around their heads.

Painted moons and crescents adorned their faces, with black charcoal ringing their eyes.

"Looks like those old men are his scribes and advisers!" said Marcellus in a low voice. Two Nubian slaves holding long gold-painted poles with large white ostrich feathers at their tips fanned the king as he sat waiting.

Large bronze bowls on stands had been placed at the floor's edges, burning incense, creating a strong, potent smell.

Probably to kill the stench coming from spikes dug into the sand in a row where the heads of men were displayed on their tips. Flies buzzed around, crawling over them, feeding. It was by no means a pretty sight.

Artabanus noticed the Roman legate staring at them as they approached and dismounted in front of the great tent.

"If you're wondering, those are the heads of the officers who allowed your column to break through to your fort and capture my son!" said Artabanus. This had also been designed to unease his Roman guests.

Artabanus then smiled and stroked his long narrow dark beard feeling the discomfort on the Roman Legates face. Making Artabanus feel good in the knowledge it had seemed to unease the officer in charge of his Roman enemy.

"At least you have saved me having to kill them on the battlefield!" said Atticus after he had dismounted.

"And who are you to address me?" retorted Artabanus gripping the handrails on his throne in anger.

He then returned his gaze to Marcellus. "I told you it wouldn't take Atticus long," whispered Adelar to Edelgard.

"Are you not the officer in charge of that fort!" demanded the king. Marcellus dismounted, bowing his head slightly towards the king as protocol demanded.

"I am Marcellus, the legate of the 111 Galicia Raphanea stationed at the fort." he went on to say.

"And who is this impertinent boy I see before me!" growled Artabanus, Marcellus turned and faced Atticus.

"May I introduce Atticus the First Centurion of the Augusta 11 legion sent here by our great Emperor Augustus," replied Marcellus. Who then returned his attention and faced the Parthian king.

One of the old men bent his head and whispered into the king's ear for several moments which seemed to anger the king more as he glared at Atticus. Who simply stood looking back at the king with no expression at all on his face.

"Is Rome running out of men that it needs to put boys into officers' uniforms!" shouted the king trying his best to belittle Atticus.

"Have you just brought us here to trade insults or do you have something worthy of our time to discuss?" replied Atticus, with a long sigh.

Atticus then pretended to brush sand off his tunic. Again, doing his best to anger the king even more if that was possible. Edelgard and Adelar were trying their best not to laugh and sat on their horses trying to hide their grins. A large, broad Parthian bodyguard with an ear missing and many battle scars cut across both his bare arms and a long scar running down the full length of the right-hand side of his face.

Stepping forward. He unsheathed his sword, pointing it in the direction of Atticus.

"Put your sword away, Masood, you will have your chance to kill him on the battlefield, but today they are my guests," said the king not wanting things to get out of hand while his son was being held captive.

The king returned his attention to Marcellus, as Masood the Parthian bodyguard stepped back and replaced his sword in its scabbard while not taking his eyes off Atticus.

"So which one of you speaks for Rome?" asked the king, lowering his tone trying to hide the deep anger within him.

Marcellus looked over at Atticus, then faced the king once more.

"Atticus has been awarded the emperor's full authority to speak for Rome. I am therefore quite happy for him to take charge of these proceedings," said Marcellus taking a step back. Artabanus looked at Atticus for several moments before speaking.

"Surrender the fort, give me my son and I will grant you safe passage out of Mesopotamia."

Atticus stepped forward and looked directly into the king's eyes, "This land is under Roman rule. You have invaded, I will not surrender the fort. And when General Maximus arrives with his legions, you and your army will be forced back into Parthia. The ground between here and Parthia will be littered with your dead!" replied Atticus coldly and without any sign of hesitation.

Artabanus struggled to keep his anger under control and shouted, "I WANT MY SON RETURNED TO ME OR YOU WILL ALL DIE!"

Atticus just looked at the king and without any expression replied, "You can have your son back, but it will cost you."

"What do you want, Roman?" demanded the king, lowering his voice a little.

"That small chest there," Atticus pointed.

"I want seven of those filled with gold coins."

"WHAT! SEVEN?" yelled the king looking at the small chest.

"Yes, and a further three filled with silver is your son not worth that to you?" asked Atticus trying his best to provoke the king further.

The king, wishing not to demean the value of his only son, sat back in his throne to gather his thoughts. He glared full of hatred towards Atticus, he regarded this Roman as nothing much more than an over privileged young upstart. Silence now descended as everyone awaited the king's reply. Artabanus stood up and stepped forward glaring at Atticus.

"You can have your gold and silver...It will be brought to the fort's gate tomorrow. Have my son ready to return!" growled the king angrily.

"He will be ready," answered Atticus with a slight nod of his head.

"Now, go before I change my mind! And have you all killed," shouted the king.

Atticus mounted Fury, who snorted loudly, stamping one of his legs into the sand. Marcellus quickly mounted his horse. They turned their mounts facing towards the fort and began to make their way through the Parthian lines. Atticus was leading the column slightly in front of Marcellus. It wasn't long before they were back out on the Parthian lines. As soon as they were well away, Marcellus began to grin. "I thought Artabanus was going to explode, I really thought at some point he was going to have us killed."

"He knew his son would die, not only that he knew I was capable of killing him first before we perished," replied Atticus. Edelgard along with Adelar and the men were very glad to be returning to the fort alive to fight another day.

"Why did you agree to the demands of that Roman dog, my king?" asked Masood. He was the king's champion and most trusted bodyguard. Artabanus favoured Masood over his son Mithridate, whom he regarded as weak, but blood is thicker than water.

"Don't worry Masood, as soon as I have my son back, we will attack that fort and kill everyone inside it. Every man, every woman, every child. I will get back my gold and silver and much more. Then I will kill Maximus and annihilate his legions"

This made Masood smile as the king's scribes and advisers argued amongst themselves. "SILENCE!" demanded the king. "Bring my Generals here at once!" Artabanus shouted. He then retired back inside his lavish tent. His scribes and advisers were left outside still arguing amongst themselves.

Chapter 20

The following morning Atticus walked along the battlements with Edelgard at his side.

"I can't believe how fucking hot it gets so early in the morning after such a cold night," said Edelgard, wiping his forehead.

Adelar stood below in the courtyard with several soldiers guarding the prince standing in the middle of them, his head held high in defiance.

"Look at that pompous runt down there!" growled Edelgard, Atticus stood for a while looking down at the prince.

"The apple didn't fall far from the tree, he's just like his father rotten to the core. His father rules with an iron fist and has no regard for his people. They do his bidding out of fear, not loyalty" answered Atticus.

"SIR!" shouted one of the lookouts above in the tower and pointed. "Riders and a waggon approaching from the Parthian lines!" he went on to say.

Atticus shielded his eyes from the sun and looked out from the battlements, he could see a dozen riders and a waggon being pulled by a team of mules.

"Looks like they are bringing your gold and silver for the runt," said Edelgard with a grin.

"It's not my gold and silver that belongs to the emperor," replied Atticus.

The legate Marcellus walked down the courtyard accompanied by Justus, Atticus saluted as he descended from the battlements.

"Looks like your father has sent the ransom for your release Mithridate," said Marcellus.

"My father will have you all killed, Roman dog!" retorted the prince in defiance.

"We'll see about that I would keep a civil tongue in your mouth, you're not free yet," answered Marcellus.

The waggon and escort came to a standstill outside the gate. "Open the gate!" ordered Marcellus. It took six Roman soldiers to lift the giant wooden bar and stand it to one side and a dozen more to open the giant gates.

Marcellus and Atticus, followed by Edelgard, walked out to address the Parthians.

"I take it you have the ransom in full on that waggon?" demanded Marcellus.

The Parthians were being led by the Parthian champion Masood, the one with his ear missing. Masood glared at Atticus, his face filled with the look of anger and hate for all to see.

"Unload those chests," said Masood through gritted teeth.

"Your friend has brought the ransom, Atticus," said Edelgard with a chuckle.

"It appears so," replied Atticus.

Two men jumped down from the waggon and two more began to pass down the small heavy chests filled with gold and silver. It took two men to carry each of the small chests. They placed them at the feet of Marcellus.

"Release my prince!" growled Masood glaring at Atticus.

"All in good time…first, I will check the contents of those chests," replied Atticus doing his best to antagonise Masood.

He then opened the lids one at a time and slowly ran his hand through each of the chest's contents making sure it was all gold and silver pieces.

"Well, Roman, are you satisfied?" growled Masood angrily.

"Yes, it appears everything is as I asked Parthian," retorted Atticus with a smile.

"Don't worry, Roman, it won't belong to you for long, my king will have you all killed soon, and that gold and silver will belong to him once again. I will have the pleasure of personally killing you and pissing on your bones!" shouted Masood in anger.

"Is that so?" replied Atticus with a grin.

"I will only give you one chance to kill me! But mark my words ugly one…It won't be easy, don't miss your chance…for I won't miss mine."

The tone in Atticus's voice sent a chill down the spines of the Parthians sitting on their horses at the side of Masood.

"Bring the prince!" shouted Marcellus, as the prince was escorted out of the fort several soldiers ran forward, picked up and carried the chests of gold and silver into the fort.

One of the Parthians dismounted and gave his horse to the prince and climbed onto the waggon. Once the prince had mounted, he turned to look at Atticus, leant forward and spat at the ground in front of him before saying, "I will see you die Roman dog!" Mithridate then turned his horse and rode off fast towards the Parthian lines. Followed closely by Masood and the others.

"Well, Atticus, looks like your plan has worked; how long do you think it will be before they attack?" asked Marcellus.

"Tomorrow, at first light, I think we should get ready," replied Atticus.

"Have the men store those chests in the strong room Justus," ordered Marcellus.

The fort became a hive of activity, piles of arrows were placed at intervals all around the battlements stockpiles of iron bolts were placed at every Ballista. Spears were neatly placed every few yards along the fort's walls. The vipers were already loaded with their large, barbed arrows but more were piled at their side. Buckets of water were lined up all around the base of the fort's walls ready to put out any fires.

Stretchers were hurriedly made and placed neatly ready to carry any wounded to the infirmary. Bandages were prepared and placed on long wooden tables along with all manner of medical equipment needed.

Some of the soldiers preparing the infirmary grimaced at the sight of the saws and blades needed for amputations but calmly went about their duties.

Many of the civilians offered themselves to be stretcher bearers, the women were wanting to help the legions medics who were small in number wherever they were needed.

Quickly the medics showed them how to bandage wounds on volunteers, others were shown how to stitch, clean, and dress wounds.

Men, women and older boys were put into groups and would help put out any fires with help from the fort's orderlies. They were shown where they would gather when the fighting started. This would enable all the Roman soldiers to do nothing but fight and defend the fort. Every able-bodied soldier was needed to do his duty for Rome.

"Everything seems to be ready!" Atticus addressed Marcellus saluting, "Good," he replied.

"Hopefully, Abass should be returning within the hour, so I need to be on the wall to meet him."

"I won't keep you any longer then," replied Marcellus Atticus saluted and left.

Edelgard and Adelar were both waiting on the battlements for Atticus with the rope. When Atticus arrived, they both smiled, "Thought you'd forgotten about meeting us," teased Edelgard.

Dusk had descended but with a full moon they could see reasonably well for at least fifty yards.

"At least you remembered the rope!" replied Atticus grinning.

It was getting close to the time Atticus had arranged with Abbas for his return. There was no sign or sound of him yet only a stillness and eerie silence. The Parthian campfires had been lit and glowed in the distance filling the dark sky with a red haze.

"Fuck me, look at all of them fire's his army has got a whole lot bigger since we arrived," said Adelar.

Edelgard and Atticus were straining their eyes looking for any sign of Abbas.

Another half an hour passed, which seemed like an eternity, and nobody had spoken a word. Atticus could feel a knot of anguish grow in the pit of his stomach and wondered to himself had he been wise to send Abbas out into so much danger. Was his life worth it for any information he might or might not have gotten?

Edelgard could sense Atticus's discomfort.

"Don't worry, my young friend, he will return," he said quietly, as more minutes passed slowly.

Atticus was gripping the fort's stone wall still looking hard out into the night for any sign of his friend.

Atticus could see a shadow appear from behind a small bush in the distance and then heard the call of an eagle twice. Atticus felt the knot in his stomach disappear.

"There he is," pointed Atticus to the others.

"Drop the rope!" he shouted.

Abass quickly ran to the wall grabbing hold of the rope. He started to climb up aided by Atticus who pulled hard on the rope.

Abass dropped down off the wall onto the walkway with a grin and clasped forearms with Atticus's as Edelgard patted him on the shoulder.

Atticus could see a large swelling under the left eye of Abbas, "What happened to you?" asked Atticus.

"Oh, nothing really, I pretended to need a shit so I could make my way back here but one of the Parthians I met didn't really trust me and followed. I had to kill him the first chance I got. He caught me with a good punch before he died, that is why I was a little late," answered Abbas. Who was still grinning but gasping for breath from the climb up the fort's wall.

"What have you learned?" asked Atticus.

"It's not all good news," replied Abbas, and hesitated a little as he gathered his thoughts.

"Go on, my friend," said Atticus.

"Well, they have over seventy thousand men now ready to attack this fort, over fifteen thousand men joined his army yesterday crossing the border the previous night."

"Fuck me!" Adelar said, "The General will only have about twenty thousand men, I know they were far better fighters than the Parthians but that's not good odds by any means," Adelar went on to say.

"That's why we need him to attack these walls and kill as many as we can before Maximus and his legions arrive." stated Atticus.

"Don't worry, you pissed off their king so much that he attacks at dawn; he intends to attack all four of these walls at once," said Abbas. Atticus paced up and down while thinking to himself.

"Their main goal will be to break through the main gate, they have made a heavy battering ram with a roof of animal skins to stop your arrows penetrating it," said Abbas pausing for a while, waiting for Atticus's reply.

"Anything else you found out that might be of use?" asked Atticus.

"Not really, other than a lot of the Parthians arriving to do battle with us are not trained soldiers. There are goat herders, market traders and beggars dragged off the streets. Artabanus has declared all those of an age to fight will be conscripted into his army."

"No doubt, he will use them to attack these walls first, and use them as fodder to find out where we have any weakness for his best soldiers to exploit!" said Edelgard.

"You're probably right, so I might use that to our advantage at some point," replied Atticus.

"How do you mean to do that?" enquired Abbas, "I will weaken the defence of the wall at the north end of the fort. Giving the impression that is our weakest point. Hopefully we can repel his attack. When he attacks that wall again later with his best soldiers, I will prepare a nice surprise for them!"

This made the others grin and Edelgard took the stopper off his wineskin and shouted, "I will drink to that!" and swallowed a large mouthful.

"You'll drink to anything," teased Adelar, which made Atticus and Abass laugh out loud.

"Go Abbas, Aisha will be awaiting your return, and probably biting her nails with worry," said Atticus.

"Thank you, Atticus, I will," replied Abbas.

Who then turned and ran down the stone steps and up through the large courtyard and disappeared.

"We better place some heavy stone slabs above the gates on the walkway ready to drop on those Parthians carrying the battering ram and crush those fuckers!" said Atticus.

It took almost an hour of toil and sweat but soon there was a large pile of heavy stone.

"Right lads, better get some sleep, we will have a long day tomorrow," said Atticus.

"Yes, you're right, plenty of killing," grinned Edelgard with his reply and off they strolled to their beds.

Chapter 21

"Look at the horizon over there!" shouted Yassur, they could see a large dust cloud being kicked up.

"That's got to be Maximus's legions."

They both shielded their eyes from the sun while sitting on their horses looking and watching the dust cloud slowly moving in their direction.

"We better ride to that ridge on the left of the trail over there," Abdul pointed it out to Yassur.

"We need to get a better look just in case it's not Maximus, they are still too far away to make out who they are from here."

Yassur dug his heels into the side of his mount and his horse immediately bolted in the direction of the ridge followed closely by Abdul riding his mount hard and fast. As soon as they reached the ridge, they found a spot high up, slightly out of sight from the trail below.

They both eagerly watched the dust cloud being blown in their direction by a stiff breeze.

Looking for any sign it was Maximus and his legions.

"What if it isn't Maximus?" asked Abdul. "Then we go around them and on towards Tarsus and fucking find him," retorted Yassur, still feeling upset at the loss of his cousin.

"Sorry my friend, I didn't mean to sound disrespectful," said Yassur in a low voice with a deep sigh.

"Don't worry, my friend, I understand," replied Abdul.

He then put his hand on his friend's shoulder reassuringly. Another hour passed rather slowly. It was now midafternoon.

"Look, that's definitely Roman soldiers marching at pace with the General and several officers riding at the front," said Abdul.

They could also see a large contingent of Roman cavalry scouting ahead of the column and more on each flank coming into view.

"Come Abdul, we must ride down fast and meet them."

As they got nearer, the Roman cavalry on the left-hand side turned towards them. Abdul and Yassur pulled up their horses to a standstill and waited as the Roman cavalry charged towards them. Yassur put his hands in the air to show they were not a threat, followed quickly by Abdul.

The Roman cavalry encircled them and the officer in charge had drawn his sword pointing it at Yassur.

"Who the fuck are you two?" he snapped.

"My name is Yassur, and my friend here is Abdul," as he spoke one of the Roman soldiers dismounted and began to grab one of the saddlebags on Yassur's horse.

Yassur bent down and stopped him from opening it. The soldier was about to draw his sword when his officer intervened and shouted, "Leave it, Clictus!" He had seen the emblem of the Augusta 11 legion stamped on its flap.

Clictus let his sword slide back into its scabbard and stood back.

"State your business and what is so important in that saddlebag that you would dare risk your life for?" demanded the Roman officer.

"As I was saying my name is Yassur and this is Abdul," he then bowed his head to the Roman officer.

"And who are you if I may ask? In my country it is polite to know who one is addressing," asked Yassur again, bowing his head.

But before he could reply, an officer with several Roman Praetorian soldiers riding hard pulled their horses up at his side.

"What have we here?" the Roman officer demanded, "Sir I was just finding out when you arrived Tribune Marcus," he then saluted.

"I will take it from here," said the Tribune.

"SIR!" came the reply from the other officer, who then pulled his mount out of the way. "Well gentlemen as you are now aware I am Tribune Marcus, of the Roman Praetorian guard accompanying General Maximus and his legions. Who may I ask, are you two?"

"Yassur bowed his head once again, "I am Yassur, this is Abdul. We are currently on pay in Rome and employed by your great General Maximus to scout and assist First Centurion Atticus of the Augusta 11 legion," replied Yassur."

Marcus smiled when he heard Atticus's name. "How is my young friend Atticus and where is he?" Enquired Marcus.

"He is well and at the fort in Tadmor, and when we left, he was due to have a parley with Artabanus the king of Parthia!" replied Yassur with a smile.

Marcus laughed out loud, "Bugger me! It didn't take long for the young lad to make his mark. I would bet my life he's been causing havoc for those Parthians since he arrived," said Marcus.

"He most certainly has, and I have urgent dispatches in my saddle bag for General Maximus's eyes only," replied Yassur. He then turned and looked at the other Roman officer sitting on his horse and bowed slightly.

"We better go meet the General immediately and give him them with all haste. Ride by my side if you please and tell me what Atticus has been up to." asked Tribune Marcus, smiling.

All the way as they rode to meet the General Yassur and Abdul enlightened Marcus about everything that had occurred up to them leaving Tadmor.

"Yassur…Abdul my friends it is good to see you both!" shouted Maximus, as they approached him and dismounted. Maximus jumped down from his giant white stallion and clasped forearms with Yassur.

"How is my friend Abd-El-Kader and where is he?" enquired Maximus. Yassur hung his head a little.

"I have grave news that my cousin Abd, was killed as we broke through the Parthian lines to bring these dispatches from Atticus," Yassur replied. The pain of his loss returned as he spoke.

Maximus sighed deeply.

"He was a good friend and a great servant of Rome; he will not be forgotten. I will make sure the emperor hears of his service to Rome and make sure his family is taken care of; they will want for nothing," replied Maximus.

"Thank you, General, but we have pressing matters to deal with here. These are from Atticus, he told me to give them to you without delay."

"Marcus, have the legions make camp with all haste and as soon as it is all done, I want all officers of the rank of Centurion and above to be at my quarters as soon as it's done!"

"Yes, sir it will be done."

He quickly left and started barking out instructions. It was by no means an easy task out in the middle of the desert with over twenty thousand men needing to be camped and defences built, but that is what they were trained to do.

While the camps were being constructed and strong defences set all around Maximus had instructed Optio Paulinus to erect a temporary sunscreen and place several stools for him and the two scouts to sit underneath it. Orderlies quickly brought fruit, dates, and dried mutton for them to eat along with some watered wine.

Yassur and Abdul gave all the details of the reinforcements' demise under Titus's command and the rescue of the Roman captives and hostages. Explaining the Parthian kings plan to kill them all if the legate Marcellus didn't surrender the fort. Yassur also gave a full account of the capture of Prince Mithridate.

"Atticus seems to have been very busy…but I wouldn't have expected any less of him," said Maximus. He then sat quietly reading the dispatches from Atticus while Abdul and Yassur ate hungrily and drank the watered wine.

After a while Maximus looked up after finishing reading them. "Atticus says there are at least over fifty thousand Parthians surrounding the fort?"

"Yes, and it is increasing every day, my General," answered Abdul with a worried look on his face.

Tribune Marcus arrived at the makeshift tent, "General! Your quarters are ready, the camp's defences are built, and guards are posted. The officers are waiting as you requested," Marcus then saluted.

"Come, you two, no time to waste, thank you Marcus," said Maximus.

"I have instructed all Optio's to be on duty and take charge of the men while our meeting takes place!" answered Marcus.

"Good," replied Maximus.

All the other officers were standing outside the General's large tent talking amongst themselves eagerly awaiting any news from Tadmor.

Once inside, Maximus stood behind a large table and unrolled a map of the region around the fort at Tadmor and placed weights on each corner to keep it flat.

Several benches had been placed in rows for the officers to sit but several had to stand at the back. Tribune Marcus and Tribune Matias stood to the right of Maximus, with Yassur and Abdul on his left.

"Silence!" shouted Tribune Matias. The room fell quiet. Maximus looked hard at the map and read one of the dispatches from Atticus.

"Before we start in case any of you are wondering who the two gentlemen are standing at my side…"

"Tribune Marcus and Tribune Matias!" shouted Centurion Decimus cutting in. Laughter filled the General's tent, "Very funny Decimus always the joker," replied Maximus smiling. He wasn't one not to appreciate a little humour.

"May I introduce you to my scouts from Tadmor, Yassur and Abdul," said Maximus as soon as the laughter had died down.

Maximus pointed at a place on the map, "Is this the slight ridge Atticus wants us to form our battle lines to face the Parthians Yassur?"

"It is General!" he replied, looking down at the map.

"Why? It's a fair distance from the fort's defences, a little further than I would have expected for us to face the enemy!" Enquired Maximus.

"The ground that slopes up to that ridge is very soft sand, blown by the winds over many years. Atticus is sure that when the Parthians attack your lines with their chariots the horses will struggle, and the wheels will sink causing disarray. Thus, faltering their attack, their lines of infantry will be bogged down behind." Yassur paused for a moment for his words to be pondered over by Maximus as he looked at the map in deep thought.

"Atticus thinks this will give you a great advantage over their numbers," finished Yassur.

"Yes, he is probably right. Atticus is very good at reading maps and terrain. Romulus has trained him well," replied Maximus.

"He knows how to kick arse as well!" shouted Decimus, creating more laughter.

Maximus couldn't help but smile and didn't mind the interaction from his men; he knew that within a few days they would all be putting their lives on the line in the service of Rome.

"Would you like to come up here and take over proceedings, Decimus?" answered Maximus with a grin.

"Err no sir, you're doing a fantastic job," replied Decimus, a little sheepishly.

"Good then, I will carry on," said Maximus.

"What else does Atticus have in mind while the Parthians attack us?" enquired Tribune Marcus.

"According to this dispatch he will then lead his men out of the fort and attack the Parthians in the rear. He will have the fort's cavalry attack their flank," replied Yassur.

"That will be a bold move even for him," said Tribune Matias.

"It may be, but necessary if we wish to trap them causing panic amongst the Parthians."

"As we speak Atticus will have angered the king of Parthia so much, he will be attacking the fort with all his might. Atticus wants to kill as many Parthians as possible against its walls before you arrive out in the open," said Abdul.

"Knowing Atticus as I do…he will have plenty of tricks up his sleeve. I just hope the fort can withstand an attack from such a large force."

"I know that if anyone can, Atticus is the one," stated Decimus interrupting once more.

Cheers rang out in the tent as the Roman officers stamped their feet on the wooden floor. The Praetorian guards outside the tent looked at each other in amusement wondering what the hell was going on inside the tent.

"Alright lads that's enough," said Tribune Marcus. General Maximus gave them their orders to be carried out to the letter and the meeting concluded.

The following morning at dawn, General Maximus and his legions marched at pace towards Tadmor. Word had spread among the ranks of Roman legionaries of Atticus's actions before and after reaching the fort. Many ignored the heat and toil of marching; songs rang out as they marched with renowned vigour.

Chapter 22

Atticus, along with Edelgard and Adelar, stood on the fort's battlements walkway above the Maingate. The legate Marcellus and his Tribune Justus were high above in one of the towers.

"Fuck me! There's thousands of the buggers," said Justus, as they surveyed the Parthian battle lines surrounding the fort. There were too many lines standing deep to count.

The Parthian king, his son, and his champion sat on their horses in the middle, facing the Maingate just out of range of the fort's catapults. Hundreds of Parthian banners fluttered in the breeze facing all four of the fort's walls.

Atticus had instructed Abbas and his Mesopotamian auxiliaries to allow some of the Parthians to scale the rear wall. He wanted to let them manage to gain a small foothold over the wall before repelling them.

Atticus had placed two hundred legionnaires of the 111 Gallicia Raphanea under the command of Centurion Crassus. Hidden out of sight to make sure the Parthians were pushed back over the wall if necessary.

He hoped this ruse would convince the king it was the fort's weak point. Atticus surveyed the Parthian hordes lined up. He noticed a young legionnaire still probably two years older than Atticus standing to his left trembling as he gazed at the multitude of Parthians waiting to attack the fort. His face was pale, his eyes bulged with fear, his lower lip was trembling. Atticus strode over to him and stood at his shoulder. Atticus kept his focus on his enemy as he stood at the legionnaires side for several moments without saying a word. The legionnaire that was transfixed staring at the enemy hadn't noticed Atticus now standing at his side. Atticus then calmly spoke without looking directly at the legionnaire and asked, "What's your name, soldier?" The soldier flicked his eyes to his right to see who was addressing him. He immediately stood to attention and puffed out his chest.

"My name is Brutus sir!" he replied.

"It is alright to fear the enemy…It's how you respond to them when the time to fight comes," said Atticus, in a low, calm voice.

"It's the waiting sir…why don't they just attack and get on with it, sir?" Brutus replied still in the grip of fear.

"We are all a little nervous before battle, that is only natural. They will attack all in good time, they're just trying to scare us with their numbers. Don't worry I have every confidence that you will fight well at my side," answered Atticus.

"Yes sir! I will, sir!" replied Brutus, feeling a little less nervous knowing Atticus believed in him and smiled. His lower lip stopped trembling.

Atticus turned and began to descend the stone steps leading to the courtyard in front of the gate where Centurion Cyrus and the rest of the Augusta 11 legion were standing in line ready to protect the gates. Just in case the enemy managed to break through them. Atticus tightened the chin strap to his helmet so it wouldn't move.

"What are you up to, Atticus, my friend?" shouted Edelgard from up on the battlements.

"I'm off to pick a fight and put some fear into those Parthians at the same time, two can play mind games!" shouted Atticus in reply. Edelgard took hold of his wine skin and swallowed a large mouthful. After replacing the stopper, he looked at Adelar and said, "Looks like the fun's about to begin my friend," he then promptly belched out loud.

Adelar stroked his unkempt beard then ran his hands through his greasy hair, smiled and replied, "About fucking time…I've never been one for waiting. Bet you two sesterces I get a kill before you!"

"Make it five. I'm feeling lucky," replied Edelgard with a grin.

"Five it is then," answered Adelar.

"Thaddius!" shouted Atticus, "Yes sir!"

"Give me your spear!" Thaddius took a couple of steps forward and presented it to Atticus. Many of the other soldiers standing in rank looked at each other wondering what the fuck was happening.

"OPEN THE GATE!" shouted Atticus.

Several soldiers dropped their spears and ran to the gate, straining as they lifted the heavy wooden bar then laying it to one side. A dozen others dragged the large, heavy gates wide open and sand and dust blew in as they creaked open. Atticus strode out of the fort alone and headed towards the Parthian lines, as he did a large wind funnel swirled. Causing a cloud of sand to seemingly dance eerily across the ground between the lines of Parthian soldiers and Atticus. He was now standing alone outside the fort facing the Parthian king holding the spear given to him by Thaddius.

"Look father…the gates are opening; a soldier is approaching," shouted the Prince Mithridate.

"Looks like they want to surrender after all," grinned the king in reply, his fat cheeks wobbled as he spoke.

Atticus had stopped about fifty yards out in front of the gates, he thrust the butt of his spear into the ground making it stand erect. He then bent down on one knee, filling one of his hands with sand and began rubbing his hands together.

He stood up tall, his full height was six foot six, his body's frame was the size of a barn door, arms as thick as most men's legs. Not an ounce of body fat for anyone to pinch. Atticus took hold of the spear once more, still looking in the direction of Artabanus the Parthian king.

Silence hung in the air for what seemed like an eternity but in reality, it had only been a matter of seconds.

Atticus then roared the name of "MASOOD!" His voice sounded like a crack of thunder, shattering the silence. Several of the Parthian horses, including the king's mount, shifted backwards. This caused the king to settle and reassure his mount.

Again, Atticus shouted "MASOOD!" Atticus took another step forward gripping his spear. The sand on the palms of his hand had soaked up any sweat, giving him a solid grip.

Edelgard, above the fort's battlements, looked down at his friend and shouted out loud,

"Balls of steel!"

"Balls of fucking steel!" Marcellus looked at Justus raising his eyebrows.

"Who is that my king?" asked one of his Generals as his horse reared up slightly. "That is the young Roman dog Atticus!" the king snarled his reply. Many of the men in earshot of the king grimaced with fear at the mere mention of the name Atticus.

Masood looked at his king, nudging his horse forward. "Let me kill that itch of his mother's cunt!" The king didn't answer, he just stared in the direction of Atticus.

"My king…he challenges me in front of the army! He said he would give me one chance to kill him. Let me kill him! Look at the faces of fear in our soldiers, they think he's a demon sent by the Roman gods!"

The king looked at his champion with pride, knowing Masood had killed many of the king's enemies. "Go kill him, bring me his head and I will feed it to the rats!"

Masood edged his horse forward; cheers rang out from the Parthian army and the chants of Masood! Roared at them as he rode fast and hard, waving his sword above his head, charging at Atticus.

Masood was filled with hate for the young Roman, he kicked his heels into the flanks of his horse hard making it charge forward faster. He was still over five hundred yards from Atticus but bearing down fast.

Atticus gripped his spear and waited without so much as a flinch.

"You will die, Roman dog!" shouted Masood as he charged his mount forward.

Masood was now two hundred and fifty yards away, his horse kicking up a cloud of dust as it charged on.

An eagle circled the sky above, Atticus ran three steps forward and jumped as his third stride hit the ground, launching his spear with all his strength.

It flew straight and fast with such force and accuracy; Masood never saw it coming as it punched through his chest, penetrating his heart, smashing through his rib cage.

The tip of the spear protruded out of Masood's back; such was the force of the spear as it struck. It knocked the Parthian champion backwards off his horse, crashing to the ground.

The Parthian lines of soldiers were stunned into silence as the chants for Masood faded and disappeared.

Tribune Justus turned to Marcellus and said, "By the gods! I have never seen a spear thrown so far."

Edelgard, standing below within earshot, answered while looking at his young friend Atticus, "I have, when Atticus saved the General's life and mine in that forest back in Ostia." Marcellus looked down at Edelgard feeling the hairs on the back of his neck prick up. He then returned his gaze towards the Parthians and Atticus.

Atticus walked over to the body of Masood, drew one of his swords with the inscription MORI QUAM FOEDARI – 'DEATH BEFORE DISHONOUR' and with one swift stroke cut off his head.

Atticus lifted it up for all to see and threw it definitely towards the Parthian king; the eagle swooped down and landed at the feet of Atticus.

The eagle stretched out its wings facing the Parthians and screeched out an ear-piercing call before ascending high up to the skies and out of sight.

Atticus turned slowly and walked slowly back to the fort's gates to the chants of "Atticus! Atticus!" over and over again. The gates were then closed and bolted behind him.

"Sorry Thaddius, looks like you will need to get another spear," said Atticus, with a grin causing large amounts of laughter among the men of the Augusta 11 legion.

King Artabanus's face filled with anger, shouted, "10 thousand gold pieces to the man who brings me the fucking head of that Roman dog Atticus."

Some of his soldiers cheered filled with greed, but others felt a deep fear of the one they called the Demon of Rome. They also regarded the eagle as a bad omen.

"ATTACK!" shouted Artabanus as he pointed a golden spear towards the Roman fort. The call to attack rang out all around the fort as it was repeated by his Generals.

The Parthians marched forward somewhat gingerly but were forced forward by the men behind. Over fifty men carried the heavy battering ram towards the gate, others carried the screen of animal skins above it hoping to block out the Roman arrows.

Others carried large wooden screens, logs fastened together with rope for their archers to hide behind and fire at the fort's walls above the gate to try and protect the men with the battering ram.

The king had kept all his chariots and horse archers along with many of his finest men in reserve for the battle with Maximus. Not wanting to waste them attacking the fort. King Artabanus was relying on the sheer weight of numbers to capture the fort and was blinded with rage and a deep hatred of Atticus.

"Justus take charge of the catapults! make sure they fire as soon as they are in range and shout out the distance for them to reset, I don't want any mistakes!"

"YES SIR!"

"Atticus, you take charge of the front wall," shouted Marcellus, as he returned to the battlement's walkway.

"Farrokh, form up your Cilician archers and wait for my order to fire!" ordered Atticus.

"Yes sir!" came the reply.

All along the walkway above the main gate the archers readied themselves as Justus shouted for the catapults to ignite the fireballs and release.

Loud cracks rang out from the catapults as the pins were pulled out, firing their large, heavy, burning missiles out from within the fort's large courtyard.

Up and over the walls they streaked, thick black acrid smoke trailing behind them as they flew towards their targets.

Down they crashed out of the blue sky amongst the attacking Parthians, crushing men as they struck. Flames burst out in all directions, igniting the clothes of many more. The burning liquid sticking to their bodies setting them on fire.

Many rolled themselves in the sand, trying, as they screamed, to extinguish the flames, to no avail. The other hordes of Parthians marched around them to avoid the flames. Men at the back holding bullwhips lashed out at any soldier faltering in fear, pressing them on with the attack.

Again, the catapults fired from within the fort sending out their burning missiles killing many more Parthians as they marched forward. The stench of burning flesh filled the air along with the men's dying screams.

The Roman officers in charge of the bolt throwers and vipers shouted for them to be fired as soon as the Parthians came into range.

Large arrows and heavy barbed bolts flew out from all four walls of the fort, punching into the bodies of the marching Parthians, too many packed together for them to miss. The soldiers quickly reloaded and fired repeatedly.

Then as soon as the Parthians were in range of the archers, Atticus shouted "Fire!" and little grey specks filled the blue sky before descending down into the lines of marching Parthians striking their bodies ferociously. Punching into faces, arms, and legs indiscriminately. Many of the Parthian conscripts had no armour to protect them, some didn't even have shields. Artabanus didn't care how many conscripts were killed; he wanted nothing more than to take the fort and kill all those inside.

Arrows were now being fired from all four walls repeatedly into the Parthians attacking the walls, killing hundreds, bodies fell blood seeping into the sand but still the Parthians charged forward.

The Parthians, carrying the wooden screens, now placed them ready for their archers to hide behind and fire at the fort's walls which began straight away.

"legionnaires raise your shields and protect our archers!" shouted Atticus. All around the fort's walls the order was repeated and carried out.

The Parthian archers were now firing their arrows as fast as they could from behind the wooden screens. But had little effect, most of their arrows struck the stone walls or the Roman shields.

Some arrows found their targets, killing several legionnaires, others were struck but were quickly taken to the infirmary. The fort's surgeons acted quickly to remove the arrows and stem the flow of blood.

As soon as they had been treated, many who could still fight returned to the walls, one of them was Brutus, the young legionnaire who had been struck in his left arm.

Atticus acknowledged Brutus on his return and smiled in admiration of his bravery.

"Farrokh!" shouted Atticus.

"Yes sir!" came the reply. "You need to keep those archers behind those screens from firing concentrate on them the artillery will take care of the rest."

'BOOM!' came the sound from the gate as the battering ram struck. Dust and splinters covered Thaddius and the other Roman soldiers standing in line behind them. But before it could strike again, Atticus and Edelgard, along with several burly Roman soldiers, lifted the heavy stone slabs and boulders. Dropping them over the wall, crashing down through the animal skin canopy protecting the men with the battering ram below.

Screams could be heard as the men below were crushed; skulls were cracked open as more boulders were dropped from the walls above.

They crashed through the screen with ease, It was poorly designed and only fit to stop the arrows being fired from above.

As the men below were crushed the heavy battering ram was dropped and any survivors ran in fear for their lives causing panic.

Many of the conscripts turned and began to run and retreat from the fort's walls in fear. Farrokh and his Cilician archers fired as fast as they could. Spears were being thrown by the legionnaires striking many of the fleeing Parthians.

The Parthian archers behind their wooden barricades abandoned them and ran, seeing their comrades flee.

But at the rear wall of the fort Abbas and his men had allowed the Parthians to scale the wall up their ladders. A ferocious fight with swords and spears ensued all along its walkway. Centurion Crassus and his men now joined the fight, shields held tightly together. Their short swords sliced the enemy between the slight gaps in the shield wall.

They killed indiscriminately and without mercy.

The Parthians were soon repelled back over the wall, many of whom fell to their deaths from the high stone walls. Their screams echoed off the walls as they fell dying. The attack on the fort was beginning to falter.

"Father, many of your men run in fear while others fight. We need to call a full retreat and regroup and attack again or many will die getting in the way of others," said Mithridate, quietly in his father's ear not wishing to anger the king.

Artabanus glared at him, but realised he was right and shouted for the call for retreat to be announced.

The sound of trumpets could be heard blaring out three long blasts followed by two short ones, giving the clear signal for the army to retreat. The Parthian army gained some momentum, and an orderly withdrawal began to take place.

"Have all my Generals come to my tent immediately. They return," screamed the king, as he and his bodyguards rode off in the direction of his tent followed closely by Prince Mithridate.

The Parthians had fully retreated to their lines well out of range of the fort's heavy weapons. leaving behind a scene of carnage, bodies still burned. Wounded men crawled or limped back to their comrades, some screaming for help as they did so.

Dead bodies littered the battlefield, too many to count all around the four walls of the fort. The attack lasted not much more than a couple of hours and was repelled with relative ease.

Marcellus descended from the tower and approached Atticus, "Was that wise of you to put yourself in such danger outside the fort earlier?" enquired Marcellus.

Atticus smiled at the legate, "Yes sir, it had the desired effect…it got the king to attack recklessly. I think many of his advisers will be feeling a little uneasy about it now, having to face the wrath of their king. His army has received a bit of a bloody nose and by my reckoning he has a couple of thousand men less to face Maximus," replied Atticus.

"Even a young man like you if you fall it will have a deep impact on the morale of the men," responded Marcellus.

"Sometimes, it is a risk we all have to take for the good of Rome," answered Atticus.

Marcellus sighed and smiled, "Yes, Atticus, you're probably right and anyway thanks to the gods you prevailed. I'm going to my quarters, have a report sent to me regarding our losses, carry on with your duties."

"Yes, sir, I will. I don't think the Parthians will attack again until tomorrow," replied Atticus.

After Marcellus had departed, Atticus could hear Edelgard and Adelar teasing each other.

"What's up with you two?" asked Atticus, grinning. "This turd owes me five sesterces," grinned Edelgard.

"What for?" enquired Atticus.

"We had a bet whoever killed the first Parthian boyfucker won. My spear struck first!" shouted Adelar.

"Yes, it did but my spear struck another and he died first, yours was still wriggling around in the sand. He was whimpering like a child and clearly not dead!" said Edelgard. Who then opened his wineskin, taking a large mouthful of its contents before smacking his lips together with a grin.

Atticus couldn't help but laugh out loud, "Come you two, we need to go see Abbas and find out what went on at the far wall." Adelar finally placed five coins into the open hand of Edelgard.

They walked the full length of the battlement looking out at the devastation. Parthian bodies littered the battlefield; some still hadn't died of their injuries and could be seen trying to crawl back to their comrades.

Atticus shouted for Centurion Cyrus to have the archers kill and put the surviving Parthians out of their misery. It wasn't long before the order had been carried out.

Abbas could be seen receiving treatment for a cut to his arm as they approached. "Are you alright Abbas?" enquired Atticus.

"Yes sir, it's only a scratch."

The medic treating him shook his head and said, "That's what you buggers always say. I need to put at least four stitches in this so-called scratch so keep still."

Atticus smiled at his friend and asked, "Well, do you think the Parthians will take the bait and attack this wall with some of their best men tomorrow?"

"I would be very surprised if they didn't. We let them gain a foothold on this wall and to be honest the Parthians attacking here were not wearing much armour and looked more like traders and goat herders than fighters! Many were too old to fight."

"Let's hope they take the bait! Adelar, go find Thaddius and have him and some men bring those cases of caltrops to this wall. And have him go to the fort's armoury and see if there are any more stored there. When it's dark I want to spread them all over the ground outside this wall," said Atticus.

Edelgard grinned, knowing the devastating effect the caltrops had when they rescued the women and children along with the Roman soldiers. Atticus smiled, "well it worked once, might as well give it another go" he said looking at Edelgard.

"I wonder how that idiot Titus is recovering, locked up in his quarters?" enquired Edelgard.

"The last I heard he was still delirious, and his Tribune just sits there staring at the wall! Probably realising it won't go well for them when they return to Rome in disgrace. I wouldn't be surprised if one or both of them will fall on their own swords," replied Atticus.

"That will be no loss to Rome," said Abbas, wincing a little as the medic stitched his wound.

Adelar had left to carry out Atticus's instructions, Atticus made sure the walls were still properly manned but had allowed every fourth man to take two hours rest for food and water. Then to rotate so every man was fed and rested but ready to return to the walls if an attack took place.

Atticus and Edelgard had arranged to meet up with Abbas and the others just before nightfall to place the caltrops all over the ground outside the rear of the fort.

"What now?" enquired Edelgard.

"Now we eat, bathe and then it's off to see Fury. I want to make sure he's behaving." Atticus grinned.

"It won't be dark for at least another four hours," responded Edelgard.

Artabanus sat on his throne in his tent feeding his fat face with a large, salted mutton leg, while his Generals and advisers stood waiting anxiously outside. They waited in silence, some shovelling their feet wondering who would be punished or even killed for the failed attack on the fort. The heads of the officers were still displayed outside the king's tent; the smell of rotting flesh was quite repulsive even to those with a strong stomach.

Still, the Parthian king ignored them, knowing full well of their discomfort. His feet were being washed by a young Persian slave girl.

When the girl had finished washing his feet and drying them, she kept her head down and left the king's tent.

The girl felt a huge sigh of relief once she was outside the king's tent. She knew of many other young slaves that had been flogged to within an inch of their lives, If the king had felt any displeasure towards them while they attended to his needs.

Artabanus now looked up as the gold tray of leftover food was taken away by one of the servants. Artabanus waved his hand towards one of the many bodyguards standing just inside the curtained entrance to his inner sanctum. Who immediately pulled back the silk curtain and beckoned the Generals to enter. They were led in by one of Artabanus's most trusted advisors, Yusef-El-Bashir. Artabanus looked directly into the faces of his Generals as they walked in, making them feel very uncomfortable. The Generals did not return the eye contact but bowed very low knowing all too well the wrath of their king would soon descend upon them. All of them wished not to meet the king's gaze as they stood staring at the floor in silence.

King Artabanus suddenly erupted with rage, "What the fuck just happened?" He yelled standing up.

"Are you so weak? Are your men cowards? They ran from those Roman dogs far too easily."

Nobody dared answer or meet his gaze.

"Lift your heads and look at ME!" demanded the king.

Slowly, one by one, they raised their heads looking towards their king not daring to utter a single word.

"WELL! Answer me!"

Silence fell within the king's tent as soon as Artabanus finished shouting in anger. Prince Mithridate walked in from a room behind the king's throne and stood at his father's side. Still, nobody responded to the king's demand for answers.

Prince Mithridate then asked calmly, "Who will offer an explanation to my father?" One of the Generals coughed to clear his throat before speaking from behind the other Generals. He stepped forward, making his way through the other Generals and stood at the side of Yusef-El-Bashir.

He was a man in his early fifties with a long thin greying beard, slender, quite tall, a little over five foot ten in stature. His armour was well made and immaculately polished.

He was a man clearly from a wealthy background, "If I may, my king?"

Prince Mithridate beckoned him to step closer, the General swallowed hard and stepped closer to the king's throne.

"At last, someone has grown a pair of balls, speak, explain, tell me what is on your mind?" enquired the king in somewhat of a calmer tone. But still demanding an immediate response.

"I am General Asiff," he spoke quietly and bowed his head as he spoke,

"Speak up so we can all hear!" demanded the king.

"We attacked today with our conscripts at the front, many of whom had no armour."

"So you expect me to waste our best men on those walls!" shouted the king angrily, cutting in leaving Asiff with his mouth slightly open.

"No...I only wish to offer an explanation," Asiff bowed his head again to his king. Artabanus shifted a little in his throne, "Then explain, I will allow you to speak on." he then waved his hand in the direction of Asiff for him to continue.

"I led the assault on the fort's rear wall even with the conscripts we managed to scale the wall and take a foothold inside." Artabanus interrupted again sharply, "And? Speak up man, I can hardly hear you." The king was getting very impatient.

Asiff cleared his throat and said, "If you give me three thousands of our best men when we attack tomorrow. I will get us back inside that fort and hold us there until more men get inside and the fort will be ours, my king."

Asiff bowed and took a step back, Yusef-El-Bashir, the king's most trusted adviser, an old man in his seventies, stepped forward. The king beckoned him to approach, Yusef then bent forward and began to whisper into the king's ear for several minutes. Artabanus listened intently the whole time before Yusef-El-Bashir stepped back and left the tent. The room stayed silent, everyone waited for the king to speak wondering what Yusef had said. Artabanus sat quietly reflecting over what Yusef-El-Bashir had advised him to do while everyone else still stood in silence, awaiting their king.

King Artabanus finally broke the silence, "Asiff, I will give you three thousands of my finest men, give me victory tomorrow or I will take your head personally."

"I will give you your victory," answered Asiff.

"Go all of you, make the preparations for tomorrow's battle," demanded the king.

As they left, the king shouted, "Not you, Abilsin!"

He was the General in charge of the attack on the main gate. He stopped and turned to face his king and bowed. Artabanus walked towards him, drew his dagger and slit his throat without so much as a second thought. Abilsin grabbed his throat, trying to stem the flow of blood now pouring down onto his tunic. His legs buckled as he fell, dying to the floor.

"Take this worthless piece of shit outside, remove his head and place it on a spike my son," The prince dragged Abilsin's dead body outside, unsheathed his sword and sliced the blade through his neck. He then instructed one of the bodyguards to stick it on a spike for all to see. This was done in full view of the Generals who had just left the tent. Asiff looked down at the dead body of his friend, knowing full well that it would be him if he didn't give the king the victory he'd promised.

A new carpet was rolled out replacing the blood stained one that had been removed. Artabanus instructed one of his guards to bring two fine slave girls to attend him and warm his bed for the night.

Chapter 23

Night had fallen and Atticus and the others gathered on the rear battlement. Large cases of caltrops had been placed with ropes tied to their metal handles ready for them to be lowered over the walls.

Thaddius and twenty others from the Augusta 11 first cohort had volunteered for the mission, "Right men listen up, we're going over the wall now. Abbas, you and your men lower the cases as soon as we are on the ground. We take them five hundred yards out and scatter them everywhere, move slowly, our vision won't be good, It's only half-moon tonight." Atticus paused looking around at his men and asked, "Any questions?"

He could see the smiles on their faces in the flickering light from the burning torch held by Abbas.

"Don't forget there are dead bodies littering the ground out there if any are still alive kill them. We don't want any dying Parthians alerting as to our presence."

Edelgard and Adelar lowered themselves down one of the dozens of ropes now dangling from the fort's walls, followed by Atticus and the others. As soon as they were all down, Abbas and his men lowered the cases of caltrops slowly and carefully. Dark shadows hung on the great stone walls of the fort and the hiss of a rattlesnake could be heard not far away. The ropes were untied from the handles, each case was to be carried by two men as instructed by Atticus. They carefully picked their way forward, striding over the many dead bodies. Thaddius slipped and almost fell as one of his feet slid into the intestines of the body, spilling out.

"Fuck me!" he whispered feeling the cold, slimy fluid seep through the holes in his sandals. He then felt tiny claws scratching his toes as a large rodent that had been feeding scurried over them and disappeared into the dark. Thaddius almost emptied the contents of his stomach at the stench, he pinched his nose and covered his mouth with his free hand. Adelar, who was carrying the other end of the case, gripped the handle hard so it didn't fall as Thaddeus steadied himself, managing to stay upright and not dropping his end of the case.

Adelar strode over to the body to the side of Thaddius, looking at him and grinning at Thaddius's discomfort. Adelar could hear a dull moan coming from his left side not too far away and gestured for Thaddius to take the full weight of the box. He then slowly made his way to the sound still coming. Adelar took hold of his knife, bent down on one knee and finished off the dying Parthian. He was lying almost face down with an arrow sticking out from his back. Adelar quickly returned to Thaddius and began distributing the lethal caltrops, smiling as he did.

Atticus and Edelgard had made good time and were now placing the caltrops in front of them and taking care walking backwards. They didn't want to step in their own trap, it was very dark, and it was painstakingly slow hard work. But a couple of hours later Atticus and his men had returned to the base of the fort's walls where Thaddius and Adelar were already waiting. The empty cases were tied to ropes and pulled up by Abbas and his men. The ropes were quickly dropped to enable Atticus and the others to climb back into the fort. Adelar was the first to haul himself upwards followed by Thaddius and the others.

Atticus was the last man to get back in the fort wanting to make sure all his men were safe inside the fort first.

"Well done men, let's hope the Parthians have taken the bait. If not, the caltrops will still do their job on whoever attacks this wall."

Thaddius and the others grinned in response, knowing the devastation the caltrops would bring to anyone attacking that wall tomorrow.

"Let's hope it will be some of their best fighters," said Abbas.

"Get some rest, we still have at least four hours before dawn," said Atticus. The guards on the wall were now relieved of their duty and replaced by others who'd rested. It would be a long, hard day of fighting ahead. The men needed to be at their best.

As soon as Atticus laid on his bed, he was fast asleep dreaming of home and Naomi.

"Look at him sleeping like a baby already," said Edelgard to Adelar with a smile.

"Better get some sleep ourselves, something tells me we're in for a bit of a fight tomorrow," answered Adelar with his thick Germanic accent as he laid down on his bed and promptly farted.

Tribune Marcus was leading a column of Praetorian cavalry scouting on the right of General Maximus and his legions marching hard in the heat of the sun.

The column strung out in perfect order for over several miles; the baggage train at the rear carrying the heavy equipment, food and water, was flanked by over a thousand Roman cavalry under the charge of Tribune Matias.

"Look sir, several riders coming towards us from the west," shouted Centurion Metelus. Marcus shielded his eyes from the sun's glare, squinting, trying to focus on the dust cloud being kicked up.

"I see them, they're definitely Roman Halt!" shouted Marcus turning his mount to face the direction of the oncoming riders.

As they drew close the riders slowed their horses to a trot; there were ten in all, covered in dust, each with scarves covering their mouths and noses.

When they'd pulled up in front of Marcus and his men, an officer at the front pulled down his scarf covering the lower half of his face and saluted.

"I am Tribune Gaius of the V1 Ferrata, Raphanea and Judaea legion, stationed at Damascus on my way to find General Maximus and his legions, sir!"

"Well, my friend you have found us. I am Tribune Marcus of the Praetorian guards accompanying the General," replied Marcus.

"I have urgent dispatches for him from my legate Magnus Cassius Antonius," said Gaius.

"You and your men better follow me. Metelus, hold the men here and keep a sharp eye!" shouted Marcus, looking over his shoulder at him.

Maximus shouted for the column to halt as soon as he saw Marcus and the small group of Roman cavalries arriving. Marcus saluted and introduced the Tribune of the V1 Ferrata, Raphanea and Judea legion.

Gaius handed the dispatches to Maximus and dismounted to stretch his legs from the hard ride out from Damascus. He began stamping his feet in the sand to pump the flow of blood down to his legs.

"Marcus, have the column rest, eat some rations and make sure they all have plenty of water before we head on. We still have plenty of daylight left to make progress," demanded Maximus.

"Yes, General!"

Maximus then read the dispatches intently, as the others dismounted and drank from their waterskins.

"When did you leave Damascus?" asked Maximus.

"Two days ago, other than resting the horses at intervals we haven't stopped riding."

"How did the legate come to the attention of our whereabouts?"

"We received a dispatch from a Tribune at Tarsus by the name of Tiberius. He'd captured a couple of spies hiding in the town, interrogated them and thought due to the size of the Parthian army you would require assistance. And any further information we might have that could be of help to you sir. they apparently number over seventy thousand and the number rises each day." Maximus pulled out a map from his saddlebag and laid it out on the ground.

"Show me on this map where Magnus and his legion are?"

"The legate will hold his legion here," Gaius pointed to the map.

"He will wait there until I return with your instructions sir."

Maximus knelt quietly deep in thought for a while. "How good is your memory or do you require me to write my instructions down?"

"No need to write, my memory is good, and if we are intercepted on our way back to my legion, they will find nothing. I will fall on my sword before they can torture me," answered Gaius, standing tall with pride.

Maximus looked into the eyes of Gaius for a moment then said, "I believe you would," with a smile. "What happened in the region around Damascus after the Parthians invaded?" asked Maximus.

"The first news of the Parthian incursion came to light when one of our patrols whose job was also to take supplies to two of our small outposts stationed along the outer reaches of our empire on the Parthian border." Gaius coughed slightly and spat out some sand from his dry mouth.

"Sorry General, I've been breathing in that dust for most of our ride to find you."

"Here drink some water," replied Maximus, passing him a waterskin.

Gaius swallowed a large mouthful then carried on with the story.

"The garrison of the first outpost consisted of some fifty auxiliaries under command of Centurion Decimus, a very capable soldier. They had all been killed and their bodies were stripped of any clothing and staked out in rows. The men of the patrol couldn't tell if all of them had been killed first or some had been staked out alive." Gaius paused for a moment, hanging his head low.

"Take a deep breath and carry on" said Maximus quietly, Gaius coughed again and spoke on.

"Most of their bodies had been eaten by ants, vultures and other scavengers, Decimus's body had been mutilated and strung up to a post. All his limbs had been hacked off. It looked like, according to the patrol officer; the outpost had been attacked during the night. There were very few Parthian dead bodies to be found unless they had carried some off."

"Highly unlikely they don't remove their dead unless they are staying, not wanting disease to spread. What had become of the second outpost?" asked Maximus.

"The second outpost was the larger it was manned by over a hundred auxiliaries and a further thirty legionnaires, an Optio and a Centurion from our legion. They were all very capable soldiers handpicked by our legate Magnus. The outpost was situated at the top of a small mountain range and could be well defended. They had fought fiercely to the last man; the patrol counted over four hundred dead Parthians wearing good armour. They must have been in a hurry; they didn't bother to gather up their weapons, bury their dead or take their armour!"

"Don't worry the lives of your brothers in arms and soldiers of Rome…will be avenged!" answered Maximus with a strong tone of determination in his voice.

"The men of the V1 Ferrata, Raphanea and Judea legion will do our duty for Rome, but we will also seek revenge for our dead comrades. You can be assured of that, General."

Maximus smiled at Gaius before returning his attention to the map. "We will form our battlelines here on this ridge facing the Parthians and force them to attack us. I want your legate and his legion to attack the Parthians right flank here," Maximus paused and pointed at the map allowing Gaius time to absorb the detail.

"I will position my cavalry here protecting our left flank, when the battle has begun, I expect Atticus and his cohort along with the forts legion to come out and attack the Parthians left flank. Hopefully between us we will defeat that inbred Artabanus and hit them so hard they will never underestimate the power of Rome again. He might think he outnumbers us but there is no army more powerful than the legions of Rome," stated Maximus proudly.

"I keep hearing the name Atticus but for all the years I have fought with the legions I cannot place him," answered Gaius.

"You won't have met him; he has been with the legions of Rome for only a couple of months now," replied Maximus.

"He must have come from a wealthy family then?"

"No, he saved my life and to fight for Rome only reward he craved was at the ripe old age of 18 was to fight for Rome."

"I see…really nothing but to fight for Rome!" Gaius, who came from a wealthy family, also had several wealthy benefactors was given a commission and had not come up through the ranks. He was in his early forties, but all said and done Gaius was more than happy to give his life for Rome and go to the afterlife if it was his time to die.

"Well, General, with your leave I will return to my legion and give your instructions to my legate?" answered Gaius.

"Go with all speed and I hope to see you safe after the battle."

Gaius saluted, mounted his horse and left followed by his men kicking up a cloud of dust as they rode off.

"Have the men ready to march on in ten minutes Marcus we have a battle to win!" shouted Maximus.

Dawn had broken at the fort in Tadmor, and the Parthians were lined up ready to attack all the fort's walls again.

Atticus and his cohort, along with his Cilician archers, were positioned out of sight, kneeling down along the rear wall. Only a hundred soldiers could be seen spread out by the Parthians along it's battlements.

The Parthians under the command of General Assif containing three thousand of the king's finest fighters stood waiting to attack the rear wall. Along with another thousand conscripts at their rear. Assif didn't want them faltering and getting in the way of his desire for glory, a victory at any cost. He knew failure would cost him his head. He felt very confident seeing how sparsely the wall looked of defenders, all it needed now was the king's order to attack Atticus had moved the bolt throwers from the rear wall and placed them above the main gate having taken his Cilician archers to the rear wall not wanting the gate breached. The battering ram had been hauled inside the fort, so the Parthians were not able to use it again. Asiff had also been emboldened, noting there weren't any deadly bolt throwers on the wall his men faced.

"Won't be long now," said Edelgard, gripping his double-headed axe. Atticus smiled in response; Thaddius was one of the soldiers looking out from the battlements.

"I can see plenty of Parthians well-armed and wearing good armour," said Thaddius, Without turning around. knowing Atticus was crouching holding his bow not far behind him.

"Good looks like we will kill plenty of their finest today," answered Atticus.

The sound of trumpets filled the air outside the fort signalling the Parthian army to attack, and hundreds of drums could be heard pounding out a deafening beat. General Assif gave the order for his men to attack. They immediately marched forward in perfect lines, not like the day before when the Parthians charged the fort screaming in anger.

The Parthians attacked all four walls again, The fort's catapults fired as soon as they came into range. This time they were launching heavy boulders at the enemy.

The bolt throwers and vipers fired their deadly bolts and arrows into the lines of attacking Parthians, killing indiscriminately. Men died, limbs were torn off, bodies were crushed under heavy boulders as the battle for the fort was in full swing.

This time many Parthians carried ladders to scale the walls, having no heavy battering ram to smash the gates open.

"Wait men, not yet let the caltrops start to do their job, Archers wait for my signal. I want all of them engaged in attacking this wall, stay down out of sight. Thaddius felt his heart pounding in his chest, waiting to let Atticus know when to appear at the wall with his archers, not wanting to give the signal too soon." An arrow bounced off his helmet and clattered to the floor in front of Atticus and Edelgard.

"Careful Thaddius, keep your shield up, wouldn't want you losing an eye…you need to keep your pretty look for the ladies," shouted Edelgard.

Nobody moved. Atticus and his archers waited patiently; screams could be heard outside the wall as many of the enemy sliced their feet wide open on the caltrops.

The Parthians now struggled to keep formation as many of their comrades fell, blood pouring into the sand from their feet.

But these were battle-hardened, well-trained men who kept going forward, striding over their dying or maimed comrades. The conscripts marching behind hadn't yet reached the ground laden with caltrops, but death would soon be upon many of them.

Some of the Cilician archers fidgeted with their bows and quivers of arrows, eagerly waiting for the order to join the battle.

King Artabanus and his son Mithridate sat on their horses surrounded by the king's bodyguards. They were impatient, looking for any sign of a breach in the fort's wall.

The king was growing more impatient with every minute, rubbing one of his hands on the golden painted armour covering his left thigh vigorously. He began puffing out his cheeks and wiping the sweat off his forehead with a cloth.

"Send riders to the rear wall, I want to know the moment that wall is breached!" yelled the king.

Four riders were dispatched to circle round to the other side of the fort behind the attacking Parthians. Rows of chariots stood idle with lines of Parthian cavalry behind them. The king wanted them for the fight with Maximus.

Thaddius turned to Atticus.

"They have reached the range of you and your archers!" he shouted eagerly.

"Not yet!" Atticus shouted making sure he could be heard above the sound of the dying screams of the Parthians. Atticus stood up and moved to the side of Thaddius, looking at the advancing enemy lines now no more than several yards from the fort's wall.

"Now with me to the wall but wait for my signal to fire!" shouted Atticus.

Atticus could now see the devastation the caltrops had caused. Scores of Parthians had fallen, many of whom died from the loss of so much blood. Others screamed, holding their feet, trying to stem the flow of blood seeping into the sand.

The conscripts behind were being lashed with bullwhips, forcing them forward, clambering over the dead and dying men in front of them.

Atticus gave the order to fire! as he took aim at an officer and fired, his arrow struck the officer in the face, who then fell face down to the floor.

Hundreds of arrows fired from the Cilician archers struck their targets with ease, but many arrows bounced off the well armoured men. "Aim at the weak points in their armour!" shouted Atticus.

On came the enemy, the archers reloaded their bows with arrows time and time again killing hundreds of the enemy but on they came. Many of the Parthians had reached the base of the wall. Edelgard and Adelar, along with the legionnaires of the Augusta 11 launched their spears down from the walls into the mass of Parthians below.

Asiff, now realising he'd been duped, unsheathed his sword and attacked the wall alongside his men.

He would rather die in battle fighting, than return in disgrace to his king knowing full well he would be executed.

To die in battle meant he died with some dignity and honour; it also gave his men a sense of valour to fight on at their Generals' side.

The battle for the wall was still far from over, ladders were now hurled up against the wall and men started to climb up them gritting their teeth, staring death in the face.

Atticus drew his bow, firing arrows down as fast as he could, aiming at the men climbing the ladders killing many. Down to the ground they fell, landing on their comrades below. Edelgard grabbed the top of a ladder and pushed with all his might, sending it crashing to the ground below with several men falling from it to their death.

Adelar and the other soldiers relentlessly threw spear after spear down at the enemy, killing dozens.

The Cilician archers were running out of arrows fast, Farrokh called for more arrows to be brought quickly.

Then came the Parthians, these men were no cowards, up the ladders they climbed, more ladders were hurled against the wall for men to climb.

It was without doubt a killing field, with bodies piled up littering the floor all around the fort, such was the ferocity of the battle.

Asiff had now reached the fort's wall and climbed, sword in hand, up one of the ladders. He hauled himself up, his strong, powerful legs pumping him up one rung at a time.

As soon as he reached the top, the giant figure of Atticus awaited him, a sword in each hand. Atticus met Asiff head on. He punched both swords into the chest of Asiff with such force they smashed through his armour with ease, killing him instantly.

Atticus then pushed the body of General Asiff over the wall, sending him crashing to the floor. His men, seeing their General die, started to retreat. Many of which were now totally exhausted from the fight which had gone on for well over an hour.

All their blood lust and fighting had evaporated, replaced with fear at the thought of certain death. More arrows had been brought, and any Parthians who had reached the fort's battlement and managed to get inside the fort were killed without hesitation. Their bodies were then thrown back over the wall to the ground below. The Cilician archers now resumed firing arrows into the retreating Parthians; no quarter was given.

This was war, it wasn't a place for the faint hearted, it was kill or be killed. Voices of the men dying below, screaming in pain, filled the air. Some sobbed, crying in the throes of death for their loved ones.

"Archers stay here to protect the wall! I want twenty men to help take our wounded to the infirmary and carry the dead below," shouted Atticus.

The battle for the fort still raged on at the other three walls. "The rest of you line up in columns of two, shields up, swords at the ready follow me. We fight where we are needed!" demanded Atticus.

Edelgard proudly marched at the side of Atticus along the stone walkway of the battlements looking out over the heads of men fighting ferociously keeping the Parthians at bay. Atticus looked down below at the courtyard leading to the prison holding the Parthian prisoners; he could see scores of dead bodies, amongst them several dead Roman soldiers.

Atticus shouted to a group of legionnaires standing below, guarding the prison gates.

"What's happened down there?" one of the soldiers saluted and shouted. "Several of the prisoners overpowered one of the guards, took his keys to the gates and charged out trying to escape. We have them back under control and locked up, sir."

"Good carry on!" replied Atticus.

"Doesn't look like they will breach these walls today," grinned Edelgard, as they approached the front wall above the main gate.

Abbas and his men, under the watchful eye of Tribune Justus, had fought well. The Parthian trumpets sounded calling their men to retreat, the Parthian drums had fallen silent.

"Looks like they have had enough fighting for the day," said Adelar while sheathing his sword.

"It does! our men have fought well, how did it go at the rear wall?" asked Justus, "It all went to plan," answered Atticus.

"Good."

"Where is the legate, Marcellus?" asked Atticus.

"He's gone to the infirmary to check how they are coping with our wounded. We have lost some good men today," replied Justus.

"We have, unfortunately, but a tiny fraction of our enemies' losses. By the looks of it," said Atticus.

"The Parthian king will not be happy, some of his officers will be feeling his wrath shortly I presume," said Justus with a wry smile.

"We better rotate the men from the battlements for food and rest, just in case the Parthians fancy another attack before dark," said Atticus.

"I will organise that myself straight away," answered Justus.

"Come with me Edelgard to the infirmary, we better get a report as to our dead and wounded," said Atticus.

"What do you want me to do?" asked Adelar, "Bathe, you smell like a dead camel's fart." shouted Edelgard grinning. This made many of the soldiers within earshot laugh loudly.

"Adelar, I need you to check and make sure the prisoners are locked up securely. I don't want them to be able to break out again," replied Atticus.

"Yes, I can do that, the prisoners will have more chance of getting up Edelgard's arse than escaping again when I've finished," grinned Adelar in reply. "Good! then you can bathe, Edelgard's right you do smell," replied Atticus, laughing.

"And I thought you were my friend?" shouted Adelar as he descended down from the battlements making his way to the prison with a chuckle.

Atticus and Edelgard made their way to the infirmary and came across Aisha helping one of the Roman auxiliaries make his way to the infirmary. The soldier with an arrow sticking out of his shoulder tried his best to salute Atticus.

"Gooday Aisha, let me help you!" Atticus lifted the soldier up with ease and began to carry him in his strong arms towards the infirmary. "You make things look so easy Atticus," said Aisha smiling, "I'm just glad he's not as heavy as Edelgard," replied Atticus grinning at his friend Edelgard.

The soldier chuckled slightly but winced with pain, "What is your name soldier?" asked Atticus.

"My name is Dacius sir," he answered, again wincing with the pain he felt from his wound.

"Well, Dacius, we are nearly there, and the surgeon will have that arrow out and your wound stitched up in no time."

As they approached the infirmary several soldiers were laid outside on stretchers being attended to by the women of the fort helping the medics.

Atticus glanced to his left and could see at least twenty dead legionnaires laid in a row under blankets which gave him a feeling of pain and sorrow for their loved ones.

Atticus stepped inside the doorway still carrying the wounded soldier and was quickly met by two orderlies.

"Here, sir! Let us take him from you and we will attend to his wound straight away."

Marcellus appeared from a side room, "Ah' Atticus how has today's fight gone?" Marcellus looked tired and sighed as he spoke.

"All is well, sir! It looks like they have had enough for the day, we are rotating the men for food and rest. The heavy weapons are being replenished, more spears and arrows are being taken up to the battlements as we speak. Some prisoners apparently tried to escape during the battle but are now back under lock and key. Do we have the numbers of our dead and wounded?" enquired Atticus.

"Yes, I have the latest report here, but it will need updating slightly as more men are still being brought in." Marcellus fumbled a little with the report before reading it out.

"Up to press we have sixty-seven dead, twenty-four of which are from your Agusta 11 cohort." Marcellus paused to read a little more of the report, "We have a further ninety-two wounded of which fourteen are from the Agusta 11 cohort and according to the surgeon seventeen of the wounded will not see the light of another day."

Marcellus closed the report and looked up at Atticus, "Well, it could be a lot worse the fact that we have been attacked by such a large force for a couple of days now," said Marcellus.

"We must have killed over ten thousand of the enemy by my estimates."

"Sir!" shouted Centurion Cyrus from the doorway while trying to catch his breath.

"What is it you want?" asked Marcellus.

"Several Parthians have approached the main gate under a flag of truce sir."

"We better go find out what the enemy wants," replied Marcellus. Atticus, Marcellus, And Edelgard joined Justus on the walkway above the main gate.

They looked down at the Parthians on horseback below, surrounded by hundreds of dead bodies, many impaled with arrows and spears, some crushed under boulders.

"My name is General Girish, I have been sent by my almighty King Artabanus, king of all Parthia, to request a cessation of hostilities until sunset for the purpose of removing the dead bodies."

"Give me a moment to answer while I discuss this with my officers!" shouted Marcellus in reply.

Marcellus turned to face Atticus out of sight and earshot from below, "What do you think? Could it be a ploy or trickery to catch us off guard. They might try to get waggons close filled with men hidden?"

"It would also be in our interests to have those bodies removed; many of them have been laid there for over two days. In this heat they decompose quickly, and disease might spread if left for too long," answered Justus. Atticus thought carefully for several moments before answering.

"I have to agree with Justus, I don't think they would be so stupid knowing we will be watching their every move from these walls. Any outbreak of disease will affect us just as much as them. Let them take and burn their dead; it can't be long now before Maximus and his legions arrive."

"It is agreed then...Atticus give them our answer. I need to file the reports and rest we will all meet at my quarters after sunset. You will all need to eat and rest, take my advice, but have the walls fully manned while the bodies are being removed."

"Your orders will be carried out sir," answered Justus.

Atticus went back to the wall with Edelgard and looked down at the Parthian General and his escort.

"We will allow you to remove the dead! But mark my words carefully, any sign of trickery will be met without quarter, and I will personally remove your head."

Such was the venom in the words of Atticus it sent a slight shudder down the spine of the General.

Girish bowed his head slightly in acknowledgement, turned his horse and signalled his men to return to their lines and rode off at a gallop.

Atticus ordered Centurion Cyrus and a squad of men to stand outside the main gate, in battle formation and retrieve any dead Roman soldiers who had fallen from the walls.

Atticus and Edelgard went to the bathhouse for a well-earned massage and bathed. One of the servants brought mutton, bread and fruit for them to eat.

Maximus and his legions were camped a short distance away, just far enough out of sight from the Parthians camped all around the fort. They were close enough to the ridge for his battlelines to be deployed at short notice. A scouting party that had been sent out by Maximus the previous night had come across a small group of Parthian lookouts. They were situated on the summit of a small cluster of rocks giving them a good view of the trail leading from Tarsus. A beacon had been constructed ready to be lit if there was a sighting of Maximus's legions to warn the Parthian army. Stupidly they had lit a fire for cooking which was seen by the Roman scouts. The Romans had crept up and killed them while most of them slept. The main Parthian army had no idea how close Maximus was and would soon pay a high price for their folly.

With only a few hours of daylight left, Maximus summoned Yassur and Abdul to a meeting with him.

"I want you both to head for the fort and sneak back in." Yassur looked at Abdul with a feeling of trepidation.

Maximus had noticed the look on Yassur's face.

"I know it will be dangerous, but it is important to get this message to Atticus." Maximus put his hand on his shoulder and handed it to Yassur.

"Yes, General! we will get in the fort…Come! Abdul, fetch that water skin."

Yassur and Abdul quickly left, mounted and rode off in the direction of the fort.

"Marcus have the bolt throwers brought up from the baggage train, I want to prepare our defences along that ridge as soon as it's dark."

"It will be awkward, we're going to be very close to the Parthians, if we are discovered your plan to surprise the enemy will disappear," Marcus replied.

"I know that's why I have sent Yassur and Abdul to the fort with a message for Atticus to cause a distraction at the far side of the Parthians main position."

"Let's hope they get through, it will make our job tonight a lot easier," answered Marcus, who saluted and left to carry out his order.

"Centurion Metelus!" shouted Maximus.

"Sir!"

"Have the other Centurions come to me here quickly!"

"Yes, sir straight away!" replied Metelus.

Maximus had his meeting with the Centurions, giving them their instructions for the night's mission and to prepare the men for the battle tomorrow.

Excitement had filled Maximus's legions upon hearing the news of the following day's battle; they had marched long and hard, and it had not been easy in the heat and harsh terrain. Men sharpened their swords, ate heartily and readied their equipment. The legions had been well-trained and most couldn't wait to get stuck in.

Some of the veterans of many battles were a little more subdued, knowing full well what lay ahead, standing in line, fighting a determined enemy.

Maximus knelt alone in his tent praying to the Roman gods Mars and Jupiter for victory in battle.

Chapter 24

Yassur and Abdul had managed to slip into the Parthian camp unnoticed, such was the disorganisation. Many were having their wounds tended to after days of fighting. They could see the main gate of the fort not too far away from their position, "What plan do you have to get us into the fort?" whispered Abdul, not wanting to be overheard by the many Parthians gathered all around them.

Yassur and Abdul were dressed in very similar attire to most of the poor conscripts in the Parthian army and did not look out of place.

"I'm not sure yet, let me think," Yassur was looking towards the Main gate and could see a group of riders returning to the Parthian lines not far to their left.

"Looks like the Parthians have been having a parley with the Romans at the fort," said Yassur.

"Wonder what that was about?" asked Abdul, while stroking his thin, wispy beard.

"Wish I knew!"

Yassur turned his focus to the Parthians around them wondering whether to ask if anyone knew what was going on, but thought better not draw any attention to themselves.

"We sit here for now and give me time to think," said Yassur, who promptly lay back, resting his head on a small boulder, and closed his eyes, deep in thought.

Half an hour later they were disturbed by a Parthian officer shouting and kicking men sitting on the ground as he walked by them.

"I want volunteers for burial duties to clear our dead comrades from around the fort," he demanded.

Yassur looked at Abdul, realising their chance to get near the fort had come.

"You two lazy buggers, you don't look injured from battle," and promptly kicked Abdul in his side as he lay on the ground pretending not to be taking any notice of the Parthian officer. Abdul groaned, exaggerating the pain he felt.

"Yes, sir, we volunteer, please don't kick me again," Abdul gave a sly wink to Yassur as he got to his feet, rubbing his side.

"Follow me then before I change my mind and kick you harder," Yassur dusted himself off as they both followed the Parthian officer.

"You four you're not injured come with me!" shouted the officer pointing at some men sitting on their left as they passed them by.

Yassur and Abdul were doing their best to try not to look overly enthusiastic and were now joined by the others.

As they walked on, the officer enlisted many more for the burial duty, and they now numbered well over a hundred.

They were escorted to a line of waggons waiting ready to head towards the battlefield around the fort. One of the waggon drivers was giving his team of mules some water.

"Hey, you!" shouted the Parthian officer angrily, the man watering his mules looked up at him in bewilderment. The officer walked towards him, "What do you think you're doing? We're short of water as it is!" bellowed the officer. "My mules have barely eaten for two days and it's their first water today. If you want them to pull these waggons without collapsing, leave me to water them." came the harsh reply.

The officer glared at him but walked away, knowing the waggon driver was probably correct the last thing he needed right now was further confrontation. The task at hand needed to be done and done quickly before nightfall. He made his way to the front of the line of waggons. There were many more men waiting beside the waggons, all were conscripts. The real soldiers were being left to rest for the battle ahead.

"Right, you lazy good for nothing useless sons of whores get those waggons moving we have only to nightfall to clear the dead!" shouted one of the other officers in charge.

Large funeral pyres were being erected in a long ravine behind the Parthian camp, well away from the tents, ready to burn the bodies.

The column of waggons started making its way towards the fort. They began to span out in all directions, bodies were being dragged up from the ground and thrown on the back of the waggons. As soon as a waggon had been filled with bodies it turned and made its way to the ravine. Many of the bodies were quite mutilated. The men lifting them had tied scarves around their mouths and noses. The smell of the rotting flesh was quite nauseating. Some of the waggons were stacked so high with bodies the mules strained pulling their heavy load. This made it hard work for the waggon drivers who now lashed them with whips. The bodies were unloaded, and the pyres were ignited, sending flames shooting upwards.

"Keep moving, stay with the waggons heading nearest the fort's gates," whispered Yassur to Abdul.

The waggons creaked forward, they were slowly getting nearer the fort, now and again they would drag up a body and throw it on the back of a waggon. The heat and smell were quite unbearable.

Abdul kept looking towards the gate getting closer and closer, his heart seemed to be thumping inside his chest. Their eyes flicked from one to the other as they edged nearer the gates.

They could see a line of well-armed Roman soldiers outside the gates, as other Roman soldiers carried their dead comrades inside the fort.

Archers above the gates had strung their bows and waited for any sign of attack on the open gate's.

"You two!" a voice shouted from behind Abdul and Yassur. Abdul turned around, "Pick up more bodies up you lazy buggers we haven't got long before dark!" shouted the waggon driver. He wanted his waggon filled as quickly as possible so he could return to the Parthian lines and out of harm's way.

Abdul and Yasur promptly picked up the half-eaten body, covered in ants feasting on it, and big fat meat flies buzzed about them as they threw it on the back of the waggon.

Yassur judged they were now only fifty yards away from the open gates and line of Roman soldiers. "That's enough, my waggon is full, we need to return!" shouted the waggon master.

"It's only two thirds full," retorted Abdul, "I don't give a fuck, I'm taking it back."

Abdul looked at Yassur, then back at the fort.

"We will wait here for another of those waggons approaching!" shouted Abdul in reply and pointed to two more waggons making their way forward.

"Suit yourself!" replied the waggon master, turning his waggon around. He spat on the floor in front of them as he did so and began making his way back, lashing his mules with his whip.

Yassur looked about surveying the scene he was engulfed in, the stench filled his nostrils, vultures circled the sky above and many more were pecking and feeding on the dead bodies which still littered the ground. Flies buzzed everywhere, ants filled the ground where they stood and crawled looking for another body to feed on.

"Looks like the fighting has been very intense since we left. Come on Abdul, quick, let's get inside that fort." They both walked faster, eager to get safely inside. There were many Parthians collecting their dead not far away from them, but they weren't taking any notice.

"Not far now!" said Yassur, smiling, striding fast towards the line of Roman soldiers.

"Don't get too close! you two unless you want to feel my spear up your arse!" shouted one of the Roman soldiers lined up making the others laugh.

Yassur lowered his scarf from his face and shouted, "I don't think Atticus would be too pleased with you, Thaddius! If you did that."

"Fuck me, Yassur! Get inside quick!" answered Thaddius grinning.

"Stay here, lads, while I take these two to Atticus." All three of them quickly went in, "Atticus is at the bathhouse with Edelgard taking a well-earned rest," said Thaddius. He told Yassur and Abdul most of the events of the previous days after they had left to find Maximus, on the way to the bath house.

Atticus was laid on a table receiving a massage from one of the servants, Edelgard was sitting in the large hot bath drinking from a wine skin.

"Atticus, look who's arrived back," he shouted with glee.

Atticus sat up immediately and said, "Thank the gods. You have returned safely. I've been a little worried to say the least. Where is Abd-El-Kader?"

"I am sorry to inform you that my cousin was killed when we broke through the enemy lines." Yassur sighed and hung his head feeling the pain return in his chest as he spoke.

"I am very sorry to hear that, he was a brave man, and a very good friend, I will miss him dearly, but I will never forget him as long as I live," replied Atticus with a heavy heart.

Edelgard replaced the stopper of his wine skin before discarding it and climbed out of the bath, not happy with the news of ABD's death. Silence filled the room for a while but now was not the time for mourning.

"What news do you have for me?" asked Atticus. Yassur and Abdul sat down on a marble bench that was decorated with all manner of sea serpents. Yassur took off his head scarf, feeling the steam of the bath house fill his nostrils.

Abdul scanned the beautiful, tiled walls and mosaic floor, "Maximus and his legions are camped not far from the ridge, and will prepare it for battle tonight. He needs you to create a diversion as soon as it's dark. Hopefully he won't be discovered by the enemy as he moves his men into place." said Yassur.

Edelgard smiled and shouted, "I think that can be arranged, what say you Atticus?"

"Yes, It's about time we attacked them for a change. They definitely won't be expecting us to come out of this fort and attack them." answered Atticus.

"They seem to be very short of water and supplies from what we saw today," said Abdul.

"I'm not surprised by the number of men and animals they have. Their supply lines must reach all the way to the river Euphrates. That's their main source of water. Food and fodder for the animals will have to come from Parthia. The length of time his army have spent outside this fort will have drained a lot of their resources. Any towns and villages in the vicinity will have been plundered long ago." replied Atticus.

Atticus stood up and began to dress, Edelgard dried himself with a towel before retrieving his wine skin and dressed. When Adelar walked in, "The prison was secure," Adelar claimed.

"Better have your bath then!" said Edelgard.

Adelar then noticed Yassur and Abdul sitting at the far side of the room, slightly obscured by the steam rising from the bath.

"Welcome back my friends, what news of Maximus have you?" asked Adelar, "He has arrived with his legions and is ready to do battle my friend!" answered Abdul.

Atticus and Edelgard quickly finished getting dressed while Yassur told Adelar of the grave news of Abd-El-Kader's death.

"Come we better go inform Marcellus and make preparations for tonight's little diversion," said Atticus heading for the exit.

"What diversion?" asked Adelar.

"I will explain everything on the way to see Marcellus, but we have much to prepare and not much time to do it, come," replied Atticus.

The guards outside Marcellus's quarters stood to attention and saluted as Atticus knocked loudly on the giant doors which were promptly opened from within by one of the servants.

Marcellus was sitting behind his desk eating dates and some fruit "Everything well I hope?" enquired Marcellus.

"Abdul and Yassur have returned with news from General Maximus."

The news made Marcellus stand up from behind his desk with a look of relief, along with an expression of excitement on his face.

"Well don't keep me waiting! Tell me!" demanded Marcellus, "Have you that map?" enquired Atticus.

"Yes, I have it here," replied Marcellus, walking to a table placed at the side of the room with several scrolls laid neatly on it. He picked one up and spread it out on his desk for them all to look at.

The fort was at the maps centre and showed the landscape of the whole area around it as far back as Damascus to the left of the fort's main gate.

The map also showed the river Tigris-Euphrates river system running down to the far rear of the fort between Mesopotamia and Palmyra. It showed Parthia many miles away to the front of the fort, small mountain ranges were scattered about. Some of the larger cities were also shown on the map including Edessa, Carrhae, Seleucia and many more.

"According to Yassur's report Maximus has camped his legions here," Atticus pointed out.

"He plans to fortify that ridge ahead of him and move his men into position there as we planned tonight hopefully and without being discovered."

"That will be rather risky, It's quite close to the Parthians main encampment," replied Marcellus.

"I know that's where we come in, he wants us to create a distraction so he can do it without being discovered."

"And how do you propose to do that? No doubt you have a plan in mind already," enquired Marcellus.

"You are correct! To be frank it's quite a daring plan and before you ask rather dangerous, but they will not be expecting it." Atticus then paused.

"Don't keep us in suspense, Atticus speak on," said Marcellus. Edelgard was standing there also eagerly awaiting Atticus's plan, "Come on, Atticus!" he quipped, grinning.

Atticus smiled as he looked at them both, "I intend to attack the king's tent and their main camp around it!"

"Fuck me!" Edelgard blurted out.

Marcellus stood staring at Atticus unable to answer with his mouth wide open trying to comprehend what he thought he'd just heard.

Atticus smiled and said, "Well, that seems to have got your attention, who dares wins. You two have just confirmed my plan."

"How?" asked Marcellus.

"It's that bold and unthinkable, what better way to distract the enemy, they won't ever expect it."

Atticus paused again, letting his words sink in, "I think I need a drink, pass me that amphora of wine Edelgard?" asked Marcellus.

He then sat down behind his desk as Edelgard poured the wine into several cups. The room went silent for a while before Marcellus, after drinking a full cup of wine, asked, "It is without doubt a very bold plan and how do you propose doing that?"

"Yes, it will be very dangerous, I will require volunteers only, five hundred cavalries to be precise. We attack as soon as it's dark enough, I will have some of the men make large balls of hay coated with flammable liquid. We will have them secured with ropes which will be hauled between two men on horseback. I want at least thirty of these, we charge in ignite and launch the fireballs amongst the tents, hopefully the king's tent as well, setting many alight causing as much mayhem and destruction as possible."

"Then what?" asked Marcellus.

"Then we fight, killing as many as possible, charging within their camp, causing as much panic as we can for as long as we can. Hopefully Maximus will get that ridge manned and ready for Forthcoming battle undiscovered." said Atticus.

"Your plan is very bold…But knowing you, Atticus, if anyone could pull it off, it would be you! I wish you well, go prepare. I will watch from the battlements and pray to Mars and Jupiter that you return safe."

Atticus saluted and left followed by the others, once outside Edelgard said, "Goes without telling me and Adelar volunteer," Atticus smiled at his two friends.

"I had hoped you wouldn't, but I knew you would," responded Atticus.

Everything was quickly prepared; every single man of the Augusta 11 cohort volunteered, including Farrokh and his Cilician archers. Abbas and his auxiliaries of the 111 Gallica and Raphanea all volunteered. Atticus wanted only five hundred so between him and Abass they chose their best riders which included all the Cilician horse archers.

Darkness descended as Atticus and his five hundred men rode out of the fort's gate at a steady trot.

Atticus held one of the ropes, dangling one of the balls of hay tied tightly and doused in flammable liquid, while Edelgard held the other rope. They rode out in a column of twos twenty feet apart with the hay balls hanging between the first sixty riders.

They rode forward at a trot in complete darkness, the men carrying the balls of hay between them also carried a small thick clay pot filled with red hot ashes to ignite them as soon as Atticus gave the order. Torches were not an option; they would only alert the enemy to their presence.

They were now only several hundred yards away from the Parthian lines with the king's tent well behind in the centre of the main camp behind hundreds of tents situated in neat rows. Campfires could be seen but they were able to ride on undiscovered. Atticus nudged Fury to go faster, and the pace picked up.

Atticus gave the order quietly for the cavalry to pan out into one single line.

A shout of alarm rang out from the Parthian lines as Atticus and his men were discovered riding fast towards them.

Farrokh fired an arrow killing the Parthian but many more shouts of alarm rang out into the night sky.

"Charge!" shouted Atticus, they were less than a hundred yards now from the Parthians as arrows and slingshots were now being fired at Atticus and his Roman cavalry.

"IGNITE!" came the order from Atticus and the hot ashes were poured onto the large balls of hay from the clay pots.

Flames sprung up, turning them into fireballs in midair between the two men on horseback hauling them.

Atticus and Edelgard launched theirs forward at the Parthians. It spun ferociously, spitting flames, and landed directly on top of one of the tents, igniting it. Screams could be heard as men clambered out, some with their robes alight, rolling themselves in the sand trying to put the flames out.

The other balls of fire were thrown amongst the Parthians causing chaos, death and destruction.

Fury reared up and stamped on a Parthian, crushing his skull as he charged into the camp. Atticus slashed another Parthian with his sword, sending him falling to the ground holding his face. On one side, the flesh of his cheek had been sliced cleanly off, along with most of his jaw.

Atticus and his men charged amongst the Parthians slashing and cutting the enemy, who were in total disarray. Smoke from the burning tents filling their lungs making it hard for all to breathe.

"Protect the king!" shouted one of the Parthian Generals as the king's tent almost went up in flames, the ball of fire falling short of its target, but still engulfing men in flames. The king clambered out of his bed, pushing one of the two Persian slave girls off him to the floor as he got to his feet.

An officer poked his head inside the tent, "What is going on out there?" shrieked the king while dressing himself.

"We are being attacked!" replied the officer, "By Maximus and his legions?"

"No, my king, Roman cavalry from the fort!"

"THE FORT!" Artabanus replied angrily.

"Yes, my king!" answered the officer, "Stay inside the tent I will surround it with your bodyguards until we gain control. It looks like they are trying to kill you, my king."

"KILL THEM! KILL THEM ALL!" screamed the king. The officer bowed, turned, and went outside.

General Maximus and Tribune Marcus could see flames erupting from within the Parthian camp far in the distance.

"Looks like Yassur and Abdul made it to the fort and Atticus is attacking them from the far side. Quickly have the engineers place the Ballista, and get the men to fortify the ridge!" Marcus saluted and went with Centurion Metellus to carry out his orders. The engineers were already waiting for the order to proceed, and with stealth, speed, and perfection they went about their task.

All along the top of the ridge sharpened wooden steaks were dug into the ground pointing forward.

The Ballista were placed spread out from one end of the ridge to the other, piles of iron bolts tipped with sharp pointed barbed heads were placed behind them.

The task of preparing the defences had been completed an hour before dawn, and Maximus's legions now stood in battlelines. Thousands of shields were now facing the Parthian camp all along the ridge in the darkness of night.

The men of the legions stood in silence, shields on one arm, spear in the other, staring forward showing no emotion, ready to kill or die for Rome.

The archers lined up silently behind the front row, three rows deep, stacks of arrows at their feet, bows held firmly in one hand. Behind them another ten rows of legionnaires were ready and waiting for their turn to join the fight as soon as the order was given.

Maximus sat on his great white stallion in the middle of the legion's standard bearers. Behind him stood twenty men with long trumpets ready to sound the signal for battle. The standard bearer wearing his bear skin was standing just in front of the trumpets along with several Roman officers holding the banners of the Augusta legions.

Marcus had been placed in charge of four thousand cavalry protecting the legions flanks along with five thousand auxiliaries. Thousands of which were the Batavians of Atticus's Agusta 11 legion.

The Parthians still had no idea they were there, such was the fight around the king's tent which was still going on as they stood in silence.

Edelgard pulled his horse up to the side of Atticus who was covered in blood from the fight as was Fury.

"We need to get back to the fort, it will soon be sunrise, the men need to rest for the battle ahead," shouted Edelgard. He was coughing due to the thick smoke drifting in all directions.

Smoke hung in the air and it was hard to see in the dark of night, the fight was raging on, illuminated by the burning fires. Several riderless horses charged around in fear trying to get away from the danger.

"Your right my friend," replied Atticus, breathing hard through a scarf covering the lower part of his face.

An arrow cut the air between the two of them as they spoke, "Fuck me, that was close," said Edelgard with a grin. He then spat at the floor trying to get rid of the bad acrid taste in his mouth from the toxic smoke.

Atticus quickly looked around himself in the dark, the light from the burning tents and fires was diminishing rapidly.

"There he is," Atticus said with a smile.

"Cyrus sound the retreat then make your way back to the fort!" shouted Atticus. Adelar pulled his horse up and joined them, blood pouring from a cut to his arm as the call to retreat went out.

Quickly the Roman cavalry charged their mounts and disengaged from the enemy back out of the Parthian lines and headed for the fort.

"Farrokh! On me!" shouted Atticus, and he quickly joined Atticus, and the others followed by many of his Cilician archers. "We will make a line here and defend the retreat!"

Atticus sheathed his sword and took his bow off his back, knocking an arrow ready to fire at any Parthian who dared charge them.

Atticus's cavalry rode out from the camp passing them by. Abbas pulled his horse up, struggling to slow his breathing.

"Don't stop, get back to the fort with your men!" shouted Atticus.

Abbas, needing no encouragement, dug his heels into his horse and rode back to the fort followed by many of his men.

Several more riderless horses charged out from within the Parthian lines and headed towards the fort instinctively knowing where safety was.

Atticus felt a pain knowing full well every empty horse meant one of his men had been slain, Several minutes passed without any more of his men returning to the fort.

Parthians now appeared from the camp, silhouetted in the light from the fires burning behind them.

Atticus, Farrokh, and his men fired their arrows as soon as they came within range. The arrows punched into many of the Parthians who appeared, tired, choking on the smoke, many died. While others retreated, they had no more stomach for fighting, as soon as they saw many of their countrymen killed by the volley of arrows, they quickly turned and ran back to their lines.

"Come on, let's get back to the fort!" shouted Atticus. Quickly the Cilician archers turned their mounts and headed for the fort's gates. Fury pulled to his left, alerting Atticus to a lone Roman soldier on foot running towards the fort, being pursued by several Parthians baying for his blood. Edelgard and Adelar had set off with the Cilician horse archers and headed for the fort.

Atticus instinctively charged the Parthians with no regard for his own safety and attacked. He drew his blade and slashed the first Parthian nearest the Roman soldier down he went. Atticus straight away drove it hard down into the skull of another. Fury, who didn't need any prompting, trampled over the other. The remaining Parthians turned, running for their lives. Atticus cut down two more of them before heading after the Roman soldier who was too tired to run any further.

Atticus pulled Fury up to his side and thrust his arm down shouting, "Quick grab hold."

The soldier looking up at him didn't need to be told twice. Atticus hauled him up and placed him on Fury who immediately bolted towards the gates. "Thank you, sir," said the soldier, breathing heavily.

"Don't thank me. It was Fury here who noticed you and set off. I had no choice." The soldier smiled.

Edelgard and Adelar galloped to join them.

"I wondered where you'd buggered off to," grinned Edelgard, "No choice Fury spotted him."

"Better get inside," said Adelar.

As soon as they were back safe inside the fort the large gates were bolted behind them. The soldier slipped off Fury and saluted as Marcellus came down the stone steps from the battlements. Atticus dismounted Fury, hugged his long, dark neck and whispered into Fury's ear.

"Well done, my friend" Atticus then kissed Fury's cheek, who promptly shook his mane and nodded his head up and down.

Foam frothed from his mouth, his whole body was covered in sweat, but Fury was still excited and more than capable of doing battle at any given moment.

"Decimus, have Fury, and the other horses rubbed down and bathed, fed and watered. It won't be long before we are in need of them again."

Atticus stretched his long arms up and arched his back feeling a little stiff from battle. Many of his men had already dismounted and were sitting on the floor drinking fresh water, which was being ladled into cups by the women of the fort.

"Wish I had Fury's energy sometimes," said Atticus out loud, "I'm just glad to see your safe return, Atticus." said Marcellus.

"Thank you, sir," replied Atticus.

"Do you think Maximus will be successful?" enquired Marcellus.

"We will know soon enough. can't be much more than an hour until sunrise." answered Atticus.

"You and your men better rest and eat, drink plenty of water. I will prepare the men for battle. How many men do you propose to attack the Parthians with when the battle starts with Maximus and his legions?" asked Marcellus.

Other than the men needed to adequately defend the walls, and the men needed to man the fort's heavy weapons, "Everyone!" replied Atticus.

"That's exactly what I had in mind: we either win or lose this battle today, nothing else matters," answered Marcellus.

"Cyrus, find out who we have lost tonight, and give the report to the legate," Cyrus saluted and left.

"Come you two, we need rest, food and water."

"A cup of wine wouldn't go amiss if you don't mind me saying," said Edelgard, as he followed Atticus and Adelar to their quarters.

Back within the Parthian camp, General Girish had joined Artabanus and the Prince Mithridate in the king's tent.

"We have secured our camp, the Romans have been repelled my king," said General Girish, who then bowed very low and waited for Artabanus to respond.

"It looks like we have underestimated that young Roman Atticus" hissed Artabanus, "He will die, father you have my word and so will all those Roman pigs."

"That may be my son but we cannot take him lightly…Masood paid with his life for seeing nothing more than a boy in uniform. I will not take that chance. He has outmanoeuvred us more than once and whether we like it or not he is a worthy opponent."

Prince Mithridate wanted to ridicule and curse Atticus but decided now was not the time, so he stood in silence.

"I need time to think sunrise will soon be upon us."

"Shall I send for your advisers?" asked General Girish.

"No! I have listened enough to those dithering old fools for too long, leave me I need to think on my own."

"As you wish father," replied the prince who signalled for Girish to leave with him. The prince dismissed Girish and returned to his tent feeling the need to rest after the night's fight with the Romans.

Chapter 25

Dawn had broken, the glare of the sun shone down causing a slight heat haze in the distance. It was already well above 30 degrees and sweat trickled down Atticus's face from under his helmet. Beads of sweat had formed droplets on his brow which dripped onto his tunic. He'd placed a cloth under his helmet to help protect his scalp from the heat of the metal of his helmet; most of his men had done the same.

Atticus was sitting on Fury ahead of two thousand Roman cavalries perfectly formed up in ranks ready to leave the fort. Behind Atticus and his cavalry stood a further three thousand men on foot lined up three abreast all waiting eagerly to march out and fight the enemy of Rome. He had lost twenty-three brave men from the Agusta 11 legion, and sixty-seven men of the 111 Gallica, Raphanea auxiliaries during the night.

Atticus did not like to lose men, but the mission had been necessary and had been successful. He was only 18 years old and hadn't even grown any facial hair yet, which made him look even younger. But the men he led into battle, veteran or not, held him in high regard and would follow him into the gates of hell.

Maximus and his legions could be seen from the fort all along the ridge.

The sun bounced off the polished shields and armour of Maximus's legions, blinding the Parthians facing them. King Artabanus and his son Mithridate had risen from their beds in astonishment at the sight of Maximus and his legions bearing down from the ridge. They had received no warning from their lookouts high up amongst the rocks as to the presence of Maximus's legions. King Artabanus had quickly ordered his chariots and cavalry to form up ready to charge the enemy, feeling quite confident his army outnumbering the Romans would win the day.

Artabanus couldn't understand why Maximus had made his stand there, it was only a slight slope to the ridge. It was too far from the fort's heavy weapons to give him any support. General Girish tried to voice his concerns but was immediately rebuked and told not to speak. The king was in no mood to heed advice from any quarter; he sensed victory.

General Girish had realised the advantage of the windswept sand filling the slope making it appear less of a hill to climb but would impede the chariots and cavalry. The sand had formed there over many years, it was deep, soft and the wheels due to the weight of the chariots would sink and the horses would struggle to maintain a good pace up what looked like a gentle slope.

Artabanus had placed over fifteen thousand men under the command of General Kareem facing the fort hoping to prevent any assistance to Maximus getting through.

But he had no idea that the V1 FERRATA, RAPHANEA and JUDEA legions were hidden out of sight ready to attack their right flank. And unbeknownst to even Maximus.

The V1 Ferrata legion had been joined by the Mesopotamian ruler Abdulaziz, ruler in name only; he was a client king subservient to Roman rule. He was one of the descendants of Ashurbanipal, once a great king of Mesopotamia who ruled hundreds of years prior to the invasion by Rome. Abdulaziz had brought with him over ten thousand men of the various tribes living throughout the land. They were great horsemen who prided themselves with the best trained horses of all the eastern provinces and their riding skills were second to none. Artabanus had previously tried to get the Mesopotamians to rise up against their Roman rulers and join with the Parthians but thus far it had been to no avail. Abdulaziz was quite happy to pay tribute and taxes to Rome, he had made himself rich with the sale of well-trained horses.

Many of which he sold to the Roman legions at quite a healthy profit in gold and silver.

"Looks like that attack last night was only a distraction allowing Maximus to form his battle lines," Artabanus stated while sitting on his horse. Artabanus gave the order to attack Maximus.

Five hundred chariots were ready to lead the attack followed by ten thousand Parthian archers on horseback under the command of General Girish and Asif who was his second in command. The Parthian horseback archers were feared for their deadly accuracy and skill at firing arrows fast while riding at great speed. Behind them marched a further twenty thousand infantry carrying long spears, curved swords could be seen hanging from their belts. These were all well-trained men; many having fought in previous battles for their king.

Artabanus had placed all his untrained conscripts to cover his right flank. He had no reason to fear an attack on his right. The chariots kicked up clouds of dust as they picked up speed and headed towards the Roman lines. Asif led the horse archers charging forward, staying well behind the chariots.

General Girish had boarded one of the chariots to lead the attack on the Roman lines; he knew it would probably lead him to certain death but if Artabanus lost the battle he would be executed anyway. The riders under the command of Asif had to hold their mounts back from getting in front of the heavy chariots. They had sharpened blades spinning from the centre of their wheels which would slice through the horses' legs. Artabanus was counting on his chariots to smash holes through the Roman lines and make it easy for his cavalry and infantry.

The visibility for the infantry marching behind was very poor, as the choking sand dust kicked up by the horses filled the air, but regardless they marched on pulling scarves up covering their mouths to help keep the dust out. The chariots reached the incline in front of the Roman lines and charged upwards.

It wasn't long before their pace slowed, losing momentum as the wheels sank into the deep drifting sand, even the horse archers' mounts struggled to keep a good pace.

On they went, trying their best to gain traction and speed, but to no avail. Maximus, looking down at them from his mount above his lines of men, shouted the order for his archers to ready their bows.

"It seems the slope is working to our advantage," said Tribune Marcus looking across from his position on the left flank.

The Parthians were now only two hundred yards away from the front ranks of the Roman lines. The horses pulling the chariots were panting heavily as they were being whipped forward by the charioteers. Foam dripped from the horse's mouth, eyes bulging under the strain. The poor horse's eyes bulged even wider due to the pain they felt from the lash of the whips, blood trickled down their hind legs.

"ON! ON!" screamed one of the charioteers, whipping his two horses mercilessly.

One of the horses suddenly reared up, causing the chariot to tip over sideways, spilling its occupants out. One of them was immediately stamped on by a horse pulling one of the other chariots, breaking several of his ribs. Another occupant of the chariot tried to stand up but was sliced in two by the blades on the wheels of another chariot, unable to go around him, blood and entrails splattered the sand. The Parthian horse riders began to fire their arrows above the chariots at the Roman lines realising they were not getting anywhere fast and were now within range of the Roman archers.

Some found their targets and several Roman soldiers fell forward, dying from the barbed arrows hitting them, but most of the arrows bounced off the large Roman shield wall. Maximus decided the Parthians were close enough and gave the order for his archers to fire. The iron bolts from the Roman Ballista had been fired as soon as the chariots had come within range 500 yards away from their lines, with devastating effect. Large arrow tipped bolts ripped through anything in their path causing death and destruction. The wall of arrows descended down into the attacking Parthians, killing them without mercy. The slope was now in total chaos as the Parthians still made their way forward.

Bolt after bolt was fired from the Ballista killing men and beasts without discrimination. Arrow after arrow struck their targets. The horse archers worked hard and were doing their utmost to return the fire and close the distance between the two armies. One of the bolts struck General Girish, taking his head clean off. More Roman soldiers were killed in the front row but were quickly replaced from the rear ranks and with speed and precision the battle for the ridge was in full swing. The legate Marcellus watched from the fort's battlements as Atticus led his men out of the fort.

Tribune Justus led the Roman ranks of legionnaires marching out on foot; he decided not to mount his horse, wanting to march in the centre of his front rank. The standards of the two legions bristled ceremoniously in the light wind, barely kicking up dust from the sand beneath the feet of the marching Romans. Atticus charged to his left to try and out flank the Parthian lines blocking their path to Maximus. The Parthians were out of range of the fort's catapults and heavy weapons. That battle would have to be fought without them. They were outnumbered at least three to one as the Parthians waited under the command of General Kareem for the Romans to come into range.

The legate Marcellus watched as the battle unfolded. It wasn't long before the Parthians began to fire arrows and slingshots at Atticus's cavalry now passing on the right flank of General Kareem and his men. Atticus drew his bow along with his Cilician archers and began to fire arrows indiscriminately at their foe as they rode fast trying to encircle their enemy's flank. The Parthian archers fired arrow after arrow as fast as they could and a couple of Atticus's men were struck and killed, but many of the Parthians were felled by the arrows fired by Atticus and his men. Justus and the men on foot were now in range of the Parthian archers and quickly formed wedges to penetrate the Parthian lines.

Shields were held above and around them, protecting them from the arrows now falling upon them. On they marched in perfect order, arrows bouncing off their shields, unable yet to gain access to Roman flesh. This seemed to anger and frustrate General Kareem, who bellowed out further orders to fire with more accuracy. Men marching inside the Roman formation as soon as they became in range quickly threw their spears at the Parthians then returned their shields back in place to block the Parthian arrows. Now spears that were thrown relentlessly at them. The Roman shields and armour were by far better than anything the Parthians had.

This gave the Romans a lot more success at killing their foe while only wearing light armour and holding small wicker shields. The Roman spears penetrated the Parthian armour quite easily, and it wasn't long before they punched their shields into the Parthian lines forcing their way through. The short swords of the Romans came into play slicing through the narrow gaps between their shields and into the soft flesh of their foe who fell dying at their feet. The Roman killing machine marched forward trampling on the dead and dying Parthians, killing them without mercy.

Justus and his men had formed into five large wedges, they had all successfully carved their way easily into and through General Kareem's men. Atticus and his cavalry had finally outflanked Kareem's men and charged in amongst them, killing at will. Atticus slashed one of his two swords down to his right, then down to his left, killing the enemy without mercy, cutting through flesh and bone. The giant physique of Atticus charging in on his black ferocious stallion put the fear of death firmly into their hearts.

They tried as hard as they could to get out of their way, not wanting to face the one they called the Demon of Rome. Edelgard, charging in at the side of Atticus, had chosen to use a double-headed heavy hammer and bludgeoned his way through the enemy. Adelar joined in the killing spree with his sword, stabbing and slashing his foe. Thaddius rode with fine skill and hacked the enemies all around him using his oval shield to protect himself from the many Parthian blades trying to kill him, but for now at least he prevailed and was able to kill many Parthians that dared to get too close for comfort. Atticus and his many cavalry were now beginning to take control and gain the upper hand, no quarter being given.

The legate Magnus Cassius Antonius, leading the V1 Ferrata, Raphanea and Judea legion had now joined the battle, hitting the Parthians' other flank. The Parthians were taken totally by surprise, not expecting an attack on that flank.

Abdulaziz and his horse soldiers tore a great hole within the Parthians' poorly equipped conscripts. Many of whom began to flee in any direction other than to stand and fight. Mithridate screamed while pointing in the direction of the new threat.

"Over there, Father! Look, our men run!" Artabanus turned to his right and could just make out the figure of Abdulaziz leading his men cutting their way through.

"That fucking dog Abdulaziz has joined the Romans! If I ever get my hands on him, I will tear him from limb to limb and feed him to the rats!" Artabanus nudged his mount forward to gain a better view of his men fighting on the slope facing Maximus.

"If we're not careful all will be lost!" screamed Artabanus, the battle on all fronts carried on ferociously.

General Kareem looked all around at the slaughter of his men, barely managing to keep some sort of order.

He could plainly see the battle would soon be lost; he quickly turned his mount and rode fast towards his king.

Weaving his way through the men fighting for their lives, a spear thrown from one of the Roman cavalries barely missed him by inches.

"MY KING!" he bellowed, as he pulled his horse up in front of King Artabanus and the prince surrounded by their bodyguards and advisers.

"What Kareem? Why are you here and not with your men?" shrieked the king angrily.

"I fear all is lost and if we don't retreat back to Parthia now, we will have no chance of reaching our homeland!" replied Kareem. He lowered his head, blood pouring down his left arm from a nasty wound.

Artabanus was stunned into silence at what he had heard from his most trusted General, and after a few moments of reflection he looked and surveyed their situation taking place all around.

The battle for the ridge had floundered; Maximus's legions were pushing the king's men back down the slope with ease. He could see Roman cavalry charging round the chariot's right flank; what was left of them would soon be engulfed and cut off from retreat.

The flank covered with his conscripts had disintegrated, some still fought bravely But we're by far no match for the Roman legion and Mesopotamian horse soldiers who were killing with impunity.

The men holding the king's flank under the command of General Kareem were barely managing to hold but he could see it would collapse at any moment.

Artabanus looked at his son then returned his gaze towards Kareem, "Yes, I'm afraid you are right all looks lost," he sighed deeply. He then looked down at his most trusted advisor Basheir and without a moment's hesitation slit his throat.

"Have the trumpets sound retreat, gather what belongings you can retrieve from my tent, we leave for Parthia immediately. Send riders ahead and have our troops at the border ready themselves in case the Romans decide to attack and venture into Parthia," said Artabanus in dismay.

"Why did you kill Basheir Father?"

"I'm tired of his advice, look what it has brought!" The sound of trumpets blared out the call to retreat as the king and his party of bodyguards charged their horses towards the road home to Parthia. General Kareem turned his horse and galloped back to his men. They still fought against Atticus and his cavalry, some of whom now heard the sound of retreat and began to flee. Others chose to stand and fight rather than be killed running from their foe. General Kareem had decided to stay and fight with his men; he felt there was no honour in retreat.

He had told his king to leave; he felt it was his duty to inform the king all was lost hoping the king would live to fight another day. Kareem charged at Atticus wanting to kill the young Roman who he regarded as the one responsible for the Parthian defeat or die trying. Atticus turned Fury to face the challenge of Kareem bearing down on him which he met head on. Kareem lashed at Atticus with his sword, who blocked it with ease and sent him crashing to the ground. His horse bolted leaving Kareem lying on his back staring up out at Atticus sitting on Fury above him.

"Leave him!" shouted Atticus to several of his men charging forward to kill Kareem. Most of the Parthians who hadn't heeded the order to retreat were now dead, and the few who remained dropped their weapons in surrender. Atticus slid down from Fury and stood towering over General Kareem. He looking up at Atticus in defiance, filled with hatred for his Roman adversary.

"It seems you have a great wish to kill me!"

General Kareem curled his lips, "I do!" he snarled in response.

Atticus kicked Kareem's sword towards him, Kareem looked at his sword now only inches away from the grasp of his right hand. He made no attempt to take it and returned his gaze to Atticus.

"Get up, pick up your sword, I will give you that chance."

Kareem looked around at all the Roman soldiers standing around encircling both Atticus and himself.

"Don't worry, Parthian, they will not harm you. If you kill me, they will let you leave and return to Parthia."

Kareem quickly grabbed his sword and jumped up, backing off slightly from Atticus before pointing his sword at Atticus.

Without warning he lunged at Atticus who simply side stepped it leaving Kareem to slice thin air. Atticus slowly drew one of his swords, raising it above his head and waited for Kareem to attack him. Kareem looked around at the faces of the Roman soldiers who were watching the fight unfold in silence. Edelgard gave Kareem a smile. He knew there would be only one winner today and that was not going to be Kareem. His smile and the silence of the Roman soldiers seemed to unnerve Kareem who swallowed hard. He returned his attention to Atticus, still standing with his sword above his head. Kareem lunged forward again, slashing his sword first left then right to no avail Atticus parried them without blinking. Atticus stepped to his left slightly and raised his sword above his head once more. Kareem was now breathing heavily but attacked Atticus again with all his might.

Atticus spun on the balls of his feet, punching his sword through Kareem up to its hilt, and withdrew it all in one motion. Kareem fell to his knees, dying, blood flowing down his body from the gaping wound in his chest. It soon formed into a pool of thick red liquid; Kareem's body fell forward face down. Thaddius led the cheers from the ranks of the Augusta 11 legion who now broke their silence.

The Parthians had fully disengaged from fighting the Romans all over the battlefield and turned tail in an unorganised retreat; many were killed trying to flee; the battle for Tadmor was over.

Tribune Marcus rode fast to meet General Maximus, "The battle is won, General!" he shouted on arrival.

"Look, the Parthian king flees the battlefield!" shouted Centurion Metelus, his hands on his hips struggling to catch his breath back from all the fighting on the ridge.

Maximus clasped forearms with Marcus in jubilation as his men cheered, thrusting their swords dripping with blood into the air.

Many of the Parthians still on the battlefield fell to their knees, discarding their weapons and begged for mercy. Some were killed before Maximus ordered his men to take prisoners. They were rounded up under the watchful eye of the legate Marcellus who had rode out from the fort as soon as it had become apparent victory was assured.

The Mesopotamian horse soldiers were not so forgiving; they took no prisoners and killed without mercy.

Maximus rode slowly across the battlefield; vultures had already begun to feed but archers from the fort fired arrows killing them not wanting their dead comrades to be eaten. Atticus had knelt down beside the lifeless body of Tribune Justus, fallen doing his duty fighting for Rome.

As Maximus rode across the battlefield which stretched for over a mile in any direction he surveyed the aftermath. Mutilated bodies could be seen lying everywhere. He looked down at the carcasses of dead horses laid out for all to see, men groaning in pain seeking help; those who were too badly injured and beyond help were quietly put out of their misery and sent to the afterlife.

The bodies of the dead were now being relieved of any weapons and valuables; the spoils of war always went to the victor.

Broken chariots burned, sending smoke trails into the blue sky.

"The aftermath of battle is not a pretty sight, Metelus," Maximus said to him as he made his way towards the figure of Atticus who he could see not too far away in the distance.

"It is not...but inevitable...I'm just happy we have prevailed. Our emperor will be glad of the victory and surely honour you and the legions on our return," replied Centurion Metelus.

Who was riding at Maximus' side along with a section of Praetorian guards for the Generals protection. They nudged their mounts on, weaving in and out of the dead men and horses. Atticus stood up and turned around upon hearing the horses' hooves approaching, clattering the ground behind him.

Maximus jumped down and immediately embraced Atticus.

"It is good to see you well! I hope none of that blood covering you from head to toe is yours?" asked Maximus.

He looked to see if there was a wound to the body of Atticus.

"I don't think so, I'm not in any pain," replied Atticus, smiling at the sight of his General.

"Metelus, you old bugger you're a sight for sore eyes," said Atticus with a smile.

"Thank you for complimenting me young Atticus...Oh! I mean sir. Didn't mean to forget my manners," answered Metelus, puffing out his cheeks with a grin.

"Nonsense, my good friend, I'm just glad you're here safe at last and able to celebrate our victory," replied Atticus.

"Where are Edelgard and that upstart Adelar not killed I hope?" asked Maximus.

"No, they're both fine. Edelgard has taken charge of the Parthian Prisoners and has them collecting their dead comrades for burning. We don't want an outbreak of disease. And as for Adelar, your guess is as good as mine; he's probably relieving the dead Parthians of their valuables as we speak," said Atticus grinning.

"Metelus, go find the legate Marcellus. I will meet him at his quarters shortly," ordered Maximus.

"You will probably find him at the infirmary assisting the medics with our wounded. He's a trained physician also by all accounts," shouted Atticus.

"I have instructed Centurions Cyrus and Decimus to make reports as to our casualties as quickly as possible," said Atticus.

"My legate Quintus is doing the same, so hopefully, by nightfall, we will know the fighting capabilities of our legions just in case the Parthians decide to counterattack," replied Maximus.

"That will not be likely, they have suffered heavy losses not just today but since we arrived here," said Atticus with a smile.

Maximus looked at Atticus and returned his smile.

"Yes, so I have been informed by Yassur and Abdul. I hear some of your ideas were a little unorthodox but very effective. I rather liked your idea to load the waggons with archers to protect the women and children and get them into the fort safely. It was a shame that Abd-El-Kader was killed."

"It was," replied Atticus solemnly.

Hundreds of horses came into view crossing the battlefield, "Who is that, I wonder?" asked Atticus.

"That looks like the Legate of the V1 FERRATA, RAPHANEA and JUDEA legion from Damascus along with Abdulaziz, our proxy ruler of Mesopotamia. He is well respected by the many tribes wandering this land. And a good ally of Rome by the looks of those horse soldiers, they fought well alongside each other. I had no idea he was joining the battle until I could see them on the battlefield!" exclaimed Maximus.

"I wondered why the Parthians' far flank seemed to disintegrate causing the Parthians to run so early in the fight," replied Atticus.

"Early on, that battle raged on for over four hours," said Maximus with a grin. Atticus laughed in response and said, "It didn't seem that long to me," The large force pulled up in front of Maximus and Atticus.

The legate saluted and introduced himself.

"Good day, General Maximus, I am Magnus Cassius Antonius, and may I also introduce our ally and loyal subject of Rome, Abdulaziz, ruler of Mesopotamia."

He was ruler in name only, Rome ruled Mesopotamia under the Emperor Augustus, and Abdulaziz bowed his head to Maximus in greeting, then turned his attention to Atticus, who had recognised him.

"Greetings to you, young Atticus. When I heard of a young ferocious warrior going by the name of Atticus who had arrived from Rome, I knew it could be no other than the young man who saved mine and that of my son lives on the road from Ostia," said Abdulaziz, again bowing his head with a smile.

"You told me that day you were a merchant but to be honest I knew there was more to you than that, but couldn't quite put my finger on it," replied Atticus.

"It is an honour to be in your company again and it pleases me to see you are wearing the ring I gave you that day! I owe you an explanation. The assassins had been sent by my brother who wished to ally my army to Parthia for gold saying Rome had become weak and was only interested in fornication. He told me Rome was now only interested in fucking young boys at orgies rather than fighting. I travelled to Rome to see for myself and found out my brother was talking out of his arse."

"My brother alas is dead and his soul wanders aimlessly between this life and the next." Abdulaziz bowed his head again towards Maximus.

"Atticus has the knack it seems, to be in the right place, at the right time," replied Maximus. Assassins and mercenaries were easily to be found throughout the empire and beyond who offered their services to the highest bidder.

"Well, I must return to my wives. I'm sure they will be missing my attention," said Abdulaziz, causing laughter amongst his men.

"So, I bid you farewell, I have given Magnus five hundred of my men as a further gesture to Rome of my allegiance to fight as auxiliaries in his legion. I hope that will please your Emperor Augustus?"

"It will!" replied Maximus.

Abdulaziz bowed and rode off, making his way back to Nineveh.

"What are your plans, Magnus?" asked General Maximus.

"First, I need to replace the men at our border outposts and refortify them. Then with your leave I will return to carry out my duties for Rome at Damascus," replied Magnus.

"Good, I will make a report of your action here and present it to the emperor on my return."

"It has been an honour to meet you Atticus and I have no doubt at some point I will hear of your exploits fighting for Rome over the years to come," Magnus saluted both Maximus and Atticus.

They both returned the salute given to them by Magnus and watched in silence as Magnus and his men disappeared.

Maximus and Atticus rode back into the fort to a rapture of cheers from the men on the battlements joyful for the victory.

"Where is Tribune Marcus?" enquired Atticus as they rode.

"He is following the Parthian retreat making sure they leave our borders and any who don't will be slain," replied Maximus.

Atticus took Fury to the stables and made sure he was fed, watered and cleaned after which he went to the bath house to clean and put on a clean uniform before joining Maximus at Marcellus's quarters.

The reports had been completed; the Romans had lost over two thousand men with a further six hundred wounded. Over three hundred of them would never again be able to fight for Rome due to their injuries. Many would be given land and paid to enable a reasonable life and live out their days in retirement. But unfortunately, those who were not citizens of Rome would end up begging on the streets or seeking aid from family members. This caused Atticus some discomfort; he thought all those injured in the service of Rome should be looked after wherever possible.

After the meeting, Atticus took Maximus to the strong room.

"By the gods, Atticus, such wealth," said Maximus, gazing at the open chests of gold and silver.

"It's the ransom paid by Artabanus for the release of his son," replied Atticus.

"I can't believe he would pay such a huge ransom," said Maximus, still gazing at the treasure.

"He expected to take this fort and retrieve it," answered Atticus grinning.

"This will please Augustus, He likes a good victory to please the people of Rome, but victories come at a cost and this little lot will by far pay for this campaign and many more in the future," replied Maximus.

"When do you plan to return to Rome?" enquired Atticus, Maximus smiled before responding.

"Itching to get back to that lovely wife of yours?"

Atticus felt his cheeks redden.

"It would be nice," said Atticus.

"We will leave within the next few weeks. We need to allow time for the wounded to be well enough for the arduous journey. Messengers have already left for Rome with my reports of the campaign and its success. All that is needed now is to make sure our forts are properly manned and our eastern border secure. Marcellus has his orders. I've sent instructions to all the other forts so they will be fully aware. I expect our eastern border will never be so easily overrun again. With any luck we should be back in Rome within the next couple of months." Atticus was happy doing his duty for Rome but was also eager to see his family.

Chapter 26

Maximus was true to his word—several weeks later, they had left Tadmor and the eastern provinces behind. The voyage back had been uneventful; many of the wounded were recovering well. The Roman armada carrying Maximus's legions was now entering the port of Ostia.

Crowds of people lined the hills overlooking the great harbour which was crammed full of onlookers shouting in jubilation at their victorious return.

Atticus stood proudly at the side of General Maximus on the main deck of the flagship named 'IMPERIUM' meaning 'POWER' as it approached the harbour.

It slowly glided through the water, not even a slight swell of the ocean could be felt, the large canvas sails had been tethered. The ship was being powered forward by over four hundred oarsmen sitting on wooden benches, five men to each oar.

Their long ores plunging in and out of the water with hardly a splash, they cut the water at a perfect angle in then out again.

The boom of a large drum beating a rhythm to the speed of the ore could be heard from below, as slaves shackled with chains around their ankles toiled with the task.

Any failure by them to do so was met with a lash from a whip and a threat of death by one of the sailors in charge keeping a watchful eye on them.

Many of the men in chains were prisoners taken in the battle of Tadmor, some of whom now wished they had died in battle.

The pain they felt from the whip, and the strain of the hard work was taking its toll many stared blankly as if in a trance.

Atticus had said his farewells to Abbas, Aisha, and little Ava, promising one day to return if destiny allowed and the cards played their hand.

Edelgard and Adelar stood with Tribune Marcus, leaning on the handrail of the ship, absorbing the celebration of their return, drinking a fine wine.

Many of the ship's crew waved to the crowds lining the harbour walls, some recognising their loved ones waiting for them to dock.

"Well Atticus, can you see your wife and Romulus?" asked Maximus.

"I sent correspondence before we left telling them to stay at the farm. I knew there would be huge crowds, and I didn't want Naomi getting pushed and shoved amongst them; she's quite tiny," replied Atticus.

"Most people standing by your side look tiny?" said Maximus grinning.

"I want our reunion in a more private setting, and that would mean you would have to give me a few days leave before attending the emperor's victory parade and celebrations," replied Atticus.

"That's very clever of you!" replied Maximus smiling, "Yes, you can have three days, and I suppose Edelgard, and Adelar will want to accompany you?" enquired Maximus.

"They do," said Atticus, laughing.

"So, you three have already discussed this?"

"We have and Adelar has made a bet with Edelgard as to how long we get to stay at my home before returning to duty."

Maximus couldn't stop himself from bursting into a fit of laughter.

"I might bloody well have known, what are the odds," asked Maximus "four to one you give us two days," grinned Aticus in reply.

"Looks like Edelgard wins for a change, and about time, you know Adelar will sulk for hours he's not used to losing."

The ores were pulled in as the ship gently nudged the harbour wall, and the large planks were placed for them to disembark. The throng of people cheered even louder when they saw Maximus and Atticus walk down the gangplank. The soldiers on duty were struggling to hold the crowds back. It wasn't long before Atticus, Edelgard, and Adelar, were riding their horses fast for home.

Fury was extremely excited to be going home, just as much as Atticus; they were spotted not far from home and the large gate was flung inwards as the whole household ran out to greet them.

Atticus jumped down from Fury and hugged Romulus.

"Careful lad, you're crushing me! You don't know your own bloody strength." bellowed Romulus.

This made everyone laugh. Atticus let go of Romulus and turned his attention to his petite wife Naomi, who was standing waiting patiently, smiling.

He stood in awe noticing the large swelling of her womb, speechless he just gazed at her beauty.

"Would someone slap my son out of his trance?" shouted Romulus.

"Yes, my love, I am with child, twins to be precise according to the physician."

Atticus gently took hold of her and kissed her softly, "Don't worry, I won't break," said Naomi, her face beaming with love and happiness at Atticus, so glad he had returned safe and was now in her arms.

Everyone stood waiting eagerly to greet Atticus, and as soon as it was their turn hugged him regardless of their status within the household. Atticus had never regarded the servants as slaves. Zuma clasped Atticus's forearm and said, "You seem to have grown a little since you left…but it looks like you still haven't started to shave yet my little friend." Zuma promptly rubbed his hands on the bare face of Atticus causing laughter.

Atticus rubbed the bald head of Zuma and teased, "Looks like you still cannot grow any hair my big friend." Both of them embraced each other, they would always have a bond and a friendship that would never be broken in this life or the next.

Atticus quickly embraced Julia, then Lydia, he then lifted Aramea up off her feet into the air.

"I hope you have prepared a fine dinner for us all!" shouted Atticus teasing her.

"I have! now put me down you big oaf! or you're not having any," replied Aramea before kissing his forehead as he gently placed her on the ground. Atticus hugged and kissed Seema, and now noticed standing behind the throng of people Misha and Castus waiting their turn to welcome him home.

Misha stood looking at him proudly with her fat rosy cheeks, and a smile on her face that brought back the many memories of his childhood living at the small bakery. They hugged as tears flowed down Misha's rosy cheeks. Atticus then lifted up little Alesandro who'd been standing holding Lydia's hand, "Well, my little man, have you been behaving yourself while I've been away?"

"I have!" he replied gleefully.

"In that case you can have the gift I have brought you."

"What is it? what is it?" Alesandro asked excitedly, his eyes wide open.

Atticus walked over to Fury carrying little Alesandro, lifted up the flap of one of his saddlebags and took out a large wooden carving of the Roman flagship

IMPERIUM. Atticus had one of the ship's crew skilled in the art of wood carving make it while on the ship's return journey to Ostia.

Alesandro jumped down from the arms of Atticus and proudly lifted it up for all to see. Alesandro loved anything to do with the sea. He wanted nothing more than to sail the seas when he grew up to discover new lands and any wonders not yet found.

"LOOK! LOOK!" he shouted to everyone, and was quickly surrounded by his new family, Atticus clasped the forearm of Doukasi who was now able to welcome Atticus home.

Edelgard and Adelar had now dismounted and joined in with the homecoming.

"Where's the wine, Romulus?" shouted Edelgard.

"Don't worry my German friend, there is plenty awaiting us in the house, come everyone let's go inside!" shouted Romulus. Everyone other than Atticus and Naomi made their way indoors. They wanted some time to spend alone.

Atticus and Naomi, now that they were alone, kissed each other passionately and spent the next hour talking about Atticus's exploits sitting on one of the stone benches by the fountain. Atticus had kept the more gruesome details to himself. Naomi knew he was a soldier of Rome but was quite happy not pressing Atticus for anything to do with the fighting. They also discussed names for both boys and girls depending on what the gods would bless them with.

It was a night of gentle lovemaking between two people who'd grown up together, loving one another since they first met.

Laughter went on in the main house into the early hours, as Edelgard and Adelar told everyone of their travels throughout the empire to Tadmor and back.

Adelar had told them of the day of the shark attack and the death of the sailor almost being bitten in two. The look of horror on their faces as the story unfolded seemed to make Adelar exaggerate a little, not that it really needed any.

The three days passed by so quickly and it wasn't long before they had returned to the fort in Ostia.

Naomi would stay at their home until after the parade and celebrations and would then return with him to their married quarters at the fort.

Maximus had all the legions preparing themselves for the victory parade through Rome ending up at the emperor's palace in two days' time.

Maximus had already had a meeting with the Emperor Augustus, and had taken the large treasure of gold and silver as payment for Mithridates release.

Which had gone down very well with the emperor and put him in a very good mood.

Soldiers polished and cleaned their weapons and armour; their uniforms were cleaned of blood and dirt. They needed to look their best for the parade. If they didn't they would no doubt receive a clout from their Centurion with his vine stick.

New recruits were going through their paces but would not be attending the parade. This was to be attended by the men who had fought for victory; it was to be their day and theirs alone. A contingent of marines and crew from the ships were to represent the Roman navy, and were now stationed at the fort until the celebrations were over.

The day before the victory parade the emperor Augustus had sent a guard of honour to Romulus's homestead to escort Romulus and his wife Julia, along with Naomi, Zuma and Lydia to be his guests of honour and would stay the night at the grand palace. Julia and Lydia took charge of their preparations, choosing what gowns they would wear, and a lavish tunic for both Romulus and Zuma to wear.

Romulus and Zuma had pinned their medals to their tunics they had been awarded during their service to Rome.

Thunder and blaze had been groomed and had their manes plaited, and Julia and Lydia both inspected their men to make sure they were up to scratch.

Romulus protested at their interference but realised the less said the better, both Romulus and Zuma had a knack for knowing when to shut up.

As they were escorted through the palace gates, Naomi felt a little overwhelmed at the beauty of the palace, having only ever seen it from a distance.

The courtyard alone, leading to the stone steps and ornate marble pillars stretching the full length of the palace front, was big enough for thousands upon thousands of people to stand and observe the celebrations.

Romulus and his party were escorted up the vast stone steps leading to another large area outside the main palace doors.

In the middle sat a golden throne draped in the finest purple silk money could buy; two great marble statues had been placed at either side of the throne looking down towards the vast courtyard.

For the moment it was quiet, the only sound to be heard was the song of birds sitting on the edge of the palace roof.

The statues were of the gods Mars and Jupiter, the statue of Mars, the son of Jupiter and God of war, held a golden spear. His father Jupiter held a golden bow pointing skywards. Julia gazed at the statues and complemented how beautiful they looked with the sun glinting off the golden spear and bow.

"Yes, they are quite magnificent, aren't they?" a voice echoed from the palace door, as two Praetorian guards held them wide open. Emperor Augustus walked out greeting his guests.

The soldiers escorting Romulus and his party quickly stiffened their backs and saluted, standing to attention.

Romulus and Zuma knelt down on one knee, Julia, Lydia, and Naomi curtseyed and bowed their heads not daring to look the Emperor Augustus in the eye.

"Come, come, my honoured guests no formality is needed from the wife and family of Atticus, saviour of my favourite General, Victor of Rome's most recent battle. And between you and me has made me a lot wealthier! Sit here all of you on these wonderful couches!" Augustus waved and beckoned them to come forward, and he himself sat upon one of them out of the sun's glare. The emperor was wearing a fine white toga with a thick purple stripe around its edges. He wore sandals with golden cotton embroidery on the white leather straps encircling the lower part of his bare legs.

As they walked forward towards the couches, Augustus patted a cushion at the side of him, and said softly, "Naomi please if you would, sit here beside me."

Naomi smiled at her emperor while trying not to blush.

"Thank you, Emperor, it would be my pleasure," she replied gracefully and sat down.

"It would really please me if for at least the remainder of your visit, if you would all address me, Augustus Emperor sounds a little too formal."

Naomi finally found the courage to speak, "It is very kind of you to make us all feel so welcome and at ease in your presence Augustus."

Romulus still sat in silence feeling his heart pounding so loud in his chest he thought he was going to have a seizure.

Zuma sat holding Lydia's hand with a big smile, unsure of what to say.

Augustus turned his head and shouted, "Zoltar!" a servant stepped forward out of the shadows and bowed. He was tall and slender, and also wore a fine white toga. His hair was dark and set in a ponytail entwined with a golden ribbon.

"Bring wine, fine delicious pastries, and fresh fruit for myself and my guests." Zoltar bowed and rushed off to do the emperor's bidding.

Julia, also feeling a lot more at ease in the emperor's company, said softly, "Your servant Zoltar seems to be very well-dressed and well-mannered," trying her best to make polite conversation.

"His old master was a brigand of Gaul; Maximus upon killing him found that Zoltar was very skilled in writing, reading, good with numerals, and a very good manservant. He brought him back to Rome and gave him to me as a gift!"

"Good for Maximus!" said Romulus, struggling to find words to say, but finally plucking up the courage to speak.

Augustus smiled at Romulus, once the fine wine and delicious food had been consumed the conversation flowed with ease.

Polite laughter filled the air as Augustus made enquiries as to Atticus's childhood and upbringing.

The conversation carried on for the remainder of the afternoon, Zoltar returned bowing his head and waited to be addressed by the emperor.

"Yes, Zoltar, what is it?" Augustus enquired.

"Your guests' luggage has been placed in their rooms and the rooms are ready for them when they are required," Zoltar, still bowing, backed off and returned to stand in the shadows awaiting any further demands of his emperor.

The rooms were very lavish, no expense had been spared in their preparations. Fruit, dates, and an amphora of wine had been placed in each room on a small table.

That evening Augustus had given them a tour of the magnificent palace gardens and had been joined by his wife Julia and their children Tiberius, Nero, and Julia. Augustus made light of the fact that Julia seemed to be the most popular name.

The children ran around the beautiful gardens hiding from the adults. Lydia and Naomi joined in the fun, pretending at times they could not find the children. It was warm in the early evening sun and time passed by so quickly and it wasn't long before they all retired to their beds.

It would be a long few days of celebrations to come and they would all need to be up very early to ready themselves knowing they would be under the gaze of Rome's elite. The crowds of Roman citizens had filled the courtyard all the way down one side, behind a line of Roman Praetorian guards wearing their ceremonial uniform, keeping them back.

The crowd was filled with excitement, chatter and laughter filled the air.

Outside the palace, thousands of people lined the streets all the way to Rome's main gates and beyond. Eagerly awaiting the arrival of General Maximus, Atticus and the Augusta legions.

Suddenly the crowds of people lining the route screamed and cheered as the Augusta legions came into view led by Maximus and Atticus riding their great stallions in full dress armour.

Behind them rode the legions' legates and tribunes.

The legion's flags had been altered slightly with the emperor's permission.

Words in bold gold thread, 'MORI QUAM FEDEORARI' meaning 'DEATH BEFORE DISHONOUR' had been added. The legion's golden eagles shone brightly in the sun's glare as they were carried proudly by the standard bearers wearing their traditional bear headdresses.

Behind them marched the cohorts of the legions led by their Centurions, they marched in perfect order. The sound of their hobnailed boots striking the stone bricks of the road echoed from the buildings of Rome.

Centurion Cyrus was given the honour of leading the first cohort, due to Atticus riding at the side of Maximus at the front of the parade. Atticus remembered the many days as a young child he'd watched soldiers marching past and hoped one day it would be him wearing one of those fine uniforms.

Maximus looked over at Atticus riding by his side.

"I can hear you thinking Atticus," said Maximus wanting to know what was going through his mind. His words were almost drowned out by the loud cheering of the crowd.

"I was just recalling to myself the time I had spent as a very young child wanting nothing more than to join the legions of Rome."

"And here you are."

Atticus smiled at Maximus and replied, "Yes, here I am."

Over ten thousand Praetorian soldiers stood to attention in their cohorts filling one side of the magnificent palace courtyard.

As the column entered the courtyard trumpets sounded and drums began to beat loudly, barely audible due to the screams and cheers of the Roman citizens.

Women dressed in beautiful red silk gowns with flowers decorating their hair now walked in front of Maximus and Atticus. They carried baskets and began scattering the petals of thousands of flowers on the ground all the way to the base of the palace steps.

At the top of the steps sat the Emperor Augustus on his throne, to his left couches had been placed where Romulus, Naomi, Julia, Zuma and Lydia, sat proudly.

Further back behind them sat Rome's elite on fine chairs in rows, some daring not to show their discomfort at being placed behind Augustus's honoured guests. They sat stony-faced, feeling a little upstaged by those they regarded as lower class. Many knew all too well that Naomi had been a slave before being granted her freedom.

Rome's senators sat on the other side of the emperor's throne, some of which had been plotting privately to overthrow Augustus. They wanted to seize the power of Rome and the glory that went with it for themselves.

But due to recent events had decided now was definitely not the time, Augustus had the mob and the people of Rome firmly eating out of his hands.

Any attempt by them to seize power at this time would be doomed to fail.

The emperor had a new ally fighting for him who was already regarded as one of Rome's most feared warriors…who went by the name of Atticus.

Emperor Augustus stood up and walked to the edge of the steps looking down at the thousands of Roman citizens and soldiers below.

He allowed the cheers and jubilation to carry on for a while before raising his right hand and silence fell upon the proceedings.

A large eagle could be seen soaring above the palace riding the currents of airwaves. It then circled and landed on the ridge of the palace roof right above the emperor's throne. Just below the eagle engraved into the stone were the letters 'S-P-Q-R' in gold set on a purple background.

This was seen by all to be a good omen sent by the Roman gods, and fear gripped several of the senators who had been plotting against Augustus.

Emperor Augustus now began to speak in a loud voice, "Welcome citizens of Rome. It now gives me great pleasure to honour our victorious Augusta legions home from defeating our Parthian invaders."

The crowd of people responded immediately by cheering hysterically. The soldiers of the Praetorian legion banged their shields with their spears. Augustus raised his hand again and silence descended once more. Augustus looked down towards Maximus and Atticus and beckoned them to climb the steps and join him.

As they climbed the steps the citizens of Rome flew into a frenzy of adulation. The noise created was quite deafening and didn't stop until Maximus and Atticus stood at the side of the emperor.

Augustus then clasped the forearm of his favourite General and turned him to face the crowds below, presenting him once again to the citizens of Rome. Maximus had stood here several times before during his years serving Rome. And had become the most decorated General so far in Rome's history.

They needed no encouragement to show their gratitude and began to cheer again even louder. This was a day of celebration and Augustus wanted Rome's citizens to enjoy every moment.

He also knew it elevated his reign; he wanted to go down in history as one of Rome's greatest Emperors; the more victories he gained would certainly help him achieve his ambition.

"In honour of his great victory, I award Maximus, the 'Corona Obsidionalis' and furthermore, elevate him to commander of all the legions of Rome!"

The Roman citizens responded again, cheering the announcement before Augustus raised his hand for silence.

Maximus bowed his head to Augustus and spoke quietly, "I thank you, but it is too much!"

"Nonsense, you have always served me well, and I have no doubt you will again in the future. Let's enjoy the day."

Maximus bowed his head again and returned his gaze to the Courtyard, the ranks of soldiers thrust their spears skywards and chanted 'Maximus' over and over again until Augustus raised his hand.

Emperor Augustus now turned his attention towards Atticus, who was standing still like a giant, a head taller than both Maximus and his emperor.

Augustus took hold of Atticus's arm and led him to the edge of the steps facing the thousands below and raised it shouting, "Citizens of Rome! I give you Atticus! Who I now introduce to you as the SWORD OF ROME!" The crowd's response was deafening and began to shout their approval.

Augustus again raised his hand for silence…"Now, it seems I need a new General for my Augusta legions." Augustus faced Atticus and smiled.

"And therefore, I promote Atticus to General of the Augusta legions!"

Once again, the crowds went into a frenzy of adulation, the soldiers again thrust their spears skywards chanting the name of Atticus over and over. Senator Crassus sitting at the side of Janus did not like what he had just heard; he had a desire to seize power one day and rule the Roman empire. Some Generals and officers would be easily bribed to assist him in his quest for power, but he knew only too well Atticus would not be one of them. Augustus let the show of adulation for Atticus go on for quite a while; he had given Rome another hero, this one blessed by the gods.

The senators stood giving their applause as did Rome's elite, while their emperor looked over at them. He was gauging their reaction and looking for any sign of descent. He knew many of Rome's elite felt elevation to high rank should come to those born of high standing and wealth.

Augustus then presented Atticus a scroll with the emperor's seal saying, "Here is your promotion written in my own hand and may I take this opportunity to thank you personally for your valour."

Atticus bowed and saluted, not able to put his thoughts into words and glanced over to his family. Naomi blushed and smiled at her young husband.

Romulus had never felt more pride for anyone as he did today, thinking back to the day that young dirty boy sat upon that wall outside his home and how much his life had changed. The celebrations went late into the night; servants of the palace carried baskets of fresh bread and fruit and handed it out amongst the crowds of people still celebrating the victory.

Several days later, Atticus returned to the fort in Ostia with Naomi at his side, and she quickly put her mark on their lavish new living quarters. Much to the amusement of Maximus, who had taken up residence within the palace as the Commander of Rome's legions.

The gods were happy watching over Atticus's destiny but did not feel the need to intervene. They were now looking down awaiting the birth of Atticus's children.

Atticus's destiny and road to glory would go forward leading his men into battle in the book, *The Sword of Rome*.